77 RULES

a novel by

J. W. Wheeler

Dedication

This book is dedicated to the entire Canton Senior High School Class of 1977. It is a work of complete fiction, even though 90% of it happened. To all of you who see yourselves in one of the characters, be glad the names were changed to protect the guilty and forgive me for the 10% I made up.

Acknowledgments

I'd like to thank a lot more people, but I'm limiting it to the folks who, in some way or another, helped.

To Sammy Mackey and John Cox: The two of you were involved in more than 90% of the trouble I got into in high school and I am sure you couldn't be prouder of your efforts. This book is your story almost as much as it is mine, but don't think for a minute I'm sharing the proceeds.

To Lou, Bob and Brad: If I could remember everything that happened and how it happened, there would be no reason for me to write this book. If your versions are funnier let me know. I can always make edits.

To Everyone I Partied With: Thanks for the brain damage!

To Gerry and Jasmine: Your suggestions and support were invaluable in the editing process. Hearing your validation of the project was essential to its completion.

To Tonja: It wouldn't be a book without you. It would be a bunch of files with no discernable layout, illegible fonts, and an unrecognizable cover.

To Tia: Thank you for taking this journey with me. Without you in my life I'd still be reading about others' interesting lives, not creating my own, and would not understand why blessings must be shared to have real value.

The Rules

1. Be Careful What You Wish For
2. Know Your Priorities
3. When in Doubt, Hide Your Stash
4. You Better Toe the Mark
5. There are Many Ways to Steal an Election
6. If You Can't Control the Outcome, Cancel the Election
7. Never Plead Guilty Before You Get a Deal
8. Smoking Will Eventually Kill You, and It Won't Be Pretty
9. Plans Turn Out Better When You Use Some Brains
10. When It's Your Time to Go, It's Your Time to Go. There's Never a Reason to Panic
11. When Higher Status People Act Nice to You They Probably Want Something
12. Procrastination is the Most Effective Strategy Half the Time
13. Great Ideas Often Come from the Most Unexpected Places
14. There's a Possibility of Teaching a Clumsy Six Foot Eight Guy to Play Basketball, but Not to Teach a Coordinated Five Foot Eleven Guy to Be Six Foot Eight
15. Silence is Often the Most Informative Response
16. If You're Going to Be in the Spotlight, You've Got to Make an Entrance
17. You Have Twice More Courage When You're Helping Others Than When You're Helping Only Yourself
18. Love Will Keep Us Together
19. There Are Times When Its Best to Just Sit Back and Enjoy the Show
20. Choices Made for Political Reasons Often End Friendships
21. Euphoria Doesn't Last, Enjoy It While You Can
22. The Best Way to Maintain Your Innocence Is to Not Get Caught
23. Old Jokes Are the Best Jokes
24. Some People Enjoy Unraveling Your Dreams. Be Careful Who You Share Them With

25. The Best Way to Cheat is to Be the Official Scorekeeper
26. Humor is in the Eye of the Beholder
27. Messiahs Always Get the Girls
28. Whenever Someone Insults You, Consider the Source. Don't Be Surprised How Often It Turns into a Compliment
29. Don't Be a Sore Loser
30. When a Lazy Person Volunteers, Be Suspicious
31. The Most Important Talent a Cheerleader Must Possess Is the Ability to Spread Her Legs as Wide as Necessary
32. You Never Know What a Politician Will Do with the Truth, Other Than Twist It
33. If You Steal Something, Be Prepared to Run
34. Don't Let Your Friends Lack of Success Tarnish Yours
35. Displaying A Sense of Humor Is More Likely to Lower Your Grade Than Raise It
36. Most People Would Rather Be Told What to Do Than Think for Themselves
37. Don't Be Surprised if You Get Kicked Out for Trying to Be Helpful
38. Never Let Good Beer Go to Waste
39. Nervous People Make Lousy Burglars
40. Don't Buy Something You Can Get for Free
41. Learn the Rules Before You Break Them
42. Traditions with Privileges Die Hard, No Matter How Much It Costs You
43. Don't Forget to Breathe
44. Brainwashing Trumps Reality Every Time
45. Do Not Let Your Ignorance Restrict Others
46. Some Dark Clouds Are Really Cotton Candy
47. Never Follow Leaders Blindly, and If You Keep Your Eyes Open, You Won't Need Them
48. There Are More Important Things in Life Than Winning
49. Never Underestimate the Stupidity of Others
50. Always Question Generosity

51. Bid Your Hand, But Use Your Imagination
52. If You're Going to Get Heckled Anyway, You Might as Well Get Drunk First
53. Paradise for Most is Purgatory for Others
54. Don't Forget to Bring a Towel
55. Some Things You're Better Off Doing Sober
56. It Takes Two to Have a Fight, But It Only Takes One for a Beating
57. You Never Buy Beer, You Only Rent It
58. Always Avoid Risks That Have No Reward
59. Stay Away from Crazy People or You Risk Becoming an Accessory
60. Listen to Your Mother. Every Now and Then She's Right
61. Even If You Don't Hesitate, You Can Still Lose
62. It's Not Braggin' If You Can Do It
63. The Darker the Witness, The Lighter the Weight of the Testimony
64. Going Along to Get Along Leads You Straight to Hell
65. The First Conclusion Reached Is Usually the Best
66. Don't Repeat the Same Mistakes
67. Leading is Not as Important as Succeeding
68. Authority Rewards Only Those Who Happily Kneel Down to It
69. Let Dead Dogs Lie
70. Never Pull an Unloaded Gun
71. Occasionally Obedience Is Rewarding
72. There is No Reason to Lie to People Who Won't Believe You Anyway
73. Don't Throw Away Your High School Yearbook - Unless You're Not In It
74. Shit Flows Downhill
75. You'll Never Understand the Importance of Practice Until You Haven't
76. They Won't Kick You Out If They Don't Have Your Money Yet
77. Keep the Promises You Make to Your Mother

The Playlist

3.	Give Peace a Chance	– John Lennon
5.	Black Dog	– Led Zeppelin
9.	The Hustle	– Van McCoy
14.	Fifty Ways to Leave Your Lover	– Paul Simon
	Mandy	– Barry Manilow
15.	Let's Take it to the Stage	– Funkadelic
	Two Irishmen	– Old Irish drinking song
	Heigh-Ho	– The Dwarves Chorus (*Snow White Soundtrack*)
	Green Acres	– Theme Song from Green Acres TV Show
	Battle Hymn of the Republic	– Julia Ward Howe
	The Addam's Family	– Vic Mizzy and Orchestra
	The Ballad of Jed Clampett	– Flatt and Scruggs (*Beverly Hillbillies Theme Song*)
	Barny Google	– Billy Jones & Ernest Hare, Thomas & West
	Listen to What the Man Said	– Paul McCartney and Wings
16.	Why Can't We Be Friends?	– War
	Wasted Days and Wasted Nights	– Freddie Fender
	Too Young	– Nat King Cole Trio
18.	Love Will Keep Us Together	– The Captain and Tennille
	You Sexy Thing (*I Believe in Miracles*)	– Hot Chocolate
	She's Come Undone	– The Guess Who
20.	Deuce	– Kiss (*Alive*)
	Strutter	– Kiss (*Alive*)
21.	Home on the Range	– Dr. Brewster Higley
22.	Have You Never Been Mellow	– Olivia Newton-John
	You Ain't Seen Nothing Yet	– Bachman Turner Overdrive

25.	Yakity Yak	– The Coasters
	Rhinestone Cowboy	– Glen Campbell
26.	Houses of the Holy	– Led Zeppelin
	Custard Pie	– Led Zeppelin
27.	Kashmir	– Led Zeppelin
	Old Man River	– Paul Robeson
29.	Summer Madness	– Kool and the Gang
32.	Locomotive Breath	– Jethro Tull
39.	Low Rider	– War
40.	Baby I Love Your Way	– Peter Frampton
	Slow Ride	– Foghat
	P-Funk	– Parliament
41.	Jolene	– Dolly Parton
	Daydream Believin'	– The Monkees
42.	Sweet Leaf	– Black Sabbath
43.	Black Water	– Doobie Brothers
	Bungle in the Jungle	– Jethro Tull
	Take the Money and Run	– Steve Miller
	Get Down Tonight	– K.C. and the Sunshine Band
	Play That Funky Music *(White Boy)*	– Wild Cherry
	Sunshine on My Shoulder	– John Denver
	Thank God, I'm a Country Boy	– John Denver
	Livin' on the Moon	– Doug Essex
	Superstition	– Stevie Wonder
	Stairway to Heaven	– Led Zeppelin
	Don't Fear the Reaper	– Blue Oyster Cult
45.	Feel Like Makin' Love	– Bad Company
47.	The Declaration of Independence	–The Fifth Dimension
55.	Nobody's Fault but Mine	– Led Zeppelin
56.	Carry on My Wayward Son	– Kansas

70. Disco Lady   – Johnnie Taylor

    I'll Be Good to You   – The Brothers' Johnson

72. Dream Weaver   – Gary Wright

74. Love Is Slippery When It's Wet   – The Commodores

76. We Want the Funk   – Parliament

The Names and Aliases

The Seniors

Annie Royal	–	Charter Member of Zit Queens
Bart Hoff	–	Jack Hoff, Pid
Bob Fair	–	Straightest Arrow in the Class
Bob White	–	No Sense, Bub
Bonnie Midas	–	Head Cheerleader
Brad Schmidt	–	Watay
Callie Johnson	–	Shortest Status Queen
Carl David	–	Three Sport Varsity Man
Carl Murphy	–	Six Feet Eight and Clumsy
Carlo Firenze	–	Class Heartthrob
Casey Queen	–	Founder of Status Queens
Chance Gillingham	–	Potsy, Anteater, Banner Rat, Dream Reamer
Chuck Hanson	–	Hulk
Dana Pickman	–	Pick
Derek Schmidt	–	Unofficial Status Queen
Donny Gomes	–	Skull
Donny DeMoss	–	Donny Google
Gary Valon	–	Jesus
George Selby	–	Worm Chow
Grant Roper	–	The Average Jock

The Seniors

Gregory Anthony	–	Buddy
Hannah Hartford	–	Stocky Status Queen
Jack Rodney	–	Captain
Jackie Wilcox	–	Chicken-Hawk
Jana Gamble	–	Senior Class President
Jasper Waldon	–	Wrestler and Cookie Maker
Jean Keller	–	Reluctant Member of Zit Queens
Jimmy Williams	–	Whales, Spider, Stick, Dr. J, Cornbread
Joe Gurnsey	–	Apache Joe
Joe Starks	–	Crazy Joe
Katy Widner	–	Tallest Member of Zit Queens
Ken Farris	–	Vine Street Party Member
Kevin Marks	–	Weedhopper
Kevin Hastey	–	Wastey Hastey
Kirk Morgan	–	The Majorette
Kurt Haufbraun	–	Himmler, Hitler Youth, the Count
Laura Ashland	–	Homecoming and Status Queen
Mark Mueller	–	Pigpen
Michael T. Smith	–	John Denver

The Seniors

Mike Eubanks	–	No Nickname Necessary
Nancy Naughton	–	Nice Nancy
Nate Northwoods	–	none *(If I Told You, He'd Have to Kill Me)*
Nick Callan	–	Nick the Greek
Pat Hampton	–	Egg
Paul Hunt	–	Dead Dog
Peggy Wilson	–	Peg Leg
Richard Shaw	–	Richard Speck
Ron Williams	–	Jimmy's White Hippy Cousin
Sally Salt	–	Kilos' Girlfriend
Sarah Hopper	–	Princess of the Zit Queens
Scott Johns	–	Kilos Kid Colombian
Scott Michaels	–	Innocent 5 Photographer
Sonny Mathis	–	S. A. Mathis, World B Free
Tina Holden	–	Status Queen Reject
Tom Yardwick	–	Yobs
Yvonne Silverman	–	Vonny-Yonny

The Underclassmen and Women

Andrew Thomas	–	Allstate
Brad Littlejohn	–	Friar Tuck
Dale Parton	–	Dolly
Dave Chapman	–	Danny Partridge
Don Craig	–	State Farm
Donny Money	–	Dead Money
Greg Septich	–	Septic
Harry Roach	–	Driver of Innocent 5 Getaway Vehicle
Judy Davis	–	Cheerleader
Laura Morton	–	Cheerleader
Mark Bates	–	Norman
Mark Klutts	–	The
Mark Markland	–	Hoop Imposter
Marsha Rawson	–	Cheerleader
Mary Riddle	–	No Sense Conquest
Mary Stone	–	Cheerleader
Spencer Williams	–	Peppy Singer
Kim Holt	–	Cheerleader
Matt Ester	–	Garbage Time Hero

The Ones Who Could Never Be Trusted

Stewart Harbison	–	Stew-Pid
Mr. Bishop	–	Meester Beeshup
Heady	–	*(his real name)*
Maurice Wilson	–	Bucky
Fred Hart	–	Table Muscle
Walter Matthau	–	*(can't remember his real name)*
Phil Vandervort	–	Lurch
Carl Macklan	–	Mack Daniels, Charles Manson
Tom Kerranap	–	Take-A-Nap
Robert Farnak	–	Athletic Director and BB Team Sacrificer
Nellie Harms	–	Grandma
Shelton Davis	–	Chip
Dr. Turkey	–	Two Acres *(more pun than a nickname)*
Mr. Liteman	–	BiteMe
Leslie Kindle	–	The Fairy
Mrs. Cook	–	The Movie Buff
Mr. Nascar	–	Head Pervertographer
Mrs. Cannon	–	The Sheep Farmer
Coach Campbell	–	Campy
Mr. Monahan	–	The Cookie Monster

Brothers of Different Mothers:

Silas Mathis	–	Canton Dealer *(When Not Incarcerated)*
Jody Mathis	–	Sonny's Partner in Crime
Otis Mitchell	–	Canton Player
Craig Carter	–	Peoria Player
Curtis Carter	–	Peoria Dealer
Clyde Carter	–	Just Relaxin' on the Porch

Class Counselors:

Zoop
Cry-Lady
Boxcar

RULE # 1 - *Be Careful What You Wish For*

As he sat at the kitchen table staring at his mother, Jimmy Williams could not fathom what he had done to prompt a sit down. School hadn't even started yet. It wasn't his fault the Teacher's Union had gone out on strike, delaying the start of classes in this his senior year of high school. All his transgressions of the summer had already come to light. There were no reasons left to get yelled at. So why was he sitting here, watching his mother take a deep breath before starting her explanation, which was not her normal style by a long shot?

As it turned out, Jimmy wasn't the one with the problem this time, it was his Advanced Math teacher, Stewart Harbison, who had the problem. And since he was the self-proclaimed Canton Unified School District Master of Solving Delicate Problems, no one in town was better at it than him. If you ever asked him, he'd let you know that straight away.

"I got a call from the school board secretary," Hazel Williams let out between sighs.

Again, thought Jimmy, school hasn't started yet. I couldn't have done anything.

"They want you, some kid named Scott Johns, and a girl named Yvonne to take college Calculus at Spoon River College. The first day is Monday."

"What about the rest'a the class?" asked Jimmy, trying to comprehend what to him was an impossibility.

"I'm not the rest of the class's momma. They just told me about you three. You'd have to go to first period at the high school and then be excused for second and third to go the college, then be back at the high school for fourth, fifth, and sixth after lunch."

"Hel...heck yeah I'll do it!!" responded Jimmy gleefully, and not only because he'd be excused from the high school campus for

18

almost half the day, but also because he was planning on majoring in engineering in college, and he was a world class nerd and proud of it. Plus, he couldn't let Scott brag about taking Calc while he waited until the next year.

"You better take this seriously, Jimmy. They picked you because they think you're mature enough to handle it. It's an opportunity that you better not let them, or your father and I, regret," she said with her most menacing mom voice, which was rapidly becoming less threatening to Jimmy as each day passed.

He had to call Scott to get the full story. They had to mull it over.

"Pid doesn't have the gonads ta face us again," was Scott's conclusion.

"Yeah, he probly spent the whole time during the strike schmoozin' the school board instead'a walkin' the picket line," responded Jimmy.

They were right, of course. Stewart Harbison had spent many a sleepless night trying to solve this one, because there was no way could he handle another year of the abuse he'd taken the last two years. He couldn't stand in front of them again and take the constant assaults on his ego for another two days, let alone two semesters. And that's why Stewart Harbison, after having worked for many years to establish his predominance over the math department and his vision of teaching college level Calculus to high school seniors, a level of math worthy of his brilliance, was now solving the problem of how NOT to teach college level Calculus to high school seniors. At least not this group, the Class of 1977.

Back in 1971, after nearly a decade of pleading and debating and arm twisting, Stewart Harbison had finally received approval from the School Board to identify, by a special test he himself had devised, the top twenty-five math students in the seventh grade at Canton Junior High School, and to put them in a special class of pre-Algebra in the eighth grade. His plan had been for them to take Algebra as freshmen, Geometry as sophomores, Algebra II as juniors and Calculus as seniors. He would personally teach this group for the last three years, and by the time they graduated they would be on their way to Nobel Prize winning science careers, or to found corporations with their engineering skills, or to design skyscrapers and bridges, his personal favorite. If he hadn't been a math teacher, he would have been a bridge builder.

By the time he inherited his first group in 1974 the entire Class of 1977 was well known for being the most gifted and the most rebellious this town had ever seen. They had been forcing changes to the rules ever since they hit kindergarten, as they thought of things no one had before, and took the things that had been done farther than anyone had before. Even the nerds in his Advanced Math group were rowdy. And after teaching them for two years and realizing their combination of academic gifts, rebellion for fun, and synchronized anarchy couldn't be controlled, at least by him, he had had enough. His dream had crash landed into a nightmare of reality he had to wake up from. Good thing he was so brilliant.

"You know that test he gave us last year, the aptitude test?" asked Scott. "You, me and Vonny-Yonny scored high enough for Pid ta use it as an excuse ta get outta' teachin' us this year. He figured everyone else in the class would be happy about not havin' ta take math except us."

"The school board's payin' for it, so he musta' done some fancy dancin' ta convince 'em it was cheaper ta send three of us ta Goon River than teach the whole class," intoned Jimmy.

"Three books vs twenty-five. Plus, I'd rather take it from a real college professor and not Pid. You know we'll get real college credit, four per semester, that we can transfer?" continued Scott.

"No way, man," said Jimmy. "We'll be college freshman and seniors in high school at the same time. How cool is that?"

Then Jimmy had a thought. How would he get there? Scott answered that directly.

"You can ride with me, man. My dad just got me a car."

Yvonne Silverman was the kind of girl who was so brilliant and sheltered everyone assumed she was very shy whether she was or not, and she never got the chance to prove it one way or the other in high school. She was destined to be the valedictorian, an only child raised by physician parents who met as child prisoners in Auschwitz. She dressed the part and looked the part, with her dark hair cut to mid-neck and matching black glasses. She wore pants suits, with frilly bows on her blouses, and sensible shoes.

Scott Johns was not only a new car owner but also the newly elected Student Council President. He hovered in the top five in class ranking, but was never quite able to catch Yvonne, no matter how many hours he secretly studied. Not only was he a first-rate politician who won every school election he entered, he was also a first-rate class clown and prankster, which of course was a major part of the reason he always triumphed when the votes were counted. He was short, but not overly so, and had long, stringy, dirty blonde hair half-way down his neck and covering half of his be-speckled face, half of the time. He was constantly wiping it away with his hands.

Jimmy Williams was a one of a kind and relished the fact he'd never met anyone who remotely reminded him of himself. He was very skinny and becoming tall, almost six feet, with the classic 1970's big Afro and thick black glasses. Even though he wasn't in the top twenty in the class, his test scores on aptitude-based tests were always at the top, and he had distinguished himself as the most original thinker in the class. He was the quickest of the three in many ways and had a knack for contrarian thinking. He had come by it honestly, having the perspective of a black kid sur-rounded by so many whites. The brainwashing didn't work on him like it did the others. It was a good thing he was around to straighten them out.

The Canton School District had never seen a group of children come through the system like the Class of 1977. Earlier classes had their rebels, but that was more of an individual thing until the Sixties, when group rebellion became fashionable, and that was always driven by a cause which authority could see coming. The Class of 1977 organized chaos like nothing the school district had seen before, and for no discernable reason, making it much harder to see what was ahead. They seemed to have no religious restraints. No one worried they would have trouble finding a job one day. They were hell bent on enjoying themselves in the way the kids in the Sixties did, but without any of the political or spiritual claptrap. While earlier classes had ideals behind the chaos, this class thought chaos was the ideal. They were notorious from junior high on. Every year it seemed some policy had to change because of something someone from this class had managed to do.

And this was a small town in Illinois, the Midwest at its most mundane. Canton had a population of about 15,000 people, but it was by far the largest town in the county. Farms surrounded it. Strip coal mining was once the big local industry, but no more. There was no reason to lock the doors or turn the car off when going into the store on cold, winter days. International Harvester had a factory in the middle of town with a large pneumatic whistle mounted in a tower near the front gate which blew every morning at seven forty-five, Monday through Friday, loud enough to be heard for miles around, and most of the workers lived close enough to then leave their houses on foot and still saunter through the gate by the time the second whistle blew fifteen minutes later. It blew in the evening at four thirty when the shift ended so the wives would know when to put the dinner plates on the table. The men walked in the morning with full lunch pails and the flow reversed in the evening with empty ones.

There was one high school, one junior high, and five or six grade schools. Since Little League, Girl Scouts, and churches mingled the kids in the lower grades, most kids knew each other by the time they entered junior high, and everybody knew everybody by the beginning of high school.

The gist was the people were simple, country folk. There were about one hundred Negroes, as they were still called; a handful of

Indians, and a few adopted Koreans. The big city was Peoria, thirty miles and a world away. Chicago was three hours away, in a different galaxy. In this somewhat isolated, but somewhat connected, small town environment, kids could create their own slang, their own subculture. Television and radio let the outside world in, but new things could be ignored or rejected at the whim of the subculture trend setters. Someone could visit Colorado over Christmas and bring back a few cases of beer sold only out West, and that would be the new craze in town overnight. Getting invited to a party serving that beer would be the peak of social acceptance.

The Class of 1977 had learned rebellion from their older siblings. They had learned about LSD, marijuana, uppers, downers, heroin and all the people who had OD'ed years before. The Kennedys and King had been shot. In fact, many in that class had watched Oswald get shot on live TV. They had body counts given daily on how many Viet Cong were killed versus American soldiers on the nightly news during dinner throughout grade school. They had watched Nixon's fall from grace, and most of them had Republican parents, so neither their elders nor the government had much moral validity.

Jimmy Williams did not have Republican parents, but he had a knack for math. And no black kid Canton had ever seen had a talent for it like he did. He started adding up the body counts one time in the fourth grade and came up with an average, and then calculated the number in a year, then in ten years. Then he looked in the encyclopedia at the population of North Vietnam. Maybe his math was wrong, but he figured North Vietnam should be running out of people in three years. When he brought that up to his teacher and added some of those people had to be too old or too young to fight, plus some of the women at least had to help with the babies, he did not get the answer he was looking for. He did not, in fact, get an answer at all.

But Scott Johns spoke up. "I checked his numbers, and they look right ta me!!"

23

Jimmy Williams, who had known Scott Johns since kindergarten, doubted very seriously Scott could have checked his numbers that fast. He immediately realized Scott was chiming in to not allow the subject to die. The teacher wasn't having any of it and steered the class back to the lesson, but from that point on, the two of them would support each other's class mischief whenever possible, and they seemed to know instantaneously when the game was afoot, and how to take whatever the other did to the next level.

And they did have a lot of classes together, over the years, particularly math. It seemed as the years passed, fewer and fewer of their classmates could keep up with their rapid-fire wit and intellect, and they would battle it out in friendly competition to see who could finish the test fastest, who could answer the most questions posed by their teachers, and who could crack the most jokes. By the time they reached Harbison's Advanced Math program they had it down to a science.

But they were not best buddies. They did not hang out together purposely outside of school. However, it was a small town without much to do, so they did not need to be close to get to know each other well. But Stewart Harbison made them close. Once Yvonne's parents heard about the plan for their daughter to ride to the college with two boys, they bought her a car. That meant Scott and Jimmy would ride back and forth to class everyday together, as the local authorities had precluded Jimmy's parents from responding the way Yvonne's did. What happened next was a senior year like no other.

RULE # 2 - *Know Your Priorities*

There is something uniquely special about your senior year when you grow up in a small town with only one high school. Everyone in town knows who the seniors are. You have something you truly want to get away from, and you have for some time by that point, and you see the way out, and nothing can stop you. If you are planning on leaving, every day is one less day to deal with the small-town mentality. If you are planning on staying, every day is one less for you to submit to the authority of the school, and a day closer to the day you can tell your teachers what you really think of them; in the grocery store, where you will see them often. The kids who know they aren't leaving seem to know the friends who are leaving will never again be the same kind of friends, and it is imperative to create as many intense memories as possible before the chance goes away. It is no coincidence what those who are staying think will bond them closer is part of what makes those who leave know they made the right choice.

To sum it up, without thinking about it at any depth, Sonny Mathis said, "We gotta have some serious fun this year, man."

He said it as Jimmy climbed into the death seat of Sonny's car. It was a hand-me-down from his dad, an old black Caddy, with three power windows that worked, and one, the passenger side front, which did not. It was stuck about 3/4 of the way up, which was fine in the summer when it wasn't raining, but more difficult in worse weather conditions.

But that was not why Jimmy was sitting in the death seat. You see, Stewart Harbison wasn't the only one with a problem. Jimmy Williams had a problem too. Jimmy's problem was he unlucky behind the wheel of a car. He didn't drive too fast or recklessly, had never put as much as a scrape on his father's car, but speed traps and hidden patrol cars were his nemeses. The phrase 'driving while black' had not yet been coined, but Jimmy was a definite victim. Within a year of receiving his driver's license, Jimmy collected three tickets and had to serve a term of three months without the privilege of operating a motor vehicle. The suspension letter from the DMV had arrived in the mail box a few weeks earlier.

Jimmy was always thinking ahead, and after he weighed his other options against his calculations of the amount of trouble Sonny was sure to get into that year, plus the fact Sonny would probably be trying out for basketball as well, and to top it off was one of the biggest heads in the school - and a 'head' in Canton slang meant 'consumer of cannabis' - Jimmy picked this arrangement. He needed to be careful Sonny didn't go too far over the line and drag them both down; but if he was, everything would be cool, and hilarity would be maximized.

Sonny was the other black kid in the senior class. The beginnings of a beard were sprouting along the chin of his ever-smiling face, and he wore his hair in a more closely cropped Afro than Jimmy did. He was shorter than Jimmy, but normal sized, not rail thin like his friend. He was not leaving town the next year as Jimmy was. For him, a high school diploma and a factory job would be enough. He had the kind of charisma that, if he had the drive, could be developed into a serviceable career as a con man. But more likely he would adamantly avoid having that drive and would use his hustling skills and his charm with women to get by on the margins. So maybe he wouldn't need a factory job. In any case, he wasn't much worried about his future on this beautiful early September morning, the belated first day of school after the labor strife was settled. He handed Jimmy the pipe he was smoking as they pulled away from the curb at Jimmy's house.

"You got your classes yet?" asked Sonny.

"Yeah, I got 'em," answered Jimmy. "What about you?"

He knew Sonny would say no, and Sonny did not disappoint. "I gotta go to the office when we get ta school."

"I got Speech first period with Meester Beeshup," Jimmy said. His real name was Bishop, but many people pronounced it incorrectly because that was the way he did. He was an effeminate man with a pronounced lisp and the whole town thought he was homosexual until his wife turned up pregnant with twins.

"The queer?" asked Sonny. To the students it made no difference what his wife had managed to do. He had to ask because Mr. Bishop was also a twin, and his brother was another teacher in the Canton district, and a macho football coach. They were easily distinguished, despite being identical in body shape and facial features.

"Yup, the other one got the job as principal at the new elementary school," confirmed Jimmy.

Small towns in the Midwest in those days were surrounded by country roads, most of them dirt. The route Sonny chose from Jimmy's house on the east end of town to the high school on the north end was down one of these roads. It was a couple of weeks before the harvest, so the corn was taller than the car, and it was unlikely they would encounter others. If anyone was coming the other way, the dust kicked up as they approached could be seen long before the oncoming vehicle. Sammy would pull over often, refill the pipe, and they'd pass it back and forth before moving on. The three miles between home and school took thirty minutes, with all the stops.

"Then, after that, I gotta go ta Spoon River College with Scott Johns. I'm takin' college Calculus. Then after lunch I have Health with Take-A-Nap, and then I have PE and English Comp."

Sonny was always amazed at Jimmy. Jealous, but he was more proud than jealous. He knew they had little in common and would drift apart after high school, but for now he was going to be as tight with Jimmy as he could be. They played ball together, smoked weed together, and attended the same church since they were babies, but because of Sonny's need to be an over-the-top class clown, in the past Jimmy would only tolerate Sonny to a certain degree, and Sonny knew it. But in this senior year, Sonny's skills would be useful to Jimmy, and as Sonny had said, the fun to be had that year would take everyone's best efforts.

By the time they finished their journey to the school that first day and pulled into the parking lot, they had no idea what was about to happen, but they were in the proper frame of mind.

27

RULE # 3 - *When in Doubt, Hide Your Stash*

After parking the Caddy and strolling across the lot toward the school, they saw two of their closest running buddies, Chance Gillingham and Bob White, leaning against the poles which supported the corrugated metal cover of the walkway leading to the school's back entrance.

Chance was the shortest of the bunch, with the kind of extra curly hair that would be a nuisance in any other era, but during the 70's was an advantage, because he could style it as a white boy Afro. He wasn't abnormally short, so it wasn't like he needed to have a complex over it, but he was short enough to have problems on the basketball court, because his body tended toward chubbiness, not quickness. That is not to say he wasn't cocky, however, and the girls liked that cockiness, or so he thought, and he usually kept a big smile bordering the big nose on his face, to make his charms more successful. He even had a theme song, curtesy of John Lennon. When he saw a girl he liked, which was most of them, he would sing out, "All I am saying, is give Chance a piece!"

Bob was the tallest in this quartet, about six feet two, and he tried to use his height to his advantage as much as possible, which wasn't much. He had a classic follower's mentality, and the one in the group he tried to follow the most was Sonny. At this point in his life he was thin, not a stick-figure as Jimmy was, but he had the type of body that would sprout a beer gut as soon as he stopped trying to be athletic. So long as he didn't try to talk too much, the girls considered him attractive in a goofy kind of way.

As Sonny and Jimmy came to a stop, Sonny, who always wanted everyone to know he was high, asked them, "Are you up for the first day of school? I know I am."

"No," said Chance with a tinge of sadness, "and that just got a whole lot harder ta do."

"So, what's the deal?" asked Jimmy.

"You guys just missed it. The pigs just left. They took Apache Joe out in handcuffs," said Bob.

Apache Joe was another senior. He lived three doors down from Jimmy throughout their elementary school years, and he and Jimmy were each other's first best friends. They drifted apart in junior high, as Jimmy became more popular and Joe became more criminal. His real name was Joe Gurnsey, but since he claimed to be three quarters Indian, he was given the nickname of Apache Joe in junior high. The tribe he claimed to be from was the Chocktaw-Chicasaw, but Chocktaw-Chicasaw Joe just didn't flow like a nickname should. He was named Apache Joe by Donny Gomes when they were in the seventh grade, and of course it turned into a fight. That fight had started years before in Jimmy's backyard and did not end for many school years, in installments of course, and since they were nearly evenly matched, neither could clearly win. By the time they finished junior high they had called an uneasy truce, but Joe never lost the nickname.

"What for?" asked Jimmy. "Did'e get in a fight again with Skull?"

That was the nickname Donny had been given long ago as well, based on the fact his face was sunken, making it look like a skull.

"Naw, worse than that," answered Bob. "He got busted for dealin'."

Sonny smirked and replied, "Well, the shit he sold me a while back wouldn't get a fly high, so it's not that big of a loss."

"But that's not the bad part. They got about fifteen other people around town too," said Chance. "And guess how they caught 'em." Without waiting for a response, he continued, "Narcs. They had undercover Narcs goin' ta school with us last year. And it gets worse. I hear they got your brother Silas."

Silas was Sonny's older brother. He was a big, burly guy, a classic high school football lineman type, at least ten years removed from his last workout, but never more than twenty minutes away from a meal. From incidents in the past he was known as a guy with a very bad temper.

Sonny almost lost his balance and reached out to grab Chance by the shoulder. "You better not be bullshittin' me, Anteater," he warned.

Usually Chance would react rather negatively to this nickname, which had never been explained to him, which of course made it even funnier. He was anointed with the name in their sophomore year when all four of them tried out for the basketball team and were eventually cut. When they were in the shower one day after practice, Sonny saw Chance's fully circumcised penis and thought to himself, "What the hell? That looks just like an anteater's nose." He kept it to himself until he talked it over with Jimmy later. Jimmy assured him it was not some strange, contagious growth, but until then Jimmy himself did not know a boy could be circumcised in that fashion. He and everyone else he had seen still had part of their helmet intact. His first thought upon seeing Chance was maybe Chance was the only truly circumcised one of them all. Another case when the dictionary, and the special medical dictionary his mom kept high on a shelf at that, had come in handy. Jimmy would never get caught reading that one, and always carefully put it back whenever he referred to it. However, when he explained it to Sonny after doing his research, they agreed Anteater was a great nickname and they should never tell Chance why they had given it to him, but to tell everyone else so they knew. Chance knew everyone was in on the secret and wouldn't tell him, and as Jimmy predicted, that made it twice as funny. First, the word Anteater is funny itself. Second, watching Chance react to it was funnier than saying it.

"Sorry ta say he's not," said Bob.

And with that confirmation Sonny paused to think for a second, and then sped off running to his car. He did not want to be added to the list. He could register for classes later. His first thought was, "Who knows who could be next?", and his answer was, "Maybe me!", so his next thought was to hide the stash he had in his car immediately. That and the stash he had in his bedroom. Then he could see how his brother was doing, where they had taken him, and was his mom alright.

RULE # 4 - *You Better Toe the Mark*

This, in a perverted way, was the perfect start to the first day of the last year of classes at Canton Senior High School for the Class of 1977. There was no talk of how the football team would do, which girls showed the best improvements to their bust lines over the summer, who would be the Homecoming king and queen, which colleges people would choose and who would get in, who was still a virgin and who had gotten laid. There was none of that. The only topic of discussion was: Who were the undercover Narcs, and how could they be best taken care of? There would be no better place to hold that discussion than in Mr. Bishop's first period Speech class.

As Jimmy walked into the classroom, he realized immediately this class, which was known to students in past years as one of the most boring wastes of fifty minutes a day in their lives, had the potential to turn out to be the most entertaining in his life, up there with his Advanced Math classes with Mr. Harbison.

He saw, or better yet heard, Yobs first. Yobs had the quintessential personality football was invented for. He was five feet ten, a bit slighter than medium build, with dark blonde hair just long enough to peek out from under his helmet, and always had a crazy look in his eye and more than likely something crazy coming out of his mouth, but other than that he was considered handsome by the girls and popular with the boys. He was boisterous, loud, and generally happy, but constantly searching for contact. Yobs was given his nickname by the upperclassmen when he was a sophomore on the football team, even though it was never disclosed why, other than his last name was Yardwick.

Then he saw Weedhopper, who had been named so by Yobs, because he had taken Kung-Fu classes after watching the TV show of the same name. David Carradine's character was named Grasshopper, and thus Kevin Marks, his real name, was ever after renamed

Weedhopper. Yobs berated him for being the second worst player on the football team, and therefore a complete embarrassment, plus he was tall and thin with long skinny weed stem legs, so the name fit. Despite Yobs' taunts he kept coming back for more and seemed to thrive off the abuse. He was trying his best to elicit a promotion to an official Hanger-On position in the social hierarchy and move up from his current position of Tolerated Abuse Taker.

Scott Johns was also in the class, which was convenient. The football players from the Class of 1976 nicknamed him Kilos, because he was constantly lifting kilos in the weight room, attempting to strengthen himself enough to be allowed to play in a game. He was the one guy on the team worse than Weedhopper. But Kilos was popular, and therefore much more than just tolerated, and the nickname was assumed to be a drug reference which made him even cooler, even though he did not smoke weed or drink. The nickname had even been expanded to Kid Kilos Colombian in honor of the fact he didn't smoke weed.

There was also a chubby girl Yobs had named Chicken-Hawk, because Yobs had heard chicken-hawks could not fly, which of course is not true. He called her Chicken-Hawk because he said she was too fat to fly. There was also Peggy, who was long ago nicknamed Peg Leg, and not just because of her name, but because she had a bad leg and walked with a stiff-legged limp. Annie was also there. She had had a crush on Jimmy since freshman year, but like all girls, Jimmy had been afraid to act on it. She was lucky enough to not have a nickname. There was Eubanks, a quiet, moody kid who was another popular football player. His last name was cool enough to not need a nickname either. There was Chucky Hanson, known as Hulk, because he was the biggest lineman on the football team and was normally mild mannered unless someone pissed him off, and then he had quite a bad temper. Carl David was another member of the athlete group, but he didn't do anything worthy of good nickname. Also, there was Ron Williams and Carl Murphy, two unlikely best friends. Ron was poor as dirt and Carl was the son of one of the rich city fathers. Ron's claim to fame was he was white but told whoever would listen he was Jimmy's cousin; and Carl, at six feet eight, was the tallest kid in the school. There were also a few juniors in the class, who collectively were called Goon-Yers, and did not rate nicknames yet. Except one red-headed kid who looked like Danny Bonaduce from the TV show, so of course he was called Danny Partridge. His dad was rich enough to keep him from getting beaten up despite the flaming red hair, which was enough of a reason for some people to want to beat him, but not rich enough to be called by his real name.

Everyone was so hyped up about the bust no one noticed when Mr. Bishop barged into the classroom. At first, he was totally surprised the classroom was full, every seat was taken, and no one was loitering in the hall for him to chase inside. When he saw the cast of characters filling the seats, he took a deep breath and whispered a silent prayer for strength. He cleared his throat, the universal sound teachers make to get students' attention, but no one stopped their multiple conversations, spit wad throwing at the Goon-Yers, making farting noises, etc. He then rapped his fingers on the table, which raised some eyebrows, but generally did not stop what had been going on before he came in. He cleared his throat again, as loud as he could. A few people reacted to him this time and cleared their own throats.

"OK, people!" he shouted. "Lisssten up!! Classs is ssstarting."

Yobs decided to respond. "Hey Meester Beeshup, do you have any idea who the Narcs are? I mean, besides all you teachers, principals, and the school board, of course."

Mr. Bishop looked at Yobs and asked, "What's a Narc?" before he realized he had lost control of the class on the first day by responding.

"Someone without a long time to live," answered Yobs. "We need to find out who they are. It's very important."

33

Kilos, doing his part to escalate the situation, said matter-of -factly, "A Narc is short for an undercover narcotics officer. There's a story going around that three people posed as students to spy on us last year and find out who was selling drugs at the school."

Mr. Bishop pondered a response, and in hopes of regaining control of the class, said, "Are you talking about the arrests today?"

Bart Hoff, another senior, nicknamed Jack by Jimmy in their Advanced Math class, put his head on his desk and said in a disguised voice, "No shit, Sherlock!"

Mr. Bishop swiveled his head and cried, "Who sssaid that?"

Ten hands throughout the classroom shot up.

"Are you gonna kick whoever said it out of class?" asked Yobs hopefully, with his hand raised.

Mr. Bishop glared at him and replied. "No." He didn't know why he said that, because of course he would throw whoever said it out of his class.

Yobs said, "OK, I didn't say it, then."

From the time Mr. Bishop first sashayed into the room, Jimmy had been giggling along with many others. The sight of such an effeminate man was hilarious to them. And the lisp was priceless. But at this point the whole room roared.

Mr. Bishop saw an opportunity to regain control. He proceeded before the students could stop laughing and proclaimed, "In thiss classs, you will learn how to ssspeak in front of an audienccce. I had a topic in mind to ssstart with, but I think the topic Mr. Yardwick hasss brought up will do quite nicccely. Come on up and tell usss what you think."

Yobs hadn't counted on this response, but he wasn't backing down in front of this crew.

"What I think is that it's complete Bolshevik!!" The prior year, in World History, Yobs had learned about the Bolshevik revolution and had been using the word ever since instead of bullshit. Mr. Bishop was confused by the usage and made the mistake of letting him continue.

"It's complete Bolshevik ta spy on high school kids just tryin' ta have a good time. I mean, it's not like there's anything else ta do around this town. Apache Joe is one thing, but Sonny's brother had good stuff, sometimes."

Mr. Bishop knew Apache Joe quite well. He had him in this very same Speech class the year before and had kicked him out of his class in the second week. The reason for his removal was when he gave his first speech he lisped throughout it in imitation of the teacher. He had so infuriated Mr. Bishop, after warning him with his favorite line, "You better toe the mark, missster," he finally stopped him mid-speech by yelling "Get out of my classsss you sssson of a bitcsssh!!", which Joe repeated to everyone for the rest of the year. In fact, the memory of Joe telling that story, and the accuracy of the imitation, was why Jimmy couldn't stop laughing from the time Mr. Bishop first opened his mouth.

"Sonny's brother?" asked Kilos.

"Hey, Mr. Johnsss," Mr. Bishop responded, "Missster Yardwick hasss the floor." Why he was letting him continue, he didn't know.

"Yeah, Sonny's brother. I think we should start a list of suspects and kick their..." answered Yobs before being cut off.

"OK, Missster Yardwick, you can sssit down now," censored Mr. Bishop. "I like your passsion, but you need to ussse better language."

"You should use more Russian!" suggested Jimmy.

"Or French!" one of the Goon-Yers added.

"Shut up, you goon!" warned Eubanks, who didn't speak much, but was threatening when he did, especially to underclassmen.

"OK people," said Mr. Bishop. "I can sssee you have ssso much passsion that we need to talk thisss out. In order to dissscusss any topic intelligently, you need to do sssome resssearch. I was going to let the classs decccide on a dissscussion topic for next week, but I think you already have. In this classs we will ssstart with group dissscusssions, and then each of you will have to ssstand in front of the classs and ssspeak on the topic. Throughout the year we will work on different types of ssspeeches, and your grade will be based on how well you prepare for and deliver each of your ssspeeches. Being able to ssspeak in front of an audienccce is a ssskill that will take you far. You already have a key ingredient to good public ssspeaking, which is passsion. I hope you learn to use it in the right way."

Throughout this speech the class was either shouting out names to add to the list suggested by Yobs, laughing at Mr. Bishop's lisp, or not paying attention what-so-ever.

When the bell rang no one even noticed, except Mr. Bishop. 'Hey, people" he shouted after realizing the din was so loud they hadn't heard the bell. "Time to move on to second period!!"

RULE # 5 - *There are Many Ways to Steal an Election*

As the class filed out, Jimmy found Scott Johns leaning against the wall in the hallway.

"Are you ready ta go, Whales?" asked Scott. Whales was one of the many nicknames Jimmy had acquired over his high school years. Jimmy was one of those people who was called different nicknames by different people. This one came about because another nickname Jimmy had was "Wills", which in the twang of Ron Williams sounded to Scott Johns like "Whales". Most of the athletes called him Spider Man, because of his skinny all legs and arms body. But to Kilos, he was Whales.

"As ready as I'm ever gonna be," Jimmy responded.

With that they made their way through the hallways, out into the parking lot, and into Scott Johns' car. It was not a new car by any means, but at least the windows rolled all the way up. In those days only the richest of the rich were blessed with a new car. Most guys were lucky to get their parents' old car, if and when they bought a new one. Gas prices were still under a dollar for a gallon, so big bulky Oldsmobile's, Chevy's, Fords, and Pontiac's were the norm. Kilos had an Olds, an old Olds, but he had a new 8-track stereo. After turning on the ignition, he pushed in a tape. Robert Plant wailed out, "Hey, hey momma, like the way you move, gonna make you sweat, gonna make you groove."

Jimmy noticed Scott was relatively subdued, so he knew something was bothering him. "OK, what's up?" Jimmy asked, as they pulled out of the parking lot.

"They won't let us paint The Rock," was the forlorn answer from Kilos.

The Rock was the boulder which sat in front of the high school, outside the front entrance. A long winding driveway rose from

37

Main Street to the front of the high school, ending in a loop near the large glass entry doors, wide enough for a row of angled parking spaces for parents and other visitors to use next to the building. Inside the paved loop was a grassy knoll, about three feet high in the middle, which was topped by The Rock. It had been the tradition since the school was built over a decade before for the senior class to paint The Rock at the start of Homecoming week and put the graduating class's number on it as well as a design of their own choosing, with the administration's blessing, of course. Because of its prominent position at the peak of the knoll, everyone driving down Main Street could see it and know exactly which senior class year it was, just in case they didn't have a calendar.

"What?" asked Jimmy, faking shock. Jimmy couldn't care less about traditions in general, and he felt even less enthused about participating in the actual painting of The Rock. However, being told they couldn't paint it was an opportunity for rebellion, and Jimmy's interest peaked. "So, how'd this come about?"

"Well, you know how the Student Council meets with the principal before the first day of class?" queried Kilos.

"No," said Jimmy, who never bothered to keep up with the political goings on at the school.

"Well, we do," retorted Kilos disgustedly. He didn't understand how Jimmy could be so naïve about politics. In his mind Jimmy would make a great politician. "So, me and the Status Queens went in this morning, and we meet with Walter Matthau, Lurch, and Mack Daniels."

The Status Queens was the name given to the group of the most popular girls in the class, the ones who could only date the stars of the football and baseball teams. They had been so named by the less popular girls in the class in their sophomore year. This was before the unofficial leader of the group became Derek Schmidt, a newly proclaimed cheerleader and the most fashion forward person at the school.

Walter Matthau was the nickname of the principal, because he looked exactly like the actor from the Odd Couple. Lurch was the nickname of the newly appointed Vice Principal, Phil Vandervort, who was brought in the year before because Walter Matthau had concluded the other Vice Principal, Carl Macklan, had grown too old to scare the children straight as he had in decades past, and needed to be eased out.

This need was brought into focus the year before when Kilos, then the Junior Class President, had a meeting with Macklan in his office and Macklan was late. It had been rumored Macklan kept a bottle of Jack Daniels whiskey in his bottom drawer, and Kilos, in an act of bravado assuring his election as Student Council President at the end of the school year, snuck into the drawer and pilfered it before Macklan returned. He stashed it in the bottom of his gym bag and held it together long enough to survive the meeting and escape the office without cracking. It remained there until football practice when he removed it to show it to Yobs. When the seniors got wind of it, which was in seconds, not minutes, the Orr twins and Brutus McCoy seized it to drink before the next game. That was fine with Kilos, since by so cleverly leaking the story of the theft, he cruised to election without needing to campaign much. What speech or slogan could prove his leadership better?

Lurch was from the modern school, had a PhD in head shrinking, and thought he could control students through psychology instead of the paddle Macklan had used. He earned the nickname because he was very tall and gangly and had large bald spot growing on top of his head, destined to leave his hair line shaped like a horseshoe. His voice even sounded a lot like Lurch, and he talked slow. No matter how intimidating he tried to be he couldn't pull it off, because all the kids could think about whenever they saw or heard him was old Addams Family reruns.

Kilos went on. "So, we go in to talk about our ideas for Homecoming, and we start by talkin' about the design for The

Rock. Lurch stands up and says, 'Since your class couldn't wait until Homecoming week to paint it, you cannot paint it during Homecoming.'"

"Now it was a fact that during the strike someone had dumped some paint on The Rock, and of course the Class of 77 got blamed, and probly rightly so. But why should the innocent be punished along with the guilty? That's Un-American! Just cuz someone painted 'Heady Sucks' on it? I mean Heady is pretty much of a jerk. And it was never proved who actually did it."

"Free speech!!" chimed in Jimmy.

Heady was the name of the football coach. His head was the shape of the moon and about half the size.

Kilos was not deterred. "Now I was ready to argue about it, but the Status Queens wouldn't back me up, cuz Lurch said the Homecoming dance would be cancelled if The Rock was painted between the start of school and the end of Homecoming week. He said something about having ta pay a lot of money ta paint over The Rock before school started. I mean, come on. My dad has enough leftover paint in our garage from the last time he painted the house to paint over The Rock!"

"He's just tryin' ta exert his authority," Jimmy surmised. "And who cares about the Homecoming dance?"

"Well, the Status Queens do, and therefore the football players do," answered Kilos smartly.

"We'll just have ta think of somethin' else," suggested Jimmy.

And by then they had reached the parking lot of the local community college, which had been recently renamed Spoon River College. It had been renamed in honor of the title of a bestselling book by an author who had lived in town decades before, Edgar Lee Masters. Until the renaming neither of the boys had even heard of the Spoon River, and it was more of a creek anyway, but it was on the map when they looked for it.

It received a brief mention during an argument they had with Stewart Harbison during their Advanced Math class the year before, and that argument persisted for so long and was so hilarious to the class and humiliating to the teacher it had driven Harbison to his decision to not teach the class the next year. You see, Big Creek eventually trickled into the Spoon River, and Big Creek was the body of water which led to the argument which led to the end of Calculus in Canton Senior High School: The Vine Street Debate.

RULE #6 - *If You Can't Control the Outcome, Cancel the Election*

This argument began the same as so many others had in this class. It was not like it was the first time they had enraged him with their witty disdain for his authority, but it was without doubt their crowning achievement. The seed was planted the year before, when they were sophomores, when Bart Hoff came in one day and revealed to the primary class instigators his father told him he had gone to high school with Harbison, and he told him the following story:

In high school Harbison went by the name of Stew, short for Stewart. Some smart-aleck in their math class, after Stew answered a question wrong, called him Stew-Pid. That of course became his new nickname. After taunting him with Stew-Pid for a while it was shortened to just plain Pid. He bore that nickname until he graduated high school and left town for college, which was the best day of his life.

His nickname was revived in the Advanced Math class from that day forward. Every time he turned to write on the chalkboard, someone would yell out, "Hey, Pid!" and he would turn back and scan the room for the culprit, who he could never find. It only stopped when he threatened to give the entire male population of the class a detention. But that was only a temporary setback. It sprouted the epiphany Jimmy experienced when he realized Bart, one of the quieter kids in the class, should be nicknamed Jack. Everyone in the know then called him by his new full name, Jack Hoff, and would pepper him with questions. Since he had been mostly ignored before then, he was OK with it.

After a week or so of this Pid realized the joke and banned the name Jack Hoff from the class room. But that didn't stop anyone from referring to him as Jack. Even Harbison slipped up one day and called him Jack instead of Bart, and Kilos quickly shouted, "Hoff", and a new trend began. Someone would call out "Jack" and then someone else would call out "Hoff" so the words blended together. Of course, after a few days of this Jimmy was caught saying

"Hoff" after Kilos said "Jack", and they both earned detentions. While they sat in the penalty box after school, Jimmy proposed, "You know, we should just call Jack Hoff Pid instead." From that day until graduation, Bart Hoff was known as Pid.

By the day of the Vine Street Debate, it had been well established Bart Hoff was Pid, and Harbison had stopped handing out detentions for calling him Pid, despite of the fact it made him seethe. He stopped because Jimmy and Scott were two of the three sharpest students in the class. Scott and Yvonne earned straight A's in every quarter since the advanced program began and did the work strictly by the book, but, despite having many B's to go along with his A's, Jimmy could solve the Geometry proofs opposite the way the book showed, and often in a step or two less than the book showed. Harbison had never had a geometry student who could do that before. In fact, as he gave Jimmy his typical "B+" one quarter, he wrote in Jimmy's report card, 'Your thinking is far superior to the rest of the class. You should be getting straight A's.' thinking it would shame or inspire Jimmy into doing better, but instead it backfired as Jimmy showed the report card comment to Scott and Yvonne, to get under their skins. With that kind of comment in his report card, who needed an A?

The catalyst was Harbison's penchant for discussing topics which had nothing to do with the class work and the class almost universally reacted negatively every time he did it, but he never learned. This time it was how bridges were built, and how Geometry and Algebra were used in their design. He decided to use a bridge that crossed Big Creek not far from the school as an example. To prove how smart he was, Harbison told the class it was technically not a bridge, but an overpass.

Then, as he went on to describe the structural members supporting it, Pid (Jack Hoff, i.e. Bart Hoff) proclaimed proudly and loudly, "Mr. Harbison, are you talking about the bridge over Big Creek on Vine Street? My dad worked on that bridge!"

Harbison responded with his normal air of superiority, "Look Bart, it is an overpass, not a bridge."

"Not according to my dad, who helped build it," countered Pid.

Such a show of defiance was rare in Pid, but after a semester of being called Pid, he had grown bolder. Jimmy looked at Kilos, and they both knew the game was afoot.

Kilos initiated it. "Mr. Harbison, Pid's dad works construction, so he should know."

As Harbison remembered Bart Hoff's dad being one of his tormentors when he was in high school, it enraged him to be called out like this even more than it normally would, and he snatched the bait. "Vine Street is an overpass, not a bridge!" he shouted.

"Well, I think we should bring in Pid's dad to explain the difference to the class," chimed in Jimmy.

Harbison was livid. When this happened, he would run his fingers through his hair, and some of it would remain sticking straight up. That was when they knew they really had him going, and they would keep up the pressure until they were laughing too hard to continue.

"I don't need to bring Jack's dad in here to prove anything!" bellowed the enraged teacher.

The class roared, as they realized Harbison had slipped up again.

"Why, are you afraid he'll prove you wrong?" needled Kilos.

"I'm not afraid of anything! Vine Street is an overpass and that is that!" hollered Harbison in a tone he thought would make it clear the subject was closed.

Bart Hoff couldn't help himself, knowing he would be handed another detention, his third that year and it wasn't even Christmas yet, but he had to say it. "Mr. Harbison, that is just plain wrong. Vine Street is a street, not a bridge or an overpass."

Despite being correct about the detention, he earned the biggest laugh in the history of the Advanced Math Program, which made it worth it.

But it didn't end there. In fact, it led to another stunt later that school year, an even bigger, better one during the second semester. It just so happened another of Harbison's off topic subjects was politics. He had decided, since it was the spring of 1976, which was not only an election year, but the nation's Bicentennial year at that, he would teach the class about political campaigns by holding an election for just the people in his Advanced Math class. Maybe one of them would become a great politician and would trace the start of their political career back to him. What politics had to do with Advanced Math was unknown and not very well accepted by the class, but Jimmy had an idea, which he sprung on Kilos the next day.

They hadn't nominated anyone for 'president' yet, and Jimmy knew Kilos was thinking of running, but Jimmy convinced him otherwise. "We should nominate Pid, and we should nominate him to run on the Vine Street ticket."

After weighing for a fraction of a second the prestige of being the president of the math class (insignificant) vs the pleasure of pissing off Harbison (significant), Kilos agreed, and they started their campaign strategy the same day. Harbison had been hoping Jimmy and Kilos would run against each other, and that would drive a wedge between them, but when he called for nominations on the day he had scheduled, he was very surprised when Kilos stood and said, "I nominate Bart Hoff for president."

Jimmy seconded the nomination and Bart agreed to accept so quickly Harbison knew this was not going to turn out the way he had planned. Some of the others (most of the girls) who were taking this more seriously nominated Yvonne, and the race was on.

It had been decided campaign slogans and signs were to be displayed around the classroom for a week before the election. Kilos came to Jimmy's house the day before the signs were to go up and they brainstormed what they should write. They had construction paper and colored pins, and no artistic talent what-so-ever. What they were drawing, therefore, was a blank, and it was cutting into their Gilligan's Island rerun watching, so Scott wrote the obvious 'Vote for Pid' on a sheet of red construction paper.

Jimmy looked over and took the paper from Kilos. He added 'He knew Vine Street was a Steet', misspelling street the second time, but since he was running out of space, and didn't want to spend the time correcting it, he left it that way.

They had the good sense not to hang the sign themselves, but instead recruited another conspirator to hang it. The misspelling had an unknown benefit in that Harbison wouldn't assume Jimmy and Kilos had done it. In fact, Kilos, while endorsing the slogan during the campaign, ridiculed the spelling on the poster, further distancing them from the fact they had made it. Throughout the remainder of the very short campaign, Pid's supporters chanted "Vine Street's a Street, Vine Street's a Street!" as they backed their man during his one and only speech, which was focused on his one campaign theme, Vine Street's proper distinction as a street, even though no one could hear him over the chanting.

They used the same chant to drown out Yvonne's speech, so no one ever found out what her campaign themes were. In addition, they chanted, "Vonny-Yonny-Mantovani, Vonny- Yonny-Mantovani." Yvonne had been nicknamed Vonny-Yonny-Mantovani by Kilos. Earlier in the year Jimmy and Kilos heard a rumor accusing Yvonne of listening to classical music, which was unheard of to kids in the 1970s. They decided to confirm it in a sly way - because in their minds if any kid did like classical music they would have the sense to lie about it - by asking her who her favorite composer was. She replied "Mantovani" and a nickname was born. It had since been shortened to Vonny-Yonny, except on special occasions like this.

The remainder of the campaign lasted one more day, as in true totalitarian fashion, Mr. Harbison cancelled the election before the voting was to occur, once he realized he could not control the results.

RULE # 7 - *Never Plead Guilty Before You Get a Deal*

S onny didn't return to school until the following Monday. When he picked Jimmy up that morning they hadn't talked since the first day of classes. After he exhaled his first puff of smoke Jimmy asked, "So what happened to your brother?"

"Man, he's in the county jail," divulged Sonny.

"For how long?" asked Jimmy.

"Well, it all depends on if he pleads guilty or not," replied Sonny.

"So why would he plead guilty? He'll never get out if he does that."

"Well, the lawyer he talked to said the opposite. If he pleads guilty he'll be in jail for less time," explained Sonny.

"Not if he wins the case," argued Jimmy.

"Ta win the case he'd need a good lawyer, and he can't even afford a bad lawyer," said Sonny.

"Man, that sucks," consoled Jimmy, as he took another hit from the pipe. "We're gonna talk about this in our Speech class today."

"I wish I was in that class," sighed Sonny.

"Did you get your classes yet?" asked Jimmy after another puff.

"No, not yet," said Sonny.

"So, what's stopping you? You should crash it," suggested Jimmy.

Sonny couldn't think of an argument off the top of his head. And when Jimmy told him of the crew that was enrolled, Sonny knew he had to do it.

Once at school Sonny found Yobs, and Yobs rounded up a few others, and by the time the first period bell rang a group of four guys surrounded Sonny and led him into the classroom, before

47

Mr. Bishop arrived. He took a seat in the back of the room and put his head down, so the teacher would not see him.

When the second bell rang, Mr. Bishop began the discussion.

"Today isss the day that we will have a classs dissscussion conccccerning the recccent arrestsss in town. I think Missster Yardwick had the floor. Do you wish to continue?"

"Not really," Yobs responded. "I think we should have a guest speaker instead."

That surprised Mr. Bishop, and before he thought about it, he answered, "Do you have anyone in mind? Maybe the viccce-princccipal? A policcceman?"

"Heck no," responded Yobs, "That'd be Bolshevik. We need ta have someone who can tell us what really happened."

"You mean sssomeone who was actually arresssted?" asked Mr. Bishop, again before thinking about it. He was getting used to the term Bolshevik and didn't react to it at all.

"No, but we could get one of em's brother!" exclaimed Yobs.

Sonny wasn't expecting to be called on to speak and had nothing prepared, but he was no wallflower. He popped his head up from the desk.

"Now who would that be?" asked Mr. Bishop.

"How about Sonny Mathis?" responded Yobs.

Mr. Bishop smelled a rat but thought he could wiggle out of the trap. "I'm not sssure I could arrange for sssomething like that."

At that point Sonny rose from his seat, and Mr. Bishop nearly fell out of his. "Why not?" asked Sonny. "I'm available."

The class chanted "Speech! Speech! Speech! Speech!" until Mr. Bishop stood and motioned to the mob to quiet down.

'OK, sssince you are here, go ahead," he said with much trepidation. "But keep it clean or I'm kicking you out of here! Come on up."

Sonny stood his ground. "For those of you who may not know me, my name is S. A. Mathis. I'd first like to say that if anybody here can tell me who the Narcs are, please speak up."

Cheers erupted from the audience. Danny Partridge called out, "We're makin' a list!"

Sonny continued. "When I get to school the first day is when I found out. I hauled ass, uhh, I mean I got out of here as quick as I could."

"Had to hide your stash, eh?" called out Yobs.

Sonny smiled and cocked his head in the direction of the comment before he continued.

"First place I went was the Cop Shop, because I was sure that was where he'd be, but the pigs, uh, I mean the police didn't have him. They told me the County Mounties were the Narcs in charge of the bust. So, I had ta drive all the way to Lewistown, and by the time I got there, my Mom was already walkin' outta the courthouse, sayin' she'd just talked to the lawyers."

Mr. Bishop was occupied with figuring out the County Mounty reference and by the time he had, Sonny had gone on.

"So, I find out the jail is about a block from the courthouse, and I went down there to see my brother. They got him in a big cell with about eight other people. All of them got busted together. The only other one I knew was Apache Joe. Man, that place stunk worse than his house, and that's pretty bad."

The crowd cracked up over that one. Jimmy and Sonny had been over to Joe's house before, in fact Jimmy had been there many times, and it did smell bad.

"So, I'm asking him, what did they charge you with? And he says possession of turkey, with intent to sell. And I ask him, what's turkey? And he tells me, turkey is a drug that the cops can't say for certain what it is. He said it was vegetable matter, and until they got it tested, they called it turkey."

"They should bring it here, and we'll test it for 'em during free period!" Yobs volunteered.

"Yeah, you guys know he sells the real stuff," continued Sonny, "Anyway, he said the lawyers told him ta plead guilty because he didn't have the money ta hire them, and he'd probly be found guilty anyway if he did fight it. He'd get a much shorter stretch if he pled guilty."

Eubanks, who never said much, said, "My dad says never plead guilty until you get a deal."

"That only works for rich, white people who can afford a lawyer," said Sonny. "Anyway, that's what MY dad said."

The class laughed, but Mr. Bishop was not amused by the last statement. "OK, Sssonny, anything elssse to sssay?"

"Nope, that's about it," he replied.

"OK, then you should leave. You are not regissstered for thisss classs," said the teacher, breathing with less tension.

"I'm not registered for any classes, Meester Beeshup. I haven't been able ta register yet, with all that's goin' on. How 'bout lettin' me in this class?" asked Sonny.

"Sssorry, thisss classs isss full," consoled Mr. Bishop in a tone letting everyone know he was not sorry. "You need to go to the officcce. I am sssure they have a ssschedule for you."

Sonny strode to the exit to a standing ovation by at least part of the class. He waved as he reached the door, then made the V sign with both hands, imitating Nixon. "Silas is not a crook!!" he exclaimed before Mr. Bishop could close the door in his face.

RULE # 8 - *Smoking Will Eventually Kill You, and It Won't Be Pretty*

The Friendship Festival was held every September for four days in a grassy field next to Lynn Street, on Route 9. It began behind the house on the northeast corner of the Lynn and 6th Street intersection and extended for a half mile to the east without a break, until reaching the first farm house outside the city limits. There were houses south of Lynn for that stretch, but north of Lynn the field went on unbroken for a quarter mile before reaching the blacktop of the elementary school, Isaac Swann, where Sonny and Jimmy attended 5th and 6th grades.

During the first week of September the level of excitement in the town built to its highest peak of the year, as the carnies arrived in town to set up the rides and booths for games of chance, which would result in big stuffed animals for some, and emptier pockets for all. The festival opened on Wednesday of the second week of September, and until late Saturday night when the festivities ended, and the lights were shut off, Canton was the place to be.

The entire senior class had heard about the ban on painting The Rock and the mood was even fouler by the Friday of the festival than it was on the first day of class when the bust went down. The plan was for Sonny to drive and pick up Bob, Chance, and Jimmy and hang out at the festival that night. He'd picked up the other two before Sonny rolled up to Jimmy's house.

"So, what's up?" asked Jimmy as he slid into the back seat next to Chance. Bob had a cigarette and was holding it below the always open window of Sonny's car, so Jimmy parents couldn't see it from the house as Jimmy walked down the sidewalk. There was an impossible to miss column of smoke rising, however. As soon as they pulled away from the curb, Bob offered one to Jimmy and Chance.

"You got nothing better than that?" complained Jimmy.

"Nope, not right now. Maybe we can score later," speculated Sonny.

"OK, I'll take one," said Jimmy. He did not inhale cigarettes, couldn't stand the taste, but took one to go along with the group.

Parking for the festival had traditionally been, for those living too far away to walk, handled by sectioning off part of the field and directing cars to park in rows marked off in the grass. That was a good method until the year someone decided it would be a better idea to charge a fee for the privilege, which was why Sonny parked his car in the lot of Isaac Swann, and the crew walked the extra block, using the time to take the last puffs on their cigarettes before getting close enough to be seen by the adults at the festival. They couldn't let any of the coaches see them smoking.

Once they crossed the open field and began slicing through the rows of parked cars, the strangest feeling of dizziness swarmed over Jimmy. It was like the cigarette he had thrown away as soon as he exited the Caddy was filled with the strongest weed he had ever inhaled. He stumbled as he tried to navigate the stubby weeds sprinkled among the leaves of grass in the darkness.

"What's the matter with you, man?" asked Bob.

"I feel like I'm high as hell. Maybe I'm having a flashback," Jimmy wondered. He'd heard of flashbacks from some of his friends' older brothers who'd been to Viet Nam.

"Flashback to what?" countered Sonny.

Jimmy had no answer. He continued forward as best he could. The other boys ignored him, as Jimmy was constantly doing something that seemed strange to them.

In addition to the carnival attractions were livestock shows, and the smell of the manure hit Jimmy with a wave of nausea to keep the dizziness company. As they broke through the cars and up to the first livestock tent, Jimmy saw a man standing next to the door. He was fat, with dark lines running down his face, and his clothes were dirty. Jimmy couldn't tell if what he smelled was the manure or the man in front of him. As Jimmy watched, the man turned his head to the side and wretched out an enormous mass of brown, thick phlegm, which splattered on the ground at the man's feet. Even though some landed on his shoes, he did not react, as the effort to release the wad was all he could muster. He bent over, coughing uncontrollably, until a smaller chunk fell from between his lips. He stared sternly at Jimmy, as if he had made the point he needed to make.

Jimmy stared in wonder, his head unsteady, as if he may fall. Two gigantic hands grabbed him from behind. Jimmy glanced down and saw the size of the fingers wrapped around his arms, lifting him off the ground, and he knew it could only be one person.

"Guess who, Spider?" tested the familiar voice.

"Put me down, Hulk," responded Jimmy.

"How'd you know it was me?" marveled Hulk in mock astonishment. Jimmy spun around as soon as Hulk set him down. With him stood Carl David, Yobs, Crazy Joe Starks, and Dana "Pick" Pickman.

"What's happenin' guys? Hey Hulk, I hear you got voted in as captain?" queried Jimmy.

"Yup," responded Hulk.

"I bet that pissed Egg off," Sonny chuckled back.

Hulk just shrugged.

"That's too fuckin' bad," declared Crazy Joe. "If he wanted ta be captain, he should'a acted like it instead'a sayin' he didn't. He wanted us ta beg him."

Yobs studied the newcomers with his trademark mischievous smile, head tilted, and eyelids narrowed, and said, "Guys, if you wanna find out what's really happenin', you need ta meet us at the football stadium in an hour."

"You guys leavin'?" asked Anteater.

"Yeah, nothin' much happenin' here. Remember, in an hour," emphasized Crazy Joe.

As they watched the other crew stride away, Bob turned to his buddies and questioned, "Who gives a shit what those guys are doin'?"

"I don't know," retorted Chance, "I think we should check it out."

"What do you think, Jimmy?" asked Sonny.

"Let's go ride some rides, and if we're bored in an hour, we can go meet up with 'em," suggested Jimmy.

That seemed sensible to the rest of the boys. They were at the age when carnival rides were still fun but being seen enjoying them too much would be uncool, so the idea was to be there long enough to be seen, but no so long as to make it obvious they had nothing better to do later that night.

Fifty-five minutes passed before they were ready to march back across the field to Sonny's car. As soon as Jimmy passed the last car in the parking lot, the nausea and dizziness left him. It would return later, in a more traditional form.

RULE # 9 - *Plans Turn Out Better When You Use Some Brains*

T he boys were strangely silent as they made their way across town to the football stadium to the sounds of Van McCoy on the radio, doing the Hustle. The stadium was located behind the high school, on the other side of the parking lot, across First Avenue. The gleam of the metal light towers against the dim city lights and stars was visible from far down First. Sonny chose this route instead of Main Street to conceal the cigarette smoke billowing out of each car window. The stadium had been there for years, but was newly renovated, with new stands and new lights. The old lights were mounted on wooden poles and games at night were not well illuminated, so the huge banks of lights on top of the new metal light standards, as they were called, were a main point of pride for the city leaders.

As they neared the high school, passing the turn that led to the adjacent baseball field's grandstand parking lot, the boys saw Yobs, half in, half out of the left back window of Carl David's car, passing by them going the opposite direction. He was waving his arms frantically, motioning for them to follow him. Pick was in the front seat and Crazy Joe Starks was in the back with Yobs. Sonny turned his car around at the intersection of Sycamore and First and Bob watched out of the passenger side as Carl turned down the side street to the baseball field parking lot. The baseball field grandstand was an old wooden type, one bolt of lightning away from being a bonfire, and the parking lot was a dirt patch along the side of the road. In the shadow of the stand, it was dark enough for the group to be concealed from any cars passing down First Street.

The quartet in Carl's car opened their doors and jumped out. Sonny and crew did also, and they leaned against Sonny's car with their arms folded, waiting to see what would happen next. Carl popped open his trunk and Yobs reached in and pulled out a canvas cloth, which he and Pick unfurled. It was maybe five feet by three feet.

"What's up with that?" asked Chance.

"You can't read what it says?" quizzed Yobs. Then he realized it was pitch black where they were standing, and no one could read what it said. He turned to his cohorts and said, "OK, who's got the flashlight?"

Crazy Joe reached into the backseat and grabbed it. He turned it on and illuminated the canvas. Spelled out in large letters was, '77 RULES'.

"Right on!" said Sonny. "So whatcha gonna do with it?"

"Well," replied Yobs, "Since they're not gonna let us paint The Rock, we're gonna hang this from one of the light standards at the football stadium."

"How the hell are you gonna do that?" asked Jimmy, who immediately saw some design issues and knew from past experience the plan had not been thought out.

"We cut a hole in the top corner," said Pick, shining the light at the puncture, "and brought some rope to tie it to the pole."

While Jimmy knew the entire plot was not something he should be encouraging, he couldn't help himself from making a couple of specific suggestions. "If you want it ta fly like a flag, you need a couple of more holes down the side. Then you can tie it to a vertical post, and it'll fly in the breeze. Plus, if you write it on both sides, it won't matter which way the wind is blowing, you'll be able to read it no matter what!"

Crazy Joe glared at Yobs. "See, I told you it was better ta get some brains involved."

Jimmy, after blurting this out, realized he should not have said it and tried to think of how to talk the guys out of it, because climbing the light tower was dangerous enough in the daytime, but it was night, no moon was out, and he could smell beer on the breath of Yobs and Crazy Joe. He hadn't gotten close enough to the others, but there was little doubt they had all shared.

"No way can you guys do this with only two of you. How are you gonna be able to see what you're doing?" asked Jimmy.

"That's why we have the flashlight, genius," countered Yobs. "And why do you think only two of us are goin' up?"

Because Jimmy assumed only Yobs and Crazy Joe were insane enough to climb the tower at night, that's why. He kept that to himself, though.

"Pick is going up too," said Yobs.

Jimmy looked at Pick and knew immediately it wasn't his idea to make this climb, but he couldn't back down in front of his friends. He was the smallest of that group, and the only one not on the football team. He was included because he was Carl's best friend from childhood, but that didn't stop him from having to prove himself worthy of his inclusion, and he was constantly in fear of being cast out. The fear of social ostracism outweighed the more rational and real fear of falling to his death.

Trying again, Jimmy said, "So why are we meetin' here, instead of at the football stadium?"

"We saw a cop car cruisin' past the high school and we didn't want 'em ta see us goin' into the parkin' lot. Then we saw Sonny's Caddy and decided we should wait here for a while before goin' back," explained Carl.

"And we've waited long enough," said Yobs. "Let's go."

He replaced the banner in the trunk. The longer they waited the more time his mates had to locate some common sense or for Jimmy to talk them out of it. The four piled in Carl's car and he started it. Sonny, Chance, Bob and Jimmy followed suite.

"Those guys are fuckin' crazy," laughed Sonny as he turned the key in the ignition. "If one of 'em gets killed climbin' up there, I wanna be there ta see it."

The two cars navigated First and pulled into the parking lot of the football stadium. Carl turned off his headlights and stopped next to the light tower closest to the high school. When Sonny did the same, Chance jumped out of the car and said, "I've got a pocket knife."

No one had expected that. Crazy Joe reached for it, but Chance continued. "I'll cut the holes. It's my knife. And I'm goin' up with you."

This was somewhat unexpected by the others, but not totally. Chance, you see, was not as high up the social ladder as Pick and was willing to try harder to get there. He was not rich, not a good athlete, not very smart, and not the kind of guy who made the girls sigh when he approached them. He had a group of friends, and they were in no way unpopular, but still saw this as a chance to make a name for himself with the highest status group of all. If he didn't do it now, his whole life might pass without another opportunity. Plus, if Pick was brave enough, he was brave enough.

"We only need three guys max," said Yobs.

Carl, always protective of his friend, seized his opportunity, "Well, if Chance won't let you use his knife, Pick, he should take your place."

This was working out better than Chance had dreamed. Maybe he could even take Pick's place in the In Group. Yobs glared at Pick, expecting him to fight for his spot.

"No way, man," said Pick. "I'm goin' up, and we're smokin' a bowl when we get up there."

"Pick," said Carl, "If you're gonna climb up there, you're leavin' your stash with me."

Pick stared at his friend as if he wanted to argue, but then dutifully handed the baggie he had in his pocket to his buddy.

"OK, its four of us," conceded Yobs. "Let's cut the holes now, before we get up there. And give me the marker so I can write on the other side." He unfurled the banner, wrote '77 RULES' on the blank side, then handed it to Chance, who carved small holes midway and at the bottom, to match the hole at the top.

"I've got another idea," said Chance, as he looked at how badly he had carved the holes. "Got any duct tape?"

Chance already knew Sonny had duct tape in his trunk. Chance had given Sonny the duct tape he used to form a wedge to prop up his passenger side window, so it would remain level instead of tilting forward where it stuck when the motor broke, and Sonny had never given it back, so Chance knew he had it. Sonny didn't volunteer the tape however, knowing what Chance was up to.

Carl spoke up after a pause and said, "I think I have some in my glove compartment."

And sure enough he did, and he handed it to Chance. Chance tore off some pieces and used them to bolster the edges of the jagged holes he had cut.

After that adjustment, Yobs, Crazy Joe, Pick, and Chance hopped over the chain link fence surrounding the tower (barbed wire was later added to the top in response to this incident, one of the many changes made by the administration during the school year), and Carl tossed the re-furled banner over. The tower had four legs rising to a platform from which the light bulbs could be replaced, and on one of the legs pegs jutted out from either side. It took a brave man, not afraid of heights, to climb the pegs up the tower in broad daylight, and it was so dark the boys on the ground could not even see the platform the others were trying to reach.

Yobs went first and Crazy Joe second, sharing the banner between them, followed by Pick. Chance went last, with the rope looped around one shoulder, mountain climber style. It took a while for the first two boys to figure out how to climb and keep the banner in their grip, and Chance was forced to go much slower than he had thought. "Hurry up guys," he whimpered with false bravado.

"You try carryin' this thing," shouted down Yobs.

They made slow progress and before climbing halfway up the tower had disappeared from the view of the boys on the ground. Their muffled voices could still be heard, and the boys below wondered if someone in a house a block or two away would hear them and call the cops.

They weren't too worried. As soon as they couldn't see them, the boys on the ground looked at each other and shook their heads. "Those guys are even crazier than I thought," uttered Bob, to break the silence.

Carl smiled and shrugged and asked, "Sonny, did you bring your pipe?"

"Hell yeah," replied Sonny.

"Get it," ordered Carl.

Sonny sauntered to the Caddy and retrieved his pipe from the glove compartment. Carl took it and filled it from the baggie. The boys passed it around as they waited for their friends to come down, one way or the other.

"Are you tryin' out for basketball this year, Jimmy?" asked Carl as he passed Jimmy the pipe.

"Thinkin' about it," responded Jimmy. "You think Bucky'll give me a chance?"

"I think he will," said Carl to Jimmy.

Jimmy felt the dizziness he had experienced before flooding back. These rich white kids had better quality weed than Sonny ever got. Plus, Pick's stash was bigger than he, Chance and Sonny could afford to buy when they all pooled their allowances. After filling the bowl twice, all of them were so dazed they were startled by the sound of feet scurrying down the tower pegs.

It was Chance. He was first down and descended so much faster than the others he was a few steps from the ground before they came into view. The words rushed out as soon as he touched terra firma. "It was so cool up there. It was a hard climb, and I thought I was gonna slip a couple'a times, but I was holdin' on so tight I couldn't believe it!!"

"But what about the banner?" asked Jimmy.

"Well, first we tried to hang it across the top of the hand rail, but then we ended up tyin' it to the side of the rail, just like it was a flag pole. You were right, Jimmy. Three holes were much better than one."

By this time all four boys had made it down and were over the fence.

"OK guys, let's not get caught standin' around here," warned Yobs, and they spun around scrambling to find eight handles for eight hands and bounced into the cars and left the parking lot as quickly as possible, leaving dust clouds in the dark.

The cars separated at the first intersection, and no one in either car even thought about rendezvousing later that night to discuss what they had just pulled off. They didn't want any of their fellow classmates to see them, for fear they may blurt it out. In fact, they didn't even want to talk about it amongst themselves. The whole point was for the world to see the banner for the first time Monday morning, before the administration had a chance to react. Sonny took each one home in the same sequence he picked them up. It was an early night, but a good night. Nothing would happen later to match what had already happened anyway.

RULE # 10 - *When It's Your Time to Go, It's Your Time to Go. There's Never a Reason to Panic*

Monday was a chilly day. It wasn't quite half past September, but the wind was whipping across the prairies in a foretelling of the harsher months to come. Sonny was early to Jimmy's house and was sitting in the car waiting for him to finish his last bites of breakfast. Jimmy stepped outside, felt the stiffness of the breeze, and ducked back into the house to get a jacket. As soon as he saw Jimmy re-enter his house, Sonny put the Caddy in drive and pulled off.

"Hey!" called out Jimmy, running down the steps and the sidewalk to catch up with the car. Once he made his point, Sonny stopped and let Jimmy in.

"What're ya' doin' gettin' here so early?" asked Jimmy.

Sonny looked at Jimmy as if he should know the answer already and said, "I want to make sure we get ta school before the sign blows off the tower."

Jimmy had forgotten about the banner but looking at the way the trees were bending in the wind, he couldn't believe it would still be in the same county, let alone still be attached to the tower. Sonny wasn't in too big of a hurry to get to school, as he made his way slowly down his normal route through the corn fields. He had a wooden container which flipped open to reveal a compartment for crushed weed, and another that held a metal pipe. The boys passed it between themselves as they rolled along at the leisurely pace those from small towns prefer. They were, after all, going to school, so there was no rush.

After a few hits of the pipe, Jimmy's mind began to drift. Today was windy, in fact it might be the windiest day in the last couple of months, reminding Jimmy of the last truly windy day in town. It was on a summer's day the year before, in the afternoon, and Jimmy was sitting on the toilet in the back bathroom of his house, trying to lighten his load before leaving for the gym to play basketball. As his family had not yet moved into the new house where they now lived, the bathroom was next to the back door of the house. That back door led to a back porch so small it was called a stoop, a block of concrete about four feet square. A sheet metal awning was bolted to the house above the door, and it stuck out from the house to shade the back stoop. As he sat there he could hear the awning creaking, and then moaning, as the wind gathered strength. It had been a typical hot muggy early summer day when he sat down, and on days like this the weather could turn foul in a few minutes. While he moaned purposefully and worked something loose with a plop, the wind worked one of the bolts loose holding the awning, which then began whipping back and forth, banging against the outside wall of the house, on the other side of which Jimmy was sitting.

To say Jimmy was startled by this would be an understatement. The sound of the awning as it tore itself apart in the blasts of wind was something far more important than Jimmy's finishing of his call of nature. He rose from his seat without stopping to wipe and opened the door leading out of the bathroom and saw through the back door screen the raging black clouds and water drops flailing about in all directions and then he heard the pounding of the thick balls of hail followed by the blaring wail of the civil defense signal. In little Midwestern towns like Canton this siren was heard at least once a month during spring and summer. He had heard this signal so many times it did not cause the rising panic he was feeling by itself. The awning breaking loose was what did that. The rising and falling of the siren was just the topper.

Jimmy sprinted out of the bathroom, slammed the back door closed, and ran through the family room, through the kitchen, and into the living room. Once there he could hear the shouts of his mother, calling him to come and come quickly. With no basement to seek refuge in, she and his sisters were huddled in the only room of the house without an exterior window, the small bathroom the children of the family shared. Only Jimmy had not reached its safety when the chugging sound of the train that normally passed harmlessly down the tracks behind the houses across the street came barreling straight at him. It wasn't a normal train either, but a super train, fifty times more deafening than the noisiest diesel locomotive to ever screech and moan its way down the Santa Fe Line.

Three quick strides sped Jimmy through the living room, past the large picture window facing the street beyond. A quick glimpse outside revealed a wind so angry it had become a visible tumult of swirling dirt, tree parts, and miscellaneous debris. He had reached the hallway with his fourth stride when the window caved in with a mighty crash and shards of glass exploded across the path Jimmy had taken seconds before and stuck into the wood paneling behind the couch, some several inches deep. Jimmy did not see the glass, only heard it, as he stepped into the bathroom where his mother and two sisters were crouched in fear in the bathtub. Jimmy jumped in as well and the four of them sat in a circle, scrunched into the small tub, with their arms interlocked over their shoulders, waiting to die or be saved. They could do nothing else...

...except pray. Hazel Williams prayed every day. She asked the Lord for deliverance in a loud voice that could still not be heard above the roar enveloping them. Jimmy watched her in fascination. His intellect told him the law of probability would dictate whether he would be breathing in the next few minutes or not, but his spirit was happy as hell his mother was doing her part to better the odds. Plus, Jimmy was sure God would tell him when his time had come, and he wasn't getting that feeling today. His sisters were crying, his mother was praying, and all Jimmy could think about was missing basketball practice. It wasn't even a practice, it was open gym in the summer, and Jimmy had been cut from the team the year before, but any day missing a chance to make a move he had never made before, in honor of his hero, Julius Erving, was a wasted day.

That's when the roof started moaning, and pieces of it could be heard being ripped from their moorings. The walls seemed to lean at an angle. Jimmy didn't know whether the house was about to tumble around him like the snow tunnels he used to hollow out in the winter, or if it was going to fly off its foundation intact like Dorothy's house in the Wizard of Oz. When the structure reached what seemed to be the breaking point, Jimmy made a wish the girls in Oz were better looking than the girls in Canton.

And then it went silent. The silence was eerily loud at first, after so many terrible minutes of deafening noise. How could such violence disappear in such an instant? But it had. Jimmy jumped out of the tub and opened the door to look out into the hallway. He could see light streaming in from where the front window should have been, and he walked around the corner to see the glass from the windowpane now stuck in pieces to the wall on his left. He thought of the near miss, like so many others in his life, and was reassured.

"I'm gonna die one day, but not today," chanted Jimmy, louder than he had wanted to.

"Don't be so sure of yourself, Jimmy," cautioned his mother, who had exited the bathroom after him.

The sun was out and was shining brightly. Then rain poured down in a torrent. Jimmy and his mother and sisters stood in the living room and watched the rain and sunbeams mingle together, a beautifully terrible sight to behold, and then saw the destruction outside. The power poles which ran along Anderson Street were all down, and the wires were snaking along the ground in puddles of water. A large tree branch and part of a trunk were lying in the front yard. It wasn't their tree, or a neighbors' tree, it had flown in from parts unknown and was deposited five feet away from the gaping hole in the front of the Williams house, where it could do no harm. Tree limbs and trash cans, clothes blown off clothes lines, a shredded piece of tarp clinging to the mailbox came into view as Jimmy surveyed the scene.

"You've got to go check on Gramma, Jimmy," his mother told him, taking him away from his inventory. She had a look of fear on her face, as she thought of the condition of her Grandmother's rickety house, and her Grandmother's even more rickety body. She knew God's grace would keep her safe in her basement, but until Jimmy confirmed it, his mother could not be calmed.

Jimmy had not expected this. In past years his mother would have forbidden him stepping outside minutes after an event like this. She was thinking of him as a man in this time of crisis, no longer in need of protection, but a protector himself. Before she could change her mind, Jimmy opened the front door and stepped out onto the front stoop. The rain had stopped again. As he picked a mental path through the chaos before starting his journey, his mother called out, "Be careful!"

His Gramma only lived a block away, and under normal circumstances Jimmy could sprint to her house in less than a minute. But circumstances had never been less normal for the short trip he needed to take. He stepped gingerly down the front walk as far as possible until blocked by the tree, which was only a couple of strides, then climbed over and around the tree trunk blocking his path and picked his way through the grass of the front yard and into the street. The sidewalk was not passable as many of the trees which once lined the street littered it. The street was filled with so many tree branches, power poles, and wires it made an impressive obstacle course and Jimmy ensured he was not electrocuted by jumping gingerly between barriers until he traversed the block to his Gramma's. As he hopped up the front steps, he could see her sitting in her normal place, her chair in front of the television in the front room of the house. Her house did not look damaged at all. Even her porch swing was still there.

Jimmy opened the unlocked screen door and smiled at his Gramma, who smiled back.

"Already come back upstairs, Gramma?" he asked, assuming she had taken advantage of her house's basement.

"I haven't been down there all day," she responded.

"Where'd ya go during the tornado?" Jimmy asked.

"I sat right here," she said. "I opened a couple of windows, then I sat back down to watch television. When the power went out I just decided to sit still and wait it out."

Jimmy shook his head, but he was not too surprised. It was his Gramma who told him long ago the day he would die was written down in a book, and no matter how bad the situation he was in he would survive unless it was the day written in the book. And if it was the day written down, no army, no bullet proof vest, and no doctor would be able to save him, so he'd better be ready. After she told him this, Jimmy prayed very, very, hard for God to give him a clear warning when his day had arrived, so he would know it was coming and it wouldn't be a shock, and if he could live long enough to see the Bears win the Superbowl, the Cubs win the World Series, and the Bulls be World Champions, he would die happy. Jimmy was sure his prayers had been heard, because his Gramma also told him if he prayed really, really, hard God would hear, and since then, if he hadn't heard anything from God before whatever life-threatening event staring him in the face that day started, he knew he was going to make it. Gramma had probably not heard anything from God today either, and that was why she felt no need to go to the basement.

"It wasn't my day," she said, to confirm his suspicions.

"OK, do you need anything?" Jimmy asked.

"I could use a glass of water," she answered.

"OK, Gramma, I'll get it," said Jimmy, heading to the kitchen with her glass to fill it.

"I'll go back home and tell Mom you're OK, and I'll come back later ta bring you somethin' to eat," promised Jimmy as he opened the door to leave.

Gramma smiled and took a deep sip of water.

Jimmy smiled at the memory of his Gramma waving to him as he stood on her front porch.

"What's so funny Jimmy, or are you just funny looking?" asked Sonny.

Before Jimmy could think of a snarky answer, they came around a corner, and in the distance, fluttering as proudly as any flag the boys had ever seen, was the banner. As the pair stared, the wind steadied, making the sign as stiff as a teenaged boy after a whiff of perfume. The lettering could be seen for miles.

"77 Rules!!!" shouted out Jimmy.

"You know it," responded Sonny.

"I can't believe that thing is stayin' up there in this wind!" exclaimed Jimmy.

"I bet Walter Matthau and Lurch shit their pants when they saw it," laughed Sonny.

"Everyone comin' down Main Street can see it," said Jimmy. "This is much better than paintin' the stupid Rock. Every other class has done that. I wonder how long it'll stay up there," mused Jimmy.

As they entered the parking lot, a crowd of admirers was standing in a group near the edge of the lot, where the view of the banner was best. About ten football players, including Yobs, Kilos, Paul Hart, Egghead and Hulk, were there with a few of the Status Queens, namely Jana Gamble, Laura Ashland, and Derek Schmidt, and a couple of strange bedfellows, Donny "Google" DeMoss and "Captain" Jack Rodney.

Before Jimmy could get out of the car and congratulate Yobs on his handy work, Yobs jumped in his face and proclaimed loudly, "Isn't this great, Spider? I mean, whoever did this deserves a medal," and he gave Jimmy a hard wink.

Jimmy got the point. Yobs did not want to take the credit for this. It probably had something to do with the soiled trousers of certain administrators. Sonny also made the connection.

"So, who do you think did it, Yobs?" crowed Sonny mockingly.

Egghead spoke before Yobs could say something regretful. "Well, whoever did it better not be on the team, or they won't be playing football this year."

Egghead, shortened to Egg, was the nickname given to Pat Hampton; the star quarterback, the star pitcher, and the star point guard; by Hulk after he was placed in the Advanced Math Program. As the de-facto team captain, it was his duty to keep the starters on the field and out of the principal's office. He knew it was Yobs without asking.

RULE # 11 - *When Higher Status People Act Nice to You They Probably Want Something*

That put a damper on the parking lot celebration, plus the first bell rang, and the group migrated through the cars toward the sidewalk which led to the back entrance. As they walked, Egg grabbed Jimmy by the shoulder and steered him away from the others' earshot.

"I need you to do something for me, Jimmy," confided Egg.

Jimmy stared at Egg with surprise, and then with suspicion. The only thing he could think Egg could want from him was help with his math homework, and since Egg wasn't taking math this year, it couldn't be that. He sure wasn't going to ask Jimmy to try out for basketball, like Carl David had. Since he knew Egg wouldn't ask, Jimmy asked it for him, "Are you gonna ask me to try out for basketball this year?"

The look of disdain on Egg's face made Jimmy laugh and add, "Scared of the J moves?"

Egg snorted. He wasn't afraid of Jimmy in any sport. In fact, Egg played while Jimmy watched. The only times they had opposed each other without a coach to keep Jimmy sequestered was little league baseball, and Egg's team had crushed Jimmy's; and intramural basketball the year before, when Egg refused to play on the varsity for the now ex-coach, nicknamed Take-A-Nap, which was the revised version of the original nickname given to him by Sonny, T K Nap, based on his real name, Tom Kerranap. Jimmy remembered that game well, as Egg could not stop him, and his team cruised as they did every game that season. Egg did not remember the game at all. It was intramurals and he was the best varsity athlete in town, so why should he?

Jimmy not only remembered it, he had used it as motivation throughout the summer as he dribbled relentlessly up and down the blacktop behind his old grade school. Back and forth left handed, then right handed, then cross overs, then behind the back, between the legs, spinning left, spinning right. All as the sweat poured off him and the heat rose in shimmering waves from the black surface, so hot the asphalt was sticky. Pat "Egg" Hampton had not been able to stop him.

The game of basketball was, to the guys in Jimmy's circle and many other guys' circles as well, dominated by one player, Julius "Dr. J" Erving. Before having seen him on television, playing a style so startlingly artistic it was awe inspiring to behold, they had played basketball as a sport. After seeing him, basketball was played as a form of self-expression, an abstract of elegantly aggressive ballet. No longer did it matter as much what the real score of a pickup game was as much as it did to make the most spectacular, contorted, gravity defying, unorthodox moves you could imagine, and as a bonus maybe even put the ball through the basket. Scoring real points was not as important as scoring Style Points, as they became known. If you could dribble between the legs or behind the back, or even better if you could do both, then jump in the air off one foot, and if it was the wrong foot it was even better, then switch the ball between your hands while in the air at least once, and move the ball up, down, around, in or out with your hand after you changed it, or some combination thereof, and then release the ball with a scoop or a finger roll, even if you had a wide open layup, you could be awarded maximum Style Points. Since Julius loved to block shots, you could multiply your Style Points if you swatted such a shot into the stands, and the shooter received a Style Point deduction no matter how awesome the move was.

Each day that summer he was either on the blacktop by himself, dribbling and running, running and dribbling, or in the city gym, where the varsity and junior college games were played, and where Bucky and Coach Farnak, the baseball coach and athletic director, had offices. They unlocked the gym and threw out a couple of balls on Mondays, Wednesdays, and Fridays, for anyone to come and play pickup games. Jimmy didn't miss one.

There were two styles being played in those games. On the one hand, there was the group competing for Style Points, as well as to beat down the underclassmen at all costs, within the rules or not; and the straight-laced group who wanted to play the slow methodical offense prescribed by the coaches and use two handed chest passes and proper foot work on their hook shots and power moves. The Class of 77 dominated the first group, J, and the underclassmen were relegated to the second group, B, whether they liked it or not. At first games were picked by talent alone, but before long the squads were no longer picked this way, it was group J against group B, and games full of such creativity and missed layups have never been played before or since.

The J team was Bob at center, Jimmy and Brad Schmidt at forward, and Sonny and Chance at guard. The B team was a bunch of no name juniors, many of whom would make varsity over almost all the J's. The games should have all been blowouts, with the J team undefeated and unchallenged, but because of the ridiculous guard play of turnover prone Chance and never pass up a bad shot Sonny, and never make a simple layup you can miss by trying a double clutch Bob, Jimmy and Brad had to play somewhat fundamental basketball with as much style as feasible to pull half of the games out, including playing defense. They would get their thrills from stealing passes or robbing people of their dribble, and then it was off to the races for a pretty pirouette.

Brad and Jimmy played baseball together when they were both eight years old, the first organized sport for either of them, but they had not remained friends after. They had played on the same intramural team as sophomores and they connected again the next summer. By the end of their junior year Jimmy, Sonny, Bob, and Chance were an established clique, and after joining the J squad, Brad made their clique five. The original quartet made it a point to teach Brad, whose father was a minister and older brothers went straight to a seminary after high school, the finer things in life; like cigarettes, weed, and booze.

"Hardly," scoffed Egg after regaining his composure, bringing Jimmy into the present. "I need you to do something completely different," he continued. "The girls are putting together the plan for Homecoming, and we need you."

"For what?" asked Jimmy, now completely baffled. Not by who Egg meant by 'the girls', he knew Egg meant the Status Queens, but by what the Status Queens could want from him.

"We need you to play the lead role in the senior class skit during Homecoming," disclosed Egg.

"Yeah, right," laughed Jimmy, and with as much sarcasm as he could muster, "Isn't that your job?"

"Not this one. It's not possible for me to do it. You HAVE to do it," demanded Egg.

Telling Jimmy he had to do anything was a mistake, and Egg realized it the moment the words escaped his lips. If sports star Pat Hampton was asking anyone else, he wouldn't feel the need to be this open, but he knew better than to try to fool Jimmy or think he could coerce him into doing anything he didn't want to do.

"Or we need a different idea for the skit," Egg admitted.

As expected, Jimmy didn't answer.

"Did you see the movie Blazing Saddles?" asked Egg, to start his explanation.

"No, never heard of it," responded Jimmy, which was true. Jimmy didn't have money he thought was expendable enough to go to movies he had to pay for, so he didn't bother to keep up with the latest ones.

Chance, who was following behind them as closely as he could, couldn't contain himself any longer and blurted out, "You know, the one with Cleavon Little in it."

Now Jimmy understood. Cleavon Little was a black actor on a television show, so Jimmy knew him from that. They needed a black guy for the skit.

"I'll think about it," said Jimmy to both. The bell rang, and it was time for them to part ways.

Chance grabbed Jimmy by the shirt sleeve as Egg walked away. He leaned close to him and whispered, "You gotta do it Jimmy. If you do it, I get ta play your sidekick, the Waco Kid."

"And what's my role?" enquired Jimmy, even more suspicious.

"The Sheriff!!" cried Chance incredulously. He couldn't believe Jimmy didn't get it.

Jimmy was stunned, but quickly got over it. "And whose idea was this?"

"Well, there was a big argument between the Status Queens and the Zit Queens over the idea for the skit. Both ideas were stupid as hell. The Status Queens wanted somethin' ta do with Gone with the Wind, and the Zit Queens wanted somethin' about the Wizard of Oz, I can't remember what. Then it was Derek Schmidt who suggested Blazing Saddles, and he said you had ta be the Sheriff."

"When did all this happen?" asked Jimmy.

"At the senior class meeting we had ta talk about Homecoming. You know, the one you blew off?" taunted Chance sarcastically.

Jimmy stared at him blankly. He didn't know or care to know about such a meeting.

"And you know what, the Status Queens went along with it because it was Derek's idea, and the Zit Queens went along with it because a certain one of 'em likes you," teased Chance.

"Excussse me, Mr. Williamsss," screeched a high pitched nasal voice from behind Jimmy's shoulder. "Classs ssstarted two minutesss ago."

"Sorry, Meester Beeshup," apologized Jimmy, nodding to his teacher sheepishly.

"Don't you have a classss to go to, Missster Gillingham?"

"I guess," was the response from Chance.

"See ya later, Potsy," said Jimmy before the classroom door closed behind him. This was another nickname for Chance, based on the TV character from Happy Days. Not only did he look like him, he acted like him.

RULE # 12 - *Procrastination is the Most Effective Strategy Half the Time*

After an uneventful Speech class, Kilos and Jimmy were off to Spoon River College for their Calculus class. As they walked through the parking lot to Kilos' car, Jimmy asked, "So what do you know about the Homecoming skit?"

Kilos opened the driver's side door with a key and opened the passenger door by leaning across and pulling up the door lock. "Well, are you gonna do it or not?" asked Kilos, once Jimmy was sitting inside. He didn't answer Jimmy's question because he knew Jimmy knew plenty about it already, and he didn't want Jimmy to find out what he didn't know.

As they pulled out of the parking lot, Jimmy tried again. "What's the movie about?"

"OK, Jimmy, the movie's about a town in the Old West that hires a black sheriff. He's got a sidekick who's a drunk, and a big, dumb, strong guy ta help him clean up the town. There's a great scene with a bunch of guys sittin' around a camp fire eatin' beans and fartin."

"Is that gonna be in the skit too?" asked Jimmy, his interest now rising.

"Could be. It's not like anyone's written down a script," admitted Kilos. "Their idea is the town is overrun by the bad guys, then they hire you, and you clean up the town with your buddies. All they've really got is the title, "Blazing Footballs," and the lead actors: You, Potsy Gillingham, and Hulk."

"Well, if I'm gonna be in it, I'm gonna make up my own lines, and if they ask me ta do somethin' stupid, I won't do it," proclaimed Jimmy.

"Jimmy, you could write the script yourself if you want to," suggested Kilos. "You know whatever you write'll be funnier than anything the Status Queens can come up with."

"True, but that sounds like too much work. I'll have ta think about it," said Jimmy. Then something struck him as strange. Here was Kilos, the Student Council President, and he wasn't claiming any authority or involvement in the Homecoming skit. What was up with that? "So, Kilos, why aren't you writing it?" questioned Jimmy coyly.

"Because I don't feel like arguing with the Queens about it, and plus, I've got other things to plan," advised Kilos.

"Such as?" asked Jimmy.

"Hyde Park Week," said Kilos.

"What the hell is that?" asked Jimmy.

"Something the Class of 76 started. A week of commemorating the riots in Hyde Park," explained Kilos.

Jimmy had never heard of riots in Hyde Park, but more importantly, "I don't remember anything about it. What did they do last year that I missed?"

"See, that tells you how lame it was," said Kilos. "That's why I'm focusing on planning it this year. I want it ta be the event of the year!"

"That sounds like a much better thing to spend my time on than writin' a skit. I'll be the Sheriff in my spare time," Jimmy concluded. "When are you plannin' on this Hyde Park Week thing?"

"They did it the week before Homecoming last year," responded Kilos.

Jimmy had an inspiration. "Well, if Hyde Park Week is supposed ta celebrate rebellion, and you want it ta be as subversive as possible, why not do it on the same week as Homecoming? We could have pep rallies for it and the Narcs would think it was for Homecoming. Hell, half of the kids there would think it's for Homecoming. Remember what we did for the Vine Street Election? We could do the same thing times a hundred!!"

Kilos said nothing as they pulled into the parking lot of the college. But as he thought about it, a smile began to form, and by the time he exited the car, he was laughing.

"Jimmy, that may be the best idea you've ever had," he said after composing himself. "You know how the Queens put up posters the week of the game? You know, 'Victory for Varsity' and all that crap? We could come up with our own Hyde Park Week posters and put 'em up next ta the real ones, and I mean put up a whole bunch of 'em, and it'll take the Narcs forever ta figure it out."

"Like 'Peyote for Varsity," suggested Jimmy.

"We could have a Kill the Narcs rally," chortled Kilos. "We have ta get Yobs and Crazy Joe and company involved."

"Wait, Kilos," counselled Jimmy wisely. "We don't want the Narcs ta find out about it 'til after we've got everything ready. If Yobs and Crazy Joe know too much too soon they'll get out of control and it'll be over before it starts. Just let 'em know we're plannin' it, so they know ta be ready when the time comes."

"You're right about that," said Kilos. "How 'bout I come over ta your house after school, and we can start on the posters? I know where I can get my hands on the construction paper and markers we're gonna need."

And thus, the planning of Hyde Park Week began, that very evening, in the basement of Jimmy's house. They had moved into this house a few months before school started. It was brand new single level three-bedroom home, with a basement where Jimmy's bedroom and bathroom were. His father had the basement partially finished for what he said was Jimmy's privacy, but truth be told he did it knowing Jimmy would only use it for the short term, and as soon as Jimmy left for college the next year it would become his man cave. Not only was a bedroom and bathroom in the basement, but the biggest television in the house was also there, with a couch, table and Jimmy's dad's favorite chair. Jimmy moved the table to the corner, so he and Kilos could sit on the floor with their construction paper and markers and imaginations brimming, watching Gilligan's Island reruns.

Of course, the first poster read 'Peyote for Varsity'.

The next was the obvious '77 Rules'.

In quick succession, they came up with:

'Vine Street is a Street'

'Charles Macklan/Carl Manson'

'Hyde Park Week – We'll Have Watts of Fun'

'Bolsheviks Unite'

'Up With Dope, Down With Hope'

'Death to Narcs'

'All Narcs Report to Lurch'

'The Odd Couple – Lurch and Walter Matthau'

'Pid For President'

They stopped, laughing so loud Jimmy's mother opened the door to the basement and yelled down, "I never knew Calculus was so hilarious!"

"Naw, Mom," called back Jimmy. "We're watching Gilligan's Island. You know, the one about Dubov."

That inspired the next poster and started the boys off on more abstract ideas. Jimmy wrote:

'When Dubov is ready, Dubov come back!'

Absolute nonsense unless you had all the episodes of Gilligan's Island memorized, as many in the Class of '77 did, so perfect for Hyde Park Week.

'Katy Bar to the Door' wrote Kilos.

"What the hell does that mean?" asked Jimmy.

"It's something Heady says after he diagrams a play," said Kilos. "It means we should score a touchdown if we do it right."

"Who's Katy?" asked Jimmy.

Kilos didn't answer. Instead he wrote:

'Green Acres = Farm Women'

Jimmy howled again. Another inside joke.

'Free Apache Joe' wrote Jimmy, in honor of his boyhood friend.

'Stairway to Hemp'

'Smoke 'Em'

'Free Silas Mathis' came next.

Kilos wrung out his feelings about the administration with:

'Mack Daniels and Coke'

'Mack the Knife'

'Oscar the Principal'

'Lurch is a Pig'

'You Rang?'

Jimmy took a different route and wrote:

'Greetings From Panama'

'Go for the Lumbo Gold'

'Legalize It'

'Smoke 'em if you got 'em'

Kilos liked that one. He hadn't finished his thoughts on the faculty:

'Heady Blows'

'Cheap Shots for Table Muscle'

Jimmy loved that one. Table Muscle was a teacher and coach. He was the weight lifting guru and head fitness trainer at the high school. He constantly warned the football players to not add too much 'table muscle' over the summer, which was his nickname for fat. Of course, over the years he had not followed his own advice, and he had thusly earned his nickname. The cheap shots were given to Table Muscle at last year's Faculty-Student Intramural All-Star Basketball Game.

'Rednecks Support Lurch for President'

'Support the SQA: Status Queens of America'

'Kill the Pigs'

'Support the Vine Street Party'

'Free Pid'

'Chicken Hawks CAN Fly'

And they were starting to get hungry. In a final burst of creativity, they wrote:

'Goon River Country'

'Hashish is just alright with me'

'Burn, Baby, Burn'

'Peace, Love, and Peyote'

'Shaft'

'Why Can't Weed Be Fiends?'

'Narc List – Sign Below'

'Toe the Mark'

Both knew they didn't have enough left in them to top that one, so they put down their markers and surveyed their work.

"I'll hide 'em in my room until the right time. We should give 'em out ta other seniors ta hang up, so the Narcs never know it was us who made 'em," said Jimmy.

"Why are you worried about it, Whales?" asked Kilos.

"We want the posters ta stay up as long as possible, right?" explained Jimmy. "If we go into the school with a bunch of posters it'll cause a scene and the Narcs will take 'em away from us. If we hand 'em out ta people a few at a time and not make a fuss about it, the Narcs will have ta find 'em on their own. They'll never find 'em all if we do it right."

"Between now and then we need to recruit the right guys, who the Narcs will never suspect, and they can hang our posters right in the foyer with the real Homecoming stuff. If you or I try ta do it ourselves, they'll nab us for sure," said Kilos, trying to make sure Jimmy understood he was the President, and it was his idea.

"Go for it," said Jimmy.

RULE # 13 - *Great Ideas Often Come from the Most Unexpected Places*

Take-A-Nap used to be the varsity basketball coach. He was fired at the end of the last season because none of the best athletes would play for him. He instituted a list of fitness requirements which had to be passed or it meant being automatically cut. They included bench pressing 110 pounds 10 times, doing 15 dips, 5 skin-the-cats, leg pressing 250 pounds 10 times, and running 2 miles in under 15 minutes. If a guy could do those things, Take-A-Nap reasoned, he should be able to shoot a basketball and dribble.

The only kids who completed the list were a freshman who couldn't play better than half of the eighth graders in his class the year before, and a few football players who were in great shape but weren't ballers by any stretch. His downfall was when Egg quit. Egg refused to run the 2 miles in anything under 20 minutes, and then trotted off the track and into the locker room, where he quickly showered and went home. Guys like Jimmy, Sonny, Chance and Bob stuck it out only to get cut. Jimmy had worked harder than anyone in the tryout, according to Take-A-Nap, but since the only requirement he had managed to pass was the 5 skin-the-cats, he was cut anyway. Skin-the-cats were universally dreaded as the most difficult of all the tasks, and only the strangest athlete could do that one and not the others. No one was surprised because that was Jimmy through and through.

As Take-A-Nap's record did not have his phone ringing off the hook with new coaching opportunities, he had stayed on with the faculty of Canton Senior High as the Health teacher. It was one thing to teach Health to high school upperclassmen when your real job was to coach the basketball team, but if your only real job was teaching Health it was a different matter. The highlight of Health class, and the only real purpose for Health class, was to talk to the students about their sexual urges. In prior years the main purpose was to tell the students about the horrors of venereal diseases and the excruciating pain of childbirth, to instill the amount of the fear thought necessary to deter them from acting on those urges until after they graduated. As this was 1976, there was much debate among the PhD's on the school board and their city father foes about whether this strategy should change, and a more honest discussion of reproductive health be the goal. Take-A-Nap didn't care about any such debate, or the strategy of past years. He was bored, and when he was bored, he liked to tell stories. Since the class was segregated by sex, he could use the same language in the boys' class he used in the locker room, that is, if he was ever allowed inside a locker room again.

"As all of you know," Take-A-Nap said as he stood in front of his 5th period class, "The main purpose of this class is to keep all of you from knocking up your girlfriends on prom night."

That got the laugh he expected. "If you all promise me you won't do that you'll all pass this class, and if you actually learn how to prevent it, you might even get an A."

Take-A-Nap then launched into the story that made him the front runner for Teacher of the Year.

"I have a friend. I'm not going to name him because he doesn't live in Canton and you wouldn't know him anyway. He's a married guy and he gets around, if you know what I mean. Anybody out there who doesn't know what I mean? Raise your hand."

The class roared. Jimmy looked around, and saw Egg in the back row, sitting next to Nick the Greek and Carlo Firenze, then Grant Roper. In front of them were Ron Williams, Scott Michaels, and Captain Jack Rodney.

"Hey, Scott," said Jimmy. "You better explain it to the Captain."

Jimmy had known the Captain since grade school. He had been given the nickname of Captain in fifth grade, because he wore a silly looking billed, braided, white cap to school one day.

He was a chunky kid at the time, and his head was even chunkier. Until that day he had been called Big Head, but when Sonny Mathis saw that cap on his head, and how it was worn at an angle to hook onto the corner of his big head because it was too small to fit around it otherwise, he said, "Hey Captain, nice hat!!"

The Captain hated Jimmy, and it wasn't because he called him Captain. It was because later that year Captain Jack started a street gang. Half of the kids in the class thought it was a fantastic idea and joined within the first week. The other half of them didn't. When the Captain ordered a fight on the playground to get those who did not join in line, he unwittingly caused the formation of a rival gang. Jimmy, who tried to avoid joining any groups, didn't join either. That caused a problem, if the smartest kid in the class wasn't in either gang. Jack realized if he didn't convince Jimmy to join his gang, he might join the other, and Jimmy could think of things no one else could, so that made him dangerous. When Jimmy refused to join the Captain's gang, even after he promised to make him second in command, Jack had one of his minions relay a threat to him. Then the rival gang approached Jimmy and asked him to be its leader. As Jimmy recognized the need for protection, he agreed. The next recess was a decisive battle, with Jimmy directing his troops to an easy victory. By the time the bell rang, Jack was on the run, and the teacher knew something was going on.

After recess, he asked the class what had happened, and Jimmy spoke up and told him everything. At the end of the story Jimmy said it was a stupid idea to have the gangs in the first place and looked the Captain in the eye when he said it. He hadn't named names, but the look said it all. And that was the end of gang activity at Isaac Swann School in 1970.

Except one last thing, the Captain and his main enforcer cornered Jimmy in the lunch room the next day and told him they would be looking for him after school, to punish him for tattling to the teacher. So, Jimmy told Sonny to round everyone up at the end of school, and Jimmy assigned three boys to watch each exit and wait for Jack. When Jack realized what was happening he tried to run, but he and his big buddy were spied and were soon surrounded by about twenty boys. None of them cared much for Jack in the first place, but the only thing they had against Big Jim Otto was he was Jack's friend. Jimmy made a deal.

"Jim, this isn't about you. I won't let all these guys beat him up, I'll choose one guy and let him beat Jack up, OK?"

Jim shrugged, and Sonny didn't give anyone else a chance to be picked and jumped Jack immediately, taking him to the ground and smacking him in the nose. Sonny punched him a few more times before letting up and left him crumpled on the ground, bleeding and crying.

Jimmy walked over to the Captain, laying on the ground in the fetal position sobbing, and asked, "Are you ever gonna threaten me again?"

When Jack whimpered "no" in response, the crowd dispersed, and everyone went home.

Now Jack, as he stared across the room at Jimmy, remembering as Jimmy remembered, said nothing. The class laughed harder.

"Anyway," continued Take-A-Nap, "This guy starts having a burning sensation when he takes a piss. It gets worse and he has to go to the doctor, and the doctor tells him he's got the Clap."

George Selby, who had been given the nickname Worm Chow the year before, blurted out, "What's the Clap?"

Grant Roper called out, "Don't worry, you'll never get it!"

Everyone thought it was funny, but Jimmy could never laugh at anything Grant Roper said.

Take-A-Nap took control immediately, "The Clap is the nickname of a venereal disease, called Gonorrhea."

"OK, what's a venereal disease?" asked Hulk, who knew what the Clap was.

Jimmy couldn't resist, "Worm Chow!!"

The room laughed.

Worm Chow was christened with his nickname the year before when he took the same Social Science class as Kilos and Jimmy. They were given a group assignment, and of course Jimmy and Kilos paired off, and when the teacher insisted they have a third team member, George Selby jumped at the chance. George was the pimpliest kid in the Class of 1977, which was saying something, as the class was filled with pimply kids. He took Advanced Math with the other boys and was constantly trying to keep up with them in terms of wit and mischief. When things happened like the Vine Street Debate, George could be counted on to join in the anarchy.

The assignment was to create an advertising campaign, in the form of a television commercial, for an imaginary product. After adamantly denying they needed any help, Jimmy and Kilos drew a blank as to where to start. With a product, that was obvious, but what product? George had a moment of divine inspiration and called out, "How about Worm Chow?"

The other boys stared at him like the idea was completely insane. They were intrigued.

"What?" asked Jimmy.

"You know," replied George. "What you would feed your pet worms!"

After hesitating for a moment to contemplate whether he was serious, Kilos and Jimmy roared with laughter. From there they took over and worked out the campaign and the script for the commercial. Kilos would play a mad professor type in a white lab coat. He already had the wild hair and glasses, so he only needed the coat to complete his wardrobe. Jimmy would play the role of Dick Long, an unemployed executive out of TCU. The commercial opened with

Kilos drawing wildly on the chalkboard, explaining the chemical formula and benefits of Worm Chow. Then on came Jimmy, who gave a testimonial of how much healthier and happier his worms were after switching to Worm Chow, wearing his church suit and tie. Then the commercial ended with George, singing the theme song, dressed as a worm. The worm outfit was made by cutting the bottoms out of four brown paper grocery bags and taping them together to form a paper tube. George had to stand straight up with his arms by his sides to fit into the costume. He hopped in from off stage (outside the classroom door) which was so hilarious the class was in tears before he broke into his jingle.

"Worm Chow, Worm Chow, if you love your worms you'll feed them Worm Chow!!!"

The crowd went wild, and from that day forward George had a nickname which happily for him had nothing to do with his pimples. The boys, despite getting the greatest applause and having the most memorable campaign by far, all got B+'s. The reason, the teacher said, was she did not care for the name Dick Long and wasn't giving anyone an A who would use such a vulgar name.

Jimmy was glad the teacher had caught his joke, and took the B+ in stride, but Kilos went nuts.

"How can you do that? That's not fair!!" he cried when he heard her explanation.

"Sorry, Scott," consoled Jimmy after the teacher ignored Kilos long enough to confirm she wasn't going to respond to him, "I should have gone with my first thought, Harry Post."

"A venereal disease is a disease you get from sexual contact," said Take-A-Nap, who felt the need to be serious, even though he was alone in that frame of mind.

Hulk sat in the front of the room away from his buddies because he felt of all his classes, this one might have the most future benefit. He spoke up, "Listen up, Carlo. The way the girls drool all over you, you're at high risk!!"

Carlo did as he was told, because he was at the highest risk in the Class of 1977. With his long hair and smoky eyes, he didn't have to say much to get them swooning. Good thing too, because not much of substance ever came out of his mouth.

"So, the doctor, after giving my buddy the diagnosis, tells him he's gotta go tell all the chicks he's been banging that they need to go get the cure as well," plowed ahead Take-A-Nap, and then he couldn't contain himself, and broke out in a laugh. "And so, he has to go home and tell his wife that he's probably given her the Clap!" He roared on and tears came to his eyes.

The boys in the class, going through their first romances or still in the fantasy romance stage, were somewhat horrified by how funny Take-A-Nap thought contracting the Clap was.

He wiped the water from his face and squeezed his nose, so he could continue. "So anyway, he tells her, and she gets tested, and sure enough, she's got the Clap too." Take-A-Nap banged his fist on his desk as he tried to keep it together. "And then she has to go out and tell all the guys she's been banging that they have to get checked."

The class, at this point, was more fascinated by Take-A-Nap's performance than the story.

"So, it turns out, when all is said and done, it was her that had given him the Clap in the first place!!" By then his laughter had transformed into a crazy, demented wail.

No one in the class said a word for a few moments as they let it sink in. Then from the far side of the room, Ron Williams blurted out, "So, are you and your wife still married?"

As Take-A-Nap was still in revelry at his story with his mouth open, a line of drool stretched from his lower lip toward the papers on his desk as the question sank in.

"What??" he shouted, and he swung his head in the direction of the words, causing the drool to swing out and up, and splatter on his face.

That brought the class out of its stupor. The noise was so loud the teachers in the next classrooms came in to see what the commotion was about. Guys were on the floor, rolling around holding their sides to keep their organs in place while they spasmed.

"That story wasn't about me!!" screamed Take-A-Nap, after he wiped his face. "Of course, I'm still married!!!"

"Ah," said Jimmy, remembering his Shakespeare, "I think he protests too much!!"

Jimmy assumed no one would get the joke, and that would make it funnier to him, but one person did. Kurt Haufbraun, a skinny nerdy kid who was in the Advanced Math program, giggled when he heard it. In junior high Kilos found out Kurt's parents immigrated from Germany after the war, and he and his buddy Nate Northwoods looked up Nazi war criminals in the library to figure out which one Kurt looked the most like. It was no doubt Goebbels, but they decided as a nickname Goebbels wasn't funny. Heinrich Himmler, on the other hand, was funny. They called him Himmler for the next year, but they stopped when Kurt started to like it. Before Kurt was a harmless geek, but with a nickname like Himmler he started thinking he was dangerous, or at least started to make other people think he was. They decided to leave him alone after that.

In high school Yobs nicknamed him Hitler Youth, but he also got such a weird feeling from the kid he stopped calling him that too. Jimmy knew about the nicknames but didn't use them himself. To Jimmy, Kurt looked like, and acted like, the vampire Barnabas Collins. From the first year of having Advanced Math with Kurt he called him The Count. Kurt could be on the far side of the room, then all at once be right next to you, like he teleported, vampire style.

Take-A-Nap bellowed out, "Now who was the smart ass that..." and the bell rang, and the boys jumped from their seats and scampered through the exit before he could find the culprit.

From that day forward, it was treated as a fact Take-A-Nap's wife had given him the Clap and he was such a loser he stayed married to her. It was a perfect analogy to him staying on as Health teacher after being fired as the basketball coach. Since all the athletes already hated him, the story was spread like it was gospel. As it made perfect sense to the Class of 1977 to vote for the most despised teacher as Teacher of the Year, some other teacher would have to come up with an even more pathetic story to snatch the award away from Take-A Nap. No one did.

RULE # 14 - *There's a Possibility of Teaching a Clumsy Six Foot Eight Guy to Play Basketball, but Not to Teach a Coordinated Five Foot Eleven Guy to Be Six Foot Eight*

Chance Gillingham was always singing. He didn't have a skillful voice, but he could hold a tune. Spontaneous vocalizing was not totally taboo for guys of that era, but it was frowned upon. That fact only made Chance want to sing more. He was constantly updating his repertoire. Today it was Fifty Ways to Leave Your Lover. Just because he was always singing didn't mean he bothered to learn the words, so he would usually start in the middle with the part he knew best, and then fabricate words until he ran out of ideas, then move on to another fractured favorite. This song gave him more artistic license than any before. "Just get in the van, Stan. Just get on the bus, Gus. Just climb up a tree, Lee. And get yourself free," he warbled to his unappreciative audience of Bob, Sonny and Jimmy.

They were weaving through the high school parking lot, having returned from a ride around Big Creek Park sharing a couple of bowls. Bob grabbed Chance by the neck to cut off his air before he could belt out another "just". Their school day was over, but they were returning to attend the first basketball tryout meeting, in the high school gym. It was September 30.

"Will you quit singin' those Redneck songs?" pleaded Bob, in a threatening kind of way.

"What's makes it Redneck?" asked Chance, simulating innocence.

Being called a Redneck by a member of the Class of 77 meant you were uncool, unsophisticated and backward. It began as an insult the kids who lived inside the city limits flung at those who lived outside them. Rednecks drove dirty pickup trucks and listened to real country music - not the country rock that was popular at the time - and didn't have bell bottoms or wide lapel shirts. If a Status Queen was seen inside a pickup truck, she would be immediately stripped of her membership. The initial meaning gradually broadened to include anyone, or anything considered unhip.

"You singin' it," laughed Sonny.

"Fuck you, too," shot back Chance.

"Next, you'll be singin' Barry fuckin' Manilow," derided Jimmy, instantly regretting his words, because he had now given Chance a request, at least in Chance's warped mind.

Chance, having broken out of Bob's grip, was now a few paces ahead of the others as they stepped onto the sidewalk. He blurted out, as a couple of girls walked by, "Oh Annie, you came, and you gave, without taking!"

The girls giggled and but didn't stop. When they saw the three boys trailing, Annie Royal called out, "I hope I'll see you at skit practice, Jimmy!"

She was with Nancy Naughton, maybe the only girl in the class so honest, so pure, so sweet, and so nice she could be friends with the girls in both camps of the senior class hierarchy, the Status Queens and the Zit Queens. She was so nice her nickname was Nice Nancy. Annie was a charter member of the Zit Queens, and it was well known she had a crush on Jimmy.

"We're all depending on you, Jimmy," confirmed Nancy.

For some reason, hearing that from Nancy made it clear to Jimmy he had no choice but to be in the skit, and the entire senior class already assumed he was going to do it, and he had better come up with a strategy quickly to keep it from becoming embarrassing.

When the girls were at the edge of his voice's range, Chance wailed, "And I need you to stay!!!!!"

Sonny, who was perpetually trying to coach Jimmy on how to score with the ladies, said to Jimmy plainly, "You know she likes you, right?"

Jimmy didn't answer. The boys reached the door of the gym, and once through, all thoughts of girls and Homecoming skits flew out of their minds. There were about twenty boys sitting in the bleachers, mostly sophomores, juniors and now five seniors. The only other senior not with the quartet of partiers was Brad Schmidt. When he saw the group walk in, he waved them over to where he was sitting, in the top row.

"Hey, I looked for you guys after class," he said.

"We waited for you as long as we could," replied Sonny.

They were both lying. They didn't wait, and Brad hadn't tried to catch up. They all knew Brad was not the type to have the balls to show up to the first basketball meeting stoned, so why wait?

As they sat, the door to the office in the corner of the gym that held the PE equipment as well as a couple of desks for coaches and PE instructors opened and the new basketball coach, Maurice Wilson, bounded out. He went by the nickname of Buck, but everyone knew him as Bucky. At about five feet eight or nine he was tending toward stocky, had a bad toupee, and black, thick-rimmed glasses. He was wearing a short-sleeved tee-shirt and a pair of semi-tight shorts, the kind with pockets in the front and back.

He was followed by a younger man the boys had never seen. The shirt he was wearing was the same as Bucky's and he was wearing heavy cotton sweatpants, the kind with elastic at the bottom to keep them tight against his ankles. He, at least, resembled someone who in the not too distant past had played the game he was about to be coaching.

Bucky, on the other hand, did not look like he had ever played. Maybe back in the set shot days, but not since players had to be able to run and jump. He had been the assistant coach the year before, and in the brief time they had observed Bucky during try-outs he had confirmed their suspicions he was clueless about the game of basketball they saw Dr. J playing on television. Not to say he was more clueless than Take-A-Nap. At least Bucky knew the sport he was coaching was basketball, not decathlon.

"Listen up!" said Bucky as he stood in front of the boys. "I think you all know me," he continued. "I'm Coach Wilson, but you can call me Coach. I'll be coaching the varsity. You may not know our new assistant head coach, Coach Campbell. He will also coach the JV."

After waiting a couple of seconds for the murmuring to die down, Bucky continued.

"As many of you know, this is my first year as the varsity coach, and for those of you who were here last year, things are going to be different."

"Are we gonna do the same stupid conditioning stuff we did last year?" asked Chance.

Bucky smiled, but it wasn't genuine.

"No. No two-mile run, and you don't need to lift a certain amount to make the team. We will continue the weight lifting pro-gram, but once the season starts, no more lifting. Lifting during the season will mess up your jump shot," Bucky paused after that statement, which was a direct contradiction to Take-A-Nap's phi-losophy. "However, you will be running. We don't have a lot of height on this team, so we need to be in good condition. Practice starts next week, and we'll make the final cuts before Halloween. The first game of the season is right after Thanksgiving."

That caused another stir among the boys. The next stir came when Carl Murphy strolled in. Carl was about six feet eight inches tall and was as awkward as you could be at that age and height. He had never tried out for the team before, and had never wanted to, but when he grew four more inches between his sophomore year and the end of his junior year, his father had given him no choice. His gait was that of a seventy-year-old man. He sat down quietly in the front, so he wouldn't have to climb the bleachers with his creaky knees.

Jimmy could hear some of the boys in front of him, excited they may finally have a tall guy on the team. Jimmy's heart sank, because here was another kid who would make the team whether he could play or not, and one less spot for Jimmy. Jimmy knew Carl Murphy would never be any good at basketball, and it wouldn't matter, he'd get a uniform before Jimmy.

"So, if you want to try out, you need to sign the signup sheet I've got here," continued Bucky, holding up the clipboard in his hand. "You'll need to get your physical if you haven't already and be at Alice Ingersoll Gym at 4 PM sharp on Tuesday."

The boys began filing out of the bleachers. Jimmy stayed in his seat for a few extra seconds, trying to figure out the odds of his making the team. It had been so soul crushing the year before when he'd been cut, he wasn't sure if he wanted to risk that again. He counted the guys he knew would make it. He started with the football players who would not need to try out and would make it anyway. Paul Hunt and Pat Hampton, of course, would be the starting guards. Crazy Joe and Carl David would make it. Brad Schmidt would as well, and now Carl Murphy. He knew at least four of the juniors would make it. That's ten spots gone before he had a chance to really think about it.

"Come on, Jimmy," said Brad, standing beside him. "Are you gonna sign up or not?"

"Not now," replied Jimmy, as he hadn't finished his thought process yet. He had every intention of signing up when he walked in the gym, but now, with the addition of Carl Murphy, did it make sense?

"OK, suit yourself," shrugged Brad, and he hopped down the bleachers to sign.

Sonny, Chance and Bob were standing alongside Brad, but when they heard Jimmy's response, they did not follow him. They instead turned and focused on Jimmy, their eyes demanding an explanation.

"I'm not signin' up until I know Bucky's really gonna give me a shot," declared Jimmy. "Have you guys forgotten last year? I'm not runnin' all those wind sprints for nothin'."

"Well then," tested Sonny. "Are you gonna talk ta him?"

"Yeah, I'll talk to him," Jimmy replied as he surveyed the crowd surrounding the coach. "But not now. Are you guys gonna sign up or what?"

Sonny folded his arms and pursed his lips. "Naw, I'll wait too," he said.

Then all four boys climbed down the bleachers and walked out of the gym. Bucky watched them out of the corner of his eye but let them leave without stopping them.

RULE # 15 - *Silence is Often the Most Informative Response*

"Man, I can't believe you guys talked me inta goin' on the fan bus," complained Sonny.

"It'll be fun," encouraged Chance. "We can raise a lot of hell and put the moves on the cheerleaders."

"Pass the pipe, Chance," moaned Bob. "I need ta be as stoned as possible for this."

"It's our senior year and this is the first road game," scolded Jimmy.

"They're gonna get their asses kicked," predicted Sonny. "They got lucky the first two games."

"And your point?" asked Jimmy.

They left a cloud in the car, even though Sonny's front passenger window was a quarter open.

As they climbed onto the bus those already assembled let loose a rousing cheer. Chance boarded first and reacted to the hollering by holding up his hands as if asking for quiet, like he was a humble Hollywood star. Next came Bob, and he raised both hands in a double one fingered salute as he marched down the aisle.

"Hey now, I'll have none of that!" warned the bus driver.

Jimmy turned to the driver as he passed by next and, not being able to help himself, asked, "So, what are ya having? We'll trade ya some beers for some Jack, if ya have it."

The bus driver glared at Jimmy but did not answer.

The cheerleaders and their core group of friends, the Status Queens, were on the bus. There were the pom-pom girls and their friends, the Zit Queens. The remainder were juniors and sophomores, boys and girls. A group of them, boys, filled the last two rows. When the four-man crew of seniors stepped to the last row, the underclassmen vacated the seats for them. As the bus pulled away, the cheerleaders decided they could no longer contain themselves and broke into a cheer.

"V-I-C-T-O-R-Y, Victory for varsity, RAH-RAH-RAH !!!"

This went on for the first few miles out of town, until Jimmy couldn't stand it anymore. Sonny, thinking the same thing, glanced at Jimmy. They were sitting in the last row on the aisle. Chance was next to Jimmy, Bob next to Sonny. Without discussing what would come out of their mouths next, they both started, in unison, with:

Lil' Miss Muffet,
Sat on a Tuffet,
Snortin' some THC;

Long came a spider,
Slid down beside her,
Said, "What's in the bag, bitch?"

She said, "I'm laughin' at cha."

At which point both boys slapped each other's palms, then reversed their hands and slapped with the backs. It was a private joke between them. By this time even the white kids in Canton were slapping each other five instead of shaking hands, so black people had to reclaim the gesture by using the dark side of their hands instead their palms. It was called 'slapping five on the black side'. Jimmy and Sonny laughed as the others around them marveled at what they had just heard and seen.

Chance broke the silence that followed by singing out,

Two Irishmen, two Irishmen,
Were digging in a ditch.
Then one called the other one,
A dirty son of a — (now Bob, Sonny, and Jimmy join in)

Peter Murphy had a dog,
Tied him to a rock,
Along came a bumblebee,
And stung him on the — (at this point the rest of the boys on the bus join in, at least to shout out the next syllable)

COCKtails, (and at this point everyone not singing is laughing louder than the cheerleaders can cheer, so they give up)

Ginger ales,
Five cents a glass
If you don't like my story,
Then kiss my royal—
Ask me no more questions,
I'll tell you no more lies.

If you get hit in the face with a bucket of shit (or paint, for those who didn't use profanity),

You better close your eyes!!!

From that point on, the cheers came from the back row. The boys put all the naughty songs they had learned since diapers to use on the forty-five-minute ride to Morton.

Bob began the next one. They had been working on it since sophomore year.

Hi-Ho, Hi-Ho, it's off to school we go,
The principal's Walter Matthau;
He's married to a big fat cow,
Hi-Ho, Hi-Ho;

Chance knew the next verse.

Hi-Ho, Hi-Ho, it's off to school we go,
The vice principal's name is Lurch;
You'll never find him in a church,
Hi-Ho, Hi-Ho;

Jimmy had another one.

Hi-Ho, Hi-Ho, it's off to school we go,
The chemistry teacher's a real charmer;
Her real job is a sheep farmer,
Hi-Ho, Hi-Ho;

Chance had another.

Hi-Ho, Hi-Ho, it's off to school we go,
The English teacher's a real Gramma;
She taught the same class to your pa,
Hi-Ho, Hi-Ho;

Sonny had heard enough. He shouted over the crowd his all-time favorite, the theme song to Green Acres. He began with his scratchy throat full of phlegm, as it always was:

Green Acres is the place for me, (the bus joins in)
Farm women are the life for me!
Legs, spreadin' out so far and wide,
Keep Manhattan just give me that CUNT-tryside.
Duh-duh-duh-duh-duh, The Whores!
Duh-duh-duh-duh-duh, The Scores!

At which point the song broke down into howls of laughter. They had never reached any further into it before they lost it. Usually it ended at CUNT-tryside, but they were seniors now, and had better composure.

"Fresh Hair!!" Sonny gagged to end it.

Chance had an old favorite:

Mine eyes have seen the glory of the burning of the school;
We have beaten all the teachers, we have broken all the rules;
We have even made the principal and coaches look like fools;
Our truth is marching on;

Glory, glory, hal-le-lu-yah,
Teacher hit me with a rule-la;
I met her at the door, with a loaded forty-four,
And she don't teach no more!!!

One of the juniors, Spencer Williams, decided to start the next song:

Duh-duh-duh-duh
Click-click,
Duh-duh-duh-duh
Click-click,
Duh-duh-duh-duh, Duh-duh-duh-duh, Duh-duh-duh-duh
Click-Click.

The Addams Family started,
When Uncle Fester farted,
They all came out retarded,
The Addams Family!

Sonny didn't like that song. Especially since a junior had started it. Before he could react, Chance stood in his seat. He sang out:

Now listen to a story 'bout a man named Jed,
Stripped Ellie-Mae and threw her on the bed;
Down came the zipper, out came the worm,
All you could see was a-bubblin' sperm.

Sonny called out:

"Cum, that is, white gold, Texas cream!!"

With that the interior lights of the bus were turned on, the universal sign the bus driver was getting pissed off. The bus went silent.

"Hey!!" the driver called out. "We've got kids on this bus!!!"

Bob leaned down in his seat, so he couldn't be seen, and shouted, "Good, they might learn something!!"

That got a laugh, and the bus went silent again. The lights were switched off. Once they were, Jimmy started in again. This song was not dirty, but personal. Jimmy and Sonny grew up a few blocks from each other, and a kid by the name of Donny Demoss lived a couple of doors down from Sonny. His father owned a small junk yard and towing business. Donny used to be in their clique, but the year before he dropped out, so he could spend every available minute with his girlfriend. The other boys could not understand it at the time. Looking back, they were perfect for each other. Sonny composed the following to show his displeasure.

Donny Google,
With the goo-goo googly eyes.
Donny Google,
Had a wife three times his size.

She sued Donny for divorce,
Now he's livin' with Becky Morse.
Donny Google,
With the goo-goo-googly eyes.

Jimmy sang that one solo. As he finished the last line the bus swerved around a bend in the road and was blasted by the bright lights of Morton, Illinois. The cheerleaders managed to regain control of the masses and stirred the crowd with their favorite cheer.

C-A-N; T-O-N; CANTON, CANTON,

C-A-N; T-O-N; LITTLE GIANTS WIN!!!

Minus the four cohorts in the back of the bus, this chant was sustained until the bus rolled into the gravel parking lot outside the football stadium. The cheerleaders led the charge filing out of the bus, and the chaperone, who was the science teacher who would be teaching Jimmy's Physics class the second semester, stood by the bus door, waiting for the last to exit. His name was Sheldon Davis, and he was the father of the afore-mentioned children. Mr. Davis was from the South, and he prided himself on being a soft-spoken Southern gentleman. He let Sonny and Bob pass before he grabbed Jimmy by the arm.

"So, what do you think my children need to learn from you?" Sheldon asked in his soft drawl.

Jimmy looked at him quizzically, until he remembered what Bob had said earlier. He couldn't stop himself from smiling at the idea the teacher assumed he was the one who had said it. To say this teacher, who Jimmy had never spoken to before this day, was intimidating to Jimmy could not be farther from the truth. First off, he was shorter than Jimmy. Secondly, his drawl was funny. Thirdly, he had a chipped tooth. Lastly, the longer Jimmy stood silently staring at him, the more intimidated the teacher seemed to be getting. Jimmy decided silence was the best response.

Chance, stuck behind Jimmy on the bus steps, pushed his way down and grabbed Jimmy around the shoulders.

"Let's go, Jimmy, so we can get somethin' ta eat before the game starts," he said to break the tension and the teacher's grip.

Sheldon had to use all his practiced civility to remain calm as the boys skipped away.

"Don't even try to sign up for the fan bus again, boys!!" he called out as they receded into the crowd.

Chance, to emphasize the point, sang into Jimmy's ear a Wings tune, "You better listen what the man says...."

"Why in the fuck does he think I said that?" asked Jimmy, more to the thin Morton air than the boys crowded around him.

"Fuck him, Jimmy," responded Bob, slightly in earshot of the chaperone walking by with his progeny.

"Yeah, let's go watch our heroes get their asses kicked," suggested Sonny.

And so, they did. The opening kickoff was the highlight of the game. For some strange reason, Kilos was on the kickoff team. The play unfolded like a slow-motion dream sequence in a comedy movie. Canton kicked off, and Bob and Jimmy, at the same time, spotted Kilos waddling downfield with his short-legged gait. Since he was three steps slower than everyone else he was easy to spot. Then, as if he was a moth to a flame, the Morton return man faked his way past most of the swarming Little Giants and burst into the clear and was on a collision course with the last man in his path to the goal line, Kilos. Kilos lowered his body in the perfect posture of a tackler, head up, and drove his body into the runner... and bounced off. The impact launched him back on his butt, but luckily Kilos' helmet got in the way of his adversary's knee as he was run over. This slight bump, from the Morton man's perspective, wasn't enough to make him fall, but he did stumble enough to allow Yobs, chugging along a step behind, to dive onto the back of his legs and bring him down.

Kilos tried to stand, but could not, as he was dazed by what to him was much more than a slight bump. He staggered a couple of steps, like a typical high school kid after two beers, and fell to the ground. The boys in the stands were laughing so hard they couldn't stay in their seats. Yobs and Crazy Joe grabbed him by his armpits and carried him unceremoniously off the field.

"Nice hit, Kilos!!!" called out Jimmy after he could catch a breath.

The game played out as expected. Canton did not leave undefeated. Sonny and Chance scored with a couple of girls from Morton at half time, however, if you could call getting to second base scoring; and in high school, you could. Sonny lured them behind the bleachers with a rascally smile and a pipe full of cheap Mexican weed.

After the game, as the boys returned to the bus, they decided to follow as close behind the cheerleaders as they could, to avoid a possible confrontation with Mr. Davis. Bonnie Midas, the stocky head cheerleader, slowed when she saw them.

"Jimmy," she said with the sweet, simulated smile the Status Queens were famous for, "You know we're counting on you to be in the Homecoming skit."

Jimmy said nothing. He was trying to remember if Bonnie had ever spoken to him before in life. Bonnie took a few steps waiting for Jimmy's response, and in a few more they reached the bus. She stopped and stared at him for emphasis.

"I know you won't let us down," she proclaimed with the same enthusiasm she had used thirty minutes earlier, when she shouted the same line to the Little Giant defense. Her faith hadn't turned out to be well founded in that case.

RULE # 16 - *If You're Going to Be in the Spotlight, You've Got to Make an Entrance*

By Monday morning Jimmy had convinced himself that 1) he was going to skit practice and 2) he was going to try out for basketball, which meant he had to talk to Bucky. He didn't inform Sonny as they drove through the barren fields recently stripped of their corn, passing a pipe between them.

The music was too loud to talk. Sonny had been given the key to Silas's house, since Silas wouldn't be using it for a while, and he had found an 8-track tape that didn't suck among the dozens that did: 'Why Can't We Be Friends' by War.

Jimmy had heard it before, but on this very morning he realized the song Low Rider was the best 'get high' song of all time. He reached this conclusion as he listened to it blasting out of the Caddy's speakers, one of the two of which was blown. He could have listened to it over and over. Anyway, he could have if Sonny would have allowed it, but Sonny would never do that because in his mind the best song not only to get high to, but the best song of all time, was Why Can't We Be Friends. He memorized the lyrics over the weekend, or at least memorized the words he thought should be the lyrics. When he wasn't pulling on the pipe, he sang as loudly as he could, drowning out the real words.

> *Why can't we be friends?*
> *Why can't we be friends?*
> *Why can't we be friends?*
> *Why can't we be friends?*
>
> *I ain't seen you for a long time*
> *I remember you when you smoked my pipe*
>
> *Why can't we be friends?*
> *Why can't we be friends?*

77 RULES

Why can't we be friends?
Why can't we be friends?

I seen you walkin' round in Canton Town
I called you but you did not look around

Why can't we be friends?
Why can't we be friends?
Why can't we be friends?
Why can't we be friends?

I get my reefer from the Lumbo line
I see you standing in it every time

Why can't we be friends?
Why can't we be friends?
Why can't we be friends?
Why can't we be friends?

The color of your skin don't matter to me
As long as you will fill the bowl for free

Why can't we be friends?
Why can't we be friends?
Why can't we be friends?
Why can't we be friends?

I'd kinda like to rob the President
Get somethin' back from the money he's spent

Why can't we be friends?
Why can't we be friends?
Why can't we be friends?
Why can't we be friends?

Sometimes I don't talk good
But yet I know I say what I should

Why can't we be friends?
Why can't we be friends?
Why can't we be friends?
Why can't we be friends?

You know I'm spyin' on the C-I-A
And takin' money from the Maf–I-A

Why can't we be friends?
Why can't we be friends?
Why can't we be friends?
Why can't we be friends?

Sonny was still singing it when the boys walked from the parking lot and entered the school's back entrance. Jimmy entered his own world as the high enveloped him, and could hear Sonny, but it was distant background noise. Jimmy's mind was on the skit. He knew he had to come up with something. He could see himself standing on stage, and the curtain lifting, and the crowd cheering, but then a feeling washed over him like a tsunami. That was bullshit. He had to make an entrance, not be standing on stage when the curtain opened. Other people could be standing there, but Jimmy knew he had to walk on. And how should he walk? That thought was swirling in his brain when a familiar voice called out a few inches from his face.

"Hey Space Cadet!! You gonna walk right over me?" It was Bob, looking down at Jimmy with a silly grin on his face. "You look wasted, Jimmy," he said, somewhat impressed. "C'mon, let's walk it off."

A tradition at the high school was to walk in endless circles through the halls of the school from the time you dropped off your stuff in your locker until the first bell rang. The high school was made of an original two-story building which held the classrooms

109

on each floor; and an add-on one story shorter wing, where the auditorium and gymnasium were. The wings were at an angle to each other, and where they met was the building foyer and front entrance. The principal's office was to the left of the entrance as you walked in, then the classrooms were beyond. Walking straight from the entrance led to the wide front staircase, which rose to the second floor in two zig-zag flights of stairs. At the far end of the main wing was a smaller staircase which was the best place to make out if you wanted people to see you and a side door which was the best way to sneak out of the school if you didn't.

The add-on wing extended from the main entrance down a hallway with the wood paneled outer auditorium wall to the right and a trophy case along it to the left. The hallway ended at the back entrance of the school. The gym could be entered from doors along the covered walkway which led from the back entrance to a separate building, where special classrooms for practical subjects like home economics and woodshop were housed.

Sonny followed Bob and Chance down the hall toward the main stairway, to start their first circuit. Jimmy trailed the other three. He wanted to watch his reflection as he walked past the trophy cases. As he viewed himself, he was not impressed. He bounced up and down too much, took too many steps to be cool, and he didn't know what to do with his arms. He realized he had never seriously thought about how he walked. If he was going to make a proper entrance, he needed to do that now.

"Keep up, Cornbread," said Bob as they reached the stairs and started to climb.

Cornbread was another of Jimmy's nicknames. It had been given to him by Crazy Joe during basketball tryouts the year before. Cornbread Maxwell was a college star Crazy Joe had seen in a picture and thought Jimmy looked like.

"Are you so wasted that you've forgotten how ta walk?" asked Sonny.

As they climbed the stairs, Chance realized he knew a song which fit the occasion. "Wasted days and wasted nights..." he sang out in his best Freddie Fender voice as people flowed past them on either side. He didn't know any more of the words, but that was enough to get the point across. When they reached the top, they turned right and marched down the long hallway, waving to the seniors, messing with the underclassmen, blowing kisses to the girls, and in general strutting through like they owned the place.

At the end of the hall was Table Muscle's classroom, and he stood in the doorway shaking his head as he watched the endless river of circling students. As Bob passed him, he said, "Hey Coach, checking out the New Developments?"

Table Muscle tilted his head at Bob quizzically, but the boys did not slow down to explain. They kept walking and laughing. New Developments were to this group their way of describing breast size increases in the girls over the summer. That was the main reason they walked the halls as they did. It gave them the opportunity to check out all the girls and see who had filled out and who hadn't. Chance had developed a scale starting with Raisins, which meant nipples only sticking out from a flat chest; to the Grand Tetons, which had only been seen by the boys in magazines. There were a few girls who had reached the "More Than a Mouthful" stage, which to a philosopher like Jimmy meant anything more was a waste, but his was the minority opinion. Sonny had added categories for shapes, from Basketballs on one extreme, which were found only on fat girls, to Bananas on the other extreme. Bananas had the unfortunate tendency (for the girls so endowed) of no two being the same size, but fortunately that was temporary and eventually they evened out. However, for most owners of Bananas, the temporary uneven period occurred during high school.

In addition to scoping out what had sprouted, the boys also made predictions on upcoming events. Jimmy had created a special, special, category for sophomores called "Give Her Some Time," which meant the girl had potential but was, in the words of

Potsy, TYTF, meaning Too Young To Fuck. Sometimes, like this day as they walked down the back stairs past a group of youngsters, Chance would serenade such a girl with one of his old-time crooner classics, "We say, we say, you are too young!!"

And the girls, who had not heard it before, first were impressed. Then the words sunk in.

"Ehhhhhh!!" they said in unison, still not quite unimpressed.

"Give them some time," Jimmy said on cue as they reached the bottom of the stairs.

As they walked down the hall on the first floor, Jimmy walked slower than the others again, and carefully put each foot directly in front of the other. It looked controlled and forced him to swing his arms in a high arc. Most definitely not cool. Then it was up the stairs again. On the way down the second story hall the second time, Jimmy let his feet fall where they normally would, except he added a dip of the shoulders. That was a little better, he thought. He tried a different walking style each trip down the hall. After the fourth cycle, Bob couldn't take it anymore.

"Why are you walkin' so funny, Jimmy? Do you really think you're cool?" he exclaimed.

If Bob thought he was trying to be cool, Jimmy knew he must be on the right track.

"If I am, you wouldn't know," responded Jimmy, and then added for good measure, "sense."

Sonny doubled over laughing. Bob stopped walking and stood in Jimmy's face, looking down on him with a comically evil stare.

"One day I'm gonna kick your ass, Jimmy," threatened Bob.

Bob had been given the nickname 'No Sense' by Silas Mathis. It arose when Sonny took Bob to Silas's house the year before to buy some weed. After having a conversation with Bob while making the transaction, Silas had taken Sonny aside and warned him to never bring any of his No Sense friends to his house ever again. From that day on, Bob had a new nickname.

"Not today, Bub," countered Jimmy. Bub was another nickname.

Sonny broke the tension by singing his favorite song.

"Why can't we be friends, why can't we be friends, why can't we be friends, why can't we be friends?" and he laughed again.

Jimmy changed the subject. "I'm goin' ta Bucky's office after school today."

"To talk to him about basketball?" asked Bob, proving the validity of his nickname.

"No, to talk to him about woodshop," said Jimmy with a straight face.

"I didn't think you took..." Bob stopped in mid-sentence, realizing the stupidity of what was about to come out of his mouth.

Sonny and Chance were disappointed, as they were waiting to pounce on that next classically stupid thing.

"Then I'm comin' with you," declared Bob in a nice recovery.

"Me too!!" chimed in the other two.

The bell rang, and it was off to first period.

RULE # 17 - *You Have Twice More Courage When You're Helping Others Than When You're Helping Only Yourself*

As the school day progressed, Jimmy changed his mind several times about talking to Bucky. Why waste his time engaging another authority figure who would reject him on the flimsiest of reasons? He was mulling over the question again after his last class, as he stood at his locker putting his books away and had reached the conclusion it wasn't worth it when a loud bang brought him out of his trance. It was Sonny, slamming his fist against the adjacent locker, behind the open door of Jimmy's. When Jimmy pulled his head out to see who it was, he saw all three of his friends surrounding him.

"OK, Jimmy, we're ready if you are," said Sonny.

Jimmy drew a deep breath pondering how to tell them he'd decided to not talk to Bucky. Studying each of them, he knew it was impossible to do that without exposing himself as a coward. Even if he could be so convincing to them they wouldn't realize it. His hesitation was deafening. He took another deep breath.

"OK, let's go," he decided finally.

Usually the boys would fight to be the one walking ahead of the others. To be seen following was not cool. But on this walk from Jimmy's second floor locker, down the front stairs, out the back entrance, and on to the building where the woodshop was, Sonny, Chance, and Bob trailed behind Jimmy in silence. This talk was just as important, maybe more important, to his friends than it was to him. As he realized this during the short journey, it gave him a stronger resolve than he would have ever had if he had been taking this walk alone, for only himself. When he reached the door of the woodshop, he could see the basketball coach sitting behind his handmade desk, with a whittling knife in his hand.

Whatever he was carving was not obvious to Jimmy. No one else was in the room.

"Coach," Jimmy called out from the doorway, "Can I come in? I want to talk to you."

Jimmy looked behind him, and the other boys were standing few steps behind and to the left, outside the door, so the coach could see only him. If Bucky had said "no" it would have been as if they had never been there.

"Sure, Jimmy, come on in!" Bucky said with a surprised smile. He was not totally surprised. He remembered Jimmy from the tryouts the year before, and no one had worked harder. He was the new varsity basketball coach, after all.

As Jimmy walked in, the other boys crowded in behind him. Bucky's eyes widened when he saw it was a group and not just an individual. Jimmy approached the desk, but did not sit or even ask to sit, he was much too nervous for that. The other boys stood behind him strategically, so in case Bucky started yelling the sound would be deflected by Jimmy's body, or if he decided to attack with the knife they could escape leaving Jimmy to his fate. Jimmy got to the point right away.

"Coach, I wanted to find out if I have a chance to make the team before I try out. Last year I really didn't have a chance, and if this year is gonna be the same, I'm not wastin' my time," blurted out Jimmy, but not so fast the words piled up on one another.

Bucky looked Jimmy in the eye, impressed by his directness. He glanced at the other boys, who had still not said a word.

"Are you boys here for the same reason?" he questioned, looking each in the eye individually.

"Yes," they responded sheepishly.

Jimmy thought to chime in, "We all kept up with our lifting, even after we got cut last year."

"I know you have," said the coach, and he smiled. "I can tell you right now I have fifteen uniforms, and no one has their name on one. You four have just as much chance as anyone of making the team."

Jimmy stared hard at Bucky. He knew some of those fifteen uniforms had names on them already. He couldn't see any hint of sarcasm or dishonesty in Bucky's face, however, and that was rare when he dealt with authority figures. To break the tension, Jimmy thrust out his hand toward the coach, something that surprised them both. It was spontaneous on Jimmy's part, a response to what was to him a shocking encounter, maybe the most adult conversation he had ever had. Bucky reached out his own hand and they shook. A silent moment passed and then the other boys stepped forward to do the same.

"OK, boys, thanks for stopping by. See you at practice tomorrow," said Bucky, bringing an end to the conversation so he could go back to his whittling, "And be ready to run. Come by to see me anytime if you want to talk some more."

The boys stepped away from him, not turning their backs, as they eased out of the classroom. They could barely contain themselves, once a few steps out of the door, from running and jumping across the parking lot.

RULE # 18 - *Love Will Keep Us Together*

Basketball practice evolved from a fun adventure to drudgery during the second wind sprint on the first day of practice. Burning pain in the chest, stabbing pain in the legs, and nausea twisting the guts tend to take the fun out of anything. Sonny knew how important it was to bring the fun back, and the best way to do that he could think of was using the sophomores for entertainment. After the first couple of practices the coaches had split the sophomores off into a separate group, and Sonny picked up the habit of spitting, or if he could work some up, blowing snot on the basketballs that rolled onto the varsity's side of the court from the sophomore half. He would throw balls at the back of their heads. He would trip them in layup lines. He was, however, unjustly blamed when Chance stole Carl Murphy's Icy Hot and rubbed it in Brad Littlejohn's jock strap. His denials were not convincing to anyone who heard them, even to the ones who had watched Chance do it. After a week of spitting, his behavior pattern had developed to the point the facts were overlooked.

Practice was not held was at the high school. It was across town at the old, World War II hanger building that had been repurposed as the Alice Ingersoll Gymnasium. Brad Schmidt, Jimmy and Sonny rode from school to the gym with Chance, knowing they'd be returning to school afterward for skit practice. Bob drove separately, as he had decided participating in the skit was too Redneck for him.

That caused a problem, but only a slight one, because Bob was the only one in the group who had weed. Bob came from the wealthiest family of the group, which didn't mean he was rich, but it did mean he had his own car and the most extra money to buy dope with. He stored his weed in a Frisbee under the front seat of his car, and he almost always left his car unlocked. Sonny would constantly be pilfering a pinch or two from the Frisbee when Bob wasn't looking or would sneak into the parking lot and take a bud or two when he wasn't around. Since Sonny sold him most of the weed he bought in the first place, he also got a cut up front and knew when Bob was holding and when he was dry. If Bob ever realized what was happening he never let on, and his unwitting contributions were essential to the rest of the group's high times.

On this occasion, it was Brad Schmidt who provided the distraction needed to keep Bob out of his car after practice long enough for Sonny to get in it. Brad cornered Bob with a conversation about joining the Fellowship of Christian Athletes, an organization whose main function was a pancake breakfast every Thursday morning before school. Since he knew Bob would want to argue about it, it provided the exact amount of time Sonny needed to slip out, grab a pinch, and return to the gym before Bob knew he had been out. All five of the boys then left the locker room together.

After saying good-by to Bob, the other boys piled into Chance's parents' 1973 Ford LTD Country Squire station wagon, with wood paneling, which for some reason they let him drive to school that day - and the only reason the others were riding with him - and went for a round-about drive of seven miles instead of the two-mile straight shot that would have led them directly to the school. They had to get up for skit practice, didn't they? As they passed the pipe around and laughed at their friend's lack of sense, Jimmy let the others in on what he and Kilos had been planning for Homecoming/ Hyde Park Week. To a man they were wholeheartedly supportive. And as he expected, they had more destructive ideas.

"We should start some fires around the school," suggested Sonny. "You can't have a real riot unless somethin's burnin."

"We could have a march!" said Chance.

"Fuck that, Potsy," argued Sonny.

The worst thing about Chance driving was his car had a lousy 8-track player that would only play two of the four channels, and AM radio, and he would only listen to the lamest local stations. After his third pull on the pipe, and Brad Schmidt was notorious for getting really, really, stoned off two puffs of any weed, Chance's radio assaulted Brad's brain with the Captain and Tennille singing Love Will Keep Us Together.

Brad started humming a tune with a very strange melody that had never existed before. It was part science fiction weirdness coupled with West Virginia yodeling. Jimmy was in the backseat along with Brad, and Sonny rode in the front. Both boys looked at Brad incredulously.

"What's the matter with you Brad?" asked Jimmy, slightly worried.

"It's this music, man," said Brad, "If I keep listening to it, it'll stick in my brain and I'll never get it out!!!"

At this point, Toni was wailing, "I will, I will, I will..."

"Turn that Redneck shit off, Anteater!!!" commanded Sonny.

Brad stuck his head out of the window and took a few deep breaths. When he brought it back in, he said, "I've got Weed Butt Madness."

That was the boys' code for wanting a cigarette, which in their slang was called a weed butt. They had adapted it from Reefer Madness, a movie they had seen the year before. In their opinions, there had never been a movie made in the history of Hollywood that was better to smoke weed while watching than Reefer Madness. When they watched they tried to get as high as the people in the movie were acting, but they could never do it. Sonny handed him a Marlboro Light from a pack he had in his shirt pocket.

Chance turned off the radio as Toni sang her last, "Think of me babe whenever..."

"Whenever I want to throw up," said Jimmy in response.

As they entered the school parking lot, Jimmy turned to Brad and said, "You better put that weed butt out, you never know where the Narcs are."

Brad threw it out of the window, where it squirted under a car. As they rolled past, the car door opened and out stepped Lurch, the vice-principal.

"Oh shit," said Brad, looking back and then ducking down. Good thing it was dark. Lurch looked around but could not see who had thrown the cigarette. The boys parked as far away as possible and waited until Lurch's car pulled out of the lot before they got out.

"Close call, Brad, huh?" laughed Jimmy as they walked through the lot. Brad looked like he had just witnessed a beheading. Paranoia, so long as it was someone else's, was always funny.

The auditorium was not typical of schools of that era. Most doubled as gymnasiums, the stage set behind the basketball court. The Canton Senior High School auditorium was more like a concert hall, or movie theater. There was the main floor, reached by two sets of doors leading off from the school's first floor hallway. Each set of doors led to an aisle, with six theater style seats in each row outside the aisles and a wide section of twelve seats in the middle of the aisles. There were twenty-five rows, sloping gently down toward the stage to give every seat a decent view. In the back, right corner of the room was a flight of stairs leading up to the balcony. The balcony held eight more rows, with twelve seats in the back two rows, ten seats in the next four, then eight in the front two. The aisles were along the walls. The balcony, of course, was where all the coolest people would hang out.

The boys entered through the closest auditorium door to the back entrance of the school and walked down the aisle. The stage was filled with Status Queens, Zit Queens, a few football players, and assorted other geeks. Bonnie Midas and Derek Schmidt sat in the middle seats of the second row. The air seemed full of tension. Kilos saw them first.

"It's about time you got here!!" called out Kilos.

All heads turned to the quartet stumbling down the aisle. Brad had tried to trip Chance, who was walking ahead of the others, waving his arms like Julius Caesar, but tripped himself on an aisle seat. His big feet betrayed him like this often. Not as often as a few years ago, but he could still manage to do it at the most inopportune times. When Chance saw what Brad was attempting, he hopped ahead and lost his balance partially anyway. Nobody fell, but another opportunity of making a great entrance had passed them by.

As the boys reached the short flight of steps leading to the stage, Hannah Hartford, the stockiest of the Status Queens, and unofficial sergeant-at-arms, barked out, "OK, I guess now we can get started!"

"Jimmy," called out Casey Queen, the shorter, but almost as stocky Status Queen. She was the original founder of the group in junior high, and she was the inspiration for its name. "You know what your role is, right?" She said it with a contrived fondness that did not quite mask her irritation.

Jimmy looked at her with feigned innocence and said, "Nope, I'm just here for the beer."

That got a laugh from everyone on the stage except Casey and Hannah. As he looked around, he saw all the familiar faces he thought he would see. Yobs and Crazy Joe, Hulk, Carl David, Grant Roper, Carlo Firenze, and Nick the Greek Callan, the group thought of as the coolest of the cool. There was Laura Ashland, standing so Carlo could see her good side, and Nancy Naughton, with her white blouse tied securely near the top of her neck. She was somewhere between raisins and a mouthful, but she still felt the need to be careful they not fall out. Annie Royal chatted with Peggie Wilson, trying to act like she wasn't watching Jimmy and hoping he would say hello to her. Worm Chow was trying to hang with the football players while they tried to ignore him.

"Very funny, Jimmy," said Casey. "We've written down everyone's name that has a speaking part. Everyone else will be extras, either cowboys or townspeople or dancing girls in the saloon."

"You mean hookers?" asked Sonny.

Half of the crowd thought that was funny. The females didn't.

"I'll read off the names," Hannah continued. When she unfolded the paper, Peg Leg took a step nearer, so she could look over her shoulder. She wanted to make sure the Status Queens hadn't changed anything.

"Jimmy Williams is the Sheriff. Chance Gillingham is the Waco Kid. Chuck Hanson is Mongo, and Scott Johns is the Mad Professor. I am the bartender in the saloon. Bob Fair and Nancy Naughton are the Mayor and his Wife. Joe Starks and Tom Yardwick are the head Saints..."

"Crazy Joe and Billy Bolshevik!!!" called out Yobs before Hannah could state the names on the script.

"So, here's the plot," called out a feminine voice from the audience. Jimmy knew that voice. It had to be Derek Schmidt.

"We open the curtain and the scene is the saloon. The music is playing, and the girls are dancing, and the guys are playing cards. The Mayor's Wife comes in, dressed like she just came from church. She calls out, 'Oh no, there's a crazy bunch of outlaws coming into town called the Saints. What do we do?'"

"The curtain closes. Next, the curtain opens, and the saloon is full of rowdy cowboys. They are shooting and yelling and generally raising hell."

"Hey," called out Sonny, who had already decided he was going to be one of the bad guys, "How about we run across the stage in front of the curtain, acting like we're ridin' horses into town, and then the curtain opens and we're in the saloon?"

"Not a bad idea, Sonny," said Derek, but his tone of voice gave evidence to the fact he didn't think it was a good idea either. "Let's move on."

Yobs thought about it for a nano-second before he chimed in, "Yeah, that's a great idea, Sonny!"

"OK, so we run across the stage, then back behind the curtain and we're chasing the hookers around when it opens again," said Sonny.

Derek knew not to fight it. He continued.

"As the cowboys tear up the place, the Mayor and his Wife and the Bartender have a discussion in front of the stage."

"The Mayor says, 'We have to do something to save the town from the Saints!'"

"His Wife says 'Oh, what do we do!!' and then she faints."

"The Bartender says, 'We only have one choice, we have to find the Sheriff!!'"

"The curtain closes again."

Derek stopped to take a breath.

"We can't just close the curtain, and nothing happens," said Jimmy. "Why not have a few of the girls walk across the stage holding a sign or something?"

"You mean like the girls who walk around the ring between rounds of a boxing match?" asked Annie Royal, to the surprise of everyone, including herself.

"Hell Yeah!!!" was a unified roar from the males in the room.

Derek rolled his eyes in the darkness and continued, after clearing his throat to get everyone's attention.

"The curtain opens, and all the townspeople are in a meeting. In comes the Sheriff from offstage. He has the Waco Kid with him. In the meeting, the Mad Professor comes up with a plan to challenge the Saints to a winner-take-all football game, and if the Saints lose they have to leave town. The Sheriff and Waco Kid refuse to get involved and leave."

Kilos laughed and said, "I'll diagram a play called 'Katy Bar to the Door' and the Sheriff says it'll never work, because I can't tell him who Katy is."

Derek did think that was a keeper. He kept going. "Then the curtain closes, and the Sheriff and Waco Kid walk in front of the curtain from one side, and then Mongo comes on from the other side with a donkey pulling a cart. The donkey stops and refuses to go any further. Mongo gets so mad he punches the donkey and knocks him out cold. He then unhitches the donkey and starts pulling the cart himself."

Chance jumped in, "What about the pork and beans scene? How 'bout if the beans are what make him strong, like Popeye needs spinach?"

That was such a bizarre twist, it got voted in immediately.

Derek had no choice but to put it in. "The two guys are amazed at his strength. Waco asks him how he got so strong. He tells them he gets his strength from pork and beans. He says a bunch of cowboys, calling themselves the Saints, stole his horse and left him with this donkey. He swears if he ever sees those guys again, he'll rip them to shreds."

"They must'a got me drunk first!" chimed in Hulk.

Peggy, who was in charge of costumes and wardrobe, said, "We have a two-man costume with a horse head, and we can make a donkey head for it out of paper Mache!!"

"Hey, how about Worm Chow and Jack Hoff bein' the donkey?" suggested Crazy Joe, in a menacing voice that let the two of them know they had no choice.

"Write it down!!" instructed Jimmy before anyone could argue.

"The farting scene comes next!!!" shouted Yobs as he had a flash of inspiration. "The Sheriff sends the Waco Kid to the Saints camp, and he acts like he's a traitor, so he can steal their beans and get drunk, and then they sing Home on the Range."

Derek ignored him. "The curtain opens on the football game. The townspeople are taking a beating. When the game seems lost, onstage walk the Sheriff, Waco Kid, and Mongo. The Sheriff scores the winning touchdown with Mongo clearing the way. The crowd goes wild and the curtain closes."

Jimmy cocked his head toward the seats where Derek's voice seemed to be coming from. "Hey Derek, I think Yobs has a point. I think it would be funny to have a scene where the Saints sing Home on the Range and fart."

At this point, a few more football players burst into the auditorium, and one of them had a football and tossed it onto the stage. The girls squealed at the top of their lungs and scampered around hoping to get tackled as the boys scrambled for it and all thoughts of the plot were disrupted. Yobs got his hands on it and tossed it at Jimmy. "Catch it, Sheriff," he called out, hoping to catch Jimmy unaware.

Jimmy stabbed at it and somehow it stuck to his fingers. He knew the next thing to happen would be a bunch of guys rushing him and starting a dog pile, so he knew he had to get rid of it quickly. His first thought was to heave it into the balcony, but he thought better of it, he might break a light or something up there, so he didn't. Instead he tossed it to Peg Leg, and as he assumed, no one jumped her, and calm was restored.

"OK, people, listen up!!" shouted Derek, now standing and slapping a rolled-up notebook in his hand.

"We'll have to work on the next to last scene, but the last scene is clear. The Sheriff scores the winning touchdown and the curtain closes while the townspeople celebrate. Let's take it from the top!!"

After a couple of run-throughs, the attention spans of the boys had been run-through as well and practice came to an end. The next thing on the agenda was for everyone to journey to the garage where the senior class float was not taking shape. It was supposed to be taking shape, but a disagreement on the design of the float between the Zit and Status Queens could not be resolved. As the girls tried to rally the troops, Sonny whispered to Chance, Brad, and Jimmy, "I've still got a little of No Sense's stash left."

125

With little further prompting, the boys made their way out of the auditorium and back to Chance's car. Jimmy was thinking about what he should wear as the Sheriff. It had to be all white. He had a pair of tight, white, bell bottomed Angel's Flight pants. He had a white shirt. He had white tennis shoes. All he needed was a white hat.

"Wake up, Jimmy," said Brad as he passed Jimmy the pipe. "I need another weed butt."

"You sure, Brad? You don't want your dad smelling it on you," teased Chance.

"Yeah, but I need another weed butt," replied Brad. "Just don't take me home yet."

"So, what do you want to do? Just ride around?" asked Chance.

The boys did just that as they finished off two more bowls of weed from Sonny's pipe. When he took the last puff, Sonny said, "Hey, I got a better idea. Let's go visit Bucky!!"

Jimmy would have looked at Sonny like he was crazy, but he already knew Sonny was crazy and didn't bother. Sonny was serious, but Jimmy assumed the others weren't that crazy, so in his mind the best response to Sonny was to ignore him.

"Yeah, right," said Chance. "You don't know where he lives."

Brad, who should have known better, but he was high, after all, saw a phone booth on the side of the road. "Pull over!!!" he yelled at Chance, who was so startled he did not ask why, he just pulled the car to the side of the road. Brad jumped out and ran to the booth and returned a minute later with a sheet from the phone book in his hand.

"It says here he lives at Eighth and Olive," said Brad in a matter of fact tone.

Jimmy thought of telling his friends this was not a smart idea but decided to save his breath. The only reason they wanted to do it in the first place was because it was such a spectacularly bad idea. Sonny looked at Chance and Chance shrugged in the way he always did before he did something he should regret in the future, but probably wouldn't.

"Let's go," said Chance.

A song came on the radio. The lead singer from Hot Chocolate sang out, "I believe in miracles. Where're you from? You sexy thing." Jimmy saw the irony but kept it to himself.

One thing about living in a small town, there was not a lot of time to think twice about going somewhere before you got there. It was less than five minutes from the time Brad climbed into the car from the phone booth until he was getting back out at Bucky's house. The boys hadn't thought about the reason they would give for knocking on his door, or what they would say if they got in. They were just sure they wanted to get in.

The house was typical of houses in Canton. It had wooden steps leading up to the front porch, and a picture window next to the front door which allowed anyone on the porch to see in. As the boys tried to stealthily climb the four steps, Chance tripped and fell into Jimmy, causing so much noise they startled the occupants. The porch light came on before they could knock. Sonny was first, behind him stood Chance and Jimmy, and Brad tried to hide behind them all. His high was starting to be overcome by his paranoia. The top of a bald head appeared in the glass panel near the top of the door. The man inside was too short to see his face from the outside, but the boys knew instantly it was Bucky, and not only was it Bucky, he was not wearing his toupee. The door opened.

"Hey, Coach, Trick or Treat!!!!" sang out Sonny. It was Oct. 13, not 31st, but it was close enough, plus he didn't have any other ideas.

The look on Bucky's face was priceless. It should be hanging from the museum wall next to the Mona Lisa. If it was, you'd know what she was smiling about. The shock, anger, confusion, followed by the sudden awareness of the cool breeze on his head was hilarious. What a face. That exact instant was seared into the crew's brains as a moment of such comic intensity, whatever punishment came next would be worth it.

"What a surprise, boys, come on in!!" Bucky said, before having a chance to think.

As the boys stared into the house they saw a woman who looked to be Bucky's age, so they assumed it was his wife, and an old woman, who looked like she was an antique version of the other woman, straight out of Little House on the Prairie, who had to be Bucky's mother-in-law. They were sitting on a coach in the living room, watching television. Grandma was twirling knitting needles in her hands with a ball of yarn in her lap, and she wore a bonnet on her head with strings down the sides like pigtails.

"That's my wife, and my mother-in-law. Excuse me a minute, boys," said Bucky, and he disappeared out of the door on the opposite side of the room.

The boys, not knowing what to do next, sat on the floor next to the couch. Neither of the women said a word but tried at least to smile before turning their heads back to the TV screen. The boys tried to focus on it as well, but they were too high. After an awkward moment, Bucky came bounding back into the room, his toupee half stuck on his head. That's when the boys realized he was drunk.

"I haven't bought any candy yet," apologized Bucky. "So, what are you boys up to?"

"Nothing much, coach," answered Sonny. "We were just riding around, and thought we'd stop by."

No one said a word after that for about sixty seconds, which is a long time if you think about it.

Jimmy gritted his teeth to stop from laughing. The bottom of the toupee was sticking up in the back, and the woven part was exposed. Brad had seen it too, and he closed his eyes to stop the tears from streaming down his face.

"I would offer you a beer, but you're not eighteen yet!" crooned Bucky. He had to be drunk to say that.

"Aw, that's OK, Coach," said Brad, rising to his feet. This kind of composure from Brad was amazing. He must have thought this was life or death. Jimmy thought he had tears of laughter coming from his eyes, but maybe they were tears of fears.

"Yeah, Coach, I don't turn eighteen until April," agreed Chance. All the boys stood now.

"OK, Coach," said Sonny, "See you at practice tomorrow!"

Jimmy walked out first, having not said a word the entire time. The rest of the boys followed. As soon as the door closed behind them, the laughter they had been containing burst out like a blast from a volcano. It would have been impossible not to hear it inside the house.

Brad made it home OK, even though the other boys blew their exhaled cigarette smoke on him to make it more likely he would get sniffed out by his dad when he got there. Chance also helped him out by putting the only 8 track he had in the deck, The Guess Who's 'Canned Heat'. When he bought it, he thought he was buying a tape by The Who. That mistake was probably the reason most people bought a tape by The Guess Who. Their agent must have been a genius. However, it was a good thing Chance put it on, because if Brad had heard The Carpenters or Barry Manilow at this point, his head might have exploded. Jimmy thought it was extra appropriate when the song came on, "It's too late, she's gone too far, she's lost the sun... she's come undone. She didn't find what she was looking for, and when she found what she was looking for, momma, it was too late...she's come undone."

RULE # 19 - *There Are Times When Its Best to Just Sit Back and Enjoy the Show*

Hyde Park Week kicked off as intended. On Monday morning Jimmy and Kilos detoured on their way to Calculus class to Jimmy's house to recover the posters from the basement and put them in Kilos' car. When they returned to the high school they left them there, because the next step was a reconnaissance mission. They had formulated it would be best if they waited until after the cheerleaders put up their Homecoming posters, so they could determine exactly where the Hyde Park Week posters should go to make them the most inconspicuous.

They started at the main school entrance. Next to the first set of doors leading into the auditorium they found the poster they were looking for to start the ball rolling, 'Victory for Varsity'. The cheerleaders always put that poster in this spot.

"OK, you know which one goes there, right?" said Jimmy. Kilos burst out laughing. No doubt he did. Then they walked throughout the school, mapping out the places they would direct their fellow conspirators, to position each poster for maximum effect. Their plan had to include who would be assigned which. Some people, like Yobs, Sonny, and Crazy Joe, could never be put in charge of anything that required stealth. They liked getting caught too much. Guys like Jack Hoff or Worm Chow could not be counted on for anything that required aggressive behavior, but they could put up a poster like 'Charles Macklan/Carl Manson' right outside the vice-principal's office and no one would notice anything.

They passed out the posters and tape to each crew member during lunch hour and told them exactly where to put each. Some didn't care, but most did what they were told. The back stairs had the highest density of the funniest posters. At the top of the stairs, as close to his classroom as they dared put it, was 'Cheap Shots for Table Muscle'. Before the lunch break was over, all 43 posters were hung in various places around the school, and no one had been caught putting them up. There were at least twice as many legitimate Homecoming posters up, and since most people never looked at them, not a single imposter had been found and taken down when the doors closed Monday.

Part of the reason for the lack of detection was school ended thirty minutes early that day. Someone, in the mind of Lurch a senior, no doubt, pulled a fire alarm, causing the school to be evacuated. Most of the students milled around the parking lot waiting for the all-clear signal to return to their classes, but the coolest guys realized going back to class made no sense and decided to go to Big Creek Park to get high.

Once everyone was out of their cars, Yobs, Carl David, Crazy Joe, Pick, Sonny, Jimmy, Chance, Bob, Eubanks, Nick the Greek, Kevin "Wastey" Hastey, Ron Williams, Carlo, Jasper Waldon, Buddy Anthony, and Pigpen Mueller were in a circle, passing three pipes around. Buddy and Pigpen, along with Pick, were filling them. Only one junior was allowed, Harry Roach. His dad was one of the richest men in town and had given his son a 2-year-old Chevy Impala on his sixteenth birthday. Yobs and Eubanks included him, so he could chauffeur.

"We've gotta step up the Hyde Park Week activities, boys," demanded Yobs.

"What's Hyde Park week?" asked Pigpen. He was the type who would forget in five minutes anyway, so no one bothered to answer him.

"Tomorrow we should start some real fires," proclaimed Sonny.

"How 'bout we nominate Richard Speck for Homecoming King?" proposed Chance.

Most of the boys howled in agreement, except the ones who secretly, or not so secretly, were hoping to be King themselves. Richard Shaw was the biggest nerd in the senior class. There were several nerds in the class, no doubt, but no one looked and acted the part as well as Richard Shaw. He was short, skinny, wore glasses, had no athletic ability, did not have a clue what it meant to dress or act cool, did not smoke or drink, and was deathly quiet. He was the perfect candidate for not only Homecoming King, as he symbolized everything the Homecoming King was not supposed to symbolize, but also to be nicknamed after a mass-murderer, Richard Speck.

Jimmy looked around the circle and saw at least three of the real contenders, Carl David, Carlo, and Crazy Joe, and he concluded he would rather see Richard Speck with the crown on his head for sure. To see Richard Speck on the float in the Homecoming parade with one of the Status Queens would be too hysterical to not try to help make happen and seeing the looks on the most status conscious football players' faces as they watched Richard Speck float by would be a double bonus.

"That'll piss Egg off for sure," mused Yobs, who didn't need much time to come around to the idea of letting loyalty to his friends get passed over for a good laugh.

"If he can't take a joke, fuck 'em," philosophized Sonny.

He was staring at Carlo when he said it. Carlo looked down and said nothing, knowing to complain would be uncool. When all three pipes went out and no one pulled any more vegetable matter out of their pockets to fill them again, the boys split up to go to their respective practices or to a job, but no one left to crack a book.

The next morning there was another school evacuation due to a fire alarm being pulled. Except this time there really was a fire. The fire was started in a trash can outside the back entrance to the school and hanging from the wall above the can was a poster which read, "Burn, Baby, Burn." This was Lurch's first clue something unusual was going on. Jimmy and Kilos were conveniently at Goon River during this incident and could justly claim they knew

A Novel by J.W. Wheeler

nothing about it until they returned, but if they thought that made them safe from incrimination, they were wrong. Their timing was still bad.

The next clue for Lurch was a line of guys standing in front of a poster, each writing on it and passing a pen to the next to scribble on it. When he approached the boys scattered, laughing, and at that exact moment Kilos and Jimmy sauntered past, with smirks on their faces from the recently relayed news of the fire. They stopped and stared at what Lurch was staring at. The poster read, 'Narc List – Sign Below'.

Kilos, for some reason, thought it was appropriate to ask Lurch, "So who signed it? Anybody we know?" instead of acting innocent.

Lurch glared at the boys. His name, whether he realized it or not, was the first name listed, 'Lurch'. The next name was 'Walter Matthau', the third was 'Carl Manson'. Then came 'Heady' and someone had written '(Blows)' next to it. Then came 'Captain Jack', who a lot of people wanted to see beaten up even if he wasn't guilty. Lurch ripped the poster off the wall and tore it into shreds.

"Hey, if you didn't want it, I would've taken it," said Jimmy. Lurch lurched away without another word to the pair of instigators.

Weedhopper had been given the task of hanging the 'Peyote for Varsity' poster and he had taken his instructions one step further. He was supposed to hang it next to the cheerleaders 'Victory for Varsity' poster, but instead he removed theirs and tossed it in the garbage and put his poster in its place. Anyone, even someone as blind as Walter Matthau, could see it as soon as they walked into the front door of the school. That inevitable event happened by lunchtime Tuesday, and Kilos was evicted from the lunch line and dragged into Lurch's office before he could eat. When he stepped into the office, Walter Matthau was also there, holding the poster.

"OK, so is this about the nominations for the King and Queen or are you gonna warn me not ta eat the mystery meat on the lunch menu today?" joked Kilos to deflect attention from the obvious reason he had been summoned.

"So, what do you think of this?" asked Walter as he held up the poster, ignoring Kilos' question.

Kilos doubled over in laughter, as if he was reading it for the first time. "That's funny!!" he shouted.

"Would you think it was funny if I brought your mother in here and let her see it?" asked Lurch threateningly.

"Well, she wouldn't have a clue what it meant, so I'd have to explain it to her. Peyote is a psychedelic drug derived from the peyote cactus. The only thing better is to lick one of those toads. What does this have to do with me anyway?" Kilos responded so confidently Lurch was taken aback.

Walter Matthau was getting angry. "You know you are behind this poster!!" he cried. Walter, being an unknown comedian, even to himself, was much funnier when he was angry. He was shaking his head furiously, making his jowls flap.

Kilos had to look away from the flapping to keep from bursting out laughing, and even though he knew it was not the best course of action, he responded through gritted teeth, "Actually, sir, you are behind the poster from where I'm sitting."

"Get out of here!!!" shouted Walter, enormously angry now. He realized even if he was 100% sure no one could have come up with this other than Scott Johns, he could not prove it. Kilos literally jumped at the chance to escape and dashed two steps toward the door.

The vice-principal grabbed him by the arm before he could exit. "Wait a minute," said Lurch, using his psychology PhD training to keep himself calm, "We all know you are behind this," and then he paused before he continued, "I assume your buddy Jimmy Williams is in on it too." He stared intently at Kilos to see if he was agreeing with him with his body language. He was. "You guys just keep this in mind. If it was just you two, we know you know when to stop. But these other guys, and you know who they are, don't. If they get themselves into trouble I am holding you responsible."

Once Kilos was discharged he tracked down Jimmy as soon as he could. It wasn't too difficult since Jimmy was still eating lunch. He sat beside him and whispered into his ear, "They know it's us, Whales."

Jimmy leaned away from Kilos and said, "How do they know, did you tell them it was us?" Not only did he not whisper, he didn't even bother to lower his voice.

"I didn't say anything," responded Kilos in a normal tone, "But they know. Lurch is afraid Yobs and Crazy Joe are gonna get out of control."

Jimmy looked at Kilos and chuckled, "Lurch is right, and it's too late ta stop 'em now. You might as well sit back and enjoy the fun."

RULE # 20 - *Choices Made for Political Reasons Often End Friendships*

The boys hadn't finished discussing recent events when Peg Leg approached them gingerly holding a brown paper bag.

"Here, put this in your locker, Jimmy," she instructed. She opened the bag wide enough for him to see the contents: a wide brimmed, white cowboy hat.

Jimmy smiled as he looked at it. It was the perfect big hat to sit on top of his big Afro. Wearing it would perfect the walk he had been refining for some time now. After teasing him relentlessly for the first few days, Chance and Sonny decided to ignore him, and Bob refused to even look at him while they circled the halls.

"Thanks, Peggy," Jimmy said, "This is perfect."

He had just enough time to strut to his second-floor locker and deposit the hat before the bell rang for the Homecoming week assembly and pep rally. He joined a crew of seniors seated in the middle of the main floor before it rang again. The mundane purpose of the assembly was to advise the students of the upcoming activities, which included skit night on Thursday, the football game on Friday, and the parade and Homecoming dance on Saturday. The pep rally portion was to allow the cheerleaders to try out their latest cheers. The highlight of the assembly was to announce the six finalists for Homecoming King and Queen.

It was one of the many important duties of the Student Council President to announce the finalists to the cheering throng, theoretically emotionally charged by the enthralling routines debuted at the pep rally. As normal during these assemblies, the student body did not pay attention to anything the faculty, coaches, or cheerleaders said, but abnormally, they whooped and hollered as loud as they could when Kilos bounded on-stage with the lists in his hands. Since they had been working so diligently to secure the nomination of Richard Speck, the crew of seniors leaned forward in their seats in anticipation.

"OK, everyone," bellowed Kilos once the din died down. "Here's what you've been waiting for!"

"Hurry up, Kreskin!!!!!" called out Ron Williams from the back corner. Kreskin was the name given to anyone on stage who was boring. It was coined during a legendary assembly in junior high, years before. The crowd cracked up.

"The nominees for Queen are, and please come up when your name is called," continued Kilos, ignoring the heckler, something the original Kreskin hadn't done.

"Nancy Naughton."

When her name was called she jumped to her feet a little too quickly to make the others believe it was a surprise, and much too quickly to be cool about it. Her perky response took her from almost no chance to win to zero chance.

"Hannah Hartford."

She glanced at her fellow Status Queens and nodded to them in a show of appreciation before she stood, then made her way carefully to the stage like the chunky spoiled child she was. She was another politically careful choice who had no chance.

"Jana Gamble."

She rose from her seat like a queen, and peered down on her most dangerous rival, who was also her best friend, Laura Ashland, sitting next to her. She managed to have both a pitying and encouraging look on her face as she watched her friend stare up at her. Of course, she thought she would be picked too, but if she wasn't, Jana would be a good friend about it. Wouldn't that be a wonderful opportunity to show her noble character?

"Laura Ashland."

That didn't give Jana much time to gloat. Laura had grown up on the poor side of town, a couple of blocks from Jimmy. They had known each other since first grade. She was considered the second cutest girl in their class at Anderson School. The number one ranked girl was her best friend, Tina Holden. Jimmy remembered the time Laura stole his baseball glove on the playground and ran home with it, so he would have to follow. She ran into her house and left him there on the porch. Not knowing what to do, Jimmy recalled standing there helplessly, afraid to knock on the door. After what seemed like hours, but was more like five minutes, her mother came out smiling and laughing, saying Laura was in the house and was too shy to come back out, and handed him his glove. She told him Laura took it because she thought he was cute.

Upon reaching junior high Laura blossomed, and the Status Queens beckoned. Her pre-puberty best friend Tina did not blossom, and the Status Queens did not extend an invitation to her, so Laura had to choose. The choice she made resulted in her walking up the steps to the stage behind her new best friend, Jana Gamble.

"Sarah Hopper."

As she stood there were some giggles and wahh??'s from the crowd.

"They had to nominate at least one of the Zit Queens," explained Chance. In other words, she was another political choice with no chance of winning.

"And last but most definitely not least, Sally Salt!!!"

Sally was Kilos' girlfriend. It was a strange relationship, because it was so one-sided. Kilos had better things to do than get tied down to Sally and treated her like it. Sally did not act like she had anything better to do and followed Kilos around waiting for occasional attention from him. He was the wild professor, she was his blond, braced, blue eyed follower, and that was how it was.

Once all six of them were on stage, Kilos clapped his hands in hopes of engaging the crowd to join him. There was some impolite applause. It was a two-horse race between Jana and Laura, and any handicapper would have Jana as the favorite, but no one in the audience was overly excited about either choice.

"Now, for the men," announced Kilos.

"Bob Fair."

Bob must have cornered the sincere Christian vote. Unfortunately for him, there were not enough sincere Christians, or sincere atheists, or sincere people in general in the school to get him elected.

"Nick Callan."

As he jumped up, a loud chorus of "Grrrreeeeekkk!!!!" rose in the room. From the sound of it, you would think Nick was the obvious favorite. The truth was people just loved to say "Grrrreeeeekkk!!!!" and never passed on the opportunity. It was all downhill from that point for Nick's chances.

"Pat Hampton."

As the three-sport star he was, in a typical high school he would have run unopposed, and even in this one he was the favorite. Most of the boys had decided to not vote for him, even though they shouted "EEEGGG!!!!" as he trotted to the stage. He'd need to get most of the female vote.

"Carlo Firenze."

Girls in the audience sighed audibly as they watched him strolling to the stage in his tight jeans, shaking his head to keep his hair out of his eyes. Pat's chances dropped like a rock.

"Richard Shaw."

The crowd went wild; at least Jimmy, Chance, Sonny, and Bob did, along with several other assorted stoners and the others they had recruited in their campaign to nominate Richard Speck. "Speck!

Speck! Speck! Speck!" was chanted. Richard stood with the look of a man who had just won the lottery without having bought a ticket. He knew it had to be a mistake, but he walked uncertainly to the stage to join the others anyway, looking around assuming someone in authority would realize the error and call him back.

Kilos, at this point, lost his composure.

"Crazy Joe Starks!!" he called out before he realized what he had said.

As the crowd was already in full throat roaring over the last selection, they easily switched to full throated laughter when Crazy Joe stood up. No one could take him seriously. If he wasn't already pledged to Speck, Jimmy would have voted for Crazy Joe.

"Don't forget, the final voting is tomorrow, and the King and Queen will be announced during halftime of the game!! Be sure to be there. And don't forget about skit night tomorrow, and most important, 77 Rules!!!!!"

As they filed out of the auditorium, Jimmy told Bob, "Man, you've got to come to skit practice tonight. I need you to do something."

"Naw, man, I'm not gonna be in it," whined Bob in response.

"Come on, man," said Sonny. "We can get loaded after Bucky-ball, then go to Hardees, and then go to skit practice."

"I don't have enough weed..." started Bob, but Sonny cut him off.

"I got some, don't worry," he said.

"Nobody else can do it, Bob, trust me," pleaded Jimmy.

With that the plan was set, and remarkably, it was followed. After sweating through another round of Bucky's torture, which had, not so remarkably, increased drastically after the guys had gone to his house, all the while dodging the pools of spit on the floor from Sonny's missed targets, the crew emerged from the locker room and piled into Bob's car. He had a 1972 Mercury Montego, and a stereo that worked with four speakers, and an

8-track player with four working channels. As was his usual, he put on his Kiss Alive tape. As the boys chugged their way across town, the band chugged its way through "Deuce" then "Strutter."

"You've been listening to the same tape for two years now, Bub," complained Sonny.

"It's better than the Redneck shit Potsy makes us listen to," countered Bob. No one could argue with that one, so they were silent until Jimmy remembered his idea.

"Bob," said Jimmy. "What I need you to do tomorrow is sit in the first row of the balcony."

"What?" asked Bob.

"Just sit there, Bob. Trust me. It'll be great," assured Jimmy.

Skit practice went remarkably smoothly. Everyone knew their lines, sort of. No one had bothered to write them down, so no one could dispute what was said if it resembled the plot. Derek had completely lost control of the script. It was now in the hands of Yobs and Sonny, with Jimmy quietly planning his own plot twists for the night of the performance. He was not the only one. If the skit was as funny as the practice, and it did not break down into complete anarchy, which was a highly probable outcome, it would be a hit.

With the deadline fast approaching for the completion, the Status Queens and Zit Queens had come to an agreement on the design concept for the float. They had completed the hard part, which was to tape roll after roll of toilet paper to the sides of the float, in a cheap imitation of the flowers used in the Rose Bowl parade, and now all that was needed was to create the football field on top, with goal posts and the Little Giants walking around like Roman soldiers and the Saints on their knees begging for mercy. They had collected the props for the costumes and all the other materials and managed to rally the troops at the end of skit practice to help finish the float. They were mostly successful in getting the entire group (minus a sextet of football players, led by Yobs, who brandished a twelve pack and were never seen again that night) to motorcade to the garage where the float was to be completed.

The building in which the float was taking shape was more barn than building. Three lights hung from the rafters, swinging in the breeze if there was a breeze. Once the light switch was found and the lights came on, a blood curdling scream erupted from the first females to arrive, Hannah Hartford, Casey Queen, and Laura Ashland. Sonny and Bob were not even out of the car when they heard it. Jimmy and Chance were out of the car, talking to Annie and Sarah Hopper about her surprise nomination.

"How does it feel to be a princess?" asked Chance, the sly devil he was.

That's when the scream rang out. Chance made it to the door before the others. As he walked into the building, he saw the three Queens, staring at the float with looks of horror on their faces. Chance ambled to where they were standing and had to bite his tongue to stop laughing. Someone had spray painted 'Heady Blows' down the side of the white tissue with black paint. He knew the girls would never go out with him if they knew he thought this was funny, so he had to act sincere.

"That's horrible!" he cried.

Jimmy entered the building and saw it, and next to him was Kilos.

"Well, he does suck. Maybe it should read Heady Sucks," commented Kilos. He was just being honest, but his statement was not appreciated.

A crowd had now formed. Annie spoke out enthusiastically, "We can still finish it. We have enough people here to get it done."

Silence was the response.

"Screw it. We won't have a float," spat Casey Queen.

The girls in the crowd sucked in their breath in unison. This was unheard of. They were the senior class, and they wouldn't have a float in the Homecoming parade?

"Why not just use this one?" suggested Jimmy. "It's not that bad."

Everyone had to laugh at that, because it was worse than that bad. It had nothing on top, and soggy toilet paper on the sides littered with black spray paint.

Casey Queen hissed, "I'm out of here," before heading for the exit, and for once in her life, the entire senior class followed her lead.

RULE # 21 - *Euphoria Doesn't Last, Enjoy It While You Can*

Whenever the Class of 1977 planned something chaotic, they pulled it off with machine-like precision. Skit night was a classic example. The most important part of skit night was the audience. The winner between the sophomores, juniors, and seniors was decided by which skit generated the most applause. There was no judging of artistic merit, a plot that made sense, or any other objective criteria. When playing a game like this it is best to stack the deck, and the seniors did so by persuading their loudest, most obnoxious classmates to be in their seats in time for the sophomore and junior skits and not in the parking lot smoking and drinking. Their main purpose was to heckle, boo, disrupt and in even more creative ways embarrass the other classes' skits, not to cheer for the seniors.

It worked to perfection. The ruckus in the auditorium was so merciless during the junior class skit, some drivel about the Roman Empire, Lurch was launched from his seat at the beginning of the second act, when an unknown person hurled a golf-ball-sized spit wad from the middle of the mob, accurately targeting Donny Money's ludicrously designed toga. He lurched up the stairs and on-stage, to even more thunderous boos, to make a proclamation.

"OK, any more shenanigans like that and I'll stop this right now and declare a winner!!" shouted Lurch in disbelief.

No more spitballs flew out of the darkness, but the one splattered on the bedsheet served its purpose. After Lurch further disrupted what had already been disrupted by the seniors, the juniors could not get back into character, remember their lines, or do anything more than giggle through the rest of what was, from then on, an unintelligible plot. Mission accomplished. Now all that was left for the seniors to do was to get on with the show.

With the curtains closed, Laura Ashland and Jana Gamble sashayed onstage in their dancing girl outfits. The same rowdies who had spent the last hour heckling turned to howling so passionately you'd have thought they truly believed the girls were the hottest things they'd ever seen.

Jana got things underway. "Long ago in the Old West, there was a town named Canton. It was a peaceful place..." she stopped, and Laura took over, "until a group of outlaws named the Saints came to town. This is the story of how the town was saved." Then they shouted in unison, "Welcome to the Senior Class Skit, Blazing Footballs!!!!" before strutting offstage to more whoops and hollers.

The curtain opened and on one side of the stage was a bar and filling the back half of the stage were tables. Some of the guys were sitting at the tables and the dancing girls were prancing around, lifting their skirts to drum up business.

Nancy Naughton then walked on-stage wearing a long dress and a bonnet on her head. She could wear this to school on Monday and no one would notice much difference. She called out, "Oh no, there's a crazy bunch of outlaws coming into town called the Saints. What do we do?"

At this point, according to the script Sonny and Yobs had improvised, the Saints began yelling and growling off-stage, and as soon as the curtain closed, they charged from stage right, in front of the curtain, hopping around as if riding horses and pointing toy guns in the air, yelling "Yee-Hah!!" and other such cowboy exclamations. They were supposed to run across the stage and exit stage left before the curtain opened again, but once they were in front of the audience, their adrenalin took control and they lingered so long the curtain opened with them still in front of it. Instead of sitting in the saloon as the script demanded, they bounded around the stage, chasing the girls and pinching those who did not escape.

As the chaos continued to percolate Bob Fair walked out; wearing black pants, a white shirt and a bolo tie; along with his long-dressed wife Nancy. They stood at center stage, trying to stay composed as Yobs mockingly tried to pull Bob's pants down, and Crazy Joe put his arm around Nancy.

"As Mayor," Bob said, "I have to find some way to save the town from the Saints!"

Nancy, having freed herself from Crazy Joe, put her arm across her forehead and cried, "Oh, what do we do!!" and then she fell to the stage floor.

Hannah Hartford, perfectly cast as the no-nonsense saloon Bartender, had to shove her way through the Saints and was late to deliver her line. Nancy laughed as she lay on the floor but put her arm over her face to hide it.

Once she negotiated the Saintfield with her chunky dignity at least partially intact, Hannah declared, "We only have one choice. We have to find the Sheriff!!"

A fake brawl broke out among the Saints over a bottle of whiskey, and Sonny took a fake knockout punch as the curtain closed and fell on the outside of it so Crazy Joe had to pull him under. The crowd roared.

When the curtain opened the bar and tables were gone, and chairs were arranged in rows like pews in a church. Kilos was standing on the side of the stage next to a chalkboard, with his mad professor lab coat on, and his hair in its normal natural state of being all over the place.

Jimmy waited off-stage and put his hat on. Next to him was Chance, with a Mexican poncho draped over his shirt and jeans, and a straw hat. He had a can of Coke in his hand. Jimmy took a deep breath and starting walking. It was the walk he had been practicing, now down to a science. He let his shoulders droop and swung the opposite arm across his body with each slow, measured, step, and added a little bounce after he planted each foot. Chance walked out beside and a half step behind him, so Jimmy would be the one the audience could see best, and realized it was the coolest walk he had ever seen anyone in Canton use. The crowd agreed, and as Jimmy slowly strolled to center stage, the walls shook with the roar. He slowed down even further and turned slightly toward the sound, raised his hands to shoulder height, turned his palms facing up, and then he provoked an even higher decibel level by waving his fingers up and down in the coolest way he could. It worked. The rowdies in the seats decided yelling wasn't making enough noise and stomped their feet in addition. It was game over. They could have stopped the skit right there and declared the winner.

"Hey Sheriff!!" called out Kilos from his chalkboard. "We've challenged the Saints to a winner-take-all football game, and I've got the plan to win the game on one play! It's called Katy Bar to the Door!!!" He started drawing furiously.

"Who's Katy?" asked Jimmy.

"What difference does that make?" asked Chance, wavering on his feet like he could barely stand. His goal was to convince everyone the Coke had something else in it, and he was getting drunker throughout the skit.

"Well, Waco," said Jimmy. "If you weren't so drunk maybe you'd understand why it's important."

"Well, I can't really explain who Katy is, but I'm sure the play will work," assured Kilos.

"I'm sorry, folks, I can't help you," concluded Jimmy, "If you can't tell me who Katy is, I can't see how it can work."

The curtain closed with Jimmy and Chance standing in front of it. Hulk walked out from stage right wearing a flannel shirt, jeans, and a straw hat, along with Jack Hoff and Worm Chow in the donkey suit.

"Are you gonna pull the cart?" asked Hulk.

Jack shook the donkey head furiously back and forth.

Hulk let out a roar and punched the donkey head as hard as he could. He hit it so hard he knocked Jack off balance, and he tumbled to the floor splitting the costume in two, leaving Worm Chow standing by himself, bent at the waist with his head sticking out. A few seconds later he realized he should flop over and join his top half. It was the best laugh of the night, as the donkey fell in two pieces to the floor. On cue, four arms reached from behind the curtain to drag the two sides of the donkey under it.

"Wow," marveled Chance, "Who are you and how'd you get so strong?"

"Pork and beans, of course," explained Hulk, "And the name is Mongo."

"How'd you end up with such a Stew-Pid donkey?" questioned Jimmy, hoping Mr. Harbison was in the audience.

"A bunch of outlaws got me drunk and I passed out. When I woke up they had done stole my horse and left me with that dumb donkey," answered Hulk.

"Do you know the outlaws who did it?" asked Chance.

"Yeah, they was callin' themselves the Saints!" stated Hulk.

"Hey, Sheriff, I have an idea!" said Chance.

Jimmy and Chance locked shoulders and acted like they were sharing a secret plot, and then the three of them walked off-stage together.

The curtain then opened with no props and the Saints were sitting on the floor cross legged. They were eating imaginary food from imaginary plates.

"These pork and beans sure are good!!" shouted Sonny. One of the boys stuck his tongue half out of his mouth and blew, making the universally accepted farting noise as loud as he could.

'Hand me a beer!!" called out Crazy Joe. He was handed a real can of Coke.

Then Chance walked on-stage to a rousing chorus of boos from the Saints.

"Hey," said Yobs, standing up. "Ain't you the Sheriff's sidekick, the Waco Kid?" he continued.

"Yes and No," replied Chance. "I am the Waco Kid, but me and the Sheriff had a falling out. I want to join you guys!!"

"Well," said Yobs, "I'm Billy Bolshevik, the leader of the Saints. Hey boys, should we let the Waco Kid in? What do you think, Crazy Joe?"

"Only if he can sing Home on the Range," Crazy Joe responded.

Chance broke into it; "Oh give me a home, where the buffalo roam, and the deer and the antelope play. Where never is heard, a discouraging word…" the Saints joined in at this point and sang, "And the Saints are all rowdy all day!!!!"

"Home, home on the range!!!"

"Hey," said Chance, thankfully stopping the warbling, "Do you guys have a beer I can borrow?"

He then sat down, and the Saints resumed eating, drinking and loudly, obnoxiously, farting, then one by one they passed out until Chance was the only one awake. He then stood and proclaimed, "Now I'll take your pork and beans, and why not another beer or two for the road?"

The curtain closed again. When it opened the townspeople were on one side, and the Saints were on the other. A football was sitting in the middle of the stage. The Saints were cavorting with their guns out, and the townspeople were looking scared.

"Are you ready to take your punishment?" asked Yobs.

At this point Jimmy strutted on stage with the same walk he did before but this time with Hulk instead of Chance, and the crowd screamed even more raucously than the first time. Jimmy didn't need to do anything more to increase the volume. Instead he looked in the balcony for Bob. With the lights in his eyes he could not spot him. He recited his line, holding out an imaginary can of beans to Hulk. "Here Mongo, have some pork and beans."

Hulk took the can and lifted it to his lips as if he was drinking it in three gulps, then wiped his mouth and burped. Someone in the crowd of Saints farted for him.

Then the whistle blew to start the game, and Chance appeared at the back of the group of Saints and shouted, "Hey Mongo, I've got a beer for you!!!" as he held up the Coke can.

As the Saints rushed toward the ball, Hulk strode across the stage like Frankenstein, clearing a path by throwing the Saints one way or another. They fell and died as dramatically and comically as possible, each enacting the worst dying scene they had ever seen in a Western movie.

When Hulk reached him, Chance handed him the can of Coke. Jimmy used his supercool walk to casually stroll over and pick up the football, and slowly walk to the far side of the stage, and raise his hands in the universal touchdown signal, still holding the ball. Instead of a touchdown dance, he slowly paced the front of the stage with his hands aloft. The crowd went completely nuts.

On stage walked Worm Chow and Jack Hoff, now with the horse head on instead of the donkey head. Hulk started crying and ran to the horse, hugging and kissing the head to roars of laughter. This was not in any script except Hulk, Jack and Worm Chow's and even the people on the stage thought it was hilarious, as they hadn't seen it coming either. The dead Saints began returning to life, as they rolled on the floor in spasms.

Now Jimmy was ready for his final act. He peered one last time into the balcony and imagined he saw Bob, standing in the front row, waving his arms. Jimmy took a half step back with his left leg and launched the football with a perfect spiral into the night. Half the crowd gasped, some folks ducked, and no one, except Bob, hoped Jimmy, saw it coming.

Then the curtain closed. A bunch of Saints followed Sonny's lead and left their bodies half in front and half behind it, so the last act was dragging them behind the curtain, kicking and screaming for comic affect. Jimmy, now standing by himself on center stage, started the chant as he walked off with his fists clenched in the air, "Seventy-Seven Rules, Seventy-Seven Rules, Seventy-Seven Rules!!!"

The judges did not need to huddle up to declare the seniors the winners. The crowd noise was so intense they couldn't hear themselves voting anyway. As the winner was announced the seniors rushed the stage, hugging and dancing and generally using up any spare energy they hadn't used already. Most of them did, anyway. Sonny, Chance and Jimmy lingered backstage, plotting their next move.

As they huddled Annie Royal skipped over to Jimmy and said, "Jimmy, you are the coolest!!"

She looked up at him like she wanted to hug him, and he looked at her the same way, and just as they were about to accomplish the task, an arm holding a football appeared from behind Jimmy's head and wrapped itself around Jimmy's neck. Bob, the arm's owner, yanked Jimmy away from Annie.

"Nice throw, Jimmy," he exclaimed, completely breaking the mood.

Any euphoria on the part of the skit's main star, Jimmy Williams, was thusly short lived.

"Did you catch it?" asked Jimmy, smiling so broadly his teeth were beginning to hurt.

"Naw," answered Bob, "You threw it over my head. It bounced against the doors in the back. I thought for sure the glass was gonna break."

"I guess I just don't know my own strength!" proclaimed Jimmy.

He squirmed enough to loosen Bob's grip and turned his head to see Annie's reaction to his latest words, but she had walked away by then.

Sonny, who was watching along with Chance, said, "OK, let's get out of here and go get loaded!"

As they walked down the main aisle out of the auditorium, Jimmy couldn't help himself and strutted down it the same way he had strutted across the stage earlier. After they reached the doors and turned down the hall to exit the school, the other guys had seen enough. Bob grabbed Jimmy, and Sonny and Chance crowded him against the wall.

"Now look, Jimmy," said Bob. "That walk was perfect, and I mean perfect, for the skit. But the skit is over now, and if you keep walkin' that way we're either gonna pound you or we're not gonna hang out with you anymore..."

"Or both!" threw in Chance.

"Yeah, cut that shit out, Jimmy," agreed Sonny.

RULE # 22 - *The Best Way to Maintain Your Innocence Is to Not Get Caught*

Potsy and No Sense did not like each other much. The group dynamic was Bob wanted to impress Sonny, Sonny and Chance wanted to impress Jimmy, and Jimmy was not impressed with anyone except himself. That meant Chance and Bob were not impressed with, nor did they want to impress, each other. And Sonny, being the master instigator, had a goal in mind for the school year. He wanted to see the two of them have a fight.

This desire stemmed from the need to refute what he had been told throughout his life, blacks were weak as a people because they could not get along with each other. Two black boys like Jimmy and himself would eventually become enemies and could never maintain an enduring friendship. This had been repeatedly drummed into both of their heads as they grew up. No matter how hard they tried, it would never result in anything but conflict, or worse, because the only thing black people could get along well enough to do was commit crimes. Jimmy had been told point blank by the junior high principal he was better off without Sonny as a friend because Sonny could ruin any chance he had for success. But Jimmy and Sonny were so divergent they did not compete for the same things, and therefore saw no reason to be enemies. No way did Jimmy want to be the hustler Sonny was, and regardless of whether he wanted to or not, there was no way for Sonny to be the scholar Jimmy was. They only competed in one place, the basketball court, and since basketball was played five on five, they did not even have to compete there if they were on the same team. If Sonny could coerce Chance and Bob to fight and become enemies it would prove, at least to him, everything he had been taught about what kind of person he was and what kind of people they were was wrong. It was important.

The first opportunity came the night of the Homecoming game. Chance managed to score a joint earlier that day, and he told Jimmy about it and no one else. The plan was for them to go to the game together and meet up with Bob and Sonny after smoking it. During basketball practice, Sonny informed Jimmy he wouldn't be attending the game because he was visiting his cousin in Peoria over the weekend. Jimmy therefore saw no reason not to tell Sonny about Chance's joint, and once Chance and Jimmy left the gym, Sonny told Bob because he did see a reason.

It was perfectly set up. Jimmy and Chance arrived at the game and took their seats in the center of the student section. As usual, Chance was flirting with the pompom girls, the band girls, the sophomore girls, and guys with long hair before they spun around to reveal their maleness. Two rows below, Annie Royal and her fellow Zit Queens Sarah Hopper, Katy Widner, and Jean Keller were sitting side by side, and Chance broke out in his theme song to gain their attention, "All I am saying, is give Chance a piece." They turned their heads in unison.

"Hey guys!" called out Katy, "Are you going to the dance tomorrow?"

"Maybe," Chance fibbed. He and Jimmy had discussed it while smoking the joint, and since neither had any money, they weren't going.

Annie called out, "Jimmy, you have to go!! You're the best dancer!!"

Jimmy may have been the best dancer in the Canton High School Class of 1977, but it wasn't from excess talent. Having female cousins in every major city in the Midwest put him far ahead of Canton's curve when it came to the latest dance moves. Having two older sisters in college bolstered it further. He held the crown because being two years behind Chicago was still light years ahead of Canton. Jimmy shrugged in response.

"You gotta ask her out, Jimmy," counselled Chance.

"Yeah," Jimmy agreed, but he didn't have enough money to ask himself out. And when he did have it, spending it on a girl instead of weed seemed ludicrous to him anyway. In his mind, growing up with sisters eliminated most of the mystique the other boys suffered from. That had to be the reason they were so eager to make fools of themselves and he wasn't. Jimmy had been dating Rosie Palm for so long he was in no hurry to dump her. She was a girl he could afford, never nagged him, and was even more useful when he was open for a jump shot.

Out of nowhere, as Chance was in the middle of singing, "Have you ever been mellow? Have you ever triii..."

"Hey, Anteater!!!" yelled Bob, who had appeared at the end of the row. "You look pretty stoned for someone who doesn't have any weed!!!"

"So do you, No Sense!!" retorted Chance.

Chance was not really that stoned, he was just pretending to be that stoned. Jimmy barely felt a thing after smoking the joint they shared. Bob was not so easy to read. Because he talked and moved slow when he was sober, it was hard to tell if he was stoned or just his normal stupid.

"The only thing that's keepin' me from kickin' your ass right now is my girlfriend," taunted Bob with disdain.

Jimmy had been wondering what this was about. He knew immediately Sonny had told Bob about Chance's stash, but that did not rate such a public display of machismo. There had to be something more to it, and now it was apparent Bob's main purpose was to announce his conquest. Standing behind him was a girl, a junior by the name of Mary Riddle. Chance had a well-known crush on her, which was not a unique position for her to be in. Chance was one of those guys who developed multiple crushes multiple times a day. But despite this, in Chance's mind any girl he had announced he had a crush on was off limits to any of his squad without prior permission.

"Whatever," Chance mumbled with a shrug, and then he twisted his head as if the intensity of the game was more important than the current conversation, which was not a very convincing response. He was visibly depressed by the sight of Mary's hand in Bob's and had to look away.

"See ya later, Jimmy," said Bob, as he turned to walk to a different section of the bleachers with Mary in tow, "You too, Potsy."

After Bob walked away, Chance turned to Jimmy and snarled, "I hate that No Sense motherfucker. I'm gonna get him back."

Jimmy looked at Chance with great amusement. Sonny may be onto something. Chance was so livid he could not flirt despite all the girls around him, even when they flirted with him first. He even lost his singing voice.

It took Chance less than twenty-four hours, more like twenty-two, to obtain retribution. Chance picked up Jimmy as they agreed the night before, and the plan was to meet up with Wastey Hastey, who told them at the game he was going to score the next day. Wastey was also not going to the dance, and it wasn't because he didn't have any money. Wastey was short, skinny, spoiled, and shy; which was not such a good combination with the ladies. Add to that the typical white boy phobia about dancing, and it resulted in him avoiding events which included both.

Finding him was easy. On weekends, during the warmer months, one of the main activities of high school kids in small towns was to go cruising. That meant driving along the same set route through the middle of town in endless loops, honking and waving at friends in other cars; sometimes stopping and jumping out to converse or change partners. The main drag was Main Street, between Locust and Birch, which was a little more than half a mile long. The circuit was made by turning down Birch at the north end of Main, then turning again on First Avenue, then again on Myrtle to return to Main, then south down Main to Locust Street, where another loop was made by again turning on Locust, then First, then Spruce and then back to Main to go north and start over again. Following that pattern allowed everyone to cross paths with everyone within a couple of laps.

That's how they found Wastey. He was driving alone in the 1973 Mustang his parents had given him. When he saw them, he motioned for them to follow him into the bank parking lot, which was one of the designated meeting spots for cruisers. They parked parallel to each other and rolled down the windows, so they didn't have to get out of the cars to talk. Wastey was parked next to the passenger side of Chance's wagon.

"What's happenin', Wastey?" asked Jimmy.

"Not much," replied Wastey. "This town is deader than usual tonight, man."

"Everyone's at the dance!" informed Chance.

"Yeah," said Wastey, "And I couldn't score, either."

There was no good response for that news. The boys sat silently in their cars. Then Chance thought of one.

"I wish I knew where No Sense parked his car," yearned Chance.

"Who?" asked Wastey.

"Bob White, who else?" answered Jimmy.

"That's funny," said Wastey, complimenting the nickname. "I know where he parked. About a block from my house!! I saw him gettin' out of his car with some girl."

Chance reached across Jimmy, pulled him back, and shouted to Wastey, "Jump in!!"

When Wastey was safely in the back seat of the car, Jimmy turned and said, "You must live close to the school, 'cuz he was goin' ta the dance with, with…whats-her-name, Chance?"

"Fuck you, Jimmy," responded Chance.

"OK, he was goin' ta the dance with Fuck You," confirmed Jimmy to Wastey.

"So, what's the deal?" asked Wastey. He had no clue why Chance told him to jump in, but since he didn't have anything better to do, he hadn't hesitated.

"Show us where the car's parked and I'll tell you," spat Chance.

"OK, go down Main past the school and turn right at the first street," instructed Wastey.

Jimmy was thinking he may have gone down this street once before in his life. The main parking lot and main entrance were on the school's south side, and this street, Linden Street, ran along the north side of the school. Jimmy knew there were houses north of Linden, but none of his friends except Bob, whose house he never visited, lived this far north. As with so many towns in the Midwest, the poor end of town was in the south, and the more affluent and important people in Canton lived in the north. They drove down Linden past a row of houses on the left, and the school on the right.

"You live in one of these houses?" asked Jimmy.

"Naw, a block over. Keep going, Chance," said Wastey.

There it was, under the dim light of a streetlamp: Bob's green Montego. He had parked it on the same side of Linden as the school, but farther down the street. No other cars were near it.

"Why the hell would he park here instead of the school parking lot?" wondered Chance.

"Maybe because he was smokin' a bowl or two and didn't want anyone ta see him," guessed Jimmy.

Chance parked next to the Montego and jumped out of the car. Jimmy and Wastey remained seated, ducked down. Chance trotted to the passenger side of the Montego and pushed the button in the handle to release it and the door opened. All the boys laughed. He reached across the car and under the driver's seat and sure enough, there was the Frisbee. He couldn't see what was in it very well, so he brought it to his wagon and flicked on the dome light.

"Man, that's just stems and seeds," complained Wastey, not impressed.

"OK, so do you have a pipe?" asked Chance, "We can scrape something together."

Wastey produced a pipe, a metal one with a large bowl. Chance filled it with the stems, leaves, and resin he scraped from the rim of the Frisbee and grabbed a box of matches from the glove compartment.

"Wait, don't light it here," said Wastey, "My Mom could come drivin' down the street or sumpthin."

Chance handed the pipe to Jimmy and started the car. He reached for the gear selector, then stopped and said, 'Wait a minute.' He opened the door and exited with the Frisbee and placed it carefully under the seat where he had found it. Then a curious look came over his face. He jumped on the hood of the Montego, then up to the roof, and zipped open his pants. Using his hands to pinpoint his flow, he proceeded to piss as he turned in a slow circle, so it would wash over all the windows and the windshield. Then, in an act of extreme self-sacrifice, he pinched off the flow while he jumped off the car and released a squirt on each of the front door handles.

"Aaahhh," he said as he re-entered the wagon. "Sweet relief!!!"

As the boys drove away, Jimmy handed the pipe to Wastey. "You light it," offered Jimmy, unsure of how the pipe worked, plus afraid of the damage to his Afro if the wind blew the match flame the wrong way.

Chance turned on the radio. Bachman Turner Overdrive, You Ain't Seen Nothing Yet, blasted from the tinny speakers. The crackles and pops as the sticks in the bowl caught fire were the perfect accompaniment for the song. "Here's some loving baby that you never will forget...." Cough, Cough, "You ain't seen nothing yet." Hack, Hack. "You ain't been round."

After they finished the bowl, Jimmy couldn't contain his curiosity and asked Chance, "So why'd ya' piss on the passenger side door? I thought you liked the girl."

"Not anymore," answered Chance.

Chance pulled a U-turn on Linden, and at the corner turned left onto Main and passed the high school. As they drove by they saw two shadowy figures in front of the school, with what looked like a bucket.

"Someone's paintin' The Rock!!" exclaimed Wastey.

"Can you see who it is?" asked Chance.

"Naw, too far away," replied Jimmy.

Chance screeched on the brakes and swung a hard left into the driveway leading to The Rock. When the headlights of the car shone against the school windows, two shadows could be seen running in different directions but were lost in the darkness before Chance could come to a stop. He leaned out of his window and took a deep breath.

"Aaahh, fresh paint!!" he said.

"Ha-ha-ha," laughed Jimmy, "That didn't take long."

"Let's get out and take a look," suggested Wastey.

"No way," argued Jimmy, "Get the hell outta here. What if the pigs come down the street? We'll get blamed for it."

"Who gives a shit?" asked Chance.

Jimmy glared at Chance, which was enough for him to put the car in gear and drive away. He hadn't travelled a block down Main before a police car turned from Birch onto Main and passed them going in the opposite direction, toward the school.

The look of relief on Chance's face revealed he did indeed give a shit.

RULE # 23 - *Old Jokes Are the Best Jokes*

H yde Park Week wasn't over until the juniors got into the act. They came late to the Hyde Park Week party, but they brought the most unexpected gift. On the Monday morning after Homecoming/Hyde Park Week officially ended, they set up the classic Fishing Line Prank. It wasn't original, but the planning and execution were so skillful even the best pranksters in the senior class had to give them credit.

Danny Partridge, Mark (Norman) Bates, and Mark (the) Klutts arrived at school early on Monday. After spending the weekend developing their scheme they needed to make sure they had the prime positions, directly across from each other in the hallway of the add-on wing. Norman sat with his back against the wall, next to one of the main auditorium doors, and Partridge sat opposite him, with his back against the wall of trophy cases. They were manning their posts before most of the student body arrived at school.

As they expected, students arriving on buses bustled down the hall in excited groups, full of energy as their confinement on the bus was finally over after seven or eight minutes of torture. When the first group bounded toward them, (the) Klutts tried to jump in front, but he was not quick enough and before he could simulate his fall the group passed Danny and Norman before they could pull the imaginary string.

The next time they got it right. Mark moved further down the hall, so he could comfortably step in front of the next group. When he was a stride away from the other two boys, they sat up and positioned themselves as if they were pulling a rope tug-of-war style. Mark lived up to his nickname, (the) Klutts, and tripped over the nothingness stretched across his path in the most exaggerated way he could, and flailed his arms, and wailed loudly, "Aaaahhh!!"

The group behind him, half paying attention to what was in front of them as they laughed and giggled and skipped their way down the hall, saw the fall and tried to stop as a group, and failed miserably, since those in the middle and back kept walking while the ones in front didn't. Three fell, seven stumbled, and one lucky sophomore grabbed two hands full of bra, tissue paper, and nipples as a girl fell into him. She screamed. The boys, even the ones who fell, laughed. They immediately realized the only way to make amends for being tricked was to help trick the next group, so they sat alongside the original tricksters and helped provide cover and react to the imaginary rope pull to ensure the potential victims saw it. Klutts didn't have to fake a fall after that. It quickly became a study of human nature.

Some fell, some didn't because they "jumped it", others stumbled after losing their balance trying to reach down and grab it. Some stopped, figured it out, and stared at the boys unamused. Others never broke stride and glared at the boys in anger, not fooled at all. Every reaction had one thing in common. All were funny to the boys, and they rolled on the floor in laughter after every fake pull.

When Pigpen and Buddy Anthony ambled by, they didn't even notice. That might have received the biggest laugh of all. Not only was it funny they were too stoned to recognize the prank, they had even funnier looks on their faces when they couldn't figure out why people were laughing at them. Pigpen instinctively sniffed his shirt.

By the time Jimmy and Sonny arrived, heads full of the sweet leaf, and walked through the back door behind a group headed for the prank zone, the number of boys on either side of the hall had grown to the point where any sane kid would notice and assume some sort of mischief was in progress. Jimmy saw this immediately.

"Man," he said to Sonny, "What's goin' on?"

The group in front of them included Peg Leg, Sarah Hopper, Katy Widner, and Jean Keller. They were discussing the Homecoming Dance.

"Carlo is so boss!!!" proclaimed Katy. "I'm so glad he was voted in as King."

"And I guess Laura made a good queen," admitted Jean, less enthusiastically. "I wish you would have won it though, Sarah." Then she turned and said to Jimmy, following a few steps behind her, "Someone missed you at the dance, Jimmy."

"I like your shoes," said Sarah to Peggy, changing the subject.

She was wearing the most fashionable style among the girls, called "stacks", which meant they had three-inch-thick soles, front and back, and velour coverings in a multitude of colors. Hers were blue, to match her blue jeans.

"Yeah, I love them!!" responded Peg Leg, and at just that moment, Norman and Danny pulled the string. Peg Leg saw them out of the corner of her eye, thought she had enough time to react, and took an awkward step. Keep in mind every step she took was awkward. That's why she was called Peg Leg in the first place.

She tried to stop herself before she crossed the imaginary line, but she couldn't, and she turned her ankle and stepped down. Her shoe landed on its edge, and despite the wideness of the sole, once on edge it was highly unstable. Her ankle buckled, and her foot slid, and down she went. She landed on her butt, unhurt physically but undoubtedly emotionally damaged.

Jimmy and Sonny liked Peg Leg. She never did anything mean to them, but watching her fall was hilarious. Sonny grabbed Jimmy by the arm and tears squirted from the corners of his eyes. Then it really got funny. As she looked down to assess her situation, she saw the velour on her right shoe was scuffed beyond repair. She had ripped it with her left as she fell. Maybe Peggy would have seen the joke if she hadn't seen her shoe first. As Katy and Jean lifted her to her feet by grabbing her under the arms, she boiled over in anger.

"Damn it, Partridge!!!" she shouted as she rose, "I'm gonna kill you if I get my hands on you!!!"

163

The boys in the hallway knew whether she was serious or not about her murderous intentions, it was not in their best interests to let Peg Leg get her hands on them. Even the ones not nicknamed Partridge scrambled to their feet and slipped and stumbled their way down the hall toward the administration offices and the main stairs. Most ran up the stairs, knocking into the people on them already, including Grandma, the English teacher, and some ran down the hall past the offices. As usually happens with boys of this age, once they started running it turned into a race down the halls, with them yelling and laughing as they went.

When Lurch stepped out of his office to see what the ruckus was about, he saw six people at the scene of the crime; Jimmy, Sonny, Sarah, Katy, Peggy, and Jean. He also saw Grandma sitting on the stairs, a wise thing to do for someone her age in a maelstrom. If Grandma had fallen down the stairs, no one would be getting a knitted sweater for Christmas, so she had done the sensible thing and sat next to the railing as the mob rushed past.

"OK, boys," Lurch said to two of the six, "What did you get those other boys to do?"

"What??" cried Sonny, "We didn't have nothin' ta do with this, Lur..."

"It's not them!!" shouted Peggy, before Sonny could finish. "I want that little shit Partridge ta pay for my shoes!!!"

"Who??" asked Lurch.

"That little shit..." repeated Peg Leg.

"Now Peggy," intervened the vice-principal, "We can't tolerate such language."

At this point Kilos strolled up. Norman Bates had run into the library after Peggy had fallen, and he found Kilos sitting at a table tickling Sally Salt, who was sitting next to him. Kilos, like a Secret Service agent, ran toward the scene, not away from it. It was his duty as Student Council President, after all.

164

"Can I be of service?" asked Kilos.

At this point Jimmy couldn't take it anymore and burst out laughing. Lurch was not amused.

"In my office!!" shouted Lurch, and with that he turned and marched away.

As he was not specific about who he wanted in his office, the original six did not follow. Kilos, as was his duty as Student Council President, did. Jimmy waited for him in the foyer while the others drifted off.

Once behind the closed door, Lurch laid down a new law.

"I am banning walking the halls before the first period bell. Students can go to their lockers once they arrive at school, but after that no one can circle the halls any more. If anyone is seen circling more than once, they are getting a detention."

"What?" asked Kilos, first thinking he should argue circling the halls had nothing to do with the prank just executed, but then realizing arguing may lead to him having to disclose the culprits. Plus, he spent that time in the library mostly and thought circling the halls was a waste of time in the first place, so why argue?

"You heard me," said Lurch, in his most stern voice.

"OK, I will advise the council," replied Kilos in his most serious politician voice. He knew he should leave without another word, but he looked out of the window as he stood, and he couldn't help himself. The view was of the front of the school. "Hey," he said with fake surprise, "Someone painted The Rock!!" Then he walked out of the office and closed the door behind him.

RULE # 24 - *Some People Enjoy Unraveling Your Dreams. Be Careful Who You Share Them With*

A s Jimmy and Kilos sauntered to Speech class, Kilos relayed the new law to Jimmy.

"So, what're we gonna do now in the morning?" asked Jimmy.

Not wanting Jimmy to know he spent every second he could spare studying in the library, he responded, "We should play cards."

"Now that's an idea," said Jimmy.

They arrived as the first period bell rang. Jimmy sat next to Yobs, who had several sheets of white paper on his desk he was patiently tearing into strips. He stuck one in his mouth and chewed.

"Hey, Yobs," said Jimmy, trying to gauge Yobs' mood, which seemed rather devious to Jimmy. "Nice hit on Friday."

"Thanks, Spider," answered Yobs. "I could have intercepted the ball, but I wanted to knock the guy out instead."

That was exactly what happened. Yobs was playing safety and when the Saints' quarterback threw a long pass over the head of the intended receiver, Yobs had a choice. He could either run backward two steps and try to catch the ball or run forward two steps and blast the guy stretching to make the catch himself. Yobs chose the latter. That was the only play of the game Jimmy remembered. It was a good thing Canton won, or Yobs would have had a lot of explaining to do to Heady, who would have preferred he made the interception. Of course, if he had made the interception, Heady would have been pissed if they lost and he hadn't knocked the guy out.

Yobs crammed strip after strip into his mouth, chewing the mass to make it soft and wet, and the ball between his jaws grew to the point his cheeks could hardly hold it. Jimmy knew a spitball in the making when he saw it and kept an eye on Yobs as Mr. Bishop called the class to order.

"OK, people," said Mr. Bishop. "I hope you had a good weekend. Today iss the day we ssstart the presssentationsss. We are going to begin with Mr. Markss."

Weedhopper had been looking forward to his presentation speech since Mr. Bishop gave them the assignment weeks before. He saw it as his chance to shine, to show all the others he was not the loser he had been labeled as so many years before. Not only was he the only kid in the Class of 1977 with a martial arts belt, albeit brown, he was also the only one studying to be a pilot. His oft stated plan was to obtain his pilot's license in the summer after graduation and be a commercial pilot as an adult. He had been bragging about it, in fact. Weedhopper should have known better than to brag in front of Yobs.

The assignment was to give a speech with a visual aid, and Weedhopper had the perfect one. He was so anxious he volunteered to be the first one to present. Each student had to advise the teacher of the speech topic and the visual aid they would be using beforehand, a lesson Mr. Bishop learned in past years. His stated reason was he didn't want two people choosing the same topic and to ensure they had a usable aid, but the real reason was he was afraid of what topics and aids the students would use if not needing approval first. Kevin Marks was the perfect choice to start things off; with the wonderful, interesting topic of learning to fly.

Weedhopper stood from his seat in the middle of the class and walked confidently, bouncing on the balls of his feet, toward the front of the class. He had a rolled-up poster in his hand. As he unrolled it, it was revealed to be a life size picture of a plane's control panel; a myriad of buttons, switches, levers, and lights. He took the roll of tape provided by the teacher and taped each of the top corners to the wall in the front of the class, then bent over to tape the bottom corners.

Meanwhile Yobs had worked the paper into a pulpy mass the size of a baseball, which he took out of his mouth as Weedhopper taped. When he saw it, Jimmy was amazed Yobs could get so much paper in his mouth at one time. It was the biggest spit ball he had ever seen. He locked eyes with Yobs, and Yobs smiled, raising the wad in his hand. Just when Jimmy thought Yobs was going to throw it at him, Weedhopper bent over.

Yobs was never a pitcher in baseball, or a quarterback in football, but you wouldn't know it by the perfect throw he made that day. The spit wad rifled through the air with violent intent, but at the same time seemed to hang in the air as if in slow motion, giving the entire class a chance to see it in flight. Then it landed, with a loud splat, in the top middle of the poster.

Weedhopper straightened his back in shock at the sound, his eyes wide. This momentary startling was quickly replaced with the nauseating reality he would not prove he was not a loser on this day. Instead, this was the day it was cemented forever. He watched as his dignity dripped down the poster, the spit wad unravelling and spreading as it went. Yobs got the laughs he was aiming for. The only one not laughing was Mr. Bishop.

"OK people, I've had enough!!!!!" he yelled as loudly as his whiny voice would allow. "You people need to TOE THE MARK!!!!"

The chuckles circulating the room transformed into roars, and the ones already roaring lost their voices and compensated by beating their fists on their desks or falling off their chairs and rolling on the floor.

"DO YOU THINK I'M KIDDING AROUND???" screamed Mr. Bishop, totally unconvincingly. "I SSSAID TOE THE MARK!!!"

Jimmy, feigning ignorance, asked, "What does 'toe the mark' mean? If we're supposed to be doing it, it would help to know what it means."

Mr. Bishop started to choke and couldn't respond, so Kilos decided he should explain it.

"It is a reference to running track, Jimmy. If you ever tried out for the track team, you'd know what it meant."

"My brother used ta run track," responded Jimmy. "So, what does it mean?"

"It means you should run track this spring," said Eubanks, who was well known as the biggest star of the track team, the county record holder in the triple jump.

"THAT'SSS ENOUGH!!!" shouted Mister Bishop. "Go ahead with your ssspeech, Mr. Marksss."

Weedhopper, standing in front of the class with the roll of tape in his hand, had completely forgotten his speech by this point. It wouldn't have mattered, since his visual aid was now dripping with paper wad and he couldn't show the class the controls anyway.

RULE # 25 - *The Best Way to Cheat is to Be the Official Scorekeeper*

It was Tuesday, October 26th, 1976, when the Class of 1977 Pitch Festival began. On that morning Kilos and Jimmy strolled into Table Muscle's classroom, thirty minutes before the first bell rang, and Kilos asked him:

"Hey coach, you mind if we play cards in your room before first period? Now that Lur...I mean Vice Principal Vandervort has banned walking the halls, we need a place to hang out."

Fred Hart was an assistant football coach, the head wrestling coach, and an assistant track coach; and was the main advocate of weight lifting and strength training at the school. As the most patriotic member of the faculty, at least in his own mind, it was also his duty to teach Civics to the senior class. He was the first guy Lurch called into his office after he had given Kilos his new edict concerning hall walking, and he had been given the task of monitoring his corner of the building. Whenever Lurch thought he needed enforcers, Table Muscle was one of his main guys. For two of the main suspects to walk into his classroom and ask him if they could sit in his room every morning, allowing him to keep an eye on them while he graded papers instead of chasing them down the stairs, was unexpected to the point of being suspicious. He was so dubious his instincts told him to say no, but he couldn't think of a good reason quickly enough.

"You can't gamble," was all he could muster.

"Naw, we'll just play for fun," promised Jimmy, who was quite relieved no money would be on the line. It had been his only worry about the scheme.

And thus, it began.

The game they played was called Pitch. Jimmy never met anyone outside the town of Canton, Illinois who played it, so his theory was it must have been played in other places in ancient history but had died out everywhere except backwaters like Canton. The rules of the game were simple, but in a sophisticated seeming way small-town folks gravitated to.

There are four players, and only four players, and never less than four players. The two across from each other are partners and play as a team. Each is dealt six cards, and only six cards, by a rotating dealer. The other 28 cards are kept in a stack and not used until the next shuffle.

The player to the dealer's left starts the bidding. He can pass or bid, and the minimum bid is 2 and the maximum depends on whether the 4-point or 5-point version is being played. The next player must either raise the bid or pass, and if all the other players pass the dealer must bid 2. Points are scored based on who was dealt the highest and lowest trump card, who claims the Jack of trump during the hand, plus which team has collected the most "point cards" at the end of the hand.

Most times a bid of 2 will prevail. Sometimes it is raised to 3 but not usually, and on very rare occasions, so rare cheating or stupidity are always suspected, a 4 is bid. Since only 24 of the total 52 cards are dealt, players must calculate the odds of which cards are in play and which are not to bid successfully.

5-point Pitch is played by adding the Jack of the opposite suite of the same color as a point. If Hearts is the trump suite, the Jack of Diamonds is the "Off-Jack". It is treated as a trump card with a high card rank above the Ten of the trump suite, but below the Jack of the trump suite. It must be captured the same as the trump Jack to earn the point.

The odds of a particular card being in play are slightly less than 50%, and that is what makes the game interesting. The high card or low card could be any card in the suite, depending on what is in play. A hand may have three points available, or four or five. There could be 3 Tens dealt, or none.

If the bidder reaches the points bid, the team gets all the points scored. If he does not reach the number of points bid, the bid is deducted from the team score and none of the points achieved are counted. The non-bidding team's points are always counted. The game continues with the person to the left of the first dealer shuffling and dealing the next hand, and the hands continue until a specified number of points, usually 21 or 15, is reached by either team.

The players in the first few days were Kilos, Jimmy, Sonny, and Chance. They were quickly joined in the following days by Brad Schmidt and No Sense Bob - who did not say anything about his door handles smelling like piss after the Homecoming dance - and then by Ron Williams, Carl Murphy, Dana Pickman, Pid Hoff, Scott Michaels, and sometimes Wastey Hastey. A group of juniors joined but after they won a controversial game they were exiled to Coach BiteMe's classroom a few doors down. What made it controversial was the fact they scored more points than the seniors, and the argument that ensued was too loud for Table Muscle to grade his Civics classes' essays. It was a perfect choice, as Coach BiteMe, whose real name was Lightman, was also an assistant coach and patriotic citizen, but considered to be slightly less so than Table Muscle, even though he wore his hair shorter.

The guys soon realized Pitch, when not played for money, got boring very quickly. They also noticed the game could be won much more easily if cheating was allowed, and since they weren't playing for money, why not allow it? It started with subtle things, like touching the chest to signal a point in Hearts. Then came touching the ring finger to signal Diamonds. The cheaters were caught but could not be truly punished, and in no time creating comical signals, blatant but hard to decipher, became the real game. Creating a signal so obtuse no one could guess it became the highlight of the game, and after the hand the creator would have to explain it, so it could be used openly by the others in future hands, until a better signal was developed. The group decided naming them signals was not good enough, so they were nicknamed Sig-A-Nols, because that was how Ron Williams pronounced it.

Talking during games became strictly coded messages, and most not coded for long. Song lyrics were used so extensively humming a song without the lyrics could become a Sig-A-Nol. For instance, during a game when Kilos and Jimmy were partners, Jimmy signaled he had the Jack of Diamonds by scratching his finger and calling out to one of the guys watching, "Hey, Pid!!" by which he meant Jack, because that was another of Pid's nicknames. Therefore, everyone knew he had the Jack of Diamonds, as these were well established Sig-A-Nols. A new Sig-A-Nol was born when Kilos wanted to tell Jimmy to play the Jack first, which would be a dangerously stupid move unless he knew Kilos had the Ace already. To communicate this Kilos sang the song Yackity-Yack Don't Come Back, except he changed the words to: "Yackity Yack, play the Yack!!!". And from then on whenever anyone wanted their partner to play the Jack of trump, they would hum "Do-du-du-do-du-du-do da-do-da-do," and that was the new Sig-A-Nol.

Sonny had renamed the Jack the Yack in a past session, and he had also added the "look to the sky" and "look at the floor" signals to show whether you had a high point or low point of a given suite. Stomping the floor or pounding the table was the original signal for Clubs; then just making a fist was good enough, then just gritting your teeth. Jimmy and Sonny had a special signal. When they pointed to any exposed skin it meant Spades. They thought that was so funny they didn't explain it to anyone else.

Jimmy perfected a special technique that raised his game above all the others. He cheated on the score. He would cheat when he added his team's game points, when he called out the points gained by each team at the end of each hand, and he would cheat on the number he wrote on the score sheet. He would call out the incorrectly added numbers often and would complain loudly when someone tried to check his math later.

This opportunity presented itself because either he or Kilos kept score in every game they played in and some they didn't, as they were the undisputed top math students and, more importantly, the other guys were too lazy to do it. Since no one was keeping track of who won or lost these games anyway, it was just part of the fun.

As an unexpected side effect of the Pitch Festival, all the boys became experts at the game. Because no one cared who won, strategy was discussed after most hands, with opinions given on what should have been played when, and each person's playing style became attuned to their individual personalities. Sonny was aggressive and would overbid with little encouragement. Kilos was conservative, and did not like to take risks, leading to underbidding. Chance loved to sing and could send the wrong signal if he loved a song so much he hummed it at the wrong time, like the time he sang "Rhinestone Cowboy" even though he didn't have a Diamond in his hand. Bob could not strategize at all. It was obvious he would need a wife to tell him what to do as soon as he graduated high school. His partner had to tell him exactly which card to play, which was easy because of the rampant signaling. Brad Schmidt could not play if he was stoned. He would have to be shaken when it was his turn to play a card. Jack Hoff could be bullied into losing, even though he had the better cards. Jimmy liked laughing and joking more than winning but had realized long ago winning led to better jokes, so he tried to win as much as possible.

RULE # 26 - *Humor is in the Eye of the Beholder*

After another round of the Festival and first period Speech class, Kilos and Jimmy's walk to Kilos' car on their way to Goon River was untypically quiet, even though Kilos had a grin on his face.

"Whacha thinkin' about Kilos?" asked Jimmy to break the silence as they reached the car.

Kilos shared the smile making memory. "Remember when you got kicked out of German class last year for playing cards?" he laughed.

As Jimmy sat in the car, he tried to remember. At first nothing came to him, but then he asked, "What were we playin', Gin Rummy?"

"Yeah, we had that cute substitute for The Fairy, I can't remember her name," continued Kilos. He reached down to push a tape into his 8-track player. It was, of course, Led Zeppelin. The only thing that ever seemed to change was which Led Zeppelin. The song was "Houses of the Holy".

"That was back when Leslie was still in favor," recalled Jimmy.

Leslie, The Fairy, Kindle, was the German teacher until the end of the 1975-76 school year. He was even Teacher of the Year the year before, the 1974-75 school year, the year Jimmy's older sister had been named his second-favorite student. He had even created a special award for her for being second best. Over the course of years, due to his vigorous and enthusiastic support, Canton Senior High's German Club had become one of the largest high school German clubs in the United States. Not only was he one of the most loved and respected teachers in the Canton School District, he was sent to conferences and other events to represent the district because of his highly regarded status in the teaching profession throughout the state. That was why the cute substitute was in front of the class instead of The Fairy.

Jimmy did not love, or respect, Leslie Kindle and the feeling was mutual, so he never minded not having to listen to his voice on another day. Jimmy didn't like him because his sister told him the teacher had praised her, or so he thought, by telling her in front of the entire class he did not believe black people had properly shaped lips to form words in German correctly until he heard her speak it.

Kilos did not like him because he was convinced Leslie Kindle was a queer. He was one of the first to suspect it, but the tide of believers grew from the time he first took German in 1974 as a sophomore until the end of school in the spring of 1976, when Leslie Kindle was no longer employed by the Canton School District. It seems he put his hands in the wrong place on a football player, as in down his pants, during a school sponsored summer trip to Germany, or so the word-of-mouth claimed.

The problem with substitute teachers in language classes was the substitute may have been a language specialist, but not necessarily in the language the class was learning. Such was the case on the day of the memory. Since there wouldn't be any Spanish words on any future tests, even Kilos saw no point in paying attention and taking notes. He did have cards, though.

Kilos was teaching Jimmy how to play Gin Rummy, and the two boys were silently, or as silently as two boys playing cards in the back of a classroom can be, pushing the cards back and forth. Everything went well until Jimmy, who had never won a hand of Gin Rummy before, was dealt the 3 of Diamonds he was looking for.

"I'll never forget it," recalled Kilos, "Just when she asked the class, 'Now what is the Spanish word for water?' You yell out: Gin!!!"

"Hey, I was excited," grinned Jimmy.

"Then, when she asked you if you were playin' cards," continued Kilos through his laughter, over the top of the John Bonham's drums, "You said, 'No!', but you've got a buncha' cards in your hands!!"

"And then she kicked me out of class," responded Jimmy. "That was your fault."

"What can I say, it was your deal," shrugged Kilos. "Plus, I was the one who lost a deck of cards that I never got back."

Instead of continuing down Main to Hickory, Kilos turned when he reached the Square and circled, driving as slowly as possible around the half block rectangle which constituted the epicenter of Canton. Inside the rectangle were scores of stately old trees, and at the core was a covered band shell. A band had never played there in the boys' life time, but in the days before radio it was used for that purpose. Around the outside of the square were the main businesses of Canton; clothing stores, banks, and a movie theater. When Kilos rolled by the theater he pulled the car over and parked. There were three old and dirty people huddled in front of the theater, under the marquee. Kilos opened his door.

"What're you doin', man?" queried Jimmy.

"I wanna talk ta some friends of mine," Kilos explained. Just when Jimmy thought Kilos was doing some volunteer work for his church or something, Kilos called out, "Hey Zoop, is that you??"

One of the men, the cleanest of the three, but still terribly dirty looking, glared at Kilos and replied, "Zoop, zoop, zoop!!!"

Kilos jumped out and walked around the car and leaned on the passenger side, so he could talk to Jimmy, who was sitting in the front seat with no intention of getting out.

"Yup, that's Zoop, alright," said Kilos. "See the one sitting in the corner? I call her Cry Lady."

Jimmy looked at the pitiful trio and wondered why Kilos thought it was funny to stop and talk to them.

Zoop called out "Zoop, zoop, zoop," again, and the third person, who Kilos did not name, rose to his feet.

"Go away!!!" he called out. His eyes were red from continual drinking, and his clothes revealed he hadn't bothered to unzip his pants the last few times he peed. Then Jimmy noticed his pants had no zipper. Then he noticed another layer of pants underneath. The man flailed his arms, and dust and fleas swarmed out from his arm pits. The woman then lived up to her name and bawled loudly. Jimmy looked away before he could see anything else that would make digesting Calculus any more difficult.

"Who is that?" asked Jimmy as Kilos ran to the driver's side and jumped in the car.

"I don't know. I haven't seen him before," replied Kilos.

Jimmy, thinking about his clothes, called out of the window as they drove away, "See you later, Boxcar!!"

"Boxcar? Why Boxcar?" asked Kilos.

"Cuz he looks like he just slept in one," said Jimmy.

Kilos roared as he steered the car onto Main and headed for Hickory Street. Custard Pie blasted from the car speakers. The song ended by the time they turned into the parking lot of the college.

RULE # 27 - *Messiahs Always Get the Girls*

T aking a class at the junior college while still in high school was much more intimidating in theory than it was in practice for Jimmy and Kilos. For one thing, the entire college consisted of a long, narrow parking lot, at the far end of which were three buildings connected by enclosed walkways, and that was it. The combined square footage was less than the high school, even though the parking lot was bigger. Nonetheless the new, two story buildings were the pride of Fulton County higher education, as they were a tremendous improvement over the scattered storefronts that had served as the campus until then. It was built a few miles outside of Canton in the rolling hills, backed up to a stand of trees. The middle building served as the main entrance to the school, and inside it the student center, bookstore, and administration offices were housed, while the classrooms and labs were in the outer buildings. The city fathers had been so impressed they decided the old name, Canton Community College, wasn't grand enough for the new surroundings, and renamed it Spoon River College.

It wasn't long before it became repetitive, like the same boring movie playing over-and-over again. They would walk in the main building and the college students, who were mostly folks they went to high school with the year or two before, would be sitting on the brick ledge which surrounded the main stair case, trying to act more sophisticated than they were a couple of years before, and failing at it, mostly. These were the people who did not matriculate to big full-time colleges, so there was no reason for Jimmy or Kilos to be in awe of anyone. At first the high schoolers tried to join in the college level conversations, but after a couple of weeks they reverted to doing what they would have done if they were in their Advanced Math class, they focused on teasing Vonny-Yonny. She always found a way to take them seriously, so it was non-stop entertainment.

But it was college level Calculus the trio was studying, and they were mature enough to take it seriously, and extreme attention had to be paid to keep up. It was their first foray into college academics, and they were intent on knowing as much as possible about what to expect when they had a full slate of classes at this level the next year. As was the case in all the prior years of Advanced Math classes, Kilos and Vonny-Yonny were fully committed to expending the maximum time and effort possible to achieve nothing less than straight A's on every test, quiz, and assignment, and Jimmy would settle for an overall B if it left him with enough time and energy to make the basketball team, party with his friends, and watch old reruns on television. Studying Calculus was important, hard, work, no doubt, but for him it was also important to have a balance between work and play. He just had to make sure he aced the easy tests, so he could get C's on the most difficult ones and score at least a B on the final.

Jimmy's head was not consumed with Calculus as the pair drove back after class, he was thinking about what would unfold later that day. He had basketball practice after school and his oldest sister was coming home for a visit. He wondered if she would bring any gifts from Chicago, where she was now living after graduating from Western Illinois University in Macomb, and how high they would get him.

Kilos, on the other hand, was still in the same land of nostalgia he was in before class. "What about the time Mrs. Cook made us watch 'That's Entertainment!!'" he chortled.

Why was there always someone around to jar Jimmy out of a good day dream and replace it with a bad one? He wondered how anyone could remember torture so fondly. "Yeah, I remember it wasn't."

It was in American Literature class the year before. To reward the students in her favorite class for finishing the semester's work one week early, she decided to treat them to her favorite movie of all time, 'That's Entertainment'.

"What's that about?" asked Jimmy skeptically when he heard the announcement.

Mrs. Cook could not contain her enthusiasm. "I know you'll just love it, Jimmy. It's a TV special showing the best singing and dancing scenes from all the old classic movie musicals!!!"

"You mean like Fred Astaire?" asked Kilos.

"Yes!!!" Mrs. Cook cried, "And Gene Kelly, and Shirley Temple..."

"You mean from the Wizard of Oz?" asked Ken Ferris.

"That's Judy Garland!!" Derek Schmidt declared with derision.

"Whatever," said Jimmy.

"It has the Nicholas Brothers in it too, Jimmy!!!!" enthused Mrs. Cook, thinking that would interest him.

"Does it have James Brown?" quizzed Jimmy. "He's got all the moves."

'Who?" asked Mrs. Cook.

"Never mind," responded Jimmy. "Can we just quietly play cards in the back instead?"

The look of shock on Mrs. Cook's face was equal to what it would have been if she ever witnessed James Brown dancing.

"This is an opportunity of a lifetime, Jimmy!!" she said in response. "Just give it a chance, you'll love it!!"

Jimmy, having grown up in a house full of sisters, knew he would not like 'That's Entertainment'. Mrs. Cook, who had by this time firmly established she was a girls' teacher and not a boys' teacher, was saying all the things his sisters would say while trying to convince him to sit through something boring. He learned even during a good movie like the Wizard of Oz it was best to leave the room when the singing and dancing started, except the scenes with the Munchkins, and the guards singing "Ooo-Eee-Yoo, Yee-Ooo-Ooo". As the room was populated by three quarters girls, cards were not going to be allowed no matter how quietly they were played by Jimmy and Kilos. Plus, Kilos didn't have his cards anymore.

Kashmir was playing. Jimmy liked Led Zeppelin. He liked them because unlike most of the frantic rock and roll groups his white friends favored, their drummer was never in a hurry. He kept the beat and let the guitar players go wild, and the lead singer did have the white boy blues, which was to say he understood the blues artistically if not spiritually. And this was their best song by far, they would never top it. Despite this, in Jimmy's brain all he could hear was the theme song to 'That's Entertainment'.

"Three days of torture, Kilos," remembered Jimmy.

"Yeah, plus you pissed off Mrs. Cook pretty bad, too," added Kilos.

"Well, she asked for it," replied Jimmy.

Near the beginning of the first day of torture, Jimmy tried to keep his head down and sleep most of the time, but he popped his head up occasionally to see something he wished he hadn't, and what he saw first was a bare foot black boy sitting in a tree with a piece of straw hanging out of his mouth shouting something about, "He cums da showboat!!" Then he saw an older black man sitting in ragged clothes singing Old Man River. Jimmy doubled his efforts to not watch anymore.

At the end of the first day of torture, Mrs. Cook asked Jimmy what he thought. His response?

"I liked it, except for the singing and dancing," he snarled sarcastically.

"You didn't like any of it, not even Shirley Temple dancing with Bojangles?" she asked.

"My great grandma would like that, but I like music that was made after the Stone Age," responded Jimmy. It was too late in the period to get kicked out of class, so he decided to say what he really felt. "Plus, all those old musicals are so prejudiced, I just can't take them seriously."

"You didn't help your grade with that comment, Whales," reminded Kilos, in the present.

"Yeah, and Grandma didn't like it either," said Jimmy. Grandma had come into Mrs. Cook's class to watch 'That's Entertainment' as well, as the Stone Age was still in progress during her childhood.

By the second day the boys in the class were occupying themselves with farting noises, coughing, and accidentally dropping their books on the floor, inspired by Jesus Vallon, who had fallen asleep and pushed his books off his desk during a vivid dream. His real name was not Jesus, it was Gary, but since he wore his dark hair long, straight and parted down the middle, he was christened with the nickname of Jesus when the movie 'Jesus Christ Superstar' was released a couple of years before. A bunch of guys had adopted the Jesus hairstyle after seeing that movie, and a lot of girls liked it. Jesus always had a girlfriend.

The noise rose to the level Coach BiteMe felt the need to volunteer to help with crowd control midway through Day Two, about the time the Nicholas Brothers scene came on. Jimmy lifted his head when BiteMe strutted in, or he would have missed them. BiteMe walked like a rooster. He lifted weights every day and enjoyed showing off his biceps so much he wore short sleeved shirts even in the dead of winter, and he strutted like a rooster in front of the classroom, sticking his head in and out or turning it with each step.

Watching the Nicholas Brothers was like seeing Julius Erving for thirty seconds after being forced to watch George Mikan and Dave DeBushere for two hours. They were so much better dancers than any of the bigger stars, Jimmy had to shake his head. He had never seen them before, or heard of them before, and they were making Gene Kelly look like a second-class act. Typical, thought Jimmy, and he put his head back down.

"You boys need to settle down and let these ladies enjoy the show," warned BiteMe, and then he twitched the right side of his mouth, another classic trait of his. "Do I make myself clear??"

No one responded, but the boys stopped dropping books.

"What an asshole," remembered Kilos as they pulled into the high school parking lot.

RULE # 28 - *Whenever Someone Insults You, Consider the Source. Don't Be Surprised How Often It Turns into a Compliment*

The next encounter Kilos and Jimmy had with BiteMe was the day of the Hangman Controversy in Stew-Pid's math class. It happened a few weeks after the That's Entertainment viewing, cementing his status as one of the leading jerks in the faculty. It elevated him to the level of Lurch, Manson, Table Muscle, and of course, Heady, with their assholes instead of their faces carved into the side of Mount Narc.

In the middle of class one day, Walter Matthau appeared at the door and asked to speak with Stew-Pid. It had to be something important, like Stew-Pid going over his head to the school board again, to bring Walter out of his office and down a hallway where he could be accosted by one of the many students he suspected of wanting to kill him. Whatever it was, Stew-Pid knew it was going to take a while, so he told the most responsible person in the class, Kilos, to go to the board and lead his fellow students in a game of Hangman while he was in the hall conversing with Walter.

Hangman was a classroom game first learned in elementary school. It was played by first drawing the picture of a gallows on the chalkboard, and then someone, usually the teacher, thought of a word or phrase and drew a dash on the board for each letter, with a space between words if a phrase was used instead of one word. After seeing the number of dashes, the class would guess a letter, usually E, and if there were any E's in the word or phrase, the leader would put that letter above each dash where an E belonged in the word. If there was no E in the chosen word or phrase, then the leader would draw a head in the noose of the gallows. After E, A was usually guessed, and then I, then S then T, to hit all the most frequently used letters first. For each letter guessed which was not in the word or

184

phrase, the leader next drew the trunk of a stick figure, then an arm, then another, then each leg. To keep track of the letters which were guessed that were not part of the word or phrase, the teacher would write on another part of the chalkboard each incorrect letter, allowing the class to recognize which letters were still available to pick and to not be penalized twice for the same wrong guess. If the man's six-segmented figure was completed before the word or phrase was guessed, the class lost. If they guessed it before, they won.

Jimmy was offended his Advanced Math teacher, in his junior year of high school, was telling him to play Hangman, a game played by third graders, so he decided to make this the last and best game of Hangman he would play in his life. His strategy was simple. Kilos went to the board as instructed and thought of a phrase. He drew five dashes, left a space and then drew thirteen, and then followed with the gallows. While he did this, the rest of the class talked and doodled or did their homework with no intention of joining the game of Hangman, which would have been fine with Stew-Pid, but Jimmy was paying attention. Kilos knew he would be, since through the years when any game of wits was played with the two of them on opposing sides they contested it as one against one, so Kilos thought of something specifically for Jimmy. It was so clever whether Jimmy guessed it or not, Kilos would get the last laugh.

"OK, class," said Kilos in his most authoritative voice. "Go ahead and start guessing!!"

No one said a word until Jimmy broke the silence.

"F!!!!" he called out.

"There's no F, Jimmy," said Kilos, wondering why Jimmy would pick such an obscure letter. He wrote it on the board on the far left to give himself plenty of space to add more incorrectly guessed letters before they would run into his dashes and the gallows. He drew the head.

"OK, Kilos, this looks like a tough one. How about a U???" bellowed Jimmy with a smile, so loud the rest of the class could no longer ignore him.

"There's no U, Whales!!" roared Kilos, laughing and writing the U next to the F, and then walking over to draw the man's stick trunk. He didn't get it.

The entire class now dropped what they were doing and watched. Jimmy had them all paying attention.

"OK, Kilos, there has to be a C," winced Jimmy with a false tone of alarm. Half of the class laughed, and the other half asked, "What's so funny??"

Kilos was one of the clueless ones. He wrote down the C and drew an arm. There had to be something more to this than he could figure out, because it made no sense to pick these letters randomly and not start with the standard E and A. He wondered what Jimmy was up to.

Bart/Jack/Pid Hoff couldn't contain himself as Kilos drew the arm and shouted out, "K, for Kilos, K for Kilos!!!"

"OK, I might as well draw the other arm now!" laughed Kilos, and then he walked to the end of the board and saw FUC and he finally knew what his friend was up to. He froze.

"The guess was K; did you forget it?" asked Jimmy.

The boys in the class were now fully engaged. They shouted and hooted at Kilos, "K, Kilos, write down the K, we guessed K, come on Kilos, it's your job to write down the letters we guess!!!"

The boys switched to a chant, and a very loud one, "K, K, K, K, K, K, K, K !!!!!!!"

Kilos knew he had to do something, and quickly, so he decided the best course of action was to write down the K, but to put it on a line below the FUC. His plan was to then put any additional letters next to the C, so it would no longer spell anything that would earn him a detention.

Jimmy and the other boys, realizing Kilos' ploy, shifted their chant to "Wimp, wimp, wimp, wimp!!"

"OK, guess another letter!" cried Kilos, trying to speed things along past this awkward stage of the game.

"Nope!!!" replied Jimmy before anyone could screw up this classic bit of school room humor, "We're not makin' any more guesses. If those four letters aren't in the answer, who cares???"

"Yeah, we already spelled the word we wanted to anyway!!!!" called out Bart, and the room erupted in such loudness BiteMe bolted from his classroom two doors away and burst into the room. Kilos grabbed the eraser, but BiteMe stopped him before he could eliminate the evidence.

"What the fu..." started BiteMe before he realized that was the exact wrong thing to say at that moment, but he had progressed enough for it to further bring down the house. At this point Stew-Pid bounded back in, after dashing down the hall in response to the tumult.

"This is your Advanced Math class?" asked BiteMe to his colleague. Then he turned on his heels and marched out of the room, shaking his head. "More like a bunch of clowns, if you ask me."

"Class detention!!!" shouted out Stew-Pid as soon as BiteMe stepped out. "How dare you make this kind of scene when the principal is right outside the classroom!!!!"

Since he already had a detention, Jimmy saw no reason not to ask, "Hey Kilos, what was the answer?"

Stew-Pid was grinding his teeth and couldn't open his mouth quickly enough to stop him, so Kilos, midway through his return to his chair, said, "That's Entertainment."

"Hey, there's no F, U, C, or..." complained Jimmy.

"Double detentions for Williams and Johns!!!" cried out Stew-Pid, having regained enough composure to loosen his jaws.

"Well, there's not!!" concurred Bart/Jack/Pid.

"OK, double detention for you as well, Mr. Hoff," said Stew-Pid. "Any other takers?"

If you think most of the goody-two-shoes in the Advanced Math class, the top five percent of the class academically, had never had a detention in their lives, you would be correct. At least half of the class had never even been threatened with one before. So, in a reverse logic only a teenager would understand, Kilos and Jimmy were elevated that day from class clowns to class heroes. They had given the nerds something most would never have experienced otherwise, a detention. These kids, minus Egg, were never thought of as cool, and nothing was cooler to teenagers than rebels who warranted detentions. They earned a little rebel cred just by having a class with Kilos and Jimmy.

Nancy Naughton, one of those who could before only imagine the padded walls of the detention center, but was in his American Literature class as well as math, said to Jimmy after class, "Now that really was entertainment!!"

Kilos was in a different frame of mind. After class was over he was still steaming. "Can you believe BiteMe called us clowns?" he complained to Jimmy with more anger than Jimmy thought the comment merited. "We have to get him back for that."

Jimmy didn't feel insulted and wondered why Kilos was so upset. Kilos must not have a great grandma like Jimmy did, who told him at least fifty times growing up, "Whenever someone insults you, consider the source!" After hearing that again and again, most of the insults that had been hurled his way in his life had been turned into compliments in Jimmy's mind, including BiteMe's latest.

"We'll think of something," Jimmy said, and then he promptly forgot about it.

RULE # 29 - *Don't Be a Sore Loser*

"We should stop by my house before we go to practice," proposed Jimmy to Chance and Brad as they walked to Chance's station wagon after school.

They didn't need to be in the gym for another hour, and in Canton, that was a long, long time.

"My sister told me she was bringin' somethin' for me to try," explained Jimmy. "If we go now, maybe we'll get there before my mom and dad get home from work."

"You sure?" asked Brad skeptically.

"Yeah, it'll be cool," promised Jimmy.

Chance shrugged and off they went to Jimmy's house. As with any trip between any two spots in town, it took less than five minutes. Jimmy's older sister Jackie had arrived from Chicago earlier that day as hoped, and after introductions, the guys tumbled downstairs behind her to Jimmy's room and closed the door.

"Put this on," commanded Jackie to her brother, handing him an album. She could be counted on to bring home the latest music and was Jimmy's main conduit to what music was hip in the big city. He did as he was told, and the other guys sat on the floor, leaving the bed for Jackie and Jimmy to sit on. It was Kool and the Gang, Summer Madness Live. It was a long, long, song with a long, long, synthesizer solo, which was the newest musical intoxicant of the time.

Jackie pulled open the strings of the multi-colored yarn pouch she was holding and dumped a book of matches, a pack of Topps rolling papers, and a pill bottle out of it. She opened the bottle and tamped out a pile of finely crushed weed onto the album cover. The boys watched with rapt attention as she rolled one joint and then another. Their success rate when it came to rolling joints did not approach fifty percent, so watching someone roll two without a failure was to them the sign of a true expert.

She lit a match, picked up the first joint, and touched the flame to one end until fire rose from the paper. She shook it and the match, putting out both flames, and placed the unlit end of the joint in her mouth and breathed deeply.

Jimmy opened the window to his room, which was near the top of the wall, a few inches above ground level, and pointed to his sister where to blow her smoke out. She passed him the joint and lit the next. Jimmy had taken his hit and passed it to Chance who then passed it to Brad, before Jimmy finished hitting the second joint. The ladies on the record were wailing "Summmmer Madnessss!!" and Jimmy concluded, after his third hit, this was the best Get High song he had ever heard.

By the time they walked out of the room fifteen minutes later, both joints now tiny roaches, Jimmy might have been higher in his life, but not by much; Chance was trying to remember if he had ever been higher; and Brad was purely, totally, wasted and trying to remember how to walk. They stumbled up the stairs and out of the house, drove across town, and into the parking lot of the gym. As Chance rolled to a stop, he said the first words any of them had spoken since they climbed into the car.

"Man, we're so high we forgot to turn on the radio," he remarked as he slipped the gear selector into Park.

The boys laughed and grabbed their gear and trotted into the locker room to change clothes. Sonny and Bob were on the court, stretching while seated on the floor. Jimmy was the first of the trio dressed and jogged out of the locker room before his fellow partiers and sat down to stretch as well.

"Where you guys been?" asked Bob.

"We had ta stop by my house first. My sister's home for a visit," explained Jimmy.

"You look high as hell, Jimmy," observed Sonny.

"Yeah, I'm gonna hafta stay away from the coaches," agreed Jimmy.

Then Chance and Brad walked out of the locker room.

"Look at Brad, man," said Bob. Brad was staggering, unable to walk a straight line, and his face was beet red.

"We've gotta keep him away from the coaches, too," quipped Jimmy, rising to his feet.

As he stood, Bucky bounded out of his office and trotted to the center of the court.

"Listen up, boys!!" he shouted cheerfully. The group of about twenty ran from all directions to form a circle around the coach. Jimmy was too far away from Brad to grab him and pull him to the back of the crowd, and Brad ran to Bucky's front and center, smiling broadly.

"Before we get started, I want to tell you about the schedule," said Bucky. "We will be hosting a holiday tournament on Thanksgiving week," he continued.

"I heard about it!!!!" shouted Brad.

"Oh yeah?" asked Bucky, taken aback by Brad's overly extreme enthusiasm. "Who'd you hear it from?"

"From Heady...I mean Bucky...I mean Heady...I mean Coach uuuhh...I need, I need, uh, I need some WATAY!!!" blurted out Brad before blasting off in a dead sprint toward the water fountain at the end of the court, pushing people out of his way if they didn't step aside fast enough. The assembled group turned and watched him in shock, except Jimmy, Chance, Sonny, and Bob, who were doubled over in the back of the crowd laughing hysterically.

Brad turned on the fountain and put his face in the flow, the water splashing his forehead, his eyes, and running down his neck, and then he opened his mouth and drank in large loud gulps. No one moved. He finished drinking, wiped his mouth and eyes with the back of his arm, and trotted back to the group as if nothing strange had just happened.

"Feel better now, Brad?" asked Bucky.

"Yeah," answered Brad sheepishly.

"OK, I think we'll start with some wind sprints!!!" said Bucky.

This was the last time Jimmy or Brad got high before practice. In fact, Jimmy never smoked again on a practice day, even before school, until practice was over. Bucky ran them, and ran them, and ran them, and would not stop until the first guys started puking, except Carl Murphy, who stopped after the second sprint because his feet hurt. He sat in the stands and watched the others. Bucky only let the remainder rest between sprints in the "human chair", which meant leaning straight backed against a wall with their knees bent at a 90-degree angle. When the torture finally ended, someone had to pay.

Of course, it was the underclassmen. Sonny took extra care to spit on every ball before it was returned to the sophomore's half of the court and upped the ante by spitting on the ball rack and the "pass back" nets they used in passing drills. When they tossed the ball against the net it would come back with a ball of spit on it. When they picked up a ball from the rack they'd get slimed.

And then the scrimmage started. As always, because the boys picked the sides themselves, it was the seniors against the underclassmen. There were six seniors, including Carl Murphy, who could not play because of his feet, and against them were Andrew Thomas and Don Craig, both juniors and sure to make the team, plus Brad Littlejohn and Greg Septich and Mark Markland. The seniors played Sonny and Chance at guard, Brad and Jimmy at forward, and Bob was the center. The underclassmen had Andrew "All State" Thomas playing center, at six feet four, the second tallest player in town, Don and "Septic" Septich playing guard, and Mark Markland and Brad Littlejohn were the forwards.

Jimmy looked at the teams and thought of the matchups. Because Chance could not guard anyone, it made the most sense for him to guard Septic Septich, who scored as often as a stopped clock was correct, about twice a day. Bob had to guard All State, and that was a good matchup because both were equally slow, and neither could jump. Sonny, whose defensive specialty was holding guys by the jersey instead of moving his feet, was perfect for Brad Littlejohn, who could shoot, but had to be standing still in one of his special spots to score. Jimmy took Mark Markland, who was by far the worst basketball player on the court but was two inches taller than Jimmy.

Once all this was set in his mind he turned to Brad and said, "Hey, Watay, you take Craig." Brad nodded his head, and no one in the group ever called him Brad again.

As the scrimmage progressed, each player's talents, or lack thereof, were on full display.

Sonny's idol was a player by the name of Lloyd B. Free. Lloyd Free was one of those basketball players who always thought he was open and never saw a shot he didn't think he could make. Since he thought he could make every shot he never bothered to go inside fifteen feet of the basket, or even think about getting a rebound. He instead focused his energy on his next shot. He could not be stopped when he was on a hot streak, but if he was not on a hot streak he would not stop shooting, because it wasn't as if the guy guarding him was stopping him, he was just missing open shots. He would routinely make 5 out of 20 shots a game for two straight games, then in the third game make 18 out of 20. Lloyd Free was a talented enough scorer to get paid big money by the Philadelphia 76ers to be the selfish player he was.

Sonny wasn't even the most talented scorer in his crew, and they got cut every year, but that didn't stop Sonny from playing like Lloyd, and when he put up one of his long jump shots and by some miracle it went in, he made sure to shout out, "World B Free, Prince of Midair!!!" as he ran down court. Players like Lloyd deserved multiple nicknames.

The rest of the seniors, not including Carl, idolized another Philadelphia 76er, Julius Erving. Anyone who ever watched Julius Erving play knew no one in the history of mankind could ever play like him, but that didn't stop them from trying. There might have been other guys they picked things up from, like John Havlicek and George Gervin, but Julius rose above all the others, literally. When he floated through the air, time seemed to stop, even for the guys in the game trying to guard him. Even they would stop to watch in awe as he soared above them majestically.

In addition to the fundamentals the boys were supposed to be using in these scrimmages - the big man moves on the low block, the high post moves, the classic form with elbow tucked in on the jump shot - they worked on their "J Moves". Bucky had banned J Moves from practice on Day One and if anyone was caught using one he ended practice with extra wind sprints. That meant as soon as Bucky's back was turned, guys would start throwing passes behind their backs, dribbling between their legs, and shooting layups with extra hitches, changes of hands, jumping off the wrong foot or with the wrong hand, and last, but not least, the 360. The 360, for those who are not basketball fans, is when a player jumps, spins around completely, then shoots the ball. In real games there was hardly ever a reason to do it, but Julius did it during a dunk contest. No chance did Jimmy have of a 360 dunk, or any dunk for that matter, but he could make a layup after a 360 about one out of five times, and he knew with more practice he could improve it to at least 50-50.

Watay was a solid player. He was quicker than the other boys and was the best athlete. He could also play defense and wanted to play defense, so he was valuable in all phases of the game.

Bob was not big enough to match his slowness. That was his only problem. Other than that, he could shoot well enough, was tough under the boards, and played hard on defense. Against guys like All State, however, he was helpless, because All State was bigger and stronger, despite being equally slow.

Chance, as a basketball player, was about the same as Sonny in temperament, but shorter and slower. He also saw himself as a streak shooter, also never wanted to go inside, and was not interested in playing defense. His big bushy white boy Afro looked good on the court, though.

Don Craig was a fundamental ball player, the kind Bucky loved. He would do exactly what the coach instructed, even when the coach was in the office and not watching. He was slightly taller than Jimmy, stockier, and was a much better athlete than Jimmy could ever be. He would score when he was open and pass to the open man when he was not. Creativity, however, was not his strong suit.

That is how the seniors would win these scrimmages most of the time, and every time Bucky wasn't supervising. They would do unorthodox things to baffle the younger players, which the younger players labeled as "cheating", but the seniors thought of as being creative. Such as, since they had been working on their offensive schemes during practice, Jimmy knew where the next pass was supposed to go at any given time if they ran the offense as instructed by the coach. If Don Craig was at the top of the key with the ball, he would always pass to the wing next, as the offense Bucky was teaching them dictated. Jimmy wouldn't even bother to guard Mark Markland - who couldn't score unless the ball accidentally bounced off his head and into the hoop (it happened at least twice during the year) - and would run into the passing lane and steal the pass. He and Watay made this into a science, as they made steals in tandem, one of them tipping the ball to the other if they could not catch it cleanly.

Another trick was to jump off the wrong foot on a layup or shoot with the wrong hand. Big guys like All State would swap at the right hand, the one without the ball in it, because that was the orthodox thing to do. Jimmy had learned long, long ago on a basketball court, if you are the slowest, shortest, skinniest kid playing, being unorthodox was the best way to score. And since he loved to score, Jimmy spent hours on the playground by himself, working on ball handling and J Moves, to make unorthodox movements natural.

This game was typical of most. The score was 6 to 6, and the winner was the first to seven. The underclassmen had the ball and Craig threw the perfect entry pass to All State, who had Bob posted up perfectly on the low block. All State, as was his normal practice, dropped the pass.

Watay snatched it before either Bob or All State could react, and the seniors were off and running to the other end.

"Good hands, All State!!!" cried Sonny as he ran.

All State dropped almost everything he touched, and he was famous for it. The nickname was earned long before he grew tall enough to be a basketball player.

Watay passed ahead to Chance, and Chance dribbled around the top of the key trying to get off a shot but accomplished nothing other than letting the underclassmen get back on defense. Sonny and Watay were both open on the wings, screaming at Chance to pass it. Before he could raise the ball over his head and throw up a shot he had no chance of making, Brad Littlejohn swatted the ball away from him. It bounced toward Sonny, who, instead of running toward the ball to grab it, waited for it to roll to him. This gave Don Craig a chance to sprint over, but just before he could cut in front of Sonny and scoop up the ball, Sonny stuck his butt out and bumped him, knocking him off course just enough to allow the ball to roll out of bounds.

"That was a foul!!!" howled Don.

Sonny ignored him and grabbed the ball and threw it in to Watay, who drove the ball down the lane until he was cut off by All State. He threw a bounce pass to the now uncovered Bob, on the low block. If Bob had any quickness what-so-ever, he would have scored easily, but he bobbled the ball, took an awkward step, and threw it hard against the backboard. All State was sliding back and if he had any quickness would have blocked it but couldn't quite get there.

Jimmy was standing on the opposite side of the court, watching this unfold, and he knew without a doubt Bob would miss the shot. If he missed it short, the rebound would fall to All State. If he missed it long, there was nobody there. Jimmy took a couple of quick steps as he saw Bob fumbling with the ball and jumped at the same time Bob released it. It caromed hard off the glass, and barely touched the rim before bouncing off to the same side as Jimmy's hand was reaching. The ball came right to it, and he flicked his wrist to tap it softly against the backboard. It bounced and gently fell through the rim.

"Game over!!!" shouted Chance.

"Can't stop the Scoring Machine!!!!" called out Jimmy.

"That was a foul!!!!!!" snarled Don Craig, becoming more and more angry. He took a couple of deep breaths to calm himself, as his mind was filling with un-Christian thoughts.

"Don't be a sore loser," counselled Sonny.

Craig stopped trying to be a Christian. He took a step toward Sonny, who smiled at him even more broadly.

"If you're feelin' froggy, jump on it," offered Sonny to Don.

As Don took another step forward, his buddy All State grabbed him, and pulled him away.

"It's not worth it, Donny," he warned.

'OK, guys," said Bucky, who was watching this without stopping it to this point. "You must still have a lot of energy. Get on the line for some more line drills."

These were the worst kind of wind sprints. At the whistle they had to sprint from the baseline to the nearest free throw line and back, then to mid court and back, then to the far free throw line and back, then to the opposite baseline and back, and at each endpoint reach down and touch the line on the floor with one hand before turning back.

"How many, coach?" asked Markland, who had nearly passed out during the scrimmage.

"Five," answered Bucky, and the team groaned in unison. "What, you'd rather do ten???"

The boys went to the line in silence and took their punishment.

RULE # 30 - *When a Lazy Person Volunteers, Be Suspicious*

J immy dragged himself across the court after the last line drill and hauled himself up the first few rows of the stands to recover and pulled on his sweats. His sweats were unlike anything anyone had ever seen in Canton, and in fact, even when Jimmy wore them outside of Canton they drew a crowd. What made them such a magnet was their distinctive design, created by his older brother while stationed with the Army in Korea, and hand made by his own personal tailor there. Jimmy received them as a Christmas present the year before. They were made of thick, black, plush, 100% polyester. The pants had red and green stripes down the side and were wide at the bottom, almost touching the ground, not gathered at the bottom like the normal sweats of that era. An elastic waistband at the top eliminated the need for strings to tighten them. He could pull them on comfortably without taking off his shoes, and after a practice like this one, saving the energy required to take them off was crucial. The sweater had the same red and black stripes down the outside of the sleeves, and on the right front was a patch, about three inches high and an inch and a half wide, of a clinched fist outlined in red, and a red and green stripe underneath. On the left front "BRO. JIM" was embroidered in letters an inch high. The sweater zipped up, and at the top was a collar which extended around and down the back of the sweater in a large, wide flap. Embroidered onto that flap were the words "BRO." on the top line and "WILLIAMS" on the bottom line, again in one-inch high letters. Below the flap, on the back of the sweater, was another patch, six inches in diameter, outlined in red with two red fish in the middle, and the word PISCES under the fish, written around the inside rim of the outline. The sweater was cinched below the patch, so when Jimmy put it on it fit tightly around his stomach. On each sleeve was a patch, near the shoulder, sewn right on top of the stripes. The left patch read,

"BLACK IS BEAUTIFUL" and the right patch read, "BLACKS DON'T KILL BLACKS". There were pockets below each patch on the sleeves, striped to match them, with a pure black flap.

Brad Littlejohn had seen the suit countless times but still had to complement Jimmy on it. He climbed the bleachers to the row next to Jimmy and flopped down.

"That is the coolest sweat suit in the world, Jimmy," he said.

"Yeah, you're right!" replied Jimmy, but without much enthusiasm, as talking hurt too much at this point.

Brad was brimming with energy. 'You'll never guess what I saw today," he continued.

"You're right about that too," responded Jimmy.

"I saw your buddy Scott Johns in the library today."

Jimmy didn't answer, as this was not news. Kilos was always in the library.

"He was sittin' at a table with Sally Salt."

Again, not news.

"She was wearin' a dress, and he was fingerin' her under the table!"

"What?" asked Jimmy. He had been trying to not pay too much attention to Brad, as even thinking too hard hurt.

"I was sittin' at another table across the room, and I could see he had his hand between her legs under there. They didn't think anyone was watchin," Brad said triumphantly.

Jimmy thought about it and decided he didn't care. Then he wondered why Brad had felt the need to tell him about it. Before he thought too hard, Chance was standing next to them, and he was in a hurry.

"Come on, Jimmy, hurry up and get showered and dressed. I have to be to school early tomorrow," pestered Chance.

Jimmy struggled to his feet and smiled at Brad without saying another word to him. He wasn't sure what he was supposed to say to such a revelation.

As they showered, Jimmy wondered why Chance was in such a hurry and asked, "So what's happenin' tomorrow that's so important?"

"It's picture day!!" announced Chance.

"Oh, so you gotta get a haircut and brush your teeth and iron a special shirt?" taunted Jimmy.

"I'll get a haircut when you do, Jimmy," responded Chance. "I'm on the Yearbook Committee, and I'm helpin' the photographers set up."

"You're doin' the yearbook?" asked Watay, amazed lazy Chance would volunteer to do anything.

"Yup," confirmed Chance.

Jimmy thought about Chance's motives and concluded the only reason he was on the yearbook committee was to have influence on what went into it. In other words, Chance was on the Yearbook Committee to ensure as many pictures of Chance were in it as possible.

"You better get my picture from the Senior Class Skit in there, Potsy," warned Jimmy.

"Yeah, right, I'll do what I can," replied Chance.

"You know," mused Jimmy, "Another way to get in a lotta pictures is to jump in with some of the clubs' photos, whether we're in that club or not. I should try to sneak into the German Club picture. I used ta be in it last year, until The Fairy kicked me out, so I should get in the picture anyway."

Sonny was listening to the conversation and said, "Man, that's a fuckin' great idea. I'm gonna get in every picture I can too."

"OK," said Chance, "I won't say anything to the photographers."

RULE # 31 - *The Most Important Talent a Cheerleader Must Possess Is the Ability to Spread Her Legs as Wide as Necessary*

If Chance hadn't reminded Jimmy it was picture day the next day, he wouldn't have worn his favorite pullover sweater and corduroy jeans. The mirror in the bathroom let him know he was ready to face the cameras before he left the house. Once he arrived at school he proceeded to the spot he knew the picture schedule would be posted, on the wall outside the auditorium in roughly the same position the Peyote for Varsity poster had been. It listed when each club or the band or the cheerleaders were slated to be on the auditorium stage for their photos. A crowd had formed around the schedule, and it was clear someone had spread the idea of crashing the photo shoot, or others had come up with the same idea independently. It wasn't like it hadn't been done before.

The list read:

8:45 Varsity cheerleaders

9:00 JV cheerleaders

9:15 Wrestling cheerleaders

9:30 National Honor Society

9:45 Library Club

10:00 Biology Club

10:15 Band

11:00 Flag Girls

11:15 Majorettes

11:30 Thespian Club

12:00 Chorus

12:15 Art Club

12:30 Fellowship of Christian Athletes

12:45 German Club

1:00 French Club

1:15 Spanish Club

1:30 Cooperative Work Training Club

1:45 Future Farmers of America

2:00 Photography Club

2:15 Chess Club

2:30 D.O. Club

Jimmy read through the list and counted two pictures he was legitimately in, the NHS and FCA, and he was plotting jumping into the German Club picture, plus the Thespian Club, because he was in the skit, plus the French club, because he had been kicked out of German class the year before for speaking naughty French, among other things. Spanish, so he could hit all three languages. Plus, in what would be a yearbook classic, he would try for the FFA picture. With all the pictures he needed to be in, he could excuse himself from all his afternoon classes if he played his teachers right.

After Speech class he and Kilos headed for the auditorium, along with Yobs and Weedhopper. With no Calculus class that day, Jimmy and Kilos were free until lunch. They walked in on the Varsity cheerleaders in the middle of a pose where two girls, Laura Morton and Bonnie Midas, stood side by side with a girl sitting on each of their shoulders, Judy Davis and Mary Stone. They were standing the exact distance apart necessary to allow a fifth girl, Marsha Rawson, to stretch her legs from Judy's hip to Mary's, and for them to hold her by her outstretched arms to complete the pose. The sixth cheerleader, Kim Holt, sat on the floor with her legs stretched in a split in unison with Marsha's. She had to do something.

"She's got to have some talent," mused Yobs about Marsha, "Since she doesn't have any looks." He paused to contemplate his last statement before he continued. "Why aren't any of the prettiest girls, cheerleaders?"

"No talent??" suggested Jimmy in response.

"That's true," agreed Kilos, "The ability to spread your legs is much more important than looks to be a good cheerleader."

As he laughed along with the others, Jimmy had to admit Yobs was right. None of the girls he had private crushes on were cheerleaders, at least not varsity cheerleaders. In fact, he hadn't realized before today all but one of the varsity cheerleaders were juniors, the exception being Bonnie. They had short, straight, dark hair, some shorter than others, and Marsha wore glasses. Mary was a dirty blond, so she was a little different. Kim was the only one considered cute, and she had braces and was chunky enough to anchor pyramid foundations. Then he realized someone was missing.

'Hey, where's Derek??" asked Jimmy.

The other boys laughed, but Jimmy was serious. At the home football games he had attended, Derek Schmidt was one of the cheerleaders, standing alongside the others shouting out cheers wearing long pants instead of a skirt, thank goodness. Jimmy had assumed Derek was the captain of the cheerleaders from the way he led the others around.

"Derek's not an official cheerleader," explained Yobs. "They just let him go out there and embarrass the hell out of us at football games."

Jimmy looked at Kilos and said, "Well, don't you think if he's allowed to embarrass us at games, he should be allowed to embarrass us in the yearbook too, so we'll remember it thirty years from now?"

Kilos shrugged, not willing to take up this fight. He needed Yobs as an ally and didn't want to cross him.

Chance was on stage when they walked in. He was standing at the optimum angle to see up Marsha's skirt. A group of geeks huddled with cameras, comprised of the students in the Photography Club plus a couple of adult geeks. The real photographer was on a step ladder and Mr. Nascar, the Photography teacher and yearbook picture coordinator, was standing next to him to steady it.

"Hey, Anteater!" shouted Jimmy, "Where's Derek?"

Chance, despite hating the nickname, always responded to it. He turned away from his peeping mission to find Jimmy in the audience. Instead of answering verbally, he extended his middle finger.

"Are we missing someone?" asked the photographer impatiently, and loudly. His schedule was already wrecked, as the first group photo was not wrapped up and he was supposed to be on his third.

"Yeah, Derek!!" shouted back Weedhopper.

"We are NOT missing anyone," countered Mr. Nascar.

"I'm not retaking this picture again, so this better be..."

The photographer's petulant response was cut off by Mr. Nascar. "Take the picture!!" he commanded. Then he looked out into the auditorium, where not only the quartet was sitting, but scores of others were floating in for their scheduled group photos.

"Williams, are you even supposed to be here??" shouted Mr. Nascar.

"Yes, sir, the National Honor Society picture is supposed to be at 9:30, and it is 9:25 right now. Could you please hurry up? I have a lot of studying to do," answered Jimmy with absolutely fake sincerity.

Mr. Nascar shook his head and turned back to his task and waited for the next assault.

It didn't come, at least not his way. So many people were streaming into the auditorium it distracted the boys from what was happening on-stage as they laughed and joked with their classmates. The Wresting and JV cheerleaders came and went without further interruption.

Then, about half an hour behind schedule, the National Honor Society was called. As he passed Chance on the stage he slipped him a quick elbow in response to the bird flipping, catching him in the side. Chance flinched and smiled.

"I got an awesome view of one of the JV girls' panties. I hope it shows up in the picture," bragged Chance.

Portable stands had been slid into place from the side of the stage, so the large groups, such as this one, could be assembled in ascending rows. There were thirty people, most of the Advanced Math class plus a few others, and as Jimmy looked around he could not help but feel like an outsider, despite being a charter member of the group around him. His was the only black face, but that wasn't the only distinction. He also was the only one who had any hand eye coordination, or any other meaningful athletic talent, plus he was probably the only one standing on the stage who was a stoner, except most likely the photographer.

Normally in group pictures like this, the tallest take up the back row, the shortest take up the first row, and the medium size people filter in between. By this stage of life, the back row was filled with boys, and with his Afro, Jimmy was tallest. Without it he was maybe fifth tallest. Despite Kilos not being tall at least a row's worth of girls was shorter than him, but he took his place in the middle of the front row to ensure everyone in future generations knew he was the leader. Next to him stood Vonny-Yonny, who had a better claim to being shorter than a row's worth but may not have been able to prove it. At the end of the front row, another boy with a dubious height claim stood, Bob Fair. Annie Royal was in the second row, along with Nancy Naughton. Ken Farris and Scott Michaels and Mike Roper, Grant's chubby cousin, stood in the same row as Jimmy. Despite seeing the others every day for years, Jimmy would have had difficulty naming the rest. When the picture was snapped, Jimmy had a wry smile on his face, and his head was tilted slightly, as if it was in mid-shake. It was, in fact. A fraction of a second before the shutter snapped Jimmy realized the front row was where certain people thought the Student of the Year should be standing. Frontrunners stand in the front.

Yobs, of all people, tried to crash the Biology Club picture. Even the photographer, who had never seen these kids before, knew he was an imposter. It didn't help that Mr. Nascar also taught Biology, so he knew who was in the club without having to check the roster. That gave Mr. Nascar the excuse he had been looking for, the excuse to banish Yobs, Jimmy, and Kilos from the auditorium. Weedhopper, for some reason, was spared the indignities of the others, and thereby managed to sneak into Thespian Club shot.

The Fellowship of Christian Athletes met every Thursday morning at a café off the town square before school for a pancake breakfast. Most of the coaches of high school sports participated, as did the core of athletes who played those sports. At each meeting a different student would talk about God and how being a Christian helped make him a better athlete. Sonny had been dragging Jimmy to FCA breakfasts since school started, his logic being attending would look good to the coaches and help him make the basketball team. Jimmy went because he needed a ride to school, plus he loved pancakes.

The girls had formed their own group, for the first time in school history, and they far outnumbered the boys on the stage, the total reaching close to seventy. For Sonny, Kilos, Jimmy, and Yobs, this was the perfect cover. Mr. Nascar was forced to let them back in the auditorium, plus the group was so large it would be easy for them to melt into the audience for the next pictures afterwards.

It worked, almost. Jimmy made it past Mr. Nascar into the middle row of the German Club picture, but Sonny tried to climb from the back of the stand with help from those standing in the back row. That caused a commotion as he slipped and crashed back to the stage, and the boys who could no longer silently help him burst out laughing, leading to a general review of those in the picture, and Jimmy, as well as Sonny, was booted out. He tried again in the French Club, but aborted his mission before he was apprehended, but Sonny almost managed to sneak into the Spanish Club picture, along with Yobs, by hiding in the back, ready to pop up when the photographer said "cheese". Mr. Nascar foiled that attempt as well, because he was now patrolling the back row of each group photo, to catch anyone trying to climb up like Sonny again. The boys countered by waiting until he was in the back to dash up the stairs and hide, forcing Mr. Nascar to circle a few times to catch the culprits. After that he called for reinforcements, and Lurch was summoned. Jimmy did not get a chance to even watch the FFA picture being taken.

RULE # 32 - *You Never Know What a Politician Will Do with the Truth, Other Than Twist It*

The next day, Thursday, October 28, 1976; Halloween was cancelled by the Canton Senior High School administration. The reason for the cancellation began at about 8:30 that morning, as first period began. At first, it was such a faint whiff only the most sensitive girls could detect it, but by the end of Speech class it was so intense the guys in the back were debating which of them had eaten too many beans the night before. When Jimmy and Kilos left for Calculus, people were laughing about it in the halls. By ten o'clock the secretaries in the front office were calling the maintenance staff to determine if a sewer line had backed up, and by 10:30 the entire school smelled like a port-a-potty on the hottest day of the state fair. Walter Matthau made the call to evacuate over the intercom at 10:45.

A few minutes past eleven Kilos was driving into the parking lot of the high school, blasting his only tape that wasn't Led Zeppelin, Jethro Tull's Aqualung. The song billowing out of the speakers was named Locomotive Breath. Ian Anderson was singing "No way to slow down, no way to slow down, no way to slow down..." just as Jimmy noticed the crowd of students in the parking lot.

"Slow down, Kilos," said Jimmy as they passed abnormally large bunches of kids in the lot. Kilos pulled into an empty slot, next to a clutch of seniors huddled in a circle. "What's goin' on?" Jimmy yelled out of the car.

"There was a chemical attack on the school," replied Wastey Hastey, who was one of the members of the group, along with Carl David, Dana Pickman, and a few others.

Once out of the car Jimmy didn't continue his line of questioning with Wastey. He knew from his sarcastic tone Wastey didn't know what really happened. Plus, he saw Sonny standing alone with his little brother Jody, and he could hear Sonny reeling in laughter. When Jimmy ambled over close enough to see them, Sonny's eyes were red from the tears flowing down his cheeks.

"Hey Jimmy!" greeted Jody. Sonny was doubled over in a coughing fit, so he could only wave his arm instead of speaking.

"What's goin' on?" inquired Jimmy again, hoping for a better answer than Wastey gave him.

"Someone snuck into the maintenance room and put rotten limburger cheese in the main ventilation duct," confided Jody.

Sonny had managed to compose himself and take a few deep breaths by this point, but started laughing again when Jody said, 'limburger'.

"It smells so bad in there they need ta air out the whole school for a while," continued Jody.

"So, who did it?" asked Jimmy, assuming Jody knew and had already told his brother.

Jody motioned for Jimmy to step closer and whispered in his ear, "Pigpen."

Mark Mueller was a little over six feet and wore the same heavy clothes most of the year: dark jeans, flannel shirt, and long trench coat. He had wild curly hair desperately in need of grooming and long sideburns, and his beard consisted of isolated patches of hair on his cheeks. His style looked and smelled like a hobo in training. Everyone, including his friends, called him Pigpen.

He was one of those guys who started working in junior high and never played sports or joined any clubs. He had a few friends who were also fringe characters, so he was not quite a loner, but he did not need to be included in the mainstream high school society. He always looked and acted stoned, but because he had acted that way since grade school, before he ever came close to his first toke, and emitted noxious odors which repelled bystanders, no one ever knew for sure.

Hyde Park Week had come and gone before Pigpen even realized it, but a week later as he emptied the trash from his employer's restaurant he had an idea which was pure Hyde Park Week genius. Instead of tossing the old cheese in the trash can, he put it in the back of his truck, under some rags. He knew exactly what to do with it, as he had worked with the school maintenance crew in the past summer, even knew the head guy's schedule, when he made his rounds in the morning, and knew exactly when to sneak in and make his deposit. His chance came on Thursday, October 28.

"So, how'd you find out about it?" asked Jimmy.

"I've got Building Arts class with him," said Jody. "He told a few of us about it before he did it."

"Did he get caught?" asked Jimmy.

"Not yet," coughed Sonny, finally able to speak.

By then Kilos walked up, having stopped to talk to another group before following Jimmy over. "What happened?" he asked.

"Limburger cheese in the vent," responded Jimmy.

"Limburger cheese!!" cried Kilos, "What a classic!! I wonder who did it."

"We should give him a medal, whoever he is," advised Jimmy before the other two could speak. Sonny and Jody played along. They knew Kilos was a politician, after all, and you could never know what a politician would do with the truth, other than twist it to his advantage.

The "all-clear" bell rang an hour later, just in time for lunch. As the students filed into the lunch room, Lurch stood by the door, watching each move past. When he saw Kilos, he touched him on the shoulder and informed him of a meeting he must attend in his office after eating. Jimmy was still in the lunch room, playing cards before the next period began, when Kilos spun into the cafeteria after his Lurch meeting.

"You won't believe it," stated Kilos. "Lurch cancelled Halloween."

"What do you mean he cancelled it?" questioned Jimmy.

"In response ta what he said was 'tantamount to a chemical weapons attack' no students will be allowed ta dress up for Halloween tomorrow. Anyone arriving at the school in costume will be sent home and given a one-day suspension," Kilos said, repeating the message he'd heard already, but would soon be blasting across the intercoms at the start of fifth period.

"We're seniors in high school. Dressin' up on Halloween is for babies," said Jimmy. As far as he was concerned, he was once again being punished by the school for something he had no part in, but luckily in a way that did not affect him much. On the other hand, he had an indirect part in anything inspired by Hyde Park Week, so he could also take a little credit at the same time.

"I wasn't dressin' up anyway, so it doesn't matter ta me, but a lotta the girls'll be pissed," said Kilos, always thinking of the voters.

"Yeah, some of them might have come dressed as go-go dancers," envisaged Chance, smiling at the thought of other skirts to look up.

"Yeah, Chicken Hawk, for instance," said Yobs, to spike whatever image Chance had in his mind before.

The boys laughed and took their trays to the corner to be stacked and washed, as any appetite that may have been lingering was chased away by the image of Chicken Hawk's fat legs protruding down from a too tight skirt with a roll of belly fat hanging over the top.

RULE # 33 - *If You Steal Something, Be Prepared to Run*

The Halloween ban was the main topic of discussion in the locker room before basketball practice that day, and by this time Jimmy was sick of hearing it. This was just another item to add to the list of the things he witnessed his classmates do in the last six years which resulted in time honored traditions being outlawed. He looked at Sonny, and it reminded him of one such incident in junior high.

"Remember the Ex-Lax cookies?" asked Jimmy.

Sonny's face, which had a smile on it before, turned serious, and he grabbed his stomach as a reflex.

"Fuck you, Jimmy, and the horse you rode in on." responded Sonny. He remembered.

Bake sales were well known throughout the nation as a means by which funds were raised for various clubs and sports. Schools in Canton had held them for as long as anyone could remember, but they were forced to stop by decree of the school board in 1974. The change in policy was adopted because of an incident which took place during the Junior High Winter Bake Sale, at the wrestling team's booth to be specific. The stated purpose of that booth was to help pay for new wrestling mats, but the real purpose lay elsewhere.

Jasper Waldon had always been one of the shortest kids in the Class of 1977. He had the classic cocky attitude of a short guy, and when wrestling came into his life he embraced it as only a little man can. One of the things wrestlers were required to do that was unique to any other sport played in the school district was they needed to "make weight" before a match. Each wrestler had to declare what "weight class" he was in, and each class was defined by the maximum a wrestler could weigh at the time of the "weigh in," which occurred a couple hours before the match. The weight classes started at 106 pounds and worked their way up in six or seven pound increments all the way up to the heavyweight class. If a wrestler could lose a few pounds before the weigh in and then gain it back between the weigh in and the match, he would be able to maximize his strength while still weighing in below the maximum limit for his class. This made wrestlers experts at binging and purging food as necessary, and they learned the methods of doing so very early in their careers, even ninth graders like Jasper.

One of the main tricks was taking a laxative a few hours before the weigh-in to purge as much as possible, and then eating as much as possible once off the scales. When he was younger, Jasper Waldon hated regular Ex-Lax, which was a thick milky liquid that came in a tall medicine bottle, so when his mother saw it being sold in solid chocolate chip form instead, she bought it, thinking he would prefer to use them for wrestling. Because Jasper couldn't gain a pound if his life depended on it, he never needed to lose weight before a match, and the Ex-Lax chocolate chips sat in the medicine cabinet unopened for months.

When Jasper came home that fateful day and informed his mother of the impending bake sale, she told him she would bake some brownies, but he made her quite proud when he responded he'd prefer to bake chocolate chip cookies himself, if she gave him some guidance. She made the first batch for him as he watched, and made more than enough dough for two more batches, and watched him as he made the second batch, adding the chips and smoothing the batter into balls before squashing them on the cookie sheet. She left the kitchen while he made the third batch, which was when he switched the Tollhouse chocolate chips with the Shithouse chocolate chips.

The bake sale was a school wide event, and everyone who had a club that needed money, which was all of them, set up a booth. Jasper recruited his buddy Grant Roper to help him set up his folding table of a booth the next day alongside the other booths, and to help him collect the money. They began the sale innocently with the first batch of Tollhouse cookies, and the word soon spread the Wrestling Booth's fantastic cookies were the best of all. To make sure that happened, Grant let out the secret to a couple of conspirators, and they were the main ones helping with marketing in return for a couple of free cookies. By the time the intended target, Hulk Hanson, strolled up to purchase three, Jasper had switched to the special cookies.

After Hulk ambled off munching on the best cookies in the sale, things became much more interesting. Certain guys, namely Yobs and Sonny, decided to have a contest to see how many cookies they could steal from the various booths. When their marketing spies told them what was going on, Jasper and Grant purposely left the Wrestling Booth unattended and watched as Yobs and Sonny laughingly took turns swiping tainted cookies and sneaking off to eat them. Then Hulk returned and bought two more. At the precise moment he bit off the first chunk of cookie number 5 he felt a powerful flow rushing through his lower intestines.

"Aaaaaaaahhhhhh!!!!" he cried out and stampeded toward the nearest boys' bathroom.

Grant and Jasper burst into fits of laughter as they watched Hulk charge off, but they became apprehensive when they saw Yobs, then Sonny, sprinting to the same place with the same looks on their faces. Jasper wanted to toss what he thought were the tainted cookies into the trash, but they had been mixed with the second batch of the untainted and he wasn't quite sure which were which. He was staring at the remaining cookies, trying to decide whether to toss them all or to keep selling them, when a large shadow darkened the tray.

"What's the matter, Jasper?" asked Mr. Monahan, the vice principal, staring at Jasper staring at the cookies. He was a chubby, jovial man, the kind who loves children and cookies. "Don't think they're any good? I'll give them a test!"

Neither Jasper nor Grant could think of a reason sufficient to stop him before he pulled the required change from his pocket and gobbled down two.

The total tally was:

Hulk - 5 Ex-Lax cookies, 2 hours on the toilet, Jasper called into the bathroom to receive death threat.

Yobs – 8 Ex-Lax cookies, 4 hours on the toilet, school nurse dispatched to the bathroom to discuss the situation, even though Yobs asked for a priest.

Sonny – 6 Ex-Lax cookies, 3 hours on the toilet, luckily the smell emanating from Hulk and Yobs' cubicles forced him to throw up in the sink on his way to a stall, which helped.

Jasper/Grant – suspended from school for 2 days as punishment and for their own safety.

Various Innocent Bystanders – Zero Ex-Lax cookies, but more than a dozen left school early complaining of phantom nausea.

Mr. Monahan – 1 Ex-Lax and 1 untainted cookie, 5 hours on the toilet with his favorite reading material, situation normal.

And, at the next board meeting, the banning of bake sales anywhere in the Canton School District until at least 1978.

RULE # 34 - *Don't Let Your Friends Lack of Success Tarnish Yours*

While the boys trickled out of the locker room and spilled onto the court, Bucky watched, sitting in the stands with Coach Campbell. After the aspirants spread about the gym had time to loosen up, he called them over.

"Listen up, boys!!" he shouted.

They condensed into a crowd close to where the coach sat, pushing and shoving and elbowing each other, not because there was not enough space, but because that's what boys do. Bucky leaned back, his elbows propped up on the row behind. He had a semi-sick smile on his face as he began.

"Tomorrow is the day I announce the cuts. You have all worked hard, but I only have fifteen uniforms. I want to thank you all for trying out."

He paused for emphasis, and then continued rather anti-climactically, "So let's go out and have a good practice!!"

Halloween may have been cancelled at the school, but for the guys sweating in the gym, tricking and treating was still carried out on October 29. Jimmy was the last of his group to be called into the small office where Bucky and Coach Campbell sat. Bob and Chance and then Sonny had gone in before him. He was nervous, but since he was dripping with sweat from the shooting drills he had been working on seconds before, he hoped the coaches wouldn't notice. He wiped his forehead with his wrist band, more as a nervous twitch than to clear his brow, as he sat down.

Bucky smiled. He was sitting behind a metal desk in the cramped office. There was barely enough space for his desk and chair, plus two other folding metal chairs. Shelves lined the windowless walls, with various sports related books and magazines spilling from them. Jimmy had seen this smile in this setting so many times he knew not to believe it was a prelude to anything positive. Seeing it had always meant he had done well, but not well enough. Only once before, his first game of little league baseball, had it meant he was the chosen one.

"Jimmy," started Bucky, leaning back on two of the four legs his chair was constructed of, "The basketball team is the hardest team to make, because there are only fifteen players. All the other sports have at least twice as many. A lot of them don't even make cuts, but I have to. Don't get me wrong, I thought you worked harder last year than anyone I have ever seen that got cut from a basketball team. I didn't agree with it."

He stopped himself before he revealed his dislike for Take-A-Nap, but not soon enough for Jimmy to not pick up on it. At this point Coach Campbell leaned forward in his chair, directly across from Jimmy, putting the trunk of his body between the head coach and Jimmy's chair, as if to block him from lunging across the desk after hearing the words which would follow.

"I've got five football players I'm going to save spots for," continued Bucky.

Jimmy did a quick head count: Egg, Carl David, Paul Hunt, Crazy Joe, and before he could think of the fifth, Bucky went on.

"And I've got to have some juniors, so we have some guys with experience for next year," he continued.

In Jimmy's mind, that meant Andrew Thomas and Don Craig. He couldn't think of any others better than him. He assumed Watay would make it and Carl Murphy. Then he ranked Bob, Sonny and Chance in that order. By his count they should all make the team. Then he came back to reality. They would not all make it. None of them would. That was how it had always been before.

"But I've got a spot for you, Jimmy," announced Bucky with a flourish.

Coach Campbell stuck out his hand. "Congratulations, Williams, you deserve it!"

Jimmy stood as he extended his hand, incredulous, not believing the words he had just heard. It wasn't like he didn't think he had earned it. He had worked harder than anyone else the year before. Take-A-Nap had told him so when he cut him. He had never stopped working a single day during this year's tryout, even though a lot of that work was practicing J Moves. That's why he'd prepared himself to accept the reality none of that mattered. He had worked all summer on his ball handling, his main weakness, other than overall body weakness. He had been in the weight room whenever it was open to work on that and withstood the ridicule of the football players at the puny amounts he could lift. He had played when it was so hot outside the ball stuck to the asphalt and when it was so cold the snow had to be shoveled off the court before the games could start. All of that, and it had never mattered before, so why expect it to now?

He ran from the room, better yet he bounced, or more accurately still, he floated out of the room. If he could have controlled his gaping mouth, he would have smiled from the top of his Afro to the bottom of his old canvas sneakers. He burst around the corner, looking for his friends to be running and laughing as they always were, so he could run and laugh with them and they could share the joy of their mutual accomplishment. But only a few boys remained on the court, and his friends were not among those tossing balls at the various rims scattered around the gym. He sprinted into the locker room, and there he found Sonny, slowly untying the laces of his shoes.

"I made it!!!!" called out Jimmy, banging his knee against the hard, wooden bench that extended along the row of lockers. He didn't feel a thing.

"I know," said Sonny solemnly. "I asked him if you made it when he cut me."

Jimmy looked down at his friend, and then sat next to him to calm himself. He could not help but be happy, but he was also angry and sad at the same time.

"Where's Bob and Chance?" asked Jimmy, now realizing Sonny wasn't the only one cut.

"They left already," Sonny sniffed, loudly. He had to work very hard to keep the next tear from falling. Several had been shed before Jimmy walked in, and the towel covering his face was not wet with sweat.

"Well, what the hell did he tell you?" asked Jimmy, dropping his line of questioning about Bob and Chance, now knowing why they had left.

"He said I was screwin' off too much in practice, causin' too much of a distraction," moaned Sonny.

Jimmy didn't try to argue with that one because it was true, but, if Sonny, Bob and Chance all got cut, who made it? As if he was reading Jimmy's mind, Sonny answered his question.

"He kept all those worthless juniors we beat every day in practice. He even kept Septic and..." Sonny couldn't get the next word out before Jimmy.

"Markland??? He kept that worthless piece of shit???" Jimmy shouted out incredulously.

Sonny didn't answer. He put his towel over his face to confirm Jimmy's question and to end the conversation. Jimmy stood and marched indignantly to his locker; undressed, showered, dressed, and strode out of the gym as quickly as possible. Despite being upset about his friends' disappointment, he could not help but feel an elation he had never felt before and knew he couldn't act the way he felt in front of Sonny. This was one of the best days of his life. His mother picked him up, and as soon as he shut the car door, he let loose with a happy shout so loud it would have been heard inside the gym if the car windows hadn't been closed. Before the short ride was over, Jimmy had rationalized he would soon be separated from the boys he had hung out with for so many years anyway, so this might be a good transition. He would just have to make the best of it. Plus, the bragging rights would be priceless.

Halloween was not cancelled outside of school. Trick or Treaters began knocking on the front door of the Williams house promptly after sunset on the 31st of October, which in 1976 fell on a Sunday. Jimmy had stopped going out himself only the year before, and some of his classmates still did. To some, collecting candy was always cool, even if they didn't have much of a costume. Even those who were too cool to do it themselves did not laugh at their friends who did, because then they wouldn't get any of their candy. Some waited as late as nine o'clock and knocked on doors volunteering to dispose of whatever leftover candy the younger children hadn't taken earlier. The craftiest ones would volunteer to take their little brothers and sisters out and bring along a bag for themselves.

This year Jimmy volunteered to be the one to open the door and hand out the candy, something he had never asked to do before, even though he was usually forced to do it part time. He wanted to greet everyone he knew who came to his house, so he could tell them personally the same thing.

"I made it!!"

It was the best Halloween of his life.

RULE # 35 - *Displaying A Sense of Humor Is More Likely to Lower Your Grade Than Raise It*

Kilos' and Jimmy's journey from the card game to Speech class on Monday was uneventful, laughing about the Sig-A-Nols they had dreamed up during the morning's session, until a strong but familiar arm sneaking up from behind put Jimmy in a headlock before he could react.

"I knew you could do it, Jimmy!!" said the voice attached to the arm. Jimmy tried to squirm free, but the grip tightened, and his captor's knuckles were rapping against his head. When it reached the point he began to panic, he was released with a hearty laugh and a slap on the back. Jimmy turned and saw Carl David's smiling face.

"I always knew you were a Varsity Man," said Yobs, standing beside Carl.

"You'll have ta come party with us, once football is over," demanded Carl.

"Yeah, Kilos won't party with us," complained Yobs.

Before Kilos could defend himself, the boys were interrupted by Mr. Bishop, chugging down the hall toward his classroom.

"He can party after he finishshesss hisss presssentation today, and not a minute before!" he said as he passed.

What happened next was typical of Jimmy's academic career in high school. He was on-track to receive an A in the class, and his presentation going without a hitch would ensure that outcome, but fate wrapped up in mischief intervened, as it often did, and his B was cemented instead. It started well. Jimmy had completed his research, polished his outline, and practiced in front of the mirror. He had even bored his mother and sister with a dress rehearsal the night before, to ensure he could deliver it smoothly.

Although he was slightly nervous before he began, walking from his seat in the back of the room to the podium half expecting a spit wad or some other object to fly his way, the words tumbled out in the pattern they were supposed to, and flowed even easier once he spat out the first line.

"The Golden Gate Bridge was opened in 1937, after four years of construction. It was the longest suspension bridge in the world. It was built to cross the Golden Gate, which is the inlet to San Francisco Bay."

The podium was in the front and center of the classroom, and the classroom door was to his right as he stood facing his classmates, and Mr. Bishop was sitting behind his desk to his left. Before he could continue, a woman Jimmy recognized as a secretary in the principal's office approached the door and stood outside waving her hand, attempting to catch Mr. Bishop's attention without disturbing Jimmy's speech, quite unsuccessfully. Jimmy stopped and turned to his teacher, who at this point also saw the woman standing by the door.

"Keep going, Jimmy," said Mr. Bishop as he rose to walk to the door. At first, he stood just outside talking to her, but then the two of them walked hurriedly down the hall. As Jimmy watched them recede down the hallway, he had a flash of grade-reducing brilliance. He decided he should give the speech while impersonating Mr. Bishop, in honor of the unjustly incarcerated Apache Joe.

In what he thought was a perfectly pitched rendition, Jimmy continued, "Before the bridge wassss built, Ssssan Francccciisss-cansss had to jump a ferry...." Saying that line with a lisp was sure funnier to Jimmy than it was in rehearsals, and he cracked up.

That gave Kilos the opportunity to shout out, "Is it a bridge or an overpass??"

More people laughed at Kilos' joke than Jimmy's, but most of the room didn't get either one. Jimmy, not wanting Kilos to steal his thunder, stomped his foot, put his hand on his hip and roared, "TOE THE MARK, PEOPLE, TOE THE MARK!!!"

That caused the chuckles in the room to erupt into howling and hooping.

"You people jusssst aren't cccciviliessssed!!! You brutesss!!" Jimmy had his hands on his cheeks as he shouted out his response in the highest falsetto he could muster.

The class burst into hysterics, then tried to muffle it, but it leaked out from behind coat sleeves and clinched teeth.

"When I sssssssay TOE THE MARK, I mean it!" cried Jimmy with a toss of his head. He knew his impersonation was dead on, but for some reason the class wasn't laughing anymore.

A strange feeling came over him. He glanced to his right and saw the gleaming bald spot Mr. Bishop was constantly trying to pull his rim of hair over. It was tinged red, as was the man's face as Jimmy peered lower.

"Ssssssoooo!!!!" snarled Mr. Bishop, his voice full of anger and more than a little bit of pain, "You thhhhhink itssss funny to make fun of me??"

Even though Jimmy was instantly remorseful he had hurt the man's feelings, he still had to bite his lip to stop from laughing, because when Mr. Bishop was angry, he was at his comic best. He was an angry comic genius. Mr. Bishop snorted three or four times, loudly, through his nose, with his hands on his hips, palms outward. Jimmy had to grit his teeth and remind himself over and over this was not funny, this should not be funny, and he had to maintain a straight face. The class did not agree. They couldn't contain themselves anymore and burst out laughing again.

"Well, OK, ifff you thhhhink itsss sssssso funny, finishshshsh your sssspeeech imitating me!!" squealed Mr. Bishop, flopping himself down into his chair and folding his arms.

The class cheered, giving Jimmy time to compose himself.

"Naw, Meester Beeshup, I can't do it. I'm sorry," Jimmy said.

"You sssure are!!" agreed the teacher. "Go sssit down!"

Jimmy hadn't meant he couldn't go on with the speech, he just couldn't do it in Mr. Bishop's voice. He wanted to finish the speech.

"But..." he tried to respond.

"Ssssit down, now, missster!" commanded the teacher.

As he trudged to his seat Jimmy was determined to finish as much of the speech as he could along the way. He didn't have much time, so he proceeded to the last line, slightly altered.

"In conclusion, the Golden Gate Bridge is the most popular place in the world to commit suicide."

RULE # 36 - *Most People Would Rather Be Told What to Do Than Think for Themselves*

Nellie Harms had been a teacher at Canton Senior High School longer than anyone could remember, even her. She was a very sweet and kind old lady, and she was well loved by students reaching back many decades. They held her in such affection her mail box was full of well wishes every Christmas and birthday. Because of her longevity, most of the current faculty had either taken an English class with her when they were students, or she was a mentor to those she came across as young teachers, or both. She was so cherished she never had discipline problems with students despite her frail nature. No one could recall a time when she had felt the need to kick a student out of class.

That was until Yobs took Senior Composition. To the Class of 1977, Nellie Harms was universally and not complimentarily nicknamed Grandma. There may have been a few girls who maintained a soft spot for her, but most of them had been chastised for the shortness of their skirts too many times to have much sentiment left. The boys' image of her was defined by a terrible vision Apache Joe had in one of the special Ghost Dances he participated in the year before, made extra special by the mescaline trip he was on at the time.

"Man," he said, describing his vision, "It was like a porno movie gone wrong. I went back in time about a hundred years to when they were both young, and I saw Grandma bent over her desk, and Mack Daniels was bangin' the shit outta her. She kept screamin' 'double clutch me, you nasty motherfucker!' over and over again. It was so real I couldn't get a hard-on for a week."

This was one of the reasons Jimmy never did mescaline. It was proving difficult to erase the thought from his mind without the mescaline, and he was afraid if he ever went on a trip himself, he might return with even more horrible visions he could not expunge from his memory for months or even years. Jimmy and all the boys around him got hard-ons if they turned their head the wrong way, if they took too deep of a breath, if they saw a girl walk through a door, or if they were awake or asleep for more than five minutes, so it had to be a supremely powerful vision to shut a teenaged boy down for seven straight days.

It happened the day after the presidential election. Yobs, like most of his classmates, was born of Republicans. On Nov. 2, 1976, Jimmy Carter, a Democrat from the Deep South, won the election over Republican President Gerald Ford, who had been appointed Vice-President after Republican Spiro Agnew was forced to resign for cheating on his taxes, and subsequently was appointed President after Republican Richard Nixon was forced to resign for cheating in just about every phase of his political life. Like most children of Republicans, Yobs had been trained from birth to view Democrats as evil and crooked at worst, and completely naïve at best, and the only truly patriotic, honest, and hardworking citizens were Republicans. The country was held together by Republicans. Wars were fought and won by Republicans. All the taxes were paid by Republicans and the Democrats were all on welfare. Democrats were communist cowards at heart, if you really got down to it.

Jimmy, like most black people after FDR, had been raised a Democrat. Unlike his classmates, however, who defended the side they had been brainwashed to be on from their earliest memories, Jimmy thought they were all crooks. Democrats were crooks with bleeding hearts, and Republicans were cold blooded crooks. He could not believe people could forget the lies they had been told again and again, and continue to vote for the same two stupid, corrupt, political parties. Jimmy's great-grandma had summed up his philosophy by saying, "Fool me once, shame on you. Fool me twice, shame on me." Of course, as he knew by this point in his life, most people would rather do what they were told than seek the truth and decide for themselves, and to them thinking was dangerous, so it was in their best interest to forget the lies.

As soon as the bell rang to start class, Grandma asked the class for their opinion on the results of the voting. Yobs had statistics.

"Black people got Jimmy Carter elected!!" he spat out in disgust. "If you look at White voters only, Ford would have won!"

He didn't need to say the rest, as the majority of those in the room had been schooled by their parents and knew what he was implying already. These poor, deluded niggers were not sophisticated enough to know they were being lied to by the Democrats and were therefore not intellectually mature enough to vote. Yobs didn't think about Jimmy being in the room until after he said it.

He decided he needed to appease his friend. "No offence, Jimmy."

Jimmy looked at Yobs with a wry smile and responded to annoy him, "No offence taken, Yobs. I'm just glad so many Black people voted, if that's what made the difference!"

The room groaned and giggled, but that was the only response. They knew better than to debate with Jimmy. When they argued too much with Jimmy on such topics in the past, he would usually say something that made too much sense to deny and made them so uncomfortable they stopped challenging him long ago.

Grandma was passing out the students' latest graded reports while this discussion was going on and did not react to Jimmy's statement either. When Grandma handed Yobs his paper, his already bubbling anger spilled out.

"What???!!!! An F???!!!" he cried as he looked at the grade, "This is complete Bolshevik!!!"

The force of his voice alone almost knocked the old lady off her feet as she walked past him. She turned to him wide-eyed, the fear naked on her face.

"This is complete Bolshevik!!!" he shouted again as he sprang to his feet and tossed the papers she had placed on his desk in the air.

He stood with his arms at his sides, fists clenched. Anyone who knew Yobs for more than a week knew about his crazy temper, but those who knew him for much longer than that had never seen him this angry before. There was a mixture of shock, fear, and in Jimmy's case, curiosity, surging through the room at the scene he was making.

Grandma folded her arms in front of her chest, using the remaining papers she had not yet passed out for protection. She hunched her shoulders in fear and said meekly, "You copied the whole essay, Tom."

Yobs looked at her like he was going to lunge at her, but instead waved his arms up and down wildly and said "That's Bolshevik, Bolshevik, Bolshevik!!!! I did not copy it. I used footnotes!!!"

"It was copied, except for the first sentence," she responded.

"This is such Bolshevik!!" Yobs cried, and then he stomped toward the front of the room.

"Well, Mr. Yardwick, I think you should leave," replied Grandma, to officially kick him out of class, even though she could have remained silent as he was leaving anyway. As he went by, Jimmy thought he saw a tear falling from his eye.

After the wind from the passing storm abated, Grandma trudged slowly to her desk. She needed to sit down immediately, and she looked it. It was an even bet on what would happen next: A heart attack or a stroke? Remarkably neither occurred. She sat down slowly and shook her head even more slowly.

"It's all copied, right out of the World History text book," she said, as if needing to justify her actions. She said it out loud, but she was really talking to herself.

"I don't believe it!!" shouted Kilos, startling everyone in the room.

Jimmy couldn't believe Kilos couldn't believe it, but the look on Kilos' face showed he was serious and not just posturing. They both had known Yobs long enough to know what he was capable of. He might have even done it honestly, not realizing the addition of a footnote would not clear him from plagiarizing, but if Grandma said he copied it, he did.

"Look at it for yourself!!" said Grandma. She would describe herself as getting a little perturbed. "Here is the book he copied it from," she snarled at Kilos, holding up the text book.

"I'm not going to look at it!" exclaimed Kilos, becoming quite emotional himself. "If Yobs says he didn't cheat, then he didn't cheat! I don't need to look at it!!"

Jimmy was not the only person amazed at how strongly Kilos was defending Yobs.

"I'll look at it," said Bob Fair. He was no fan of Yobs' antics. As an Eagle Scout, Bob had been taught to help little old ladies cross the street, not scare them into cardiac arrest. He picked up the scattered papers and quickly scanned them and the World History book.

"They are identical!!" he declared. "Take a look," he continued, holding them out for Kilos to see.

Kilos spun away from Bob in his chair, to avoid seeing what was written. A couple of others did, however, and they agreed with Bob and Grandma.

RULE # 37 - *Don't Be Surprised if You Get Kicked Out for Trying to Be Helpful*

Nostalgia crept up on Jimmy at the strangest times. The scene unfolding in front of him caused him to think back to the many times he had been kicked out of various classes down through the years. It didn't take much calculating to conclude German was the class he was asked to exit more than any other, three times total, although remarkably the requests came from three different instructors. What remained constant was The Fairy's name on the door, and Jimmy's indignance at what he considered unjust punishment. Like the time he got kicked out for speaking French, when he was trying to be helpful.

Once again, the Fairy was off on some secret mission and a substitute teacher was taking his place. She was young, eager, and fresh; the kind of teacher who never stayed in the Canton School District a day longer than necessary. Her name was Miss Parker. As Jimmy ruminated on the irony of this, the perky instructor pulled him out of his daydream by asking the following question:

"Do any of you know any French?" she asked, after introducing herself and telling the class her specialty.

The rest of the class groaned, and Jimmy felt it was wrong to treat Miss Parker in this fashion. He raised his hand and smiled shyly but did not speak.

"OK," she said, smiling back. "What is your name?"

"Jimmy," he replied sweetly.

"OK, Jimmy, do you know any French words?" she cooed.

"Wee-Wee," responded Jimmy.

"Yes!! Excellent!! Oui means Yes!!" she said enthusiastically. She had dreaded entering this classroom and facing this group of strangers, but now she felt hopeful she could make a connection.

"Does anyone else know any words?" she asked, hoping Jimmy had broken the ice. No one responded.

Jimmy took up the challenge. He raised his hand again.

Miss Parker gave the class a chance to do likewise, but when no one did, she said, "Go ahead, Jimmy."

"Bonne Aire!" Jimmy declared.

"Good!" replied the teacher. "Does anyone know what that means?" she sang out giddily, trying to make eye contact with the others. She turned her body to face each corner of the room, hoping someone was formulating an answer.

Before any less enlightened dork in the room could say 'good air', Jimmy couldn't contain himself and shouted out, "It's what you put into the wee-wee!!"

The smile that had been splashed over Miss Parker's face quickly dried up.

"Get out!!!" she shouted, startling the rest of the class. Most hadn't been paying much attention before this turn of events and would have probably let the joke slip right past them if they hadn't been jolted by Miss Parker's shrill screech. But as Jimmy stood and started the slow stroll out of the room, the laughter began to build. It reached its peak as he walked out the door.

His mother heard about that one, which wasn't so funny. She worked at the main district office as an administrator and she was responsible for assigning the substitutes, so they all met her before long. Weeks later, when Miss Parker realized whose mother she was, she felt the responsibility to tattle on him. The first chance his mother had to confront him about it, she made a rather curious statement: "This better be the last time I hear about something like this. Next time I'll to have to come to the school to straighten things out." She was religious enough to believe in prophesy, and this one would become self-fulfilling before his senior year ended.

RULE # 38 - *Never Let Good Beer Go to Waste*

Almost all the cars from local fatal accidents spent time in Donny Google's dad's junk yard. It was truly a yard, with room for maybe twenty cars, max, packed together on the side and behind their house. Most of the time it held less than ten. It didn't even rate a mean dog, as Daddy Google kept a shotgun by the back door in case he heard any strange noises in the dead of night. They had a dog, alright, but it was the kind of dog that could only hurt you if you were short enough to drown in its drool, or more likely it might try to lick you to death. Part of the yard was fenced, but some of the wrecks were kept outside the chain link barrier. It was a small time, small town, business. Their name wasn't really Google either, it was DeMoss. The sign on the side of the fence said, 'Bob's Towing Service', Daddy Google's given name.

Donny had been Sonny's best friend when they were little boys, as they lived two doors away from each other on opposite sides of the alley that ran between Fifth and Sixth Streets. Donny's house, and the junk yard, were on the corner of Fifth and Oak. Sonny lived on Sixth, in the middle of the block. When the Anderson School playground became the place for grade school aged boys to hang out and play whatever sport was in season, Sonny and Donny came together. He was taller than everyone his age and knew how to use that fact to be the most dominant when basketball season rolled around.

Overall, however, he was a good-natured kid and was well liked by the others. His nickname back then was DD, and the Dare Devil was his favorite comic book hero. When they weren't playing sports or reading comic books, Donny would tell stories about the wrecked cars his dad would bring in, and the times his dad let him ride along. By the time they were in the fifth grade, whenever someone in town had been killed in a car wreck, the other boys would ask him if his dad had towed the car and if it was in their yard. There were a few people who took that route to paradise every year in

Canton or the surrounding countryside, and it was the talk of the town the next day, as nothing else would happen of such magnitude unless it was spring time and a tornado rumbled through town simultaneously. Whenever he confirmed it, the boys would postpone whatever ballgame they had planned and hike over to see it.

Mt. Carmel Baptist Church, which both Jimmy and Sonny attended, Jimmy constantly and Sonny sporadically, was a block away from Bob's Towing, down Fifth Avenue. A woman had managed to clock out on Friday night, November 12, 1976, at 9:38 PM, according to the police report in the newspaper, by means of the mishandling of a 1974 Oldsmobile Cutlass and the unfortunate placement of a tree on the side of the road.

Sonny told Jimmy all about it in the break between Sunday school and the main service. In fact, that was the only reason he had rolled out of bed and walked the half block from his house to the church. Donny had called him the day before and told him this was a wreck that had to be seen to be believed.

Jimmy knew Sonny loved to exaggerate, and needed to interrogate him further, "So what's so unbelievable about it?"

"All he would tell me was she wasn't wearing a seat belt," said Sonny.

With that teaser, Jimmy agreed to go see it immediately after church. They ambled down the block and across the street and knocked on Donny's front door. He opened it and came outside, zipping up a jacket against the chilly wind.

"I'm gonna hafta unlock the gate. The police want us ta keep it inside," Donny explained. "They don't want people comin' by gawkin' at it, outta respect for the family."

As Jimmy trailed the other boys, he became apprehensive he might see something he would regret, but he couldn't stop and turn away now. Donny opened the gate and when the boys stepped through and saw the car, parked alongside another, much more damaged car, Jimmy could not believe this wreck had ended in a death and not the other car beside it.

"You sure this is the one?" asked Jimmy, unconvinced.

The front end showed damage, but the car looked like it would start if the key was turned. The windshield was fractured, with cracks radiating from a bubble above the steering wheel, but all the glass was still there. As he stepped forward, and the other boys moved aside, he could see the point of impact much more clearly.

"Oh yeah," confirmed Sonny, looking queasy, "This is the one."

When the girl lost control of the car she slammed on the brakes, making matters worse, and then slid off the road and into the tree. The car stopped, but she didn't, which resulted in her being launched her from her seat and into the windshield, face first, and Jimmy realized as he surveyed the inside of the vehicle, her head exploded on impact. Bits of bloody hair and skin and bone were stuck in the cracks of the glass. The pattern of the splatter of the blood was visible on the windshield, paralleling the cracks. It had been cleaned to some extent, but not with much enthusiasm. More gobs of flesh and gore could be seen in the corner of the dashboard, and on the back of the steering wheel. A clump of hair was adhered to the roof with dried blood.

"The police already took the empty beer cans out," said Donny, smiling. "My dad cleaned off the ones that hadn't been opened yet and put 'em in the fridge." He was staring at Sonny, hoping those words would trigger him to lose his breakfast. That was why he loved showing his friends these kinds of wrecks. Despite Jimmy's having seen more than he would have liked, his breakfast was safe, but Sonny was looking very queasy.

"You're eighteen already, right, Donny?" asked Jimmy.

"Sure am," Donny replied.

"Well then, you can drink those beers yourself!" said Jimmy. "I gotta get outta here and go eat dinner. Come on, Sonny, you gotta give me a ride."

That did it. Sonny threw up. He made it out to the sidewalk, at least.

RULE # 39 - *Nervous People Make Lousy Burglars*

As Sonny spilled his guts Jimmy slowly trudged down the alley toward the Caddy, which was parked behind his house in a wide space paved with weeds and gravel. Once he had emptied his stomach, Sonny followed, and the boys jumped in the car and rolled slowly down the narrow path toward Grant Street. At the end of the block, at the corner of Grant and Fifth, was a small gas station. The pumps were on the Fifth Avenue side of the station building, and the back of the building was against the alley. As Sonny slowed even more to make his turn onto Grant, he noticed a small window, above the back door of the station, was open. It was the type that was hinged at the top and opened outward by means of a crank on the wall inside.

"The gas station is closed on Sundays," Sonny thought to himself out loud. "I wonder if you could climb through that window and get in."

Jimmy shrugged and said in response, "Maybe, but what for?"

"They might keep money in there," schooled Sonny, as if the reason should be obvious for someone as smart as Jimmy.

"Not enough ta risk gettin' caught over it," countered Jimmy, as if that should be even more obvious.

War growled out, "All my friends know the Low Rider. The Low Rider, is a little higher..."

"Man," said Jimmy, changing the subject as they rolled down Grant, "You need another tape."

The boys were quiet for a while after that, each deep in his own thoughts, listening to Lee Oskar's harmonica and the boys' favorite line, "Take a little trip, take a little trip, take a little trip with me-ee. Take a little trip, take a little trip, take a little trip and see-ee."

"Do you know any good ones?" asked Sonny. Since Jimmy had connections through his older siblings, he had the opportunity to hear music that would rarely make it on the radio stations in Peoria, and never in Canton.

"Yeah," answered Jimmy as he opened the car door at his house, remembering an album he knew Sonny would love, "Parliament, Mothership Connection."

Sonny did not bother to go into his house after he parked in his spot in the alley. Instead he hiked down the alley past the station, then turned and sauntered along the side of it to Fifth Avenue, all the while making his plan. He would need an accomplice, that was for sure. Since the perfect candidate, Jimmy, wasn't interested, his little brother Jody would have to suffice. His first thought had been to hoist his brother up on his shoulders, and have him climb into the window, but he realized his little brother was too big and heavy, plus might not fit, so he would have to be the one doing the hoisting while Sonny crawled through. They would wait until nightfall. He would take a pack of matches and wear his jeans with no holes in the pockets, and a dark jacket. That was as foolproof as it was going to get. He walked around the front of the station and finished circling his prey and then journeyed home, smiling at his plot.

The next day when Sonny picked up Jimmy for school, he told him how it went down.

"Man, I need you ta do me a favor," said Sonny as Jimmy sat down in his car.

"What is that?" asked Jimmy, always wary when Sonny was asking for a favor, but first thing on a Monday morning made it extra suspicious.

"I need you to take this money from me and spend it," tempted Sonny, handing Jimmy a small paper bag.

"What?" asked Jimmy while looking in. There must have been a hundred nickels inside.

"Me and Jody broke into the gas station last night, through that back window those dumb fuckers left open," explained Sonny.

Under normal circumstances Jimmy would be skeptical of Sonny's story, but with evidence like this, he had to take it seriously.

"I had Jody put me on his shoulders, and I climbed through. I almost broke my neck tryin' ta get down from the window. It was so dark in there I was lightin' matches so I could see into the cash registers and they're all empty, but I found four bags of change in the back room: one with quarters, one with dimes, one with nickels, and one with pennies. I grabbed 'em and then I panicked 'cuz I couldn't figure out how ta get outta the back window again without climbin' up on Jody, plus the bags were heavy. There was a desk I slid over in front of the door, but it was still too low. I almost broke out the big window in the front, but then Jody yells at me ta try ta unlock the back door. Don't know why I didn't thinka' that, 'cuz all I had ta do was turn the latch," said Sonny.

"It takes a certain temperament to be a burglar," cautioned Jimmy. "Maybe you're too nervous."

"So, I gave Jody the bag of pennies, and kept the rest for myself," continued Sonny. "But then I started thinkin', I'm gonna get caught if I start payin' for everything in change, 'specially nickels and dimes."

Jimmy shrugged in a way to show Sonny he was making sense.

"So, I need you ta spend some of the nickels. I'm givin' ya' five dollars' worth," concluded Sonny.

Jimmy did the math. Five dollars of nickels meant one hundred nickels. He smiled at his ability to guesstimate. Then he rationalized, very quickly, how noble it was to help his friend by taking the money, plus his allowance was only five dollars a week. This was like an extra payday he could stretch out until January.

"So how much did you steal total?" asked Jimmy.

"Thirty-seven dollars and seventy-eight cents. Took me half the night to count it all," responded Sonny.

Jimmy stashed the money in his gym bag where it stayed until after basketball practice, then took it out in his bedroom and hid it in his dresser behind the socks. He wondered if Sonny would be able to slowly spend the money or if he would not have enough self-control, spend it too fast and raise suspicion. Then he thought of Jody, with all those pennies. That was an even worse bet.

RULE # 40 – *Don't Buy Something You Can Get for Free*

S onny did not use the money to buy another 8-track tape, he used it to buy some good Colombian weed. In fact, he and Bob and split an ounce. That Friday night the crew got together and spent the evening driving around in Bob's car, passing the pipe and going to Hardees for a late-night snack. For the first time in longer than anyone could remember, all the boys had enough money to buy what they wanted without sharing the fries or substituting water for a Coke.

"My girlfriend got me ta buy this tape," explained Bob, thinking it was better to apologize ahead of time, in case the crew didn't approve of his music selection. He didn't realize that made it even worse, and because his girlfriend made him buy it didn't mean they needed to listen to it.

"Shadows grow so long before my eyes, and I can see them, across the stage..." Chance started singing along. He had heard this before.

"Who is this?" rasped Sonny, with much disapproval in his voice.

"Peter Frampton," answered Bob.

"Ooo baby I love your way, every day..." sang Chance.

"You need some new tapes, Bub," complained Sonny.

"Wanna be with you night and day, hey, hey, hey..." continued Chance.

Sonny handed Chance the pipe and said, "Shut the fuck up and smoke this, Chance."

Chance stopped singing, but Peter didn't.

"Any suggestions?" asked Bob.

"Parliament," said Sonny.

"Never heard of them," responded Bob.

239

"The name of the album is Mothership Connection," detailed Sonny, matter-of-factly.

Jimmy knew immediately there was no way Bob would like Parliament. He was listening to Peter Frampton, for gods' sake. The last tape he bought without his girlfriend's input was Foghat. Another of his favorite bands was Angel. Just when Jimmy was about to speak up and warn Bob, Sonny turned to him and winked. Jimmy took the pipe from Chance instead, and said nothing, and Bob took out the Frampton before Chance could start singing again and put in the Foghat. The rest of the night they took the band's advice. They rode slow and took it easy.

Jimmy had forgotten about it until he heard Sonny pulling up to his house the next week. He could hear, coming out of the open side window of Sonny's Caddy, "Good evening, Welcome to station W.E.F.U.N.K., better known as We Funk, or deeper still, the Mothership Connection. We have taken control as to bring you this special show..."

Before Jimmy could ask, Sonny blurted out, "I got that dumb fucker No-Sense to buy the tape, and when he listened to it and didn't like it, I told him he should just give it to me, and he did!"

Jimmy sat in the car and laughed and bobbed his head all the way to school.

RULE # 41 - *Learn the Rules Before You Break Them*

As always, they headed straight for Table Muscle's Card Room after dropping their stuff off in their lockers. Kilos greeted them at the door. He was exiting as they were walking in.

"Man, I was just coming to look for you guys," he said by way of a greeting. "Guess who showed up this morning to challenge us to a game of Pitch!" declared Kilos, and not waiting for a guess he said, "The Goon-Yers!!"

And sure enough, Brad Littlejohn and Mark the Klutts were sitting at the main card table, with Donny Money, Danny Partridge, and Dale Parton standing behind them for support. Ron Williams and Carl Murphy were there as well, sitting in the corner ignoring the others, and Pid Hoff was standing by nervously, but now more than a little relieved, as it would have been up to him to partner with Kilos and defend the Class of 77's honor if Jimmy and Sonny hadn't shown up. Jimmy looked at the juniors liked they smelled as bad as they looked but did not speak. Sonny stood next to him with his arms folded.

Littlejohn was the spokesman. "We're tired of you seniors actin' like we aren't worthy ta play cards with ya. We think you're just afraida' losin."

"So, you wanna get funked up?" asked Jimmy, echoing George Clinton.

Sonny laughed, and the boys slapped each other's hands, on the black side.

"And you brought Dead Money, Partridge, and Dolly Parton with you?" asked Sonny.

Dale Parton was the smallest kid in the junior class, and of course, also the cockiest. He took a step toward Sonny as if he was going to get in his face.

"Back off, Jolene," warned Sonny.

Table Muscle, who had been behind his desk grading papers, barked out, "Hey boys!! Either play cards or get out!!"

Partridge put his arm around his little classmate, as if to hold him back, and said to his elders, "Are you scared ta play us?"

Jimmy sat down in one of the seats the Goon-Yers had left for them. He looked at Partridge and said, "Are you here ta play cards or just talk?"

Sonny sat down at the other and said to Partridge, "We're gonna beat you worse than the Ugly Stick beat your red-headed momma."

"Me and Kluttzey are playing," interjected Littlejohn.

"OK," said Jimmy, "Then tell your Daydream Believin' friend ta watch and learn like you're about to."

"That's the Monkees, not the Partridge Family," clarified Pid.

"Whatever," said Jimmy, "I'll keep score."

"Are you guys still playin' four-point, or are you sophisticated enough for five-point yet?" asked Sonny.

'Uhh," said the Klutz, "We could play five-point."

Jimmy could tell by the look on Klutz's face he was clueless about five-point. Jimmy took the offensive.

"Are you sure? You guys'll have a hard enough time playin' four-point." Then turning to Sonny, he continued, "No way these lightweights can handle five-point."

"We're playin' five-point!" cried out Littlejohn.

"OK, I'll deal," said Sonny.

There were three decks of cards at their disposal, and the Cheater's Club had a favorite deck, the oldest one. Over the course of the many, many games they had played, certain cards had become marked by overuse, and the regulars like Jimmy, Sonny, and Kilos knew every card by heart. If you were using Sig-A-Nols anyway, a marked deck was just part of the fun. There was the King of Diamonds, which had a bend in one corner, in Littlejohn's hand on the very first deal. There was the Deuce of Clubs, with the faint pattern of Ron Williams dirty thumb print, in Sonny's.

Sonny didn't make a fist, the sign for clubs, but he did say to Jimmy with a look of concern, "You sound like you got some congestion, man. You gettin' a chest cold?" Or in other words, 'I have Hearts.'

"I bid 2," said Littlejohn.

Jimmy's turn to bid came next, so he used another accepted cheater's trick. He sneezed, shaking his head violently in the direction of Klutz, who was holding his cards too far away from his chest to shield them from a Fake Sneeze Peek. Jimmy saw five red cards, one of which looked like the Three of Diamonds, and all by itself, the Jack of Spades, the only black card in Klutz' hand. Jimmy looked at his own cards, and they had not changed from the first time he looked at them: The Seven and King of Clubs, the Four and Six of Diamonds, the Nine of Hearts and Six of Spades.

"Naw, I'm OK," said Jimmy to Sonny. Then he backed in up with, "I bid 3."

Klutz was looking at 4 hearts, from the Three to the Ace. Plus, the Seven of Diamonds, along with the Jack of Spades.

"Pass," he said.

Sonny looked at Jimmy and considered his options. He had the best hand of anyone, or so he thought. The Four, King and Jack of Hearts, plus the Ten of Diamonds, the Queen of Spades, in addition to the Two of Clubs. He thought of bidding 4, but Jimmy was not giving him a positive sign.

"Pass," concluded Sonny.

"The trump is Clubs!!" enlightened Jimmy.

"Clubs??" whined Sonny, upset despite the point he knew he had in his hand.

"You heard me," confirmed Jimmy.

Jimmy threw the King of Clubs. Klutz threw the Three of Hearts. This was a misplay, and Jimmy knew it, but before he spoke he realized there was no way he could know it was a misplay unless he had looked in Klutz's hand, so he gritted his teeth to stop the accusation travelling up his throat from escaping.

Sonny threw the deuce and called out "Low!"

Littlejohn hesitated, lingering over his decision.

"Hurry up, you goon!!" cried out Chance, who had now come into the room with Bob. Word was spreading about the battle taking place, and the crowd was growing.

Littlejohn threw out the Queen of Clubs.

"Nice," said Jimmy, He carefully placed the four cards in his pile. He knew he would need to show them once the hand had been played.

Then he played the Nine of Hearts, Klutz played his Ace, Sonny followed with his Four, and Littlejohn played the Seven.

"That's mine!" said Klutz as he raked in the cards. He followed with the Seven of Diamonds, forcing Sonny to play his Ten. Just when Jimmy though he could capture the Ten with his Seven of Clubs, Littlejohn threw the Ten of Clubs. Jimmy meekly threw his Four of Diamonds.

"Looks like we've got game, and your set!" shouted Littlejohn triumphantly.

"You shoulda' let me bid," moaned Sonny.

Jimmy shrugged and instructed Littlejohn, "Just play your next card."

"OK, how do you like that one?" asked Littlejohn, now throwing the out Three of Diamonds. Klutz threw his Six of Hearts, and Sonny played his King of Hearts.

"Huh," said Jimmy, throwing out the Six of Diamonds, "I'll take that one."

"Yeah, you need as much game as you can get," mocked Klutz.

"Anyone got any trump?" asked Jimmy, just as mockingly, and he threw out his Seven of Clubs.

Klutz misplayed a second time, much to Jimmy's delight, and threw the Eight of Hearts. Sonny followed with the Queen of Spades, and Littlejohn completed the round with the Eight of Spades.

"You're still hurtin' for game, boys," chirped Partridge from the audience.

"Looks like it," agreed Jimmy, with all the fake remorse he could muster. He threw his last card, the Six of Spades. Finally, Klutz threw the Jack of Spades, then Sonny threw the Jack of Hearts, and Littlejohn threw the King of Diamonds.

"Hah!!" Litttlejohn chortled happily. "We've got game for sure. You get high and low, and you're set!!"

Jimmy replaced his fake remorseful look with an even faker quizzical look, and said, "Hey, wait a minute. We're playing five-point pitch, and that Yack of Spades is the Off-Yack. Did you play trump in the first round, when I played the King of Clubs???"

Then he pulled out the first four cards played, as if he did not remember, and had to check to be sure.

"OK, I played the King," said Jimmy.

"I played the Deuce," said Sonny, slowly coming to the realization Jimmy had sprung a trap.

"You played the Queen, didn't you, Friar Tuck?" said Jimmy. Littlejohn said nothing. He knew he had, and he knew Jimmy knew he had. He looked at his shoes.

Not waiting for the answer, Jimmy continued, "Which means, Klutz, that you played the Three of Hearts instead of the Jack of Spades. You reneged."

"Re-nigger, re-nigger, re-nigger!!" shouted Pid.

"Which means you lose the game," shouted Kilos, who had returned to the room after what he said was a trip to the bathroom, and everyone knew was the library.

"It also means I would have made my bid," declared Jimmy, "If you guys knew how to play, anyway. Now get out of here and come back when you learn the rules."

RULE # 42 - *Traditions with Privileges Die Hard, No Matter How Much It Costs You*

The inaugural Canton Holiday Basketball Tournament set the tone for the entire basketball s eason. By some cruel twist of fate, Robert Farnak, Canton's athletic director and head baseball coach, had a friend who lived in the tiny metropolis of Mt. Pulaski, Illinois, who was also that town's high school athletic director. In a much more bizarre but not uncommon occurrence in isolated burgs in Illinois, and its more famous, but not as talented, neighbor state of Indiana, this town of 1,700 souls had produced three basketball players, all as white as chalk, skilled enough to propel them to the Illinois Class A state championship of 1976. They started the 1976-1977 season ranked as the best small school team in the state again.

The two friends had devised the scheme to play the tournament during Thanksgiving week, in Canton's spacious gymnasium, with not only Canton and Mt. Pulaski, but also two teams from the large school, class AA bracket, the bracket Canton was also in by the slimmest of margins, being fifteen students over the limit for Class A. After making some calls and dangling the number one team in the state, albeit the small school version, in front of the athletic directors of Peoria, Moline, and Galesburg high schools, Coach Farnak received an unexpected call from Peoria Spalding's head man, who was looking for an extra early season game or two, and he in turn brought in Galesburg. It was scheduled with two games on Monday, Spalding vs Galesburg in the first game, and Mt. Pulaski vs Canton in the second. The losers of those games would play first on Wednesday, followed by the winners in the championship game.

Canton's starting five, as proclaimed by Bucky the Friday before, were Crazy Joe and Andrew Thomas at forward, Don Craig and Egg at guard, and Carl Murphy at center. Pat Hunt was the first guard off the bench and Carl David the next forward. No one else was promised any time. When Sonny and Bob realized Jimmy would be watching the game right along with them, except with a closer seat, they made sure to pick him up from his house after school and give him a ride to the gym, with a multitude of stops along the way to properly get up for the game. Since Bob was driving, his new Black Sabbath Greatest Hits tape was blasting from his speakers.

"When I first met you, I didn't realize. I can't forget you, for your surprise..." screamed Ozzy.

"We're gonna get blown out," predicted Jimmy as he blew smoke out of his mouth and pragmatically visualized what the future held, concerning Mt. Pulaski.

"You introduced me, to my mind," sang Ozzy.

"At least you'll get to play," sneered Bob in response.

He had a point. After he made his cuts and the football players arrived, Bucky had emphasized he wanted the team to play a slow and methodical style, the way basketball was played when movies were being made that would eventually end up on That's Entertainment. He wanted none of the new-fangled fade away jumpers Jimmy was so adept at. He wanted no one-on-one moves to the basket. A fast break to Bucky was when three guys were against two, or two guys were against one, and the players had strictly defined lanes to fill even during those rare occurrences. Hook shots were taught, and bank shots were demanded, and three dribbles without a shot or a pass were not allowed. The last rule was Egg could break all the rules and did not have to rebound like everyone else, because he was the star. With that style, it was easier for Jimmy to rationalize he should be sitting on the bench.

Of course, the team was short, not counting Carl Murphy, and could only have a chance against bigger, stronger teams, which almost all of them were, if they scrambled on defense and took as many chances at speeding the game up as they could. Slowing things down played into the hands of bigger, stronger teams. That was obvious to Jimmy as he took part in the practices leading up to the first game and saw how ill-suited his teammates were to the style Bucky wanted.

A rational assessment such as Jimmy's was never going to happen, however, as it was more important in the minds of Bucky and the city fathers for the style of play used by the basketball team to reflect the values of the town. Canton was a conservative, well-ordered, patriotic, slow paced town, and that was how Authority demanded it remain. A change to the chaotic, uncivilized, style of play which was becoming more and more dominant in the 1970s could not be accepted, because that style was obviously being created by and dominated by black players, and any creation molded by black hands was fundamentally incompatible with Canton's moral values. Freedom of expression was taboo, and black people were passing their chaotic, uncivilized, immorality on to white people through the sport of basketball. White people must not be allowed to do these things, or they would lose the inherent superiority of restraint they had enjoyed for centuries, and God would punish them.

They might have fired Bucky if he had even tried it, but he didn't know how to even if he had wanted to try it, which was why he was hired in the first place. Unfortunately for Bucky and the Canton city fathers, the game had been irrevocably changed and would never be played successfully by anyone ever again in the old style. That meant, in simpler terms, the Canton varsity did not have the proper scheme, attitude, or players to win many games in the 1976-1977 basketball season, and even bench warmers like Jimmy would get plenty of playing time.

The gym was full when the Little Giants ran onto the floor to warm up for the second game. Spectators came from not only Canton and surrounding towns, but also from Peoria and Galesburg. Galesburg had been ranked as high as ninth in Class AA the year before and was expected to meet Mt. Pulaski in the championship game. They had eventually prevailed in the first game against Spalding, but the game was so close no one left early, and the crowd hadn't thinned. Even fans from the big schools wanted to see the small school state champions play.

Jimmy had never played in front of such a large crowd and was distracted by the sounds and sights as he ran through the layup line and did the other drills with his teammates. The court was ringed by the pom-pom girls, and Annie smiled at him as he ran by, in his purple and gold striped warm up pants and solid gold warm up jacket. That was when it became real, and not another marijuana induced mirage. He could smell the popcorn, and suddenly he was ravenous. He could not see them, but he could hear the shouts of his friends and classmates as his turn came to take his layup.

"Put up a J Move, Whales!!!" he heard Kilos shout.

"Can't stop the Scoring Machine!!" erupted from Sonny's scraggly voice box.

Jimmy knew better than to change hands or rock the baby on his way to the hoop and laid the ball up normally. His friends responded with a chorus of boos. He was still hoping Bucky would put him in the game before garbage time, so he did not let it affect him, and finished his warm ups without incident.

The game got out of hand in the first quarter. It seems the coach of Mt. Pulaski was not afraid of pressing on defense and allowed his players to shoot fade away jumpers and even take guys to the hole one on one. They were a fast-breaking dynamo. A ten-point lead in a high school game in the first quarter was all most of the Galesburg and Peoria people needed to see, and those remaining, plus a few early-risers among the Mt. Pulaski and Canton faithful, only needed to see the second quarter, when the spread reached sixteen.

With about 20 seconds to go in the first half Bucky summoned Jimmy from the end of the bench, where he had been eating popcorn secretly moments before, and instructed him to go into the game to replace Crazy Joe, who had by this time committed three fouls. The guy causing Crazy Joe to foul him was about six feet three, thin but strong, and Jimmy took his defensive position in front of him full of hope, fear, and anger as he stood on the right wing, a few feet outside the free throw line. It turns out he had nothing to fear, because the kid caught a pass, faked to Jimmy's right, went left, and Jimmy never saw him again. Somehow in trying to react to the kid's move, Jimmy had fallen directly on his butt without taking a step. The next thing heard was the horn, bringing the half to an end.

The second half was more of an exhibition, as Mt. Pulaski's coach took mercy on the Little Giants and took off the press defense in the third quarter after reaching a twenty-point lead and cleared his bench for the fourth. Bucky followed suite shortly thereafter and Jimmy was on the court again, this time with his fellow scrubs, Septic Septich, Mark Markland, Mark Ester, and Watay. Jimmy decided he wasn't listening to Bucky about how to play the game, as he was not interested in learning how to get pummeled by twenty points, and he was going to show Bucky how they should be playing. That meant on defense instead of waiting for a pass to come before reacting to it, he watched how the offense flowed and anticipated the next pass and reacted before it was thrown, which was the way he had learned to do it on the playground. He and Watay had played together so much they knew when the other would try for a steal and would be in position to scoop up the loose ball or race down the court for a fast break. Whenever the opportunity arose, any wild J Moves Jimmy could dream up were on the table. Fast breaks were the rule, not the exception, as Jimmy saw no point in waiting for a bigger, stronger guy to come guard him, and if there was a shorter guy on him, he saw no reason not to take him straight to the hole, regardless of the next pass Bucky's offense dictated. And it worked. Halfway through the fourth quarter, the Little Giants had brought it back to fourteen points down from twenty-two. Watay had six points, two steals and a rebound. Jimmy had four-points, a steal, an assist, two rebounds, and a blocked shot all in five minutes. Bucky got excited and the Mt. Pulaski coach got worried, and both put the starters back in. That put an end to Canton's hopes, and when the game ended, the final score was 77 to 55, Mt. Pulaski.

RULE # 43 - *Don't Forget to Breathe*

The Little Giants lost three more games before the Holiday Dance. The first was a forty- point blowout to Peoria Spalding in the not-so consoling Consolation Game of the Holiday Tournament. Jimmy had six points in the fourth quarter of that one and was second in team scoring to Egg's twelve. Those eighteen points were more than half of the team's total of thirty-five. Jimmy was rewarded by being allowed to rest comfortably at the end of the bench for the next two losses, which were close enough to be exciting to watch, at least. Egg even had a shot to tie it against Bushnell at the buzzer, but it clattered off the rim.

The dance had been organized by the Student Council, which meant it had been organized by Kilos. It was not an official event on the school schedule at the beginning of the year, but Kilos had pushed hard and had been pushed hard himself to make it happen, which was quite a feat after Hyde Park Week. He was driven not only by the Status Queens on the council he had to appease for almost ruining Homecoming week, but also by his own girlfriend, Sally Salt, who wanted him to learn how to Disco Dance. The only dance move he had was the long-haired head-bob he learned from Robert Plant.

It was held in the high school gymnasium, the small one P.E. classes were conducted in, on Friday, December 10. The available budget allowed for a few crepe paper decorations spread down the walls along with even fewer hand drawn posters, and a table and chairs were set up by the door of the gym for the ticket takers and money handlers. Other than the foot-high portable stage that had been pushed against the rolled-up bleachers along one of the walls, the gym was unadorned.

The band had not been picked by Kilos, it had been the choice of Hannah Hartford and Casey Queen. They had used their fake I.D.'s to enter a club in Peoria and heard them play a month before.

When Jimmy was told about the band, the Screaming Eagles, he was not impressed.

"They're a great band, Jimmy," Hannah told him.

"What, they play Hotel California?" asked Jimmy. He hated country rock. All of it. One of the things he planned to do after graduating from high school was to never listen to it again.

"Yes, they do," she responded dreamily. "And they play New Kid in Town, Take it Easy, Take it to the Limit. They play all of them!!!" she said.

After that endorsement, Jimmy wasn't going for sure.

Hannah decided to clinch it by saying, "And they always play Superstition by Stevie Wonder at the end!!!"

Now Jimmy was further convinced he wasn't going. Listening to a white band speed their way through Superstition was not his idea of an awesome time. If it hadn't been for Chance letting him in on the secret guest star, he would never have left his house that night.

"They're gonna let John Denver sing a couple a' songs," he told Jimmy when he called him that evening after basketball practice, which changed his mind.

"You're kidding," said Jimmy.

The John Denver Chance was speaking of was not the famous John Denver who made even worse country rock songs than the Eagles. He was referring to Michael T. Smith, a member of the Canton Class of 1977. Michael T. Smith grew up in Canton like most of the class, and he was cheerful and well-liked in grade school, an average kid in every way, other than insisting on being called by his full name, Michael T. Smith, and not just Michael, and most definitely not Mike. Then one day, when he was in the seventh grade, he experienced the event that not only changed the course of his life, it changed Jimmy's mind about going to the Holiday Dance. He heard John Denver's super-sappy Annie's Song. And then, even more amazing, to him anyway, he heard Take Me

Home Country Roads. After that he devoted his life to music, and not just any music, John Denver's music.

That day he detached from the normal world, and entered his own world of Colorado campfires, turtleneck sweaters, and playing guitar cross legged with his long, scraggly hair parted down the middle and adoring girls at his feet. He continued to attend school and did what he needed to do to survive academically, but he had one goal from that point on, and that was to be a rock star, like his icon. Although forbidden to bring his guitar into the classroom, when he wasn't inside one, he had it. He would play whenever and wherever he was allowed, and over the years he managed to collect a few dreamy fans, and by a few that meant three, one of which was Sally Salt. She was the one who convinced Kilos to put him on the bill.

To the rest of the Class of 1977, Michael T. Smith was a loser. There was a small segment who would admit to liking John Denver, the real John Denver, but to the majority, John Denver was a Redneck. He played Redneck music for sappy guys sitting around campfires. But that was not the main reason Michael T. Smith was considered a loser. This was 1976, and to be known for "doing your own thing" was very important to teen-agers of that era, even though all but a few of them were much too afraid to do anything that would be considered abnormal by the social hierarchy. To them "doing their own thing" really meant doing the same things the people they considered "cool" did. Michael T. Smith had lost himself completely in John Denver's persona, which was not considered either "cool" or "doing his own thing", he was doing John Denver's thing. That was what made him a loser.

Therefore, Jimmy could not pass up the opportunity to laugh at John Denver, and he and Chance attended the dance. It was not like there were any other options for entertainment that night anyway. The boys managed to scrape up five dollars to split a nickel bag, and they had rolled two joints in red, cherry flavored rolling papers. The flavoring was necessary, as the lack of quality of the weed needed to be masked somehow.

"You made it!!" called out Hannah, who was sitting behind the table, collecting the twenty-five-cent entry fee. Jimmy paid with five nickels. She was happy her sales pitch had worked. "Don't forget to stay until the end to hear Superstition!!"

Everyone who was anyone at the school was at the dance. The band was loud, their best quality, and they played many of the popular songs of the day, from country rock, to hard rock, to top 40 tunes, but they played them all like rock songs. Chance was no wall flower and had no trouble asking girls to dance and showing off his moves. He had a healthy philosophy about dancing; girls didn't mind guys looking foolish dancing, but they didn't like spastic guys dancing. If he wasn't spastic and acted like he knew what he was doing, he could turn on the charm and get them laughing and make dancing work for him.

Jimmy was popular at dances, his poor substitutes for his cousins' moves were cutting edge in Canton, and the girls who thought they could dance wanted to dance with him to test their skills with an expert. Now that he was on the basketball team not only were the Zit Queens on his card, the Status Queens were as well. He was more selective about the music than his partners, however, and would not dance to anything with a twang, as that was when the spastics would take over, some intentional and some not, and injuries could be expected. Plus, to be cool on the dance floor required cool music to dance to, and there was nothing cool about Black Water by the Doobie Brothers, or Bungle in the Jungle by Jethro Tull, or Take the Money and Run by Steve Miller. The band realized it too, and that's why they played Get Down Tonight by KC and the Sunshine Band and Play That Funky Music White Boy by Wild Cherry twice, once per set.

It was between those sets when John Denver took the stage. He was wearing tennis shoes and blue jeans, with his trademark white turtleneck sweater, and a thick chain around his collar with a heavy looking cross dangling from it. He was also wearing the goofiest smile Jimmy had ever seen as he stepped onto the stage holding his guitar. It was slung over his shoulder, hanging low enough to fully expose the cross. He walked from the left to the center of the stage, where the microphone was, and then he paused, trying to figure out how to lower it.

This brief pause gave Sally and her two friends time to take their positions front and center, as close to their hero as possible, and gave the boys in the crowd time to think of how they were going to react to the upcoming performance. The consensus opinion was to heckle him. It took about as long for Michael T. Smith to re-position the mike as it did for someone to get it started.

"Hello," started Michael T. Smith, with his hands in his back pockets, "I…"

"Hey, Denver," shouted Yobs, "Don't you dare sing that Bolshevik Sunshine on my Shoulder crap!!"

The crowd erupted into laughter which evolved into the shouting of approval for Yobs, not John Denver. The smile never left Michael T. Smith's face. It was now a nervous smile, not a happy smile. He cared little if ninety nine percent of the crowd hated John Denver's music and hated him singing John Denver's music even more, because he had three fans, and that was enough for him. If he had three fans now, he knew he could acquire more later, if he kept playing every chance he got. What made him nervous was the possibility of being booed off the stage before having his chance to play. Getting booed off after he played was worth it. He knew some girl would tell him later, in private, she liked it.

He took a deep breath and continued, "I am gonna play a song by John Denver." He took another and forged ahead as courageously as only a cult member can do, despite the loud groans from the audience. "But I'm gonna play a fast one. I think you should recognize it. It's called Thank God I'm a Country Boy."

"Yeee-Haaawww!!!" called out Chance.

Michael T. Smith did not miss a beat, "You can sing along if you'd like to."

He started twanging on his guitar, and then he started singing.

"Well, life on the farm is kinda laid back
There ain't much a country boy can't hack
Early to rise, early to the sack
Thank God, I'm A Country Boy"

As Jimmy listened, he thought to himself, he sounds just as good as the record, which wasn't saying much. Half the decent singers he knew could sound as good as John Denver. A lot of them would have to try hard to not sound better. The boys realized they better keep up the heckling, because they were starting to tap their feet. They howled like wolves, made Indian calls, yodeled, and made farting noises by flapping one arm with their other hand wedged into the flapping armpit. Once again, Jimmy thought, this makes the song sound better, and fits right in.

"Well, I got me a pipe, and I got me old fiddle
The sun's comin' up and I got cakes on the griddle
Life ain't nothing but a funny, funny riddle
Thank God I'm A Country Boy

Both Jimmy and Michael were relieved when that was over. The crowd cheered. Michael T. Smith went for broke.

"I've written a song of my own that I'd like to play for you," he proclaimed. "It's called Livin' on the Moon."

The crowd was quiet for the start of this one. The sound system was not conducive to clearly distinguishing the lyrics, but the song was basically a John Denver song about extra-terrestrial campfires instead of Colorado campfires, and kinky alien girls with extra orifices instead of wholesome ski bunnies. OK, Jimmy put the part about the alien girls into the lyrics himself, but in his mind, it had to be an improvement over whatever gibberish was being warbled by Michael T. Smith. The song built to a crescendo with the repeated line, "I'm livin' on the moon, I'm livin' on the moon, I'm livin' on the moon'..."

Yobs couldn't contain himself after the third moon and yelled, "OK, hurry up and blast off, already!!!!" and the remainder of the song was drowned out in laughter.

The one and only high school concert performance of Michael T. Smith in Canton, Illinois, ended with the realization he needed to take his show on the road, and leave his home town behind as soon as he crossed the stage on graduation day. They would have to beg him to come back, throw a parade, give him the key to the city, and name some park after him, and then maybe he would deign to return, triumphantly, after he was rich and famous. It would be worth it to see the looks on their faces.

The band returned and played their last set with all the enthusiasm the desire to collect a check can muster, after emptying a fifth of whiskey and snorting a gram of coke in the parking lot. They did seem to enjoy playing Superstition though. They played it like they were trying to set the world record for the fastest, longest and loudest version of Superstition ever performed. Jimmy was dancing with Annie on that one. She had hovered around him all night, and he had danced with her before, and dancing twice with the same girl was supposed to mean something.

The last song was not Superstition, however, they ended the night with Led Zepp's Stairway to Heaven, which was the best slow song ever written, if you asked the girls on the Taste and Style Committee of the Status Queens. You didn't even need to ask, they'd tell you without prompting. When the lead singer sang,

"There's a feeling I get, when I look to the west..."

The girls screamed. Those with publicly established boyfriends ran to find them, and dragged them to the dance floor, and for those without an established boyfriend it was the moment of truth, when guys stepped up to claim a girlfriend. For that reason, hovering around the right person was the preferred strategy. Jimmy looked at Annie and she looked at Jimmy, just like in the movies, but Jimmy didn't ask her to dance. He was thinking of all the times he heard

Stairway to Heaven, he had never clearly heard any of the lyrics except those first two lines and the last line, "and she's buying the stairway to heaven." All the rest of the words were garbled.

When he saw his friend hesitate, Chance stepped past Jimmy and took Annie by the waist and crooned, "Would you like to dance?"

She smiled at him and said yes and off they went, and Jimmy was left to contemplate whatever was between 'the west' and some bitch's stairway purchase, when he felt a presence on his left arm. He looked down, and it was Callie Johnson. She was almost as short as she was when he first met her, in the fourth grade. She wore her dirty blond hair short, framing the cute freckles on her face perfectly. Even though she was a charter member, she didn't act like she cared much for her fellow Status Queens. They needed her more than she needed them.

"Hi, Jimmy," she said. "Congratulations on making the basketball team," she continued with a smile.

"Thanks," answered Jimmy. Then he looked at her with a quizzical look and asked, "Do you have any idea what they're saying?"

"Who?" she replied softly, forcing Jimmy to bend closer to her ear.

"The band," said Jimmy.

"It's a song about a girl who has everything she wants but can't get what she needs," she explained, with more irony than Jimmy could fathom at this point in his life. She had a crush on Jimmy since first meeting him and told him so then. He had never responded in the eight years which had passed since, and he didn't respond this time either.

"I hope you get to play more next game, Jimmy. You're the most fun guy to watch on the team," she said as the song ended, and the lights came on and she turned to walk away to find the friends who had given her a ride.

As he watched her melt into the crowd, Jimmy felt a tap on his shoulder.

"Let's go, Virg," commanded Chance. "You'll never get laid if you don't go for it, Jimmy."

"You've never gotten laid yourself, Potsy," said Jimmy in response.

"That's true," admitted Chance, as they walked to the parking lot, "But not from lack of trying, like you!!!"

They laughed as they strolled through the parking lot past couples who were unable to wait until they reached their cars before stopping to make out. As they rambled by, they saw Annie, Katie Widner, and Jean Keller, standing next to their car. Annie and Katie were patiently waiting while Jean was making out with her boyfriend, Jesus Valon. When she saw them, Annie blew a kiss to Jimmy, then to Chance. Jimmy blew one back, but Chance said, "I'm going to give her one special delivery," and walked over to her and put his arms around her and leaned in to kiss her. Instead of the rejection both Jimmy and Chance expected, she kissed him back. They became more and more passionate as Jimmy watched, going from lips to tongues, from eyes open to tightly shut.

"Two to one he doesn't get laid," said a voice in the dark to Jimmy's left. Jimmy turned away from the passion in front of his eyes and saw Carl David. Next to him stood Dana Pickman and Jasper Waldon. "We're gonna go party. Wanna come?"

Jimmy shrugged. "I'm ridin' with Chance," he said.

"Don't worry, we'll drop you off," convinced Pick.

Jimmy left Chance slobbering in the parking lot with Annie and jumped in Jasper Waldon's new Mustang's back seat and off they went.

"You got anything?" asked Carl to Jimmy.

"I got a joint of roaches!!" responded Jimmy enthusiastically. He had taken three roaches and rolled them into one red-papered joint. He handed it to Carl, who, when he realized it was roaches inside the paper, laughed heartily.

"Keep that, Jimmy," said Carl, handing it back.

Jasper Waldon pulled the biggest, freshest looking, strongest smelling, bag of marijuana Jimmy had ever seen out of his glove compartment.

"Whaddaya thinka' that, Jimmy?" asked Carl, "Jasper got his birthday money."

"I think we shouldn't waste time thinkin' we could be usin' smokin'," responded Jimmy sensibly.

They spent the next hour cruising through the country roads surrounding the town, with the windows rolled up and the music blasting. Blue Oyster Cult's Don't Fear the Reaper was burned into Jimmy's brain by the time he fell out of the car and onto the sidewalk in front of his house, except the boys had renamed it Don't Fear the Reefer.

RULE # 44 - *Brainwashing Trumps Reality Every Time*

The day after the Holiday Dance was the Kewanee game. Jimmy had managed to collect enough weed from his roach collection, plus a bud he had pilfered from Jasper with the help of Pick, who pilfered even more, to have a nice sized joint to smoke beforehand with Watay. They stood shivering against the cold in a parking lot in Big Creek Park passing it back and forth, as Watay's dad had such a sensitive nose no smoke could be allowed inside his station wagon. Their faces were semi-frozen when they stepped inside the heat of the locker room. The more Jimmy's face thawed, the higher he felt. By the time they charged out of the locker room, Jimmy was so high he was having trouble focusing, literally, as twinkles of light were streaming through his field of vision. He was further disoriented by the blaring of the band, the screams of the fans, and the smell of the popcorn. So many things were assaulting his brain he couldn't keep them in any rational order. He felt great.

One of the ways to gauge the quality of marijuana was the effect it had on balance. Lack of balance can cause the occurrence of many embarrassing events even in normal circumstances, but in front of a gymnasium full of people watching your every move would be the worst of circumstances. After managing to keep himself together long enough to run around the court a couple of times with the team in their normal pre-game routine, he fell for the first time attempting to bend over and pick up a bouncing ball that was thrown out to start the layup drill. He looked around to see who had tripped him, but no one was close enough to blame. Then he made it through the layup line successfully, even making the right-handed lay-up, and the first time through the rebound line, but his second circuit was a disaster. He dropped the pass, for starters, and followed through on the layup with an imaginary ball as a lark, and as he trotted laughing to the end of the rebound line he thought he saw a string stretched out in front of him, across the court, and he tried to step over it, unsuccessfully. He fell face first in front of the entire Canton cheering section.

"Nice move, Dr. J!" cried out Watay.

At this point his teammates realized how high he was and started laughing. The crowd was not far behind. By the time they calmed down Jimmy was ready to treat them again. After layups and other drills, the warm-up ended with the boys taking turns shooting, with multiple balls in play, until Bucky shouted the command to return to the locker room to hear his inspiring pep talk. Jimmy's back was turned, as he was chasing down an errant shot when the command was given. That, coupled with his mental state, coupled with the very keen filter Jimmy had developed to muffle Bucky's voice, made him not hear it. When he turned around he was focused on correcting his aim and took a shot, then grabbed the ball and took another shot. It wasn't until he ran to retrieve the ball again and looked around that he realized he was the only guy remaining on the court. All the other Canton and Kewanee players were already gone.

"Hey, Dr. J.!!" called out Sonny. "Get your ass off the court!!"

Despite the crowd's enthusiastic support of Sonny's suggestion, Jimmy threw up another shot. It wasn't like Bucky's speech was going to affect either the outcome of the game or Jimmy's style of, or lack of, play. When Jimmy eventually entered the locker room, he had not been missed by anyone other than Watay, who was hiding behind as many guys as he could so Bucky couldn't see him laughing. Bucky was in mid-speech, and it was about as inspiring, understandable, and believable as the messages Jimmy gathered from the old people he heard speaking in tongues in church.

As predicted, the speech did not help. What did help, however, was Kewanee had no players taller than six feet three and they could not make any jump shots in the first half. Paul Hunt had one of his rare hot shooting nights, Pat Hampton was scoring as well, and miracle of miracles, Carl Murphy managed to coax a couple of layups over the rim against guys half a foot shorter than him, and the Little Giants had hope as they bounded out of the locker room at halftime only down by six points. That hope was crushed in the third quarter, as Kewanee's players realized they did not need to fear Carl as a shot blocker and used their quickness to score at will inside the lane. By the time Jimmy was called from his seat at the end of the bench, there were only 45 seconds left in the fourth quarter and the spread had stretched to sixteen. The frustration boiled over in the locker room after the game.

"Can you believe the way those monkeys were jumping around after they won?" asked Paul Hunt as he sat in front of his locker, dejected.

"I hate those niggers!!" spat out Pat Hampton.

Jimmy had been waiting on this reaction from his teammates. He had watched it building. Most of the teams they played against had black players, and they could usually gauge how badly they would lose by counting the black players on the other team during warm-ups. Those guys always made eye contact with Jimmy, assuming he would be the star player until warm-ups ended and they saw him take his seat at the end of the bench. Kewanee had three black starters, which meant Canton should lose by at least twenty.

Not losing by twenty made it worse. Having hope, then having that hope crushed, made it clear to the Little Giants starters they would never be able to beat a team with black players. To have to admit to themselves black people could do something better than them was more than they could take. It challenged everything they had been taught their whole lives. The only solution was to de-humanize them.

Jimmy stood in anger. Pat saw him and recognized he had said something he shouldn't but didn't care enough to apologize for it. Why should he, when he meant what he said? He did not fear Jimmy at all, as he was much stronger, faster, and had plenty of support sitting around him, but he knew it was wrong to hurt Jimmy's feelings this way.

"I don't mean you, Jimmy," he said to clarify, "I mean those niggers in Peoria, Chicago, and Kewanee. You're not like them."

Jimmy had heard this logic from white people his entire life. The black people they knew were not like the black people they did not know. He was the smartest person in the room, coaches included, and everyone knew it. If a vote were taken among them on who was the smartest, he would win it without a struggle. They also thought of him as trustworthy and reliable, more so in fact than many of their friends and family. But he was the exception and the thieves, rapists, and murderers were the rule; and there was much more of a chance he would wake up one day and be just like them than they would wake up one day and be more like him. Jimmy had learned long ago this type of brainwashing trumped reality every time.

"My mom and dad were both born in Peoria," he replied to his ex-teammate.

It wasn't like Jimmy quit the team that night, he loved basketball too much and had worked too hard to reach this point to quit playing. But he did quit playing on the team. From that point on he was strictly improving his technique, improving his fitness, and using every second of game time the lousy play of his ex-teammates afforded him to put up as many J Moves as possible, and fill the stat sheet with as many rebounds, assists, steals, and points as he could. He calmed down enough later to put Watay and Carl David back on his squad, and maybe even Crazy Joe.

By Christmas Day they had lost seven games and won once. The win wasn't really a win, as it came against Farmington. The Farmers were the only team the boys in Canton had to beat for their own sanity's sake. Farmington was such a small town they could barely field a team, and Canton was by far the biggest school they played against. Beating them by thirty points was more of a relief than a victory. Jimmy played the entire fourth quarter and scored eight points, his high for the year.

That one win did not raise the enthusiasm level when Bucky insisted on having practice on Christmas morning. It wasn't like anyone thought this was the start of some turnaround. No one on the team other than Jimmy had taken to heart the motto of the prior coach, Take-A-Nap, who had a tee-shirt with 365 written on it. Every day of the year should be a practice day, holiday or not. If you really loved the game, there was no better Christmas present than running wind sprints.

RULE # 45 - *Do Not Let Your Ignorance Restrict Others*

1977 started with a bong. No Sense Bob bought it at the Co-Op Music Store/ Head Shop in Peoria with his Christmas money, along with the Bad Company tape he was listening to in an endless loop. Feel Like Making Love was blasting from his speakers when Jimmy, in the back seat next to Chance, had a moment of clarity about something he did not feel like making, the Senior Composition paper Grandma had assigned which was due on Friday. Classes had started the day before on January 3rd, and Grandma had assigned the paper the last school day before Christmas, with a due date of the 7th. It had to be between one thousand and fifteen hundred words, which were more than Jimmy could ever remember having to write all at once. The idea came to him as he watched the smoke billowing out of Chance's lungs. After hearing Bob brag on Monday about how stoned he got taking bong hits over the weekend, the whole crew joined together the next morning to try it out. Jimmy had taken his first hit and was in the perfect mood to reflect on the shifting shape of the ejected particles floating through the air. He would write it on marijuana.

Since he had not started it before now and only had three days left to write the paper, writing about something he had already done so much research on was somewhat practical. His outline was immediately obvious: Ancient History, followed by History in the US, followed by Medicinal Benefits, and concluding with a statement on legalization. The damn thing almost wrote itself.

It started as all essays should, by stating its premise:

The use of marijuana is older than civilization itself. Some believe it is the first medicine ever used by man. Bushmen in Africa still smoke what they find growing wild as they have for thousands of years. The people of India have a weeklong festival devoted to it that goes back many centuries. It was legal in America during the colonial period and after the War of Independence, the Civil War, and World War I. The Founding Fathers all grew it and thought of it as an indispensable crop. They made clothes from it, ropes from it, and paper from it, when they weren't smoking it. Only for the last forty years has it been illegal to smoke marijuana in the United States, and like so many other laws we have today, this one needs to be changed.

Jimmy huddled in the library for the next two days, doing his research. Some time was used digging through reference books, and more was spent scanning the secret stashes of his classmates' High Times magazines, but the most was consumed reading Ron Williams' trove of Freak Brothers comic books. From High Times he took the following:

Drug laws in this country have always been prejudiced. Prohibition would have never become the law of the land if average Protestant Americans, who did not mind having a drink or two themselves on a Saturday night, weren't so afraid the Catholics from Ireland and Italy who were flooding into Ellis Island by the hundreds of thousands might become the majority in the country. They backed the religious nuts because they thought the Catholics would stop coming if they knew they couldn't have wine with communion. Of course, that backfired when those same average Protestant Americans realized they wanted to drink on Saturday night more than they wanted to keep Catholics from taking a sip on Sunday. The same politicians who got elected by promising to stamp out "demon rum" now needed another, worse demon to stamp out so they could bring booze back.

They found it in marijuana. White people in border states like Arizona, New Mexico and Texas were complaining to Congress about the lawless behavior of the workers there. They claimed the Mexicans and Indians would smoke marijuana and then get into fights and stab each other and rape white women. They begged Congress to do something about it by making marijuana illegal for Mexicans and Indians, at least in the border states where it was a problem. Members of Congress had paid no attention to their pleas until certain wealthy contributors from the now shut-tered brewing and distilling industries picked up on the com-plaints from their southwestern brethren and whispered sweet dollar signs in their ears.

Then the propaganda machine was put into operation, and movies like Reefer Madness were released with much fanfare to the public. Most white people in America were only vaguely aware of the existence of marijuana until this movie came out. As usu-al, the masses were led to believe something was bad that they had never experienced and went along with what they were told instead of being skeptical. Once it had been made clear to every-one the extent of the problem marijuana was becoming, Congress saved the day by making marijuana illegal nationwide and mak-ing alcohol legal nationwide again. Those Mexicans would surely not get into fights and stab each other if they were drunk instead of stoned, and the morality of white people would be kept intact before they started using the "evil weed."'

Jimmy did not get much to add from the Freak Brothers com-ics for his essay. He learned some good philosophy though. The Freak Brothers were three siblings whose only purpose in life was to get stoned. The two older brothers were tall and skinny and thought they were much smarter than their short and chubby younger brother - nicknamed Fat Freddie - but they were so lazy they always gave Freddie the money to buy the weed instead of buying it themselves, despite him constantly getting ripped off. Of course, if they didn't do things that way, the comic book wouldn't be funny. Their motto was: Times with no money and plenty of weed are better than times with plenty of money and no weed.

He wasted a lot of his time reading the stories of Fat Freddie's Cat. The three Freak Brothers lived in a roach filled apartment, and Freddie had a cat. The cat had its own adventures outside, but mostly spent its time in the apartment at war with the roaches that lived in the walls by the thousands. The cat did not start the war, the roaches did, and the King of the Roaches had declared every roach would die if that was what it took to defeat the cat. From that point forward the King devoted his life to procreating as many roach warriors as he could, thousands and thousands per week, and sent them out in waves to attack Fat Freddie's Cat. The cat would of course kill every roach sent its way without much effort, despite the King's constantly changing tactics. Each battle ended when Freddie returned to the apartment empty handed after getting ripped off once again and turned on the lights, which would cause the warriors to scramble to their war camps behind the wallpaper, the King to resume procreating, and the cat to get some sleep.

The clinical information was lifted from the encyclopedia:

The active ingredient in marijuana smoke is Tetrahydrocannabinol, or THC. It is classed as neither a stimulant, like cocaine, nor as a depressant, like alcohol, but as a hallucinogen, like LSD, despite not being associated with hallucinations. It can act as both a stimulant and a depressant, but the main effects of the drug are a loss of the sense of time and space, an increase in appetite, a loss of coordination, and short-term memory loss. When taken in a secure setting among friends, this may result in a pleasant experience. If the user is tense, or in insecure or depressing surroundings, the drug may cause an intense feeling of paranoia, fear, and further depression.

The medicinal purposes he learned from Kilos.

Marijuana is used by cancer patients to regulate their appetites. It increases their hunger while at the same time decreasing the feelings of nausea that accompany chemotherapy. It is also used by glaucoma patients to improve their vision. There are studies that indicate it may also help to prevent seizures.

Then Jimmy decided to add some personal observations.

Drug laws, as they are now being enforced, are prejudiced. Statistics show that most drug users are white, while most of the people in jail for selling them are black. This keeps the jails full,

270

while the number of users increases. Marijuana has been proven to be much more harmless than either cigarettes or alcohol, but white people are getting rich legally selling those drugs, while black people are in jail for selling the less harmful one.

The only 'good' argument against marijuana that I have ever heard was that it leads to other, harder drugs, in two ways. The first is once a person starts doing one thing illegal, they tend to move on to other illegal things as well. Making marijuana legal solves this problem. Since smoking it would be legal, it could not lead to other illegal activities. Making it legal would make it less "cool" for teenagers to do, as it would not be considered the rebellious act it would be if it was illegal. The second is the argument marijuana leads to harder drugs because it is not strong enough after using it for a while. That will not change whether it is legal or illegal. Some people will try anything. They are not happy unless they are doing the next new dangerous thing that comes along. New experiences are more important to them than a long life, whether they realize it or not. If they didn't move on to heroin they would move on to climbing mountains, sky diving or some other thing to get themselves killed. Sniffing glue is a classic example. Drag racing on country roads is another. The same people do all those things, because to them, the more dangerous the activity the better.

To conclude, marijuana should not be legal because it is good for you. I will not claim to use it because of medicinal reasons, even though the basketball coach does want me to gain some weight. I, like most people I know, smoke it because I like it. It is not a good habit, it is a bad one, but it is not as bad as some of the drugs that are legal. It is not such a bad habit that I want to pay for jails to house people who get caught selling it to me. It is not such a bad habit the US government should force foreign countries to go to war with their own citizens to destroy the crops Americans pay top dollar to buy.

I would rather it be taxable. I would rather those tax dollars go to honest research. I would rather have the jobs that go along

with legal marijuana, not the jails that go along with illegal mar-
ijuana. I would rather have freedom of choice, because anything
else would be un-American.

That last line was a clincher if Jimmy ever read one. He counted the words until he reached one thousand and judged from the
amount of paper still covered with letters the total had to be less
than fifteen hundred, and he was done. In past years, even maybe
in past times during the current school year, Jimmy would have
edited this down to one thousand and one words and taken out
the parts certain to lower his grade - like the bit about the Founding Fathers smoking weed - but at this point in his life he wasn't
holding anything back. He would take his B and be proud.

When he received his graded paper from Grandma the next
Monday, she told him exactly what he expected.

"Your paper was very, very, well written, Jimmy," she sang with
a smile.

He looked at the grade written at the top, a B+.

"You make good points about the benefits of legalization," she
went on, which did surprise him.

"But not good enough for an A, huh?" queried Jimmy, trying
to bait her into giving a reason.

"If you could only stop being so...well you know what you
need to stop doing if you want to get an A. The very idea that the
Founding Fathers..." she stopped and shook her head, knowing
better than to tell Jimmy what he already knew.

RULE # 46 - *Some Dark Clouds Are Really Cotton Candy*

The next game was away, at Pekin. Pekin was slightly larger than Canton and was located less than ten miles down the Illinois River from Peoria, on the east bank, instead of the west bank like Peoria. Jimmy's father had told him stories about Pekin being a whites-only town from the time it was founded, and when he was young it was legal to shoot a black person caught inside the city limits after dark. Blacks from his generation avoided Pekin at all costs in 1977, even if it meant driving miles out of the way.

Pekin's founders named it after Peking, China, in the mistaken belief it was located at the same latitude, but 180 degrees in longitude opposite that city. To show their respect and enlightened attitude toward other races of people, the town's high school varsity teams were named the Chinks. The game was therefore being played between the Canton Little Giants and the Pekin Chinks.

As the team bus rolled through Banner, Jimmy wondered if the law had been repealed, since the sun had set a couple of hours before. It wasn't like he'd be doing anything inside the city limits of Pekin other than sitting on the bench watching the action, eating popcorn like everyone else. Jimmy had trained Brad Littlejohn to sit behind the bench and hand him snacks during the first half of games. He would stop eating at halftime if the game was a blow out, but he would snack the entire game if it was a tight one. Pekin didn't have any black players, of course, so Jimmy looked forward to snack feast tonight.

As the bus cruised through Kingston Mines, Jimmy recalled the many racial slurs he had heard in his life, and the people he had heard them from first. How some were so unique he heard them only once, but those were the ones he remembered the most clearly, and how they were brought forth. Like the time he got caught telling the Two Hill Joke.

The Two Hill Joke was old even when Jimmy told it in German class the year before. He hadn't planned on telling the joke, it started with him telling Kilos the story of how Donny Google got kicked out of science class in junior high for telling him the joke, and then Kilos wouldn't leave him alone until he repeated it. The first part of the joke was to draw a wavy line to depict two hills and three valleys, and on top of one hill he drew a box, then drew an "x" in it. He then drew an "x" at the top of the other hill without a box, and then drew an "x" halfway up each side of the hill with the box on top. Next to each "x" on the side of the hill he drew an arrow; one "x" had its arrow pointing up toward the box, the other had its arrow pointing down away from the box. Jimmy made the same mistake Donny did when he told the joke, he told it too loud. The joke went like this:

"OK, Jimmy, it's a riddle," whispered Donny. "The box is a whorehouse and each 'x' is a man. The arrows tell you which direction they're goin'. What's the nationality of each man?"

Jimmy was clueless and didn't answer.

"OK, the first guy, the one goin' toward the whorehouse? He's Russian," said Donny slightly louder.

Jimmy giggled.

"This guy here?" Donny said even louder, pointing at the 'x' in the box, "Himalayan."

Both Donny and Jimmy were struggling to keep themselves contained after that one, and Donny paused to compose himself. When he thought he had it together, he blurted out, "This one," pointing to the 'x' retreating from the box, "is Finnish."

That was that. Both boys began to guffaw uncontrollably. The lecture was halted to investigate the source of merriment. The teacher slowly approached the newly purchased table Donny and Jimmy shared. The science department had begged the school board for the last three years to provide new tables for the science classrooms, and when the teacher saw Donny had broken the cardinal rule of his classroom to never, ever, write directly on the simulated wood tabletop, Donny was on his way to the principal's office without the opportunity to give an explanation, especially one that started with, "You don't understand. I was just tryin' to tell Jimmy a joke."

As Donny collected his books to carry them to his next destination, Jimmy had to ask, "What about the guy standing on the other hill?"

As he walked away, Donny turned and smiled and said, "He's a Polack. He went to the wrong hill."

Jimmy got kicked out with a twist. When he overheard Jimmy's punch line, Leslie Kindle was stooped over another student, helping him with the pronunciation of some German word. He turned and strolled toward Jimmy and Kilos' corner of the room and casually said, "Jimmy, I'm kicking you out of class for telling that joke. But before you go, I want to explain something. I want to let you know that there is no word for nigger in German. It does not exist." He stared directly at Jimmy as he said it. "We call black people Schwartzers. We don't look at it as a discriminatory term."

The others in the room were shocked a teacher would talk a student that way and so was Jimmy, but it didn't take much time for him to recover. He had lived in Canton his whole life.

"Schwartz means black, so I guess that means calling me a Schwartzer is like calling me Blackie, huh?" responded Jimmy as he exited the room, brushing past the flinching Fairy.

"Get out!!" shouted Herr Kindle after Jimmy was safely past.

The bus driver exited Route 24, merged onto Route 9 and headed over the bridge into Pekin. It was ominously dark on the streets, but no one overturned the bus or anything. No lynch mob had gathered as they trotted single file off the bus and into the locker room. There was a mural on the wall depicting the Chink in the hallway leading from the locker room to the gym. It portrayed a short, bright yellow skinned man wearing a robe with buttons down the front, all the way to the ground, and a pointed conical straw hat which sat low over his face, barely above the squinty, slanted eyes that peered out from below. He had enormous buck teeth jutting out past his nose and down to his chin and was wielding a bamboo stick with which he was preparing to deliver a beating to an unseen foe. After surviving warm-ups and Bucky's nasal droning during the pre-game speech, the depths to which the people of Pekin would go to be racist was made clear by the appearance of an actual, human, Chink mascot. A student wearing a similar robe to the one in the mural and wearing a huge Chink head ran out before the Pekin varsity was introduced and did an embarrassing dance to pump up the crowd to embarrassing Chinese music that sounded worse than the score of a Charlie Chan movie. Jimmy occupied himself with an inner debate over whether what he was witnessing was more infuriating, depressing, or bizarrely comical, and couldn't decide which before the dance was over and the game began. He kept himself warm and satiated in his favorite spot at the end of the bench the rest of the evening. Pekin had the best cotton candy of any gym on the schedule.

RULE # 47 - *Never Follow Leaders Blindly, and If You Keep Your Eyes Open, You Won't Need Them*

It was a tradition at Canton Senior High School for all seniors to take Civics. It was more than a tradition, it was mandatory. There was a rule against anyone other than seniors taking Civics, because something as serious as the study of the history and inner workings of the United States government could not be undertaken until students had reached this level of maturity. The teacher was Table Muscle, and he took the class seriously, if no one else did. He had the Declaration of Independence taped to the wall above the blackboard.

"Hey Coach," said Jimmy after Bob Fair read it to the class with the enthusiasm of someone who realized the importance of memorizing it. Jimmy had it partially memorized too, because the Fifth Dimension used it as lyrics to a hit record a few years before. "Didn't the guy who wrote 'All Men Are Created Equal' own slaves?"

"Yes, Thomas Jefferson did, Jimmy," responded Table Muscle. "That just shows you how much he wanted to change the system, but he couldn't."

Jimmy had learned not to argue this point with history teachers. Growing up he had been told by more reliable sources more about the Founding Fathers than any of his teachers knew.

His Gramma told him it was common knowledge among her mother's generation, who had been born slaves themselves, you can't find a white person named Washington in the United States because George's relatives changed their names after George had so many children by his slaves. The privilege of sharing the surname of the first president was not worth the scandal of being associated with so many shackled relatives. She told him George died of pneumonia he contracted not inspecting the slave quarters as the history book said but running naked through them

277

chasing slave girls in the dead of winter, after he became senile. In the end his brain didn't work right, but his pecker did.

She told him of Thomas Jefferson, and how he did not love his wife, no matter what the book said, he loved a slave girl. When dignitaries arrived at the White House they were greeted and hosted by Sally Hemings. When the man knew he had only a few hours to live he didn't ask for his wife, he asked for Sally. When he went to Paris he took her with him, and when she realized she could be free if she did not return with him, he promised to free her and the children they had together, because they had several, before he died. He lied.

She told Jimmy for every white child a Founding Father had, he had at least ten mulattos. Some, like George, lost track at thirty. The last thing those guys wanted was to lose their harems because of a principle. Plus, why buy more slaves, when it was much more satisfying to procreate more themselves?

It was on a Friday, January 21, 1977, a few weeks into the semester, when Table Muscle assigned the class their first big project, a report on some aspect of the Revolutionary War. It was due the next Friday, and the minimum required length was one thousand words. Jimmy joked, "How long can it be?" which caused some chuckles.

"No more than five thousand," responded Table Muscle, with the utmost sincerity.

That was the last Jimmy planned to think about it until Monday morning. He had two games to warm up for and watch between now and then. It seemed like the Little Giants had lost five thousand games after Friday and Saturday's battles, but the newspaper article on Sunday stated they were one and thirteen. Bucky now drank before home games as well as after, and Watay, who had inherited his father's nose, smelled it on him before the loss to IVC.

There was no entertainment to be had on Sunday after that beating, so Jimmy stayed home and watched television. On this night the mini-series Roots premiered, and the idea for his report became crystal clear. Roots was based on a book by Alex Haley, a half true, half fictionalized account of Alex's family from the time his ancestor was brought from Africa to America on a slave ship until the present day. The first scene, when his great, great, great, great, grandfather was captured running across a field in Africa, startled America and it quickly became the most highly watched television mini-series in history.

When he turned in his report the next Friday, Jimmy was proud of the B+ he was sure to be given, and the fact he had been able to do it in almost exactly one thousand words, with only twenty or so extra. He rationalized if Table Muscle was counting he would probably miss a few, and the extra would come in handy. He was slightly surprised when he saw the grade at the top of the paper the next Monday, until he realized Table Muscle was probably watching Roots too, and he was kissing Jimmy's ass like the rest of the school population was that week.

Slavery and the Revolutionary War

The Revolutionary War, despite the lofty goals written about in the Declaration of Independence, was all about money. It started as a tax dispute, which led to a bunch of rich guys deciding they could get even richer if they were independent from the inherent extortion of a monarchy. The only way they could have successfully broken away from the greatest military power in the world at that time, with the world's greatest navy, was first and foremost, they were able to feed themselves and survive despite a naval blockade.

That is where slavery came in, which was also all about money. The study of history reveals the civilizations which are considered the greatest, and the original beacons of freedom, were the ones with the greatest numbers of slaves. Slavery reached its peak in the ancient world in Greece, and an even greater peak in Rome. Only one in ten in Rome was a citizen with the privileges the empire was famous for. It is no coincidence the United States modeled its government on ideals championed by the greatest slave owners of ancient times. It is no coincidence the freedom the Founding Fathers were fighting for would not have been possible without the slavery that fed it, clothed it, and suckled its young. The purpose of this report is to show how the Revolutionary War could not have been fought or won without slavery.

The first successful settlement by the English in what would become the Thirteen Colonies was Jamestown, in Virginia. It was founded in 1609, and was not prosperous until 1619, when the first African slaves were imported. The tribes specifically targeted by slave traders were farmers, not warriors. They knew how to make their own tools out of wood and stone, how to clear fields with or without beasts of burden and knew how to plant and raise crops. Once they were put to work by the colonists, the settlement quickly became able to feed itself, and the colony became viable. The chief food crops were rice and corn, and the money maker was tobacco. The Jamestown model was copied many times up and down the East Coast, north and south, until the agricultural base of the colonies was firmly established.

By the time of the Revolutionary War, the population of slaves in the Thirteen Colonies was 500,000 out of the total of two and a half million, or 20% of all the people. About 1% of the colonists owned more than 50% of the slaves, and with such large numbers of zero wage workers, it was no wonder the Founding Fathers, many of whom had the biggest plantations with the largest unpaid work forces, had tax troubles. Those slaves could be depended on to raise the crops needed to support an army, and they grew the highest quality strains of the drug the world was becoming addicted to in ever growing numbers, tobacco. The British knew the kind of money to be made from slavery and drug peddling, as they had perfected the techniques of both in the decades before, and they felt justified in getting their piece of the action.

The Patriot Army had at its peak 20,000 men. Most of these men were farmers, and when they were off fighting no one was there to harvest their crops, and without the slaves performing that function the army would not have been able to feed itself. They worked on farms not only in the south, but in the north as well. In 1776 there were 17,000 slaves in New York State when the population of New York City was only 5,000.

The ending of the war did not stop business between the United States and Great Britain. In fact, the war ended in part because it was bad for everyone's business. The war had stopped Britain's slave trade to the colonies, which before the war was the biggest market for them, to the tune of 38,000 per year. Such exponential growth was occurring in the colonies at that time the demand for labor was greater there than anywhere else in the world. The last thing the British wanted was for the French to come in and steal that market. They realized it would be better to be pragmatic and *sign a treaty now and come back a few years later and take the colonies back, as they had done in other places. They needed to focus on their bigger problem, France, and once that was settled they'd be back.*

The victory of the colonists over the British was not a liberating experience for slaves in the newly formed United States, it delayed their freedom. Slavery ended in the British Empire in 1834, over thirty years before it was abolished in the United States. France abolished it in all its colonies in 1848. It did not end in the United States until mechanical agriculture and immigrants from starving Europe replaced the need for slaves, and the wealthy calculated they could make more money without slaves than with them. There was already enough good, cleared, farmland to feed the masses and keep them working in the newly created factories and the corporations that ran them. The economic engine had been stoked as much as it could be by slavery, and the momentum created by it propelled the nation by 1870 to be the richest on the planet.

The freedom and wealth some in this country enjoy today was paid for by the free labor of others, as has been the case in every other society which has become the world's wealthiest in the history of mankind. No one has ever gotten rich without exploiting some people to allow the manipulation of others. The best made money on both ends. And just like the nine out of ten in Rome who were not allowed to enjoy the true benefits of being a Roman, most of the whites living in the United States did not benefit from slavery either, other than providing them an example of how things could get worse for them if they didn't wave the flag and fight for their country when called.

"You know, Jimmy," said Table Muscle as he handed him his paper, "You could go a lot farther in this world if you just changed your attitude. You know you don't actually believe all the things you wrote in there."

"Believe it?" asked Jimmy. "You can check my facts if you don't believe it. I footnoted everything."

"You're missing the point," responded Table Muscle sadly, knowing his attempt to give Jimmy what he thought was good advice was failing.

"No, I get it," moaned Jimmy, equally sadly. "You want me to believe what you think is best for me to believe and ignore the facts."

"Go sit down, smart ass," spat Table Muscle.

Jimmy shrugged and as he trudged to his seat he muttered, so those he was passing could hear and not the teacher, "That's better than being a dumb ass."

RULE # 48 - *There Are More Important Things in Life Than Winning*

T able Muscle respected Jimmy. He recognized he was a brilliant student and was even more impressed with how hard he worked to make the basketball team. It was the year before at the last Student/Faculty Basketball game in Canton School District history where he gained the most respect from Table Muscle, or as it became known to the Class of 1977, the Cheap Shot Festival.

Take-A-Nap's last year as varsity basketball coach was the greatest in Canton High School's intramural basketball history. Almost all the best players in the school were playing intramurals, as they refused to play on the varsity even if they hadn't been cut. At the end of the intramural season an All-Star team was selected, as it had been for every year going back to at least the 1950's, and that team played the faculty in a fundraiser in the high school gym. Also, going back as far as anyone could remember, the faculty always won the game. This year, 1976, was the year the All-Stars had the best chance to win in years. They were stacked. The starters were Egg and Watay at guard, Carl David and Ben Orr at forward, and Hulk was the center. On the bench were Yobs, Sonny, Donny Google, No Sense Bob, Anteater, Jimmy, Ken Orr and Brutus McCoy.

The Orrs were twins but not identical ones, even though they were identically crazy football players who played linebacker whether the game being contested was football or basketball. Brutus McCoy was the strongest guy on the football team. They were seniors, in the class of 1976, and they picked Jimmy and Sonny for their intramural team because they played on the playground together, and Jimmy and Sonny in turn brought in Bob, Chance, Watay, and Donny Google. Their team had ended the season unbeaten and all became All-Stars.

As they huddled on the sideline waiting for the game to begin, Egg made a speech stressing how they could win this year, and finally shut up BiteMe, Take-A-Nap, Heady, Table Muscle and the other teachers who had been constantly bragging about their winning streak.

Yobs quietly listened and became more agitated with each word until he couldn't take it anymore. "Fuck that, Egg. We shouldn't even be worryin' about winnin' the game. We should give these guys as many cheap shots under the basket as we can and see if we can get 'em into a brawl with us."

"You mean like a Cheap Shot Festival?" asked Hulk, reminiscing about the Friendship Festival months after the lights were extinguished.

When the whistle blew a few seconds later, the All-Stars laughed as the faculty broke their huddle with the chant, "Let's Win!!"

It started with an elbow here and a push there, but once Yobs trotted out with the second string, along with Jimmy, Sonny, Ken Orr, and Brutus McCoy, things got interesting very quickly. Sonny put up an errant shot and Yobs plowed through the lane on a seek-and-destroy mission worthy of the strong safety he was. He targeted BiteMe, standing under the basket with his arms and legs spread, in perfect rebounding position. Yobs drove a shoulder into his back, tossing him off the court, while at the same time making the gesture of jumping for the rebound. When BiteMe collected himself enough to spring to his feet in anger, Yobs was very apologetic, and raised his hand and waved it. "I fouled him!!"

Then Brutus clotheslined Mr. Davis. He tried to make it look like he had raised his arms to ask Jimmy to pass it to him, but it was obvious to anyone watching he had done it to catch the teacher's face with his forearm. Mr. Davis's face was splattered twice as it first hit muscle and bone, and then, after a fall worthy of a comedy sketch, the floor. His feet continued when his face was stopped by Brutus's arm, and his body seemed to stretch until he took flight. He instinctively tried to turn his head when he saw the forearm inches away, so his nose at least would be spared, but he had not done so in time. It exploded in blood. He did manage, however, to give his body the momentum it needed to twist in the air, so he could land face first as well. That was when he chipped a tooth. The look on Table Muscle's face, when he saw his fallen teammate, was priceless.

"Sorry, man," apologized Brutus, but he didn't raise his hand. It wasn't a foul in his book.

From that point on, it was a hockey game. A few All-Stars, mostly Egg, Jimmy, Carl David and Watay; tried to dribble, pass, and shoot the ball in a fashion that led to points being scored. A few others, like Sonny and Potsy, heaved up shots with no chance of going in, which led to either offensive rebounds for the All-Stars or, more importantly, the best cheap shot opportunities for Yobs, Brutus, and the Orr twins. The faculty never took an uncontested shot.

The final score of the game the All-Stars cared about was:

1 chipped tooth and bloody nose for Mr. Davis.

1 busted, swollen lip for BiteMe.

2 sore balls for School Board Superintendent Dr. Turkey, after a perfectly placed knee by Yobs, who said as he trotted down court, "I didn't think he had any!!"

2 knots on the head of Table Muscle, one on the top side of his head, the other on his jaw.

3 All-Stars fouled out: Yobs, Brutus, and one of the Orrs, which meant only one Orr played at a time after the first one fouled out. They both kept playing and hacking though, just not at the same time.

47 fouls called on the All-Stars, and none were in doubt, although many were disputed.

2 fights almost started by BiteMe, one over the lip incident with Yobs, the other with Donny Google over an 'accidental' elbow to the back of his head.

94 estimated total cheap shots thrown by the All-Stars, as only about half were seen or called by the referees, who were hoarse by the end of the first half.

Keep in mind the game was played with a running clock, eight minutes per quarter, which means it did not stop when the ball went out of bounds, or someone was shooting free throws. That meant they had to keep up a pace of about one cheap shot for every 10 seconds of actual playing time, or so Jimmy calculated later. To keep up such a pace meant they had to throw as many cheap shots on offense as they did on defense. Moving screens (plowing into defenders) were a favorite. Tripping, jersey pulling, and elbowing had to happen simultaneously, no matter which team had the ball. That much fouling wore everybody out.

And how did this game result in Jimmy getting Table Muscle's respect? Because Jimmy hurt Table Muscle more anyone else, with a perfectly timed and placed elbow to the kidney. After Table Muscle had stepped in front of BiteMe to prevent the second fight he tried to start when Donny's elbow caused him to almost bite off his tongue, the All-Stars focused their efforts on the fat peacemaker. Yobs used his last foul on him at the start of the fourth quarter, and the remaining Orr twin and Hulk relentlessly pounded him under the boards throughout remainder of the game, but Jimmy got the best shot in on him with the help of his pal Sonny.

Sonny threw up a fade away jump shot about twenty-five feet from the basket with no one guarding him close enough to warrant a fade away jump shot, but he did it anyway, so he could yell out "World B Free!!!!" when he shot it. Jimmy had seen this shot so many times he'd forgotten when he had seen it a hundred times, and he knew there was about a 2% chance it was going in, and maybe a 60% chance of it hitting the rim or backboard, so he sprinted down the lane to where he thought it would carom if it did indeed manage to hit something, and as he did he saw Table Muscle, his side fat giggling as he stood his ground, waiting for the rebound himself. When Jimmy planted for his jump he threw the elbow, perfectly landing in the most sensitive spot a skinny elbow like Jimmy's could land. He then jumped, and the ball bounced right to him, and he tipped it in.

"Man, that hurt," said Table Muscle the next time he saw him in school. "You are sneaky quick, and sneaky tough!!"

Heady and Take-A-Nap, who declined to play, lost all respect from the athletes, and from then on 'Heady Sucks' was a statement of fact among them, same as the Earth was round. Even their fellow faculty members felt let down. They did not want the chance to redeem themselves the next year either, as the faculty decided they would not field a team anymore. In fact, intramural basketball itself was banned, and the guys who didn't make the varsity had to play at the local YMCA instead.

And that is how the tradition of the annual Student-Faculty Basketball game at Canton Senior High School, and the faculty winning streak, ended. The All Stars won, 42 to 36.

RULE # 49 - *Never Underestimate the Stupidity of Others*

S onny was always talking shit. All his friends, except No Sense, knew he was full of shit and didn't believe most of what he told them. He was constantly telling stories of very dubious veracity, and the other boys knew to mostly ignore him, because they had learned long ago if they went along he would lead them to places they did not want to go.

Sonny picked Jimmy up for school the morning of February 1. There was no game that night, and since Jimmy had his license back, under normal circumstances he would have driven to school himself, but today Sonny insisted on taking him. The reason given was he wanted Jimmy to go to his Y League game that night after school, which didn't make any sense either, as the Y was only three blocks from Jimmy's house and he could walk there himself in five minutes after dinner. There had to be more to it. The real reason was he had a story to tell.

"Man, you won't believe what Jody did yesterday," said Sonny.

"I probly won't care either," replied Jimmy. He knew an unbelievable tale was coming.

"He got called into the office, because they couldn't find some paperwork or somethin'. The secretary left the room for a second to get the form he needed ta take home, and he sees a bunch of school district checks in a box on the floor. That son of a bitch stuffed as many of 'em as he could into his coat before she got back," Sonny said proudly.

Jimmy rolled his eyes and did not respond.

"He says he's gonna go ta Peoria ta cash 'em," continued Sonny.

That sounded even more outlandish to Jimmy than stealing the checks in the first place. Who in Peoria would be stupid enough to cash a Canton Unified School District check made out by a teenaged kid?

Jimmy didn't think another thing about Sonny until he was in Physics class. The first thing Jimmy noticed, as always, when he walked into the class, was Mr. Davis's chipped tooth. Then he realized, for the first time since he had been coming to this room this semester, this was the same classroom he took Chemistry Lab in two years before. That was the first school year sophomores were offered Chemistry, and Jimmy was one of the few who took it, along with Nate Northwoods. Nate had been Kilos' best friend since kindergarten, and Jimmy had known him since fourth grade. The connection between Sonny and Nate was the two of them were neck-and-neck in Jimmy's ratings for the greatest bullshitters he had grown up with. They were almost as good at it as an average adult! As they were the only sophomores in the class, Jimmy and Nate were destined to be lab partners.

The Chemistry teacher's name was Mrs. Cannon, and she was the no-nonsense, analytically minded type who did not think sophomores were mature enough to take Chemistry, and she let Jimmy and Nate know it early on. Once she did, they tried their best to prove her right. Ben Orr was in the class, and he told them in the first week Mrs. Cannon had a sheep farm and of course they did not believe him, so an argument ensued.

"No way, man," disputed Jimmy, in response to Ben's claim. "I call bullshit on that!"

"Look at her biceps. She can curl more than you, Stick!!" responded Ben. Stick was the nickname the older football players had given Jimmy, for obvious reasons. "That comes from liftin' sheep over fences."

When she heard the commotion in the back of the class, Mrs. Cannon assumed the young pups had started it.

"OK, boys," she called out from her perch at the front of the room. "Can you let us in on what the discussion is?"

Nate, not one for subtlety, asked, "Are you a sheep farmer or not?"

The rest of the class had heard the same rumor before, but no one had ever had the guts to ask her. People did not know whether to laugh, or be shocked, or to ignore Nate Northwoods under normal circumstances, and this was one of them. There was a mixture of gasps and chuckles.

"Actually, Mr. Northwoods, you cannot farm sheep," she stated matter-of-factly. "You can raise sheep, however, and yes I do. My husband and I have a farm and we raise sheep."

"Are sheep as romantic as they say?" asked Nate.

The teacher paused with a puzzled look on her face.

"You need to ask her husband that one, you dork," scolded Ben.

"How many head in your herd?" questioned Jimmy, because he thought it sounded funny.

"We have 36 now. We had 42, but six of them died last year," she said wistfully.

"Did you strangle 'em by accident?" asked Nate.

He was thinking about her biceps when he asked that. It took many years to understand Nate's sense of humor, and Jimmy was the only one in the class who had put the time in, so he got the joke even though no one else did and burst out laughing, and since he was the only one laughing, that made it even funnier and he couldn't stop.

Those six, dead sheep were like children to Mrs. Cannon, and she was not amused. "This is why I don't think sophomores should take Chemistry! It is a serious subject that takes a serious mind to understand!!" she burst out, not thinking about her subject, but about her little lost lambs.

Jimmy was not deterred. Nate was not getting in the best joke in the first week of class, if Jimmy could help it.

"Mrs. Cannon," Jimmy said in a serious tone, "What do you count when you can't fall asleep?"

She hesitated for a fraction of a second as she thought of an answer before pursing her lips and resuming the lecture.

The Chemistry lab experiment which had literally burned this classroom into Jimmy's brain was the one where salt was placed in a flask, and then an eye dropper was used to slowly add sulfuric acid, with the intended result of producing hydrogen sulfide gas and collecting it in another flask by means of a tube running between the two. Once the reaction began in the first flask, a rubber stopper was placed on top of each flask with the plastic tube connecting them. A hole in each stopper allowed the gas to flow from the first flask into the second through the tube. Mrs. Cannon was very clear and repeated many times the acid must be added very slowly and carefully, hence the eye-dropper, or the reaction would accelerate too rapidly, and the gas would escape before the stopper could be put in place. The gas was not poison, but if it was inhaled it would turn into acid on contact with the water in the lungs and could kill that way.

While Jimmy was slowly, carefully, dropping in the acid, Nate was quickly growing more and more impatient because the reaction was not happening fast enough for his level of immaturity to endure, so he grabbed the beaker Jimmy had drawn the acid from and poured it all in. He then decided he could see the reaction best by standing over the flask and looking down. Just when he took a breath to say, "This reaction is a dud," a blast of gas shot up from the flask and overwhelmed him. His nose, his eyes, his mouth held moisture turning to acid, and Nate spun around blindly as the cloud grew and continued to attack him.

"Put the stopper in!!!" cried Jimmy. He was standing to the side, and Nate's wild dance kept him from being able to reach for the stopper himself.

"Gack, Gack, Gack!!!" was all Nate could say, and he bent over trying to wretch, but he couldn't. Then, like a sprinter blasting out of the blocks, he ran for the classroom door.

Jimmy watched him incredulously. Then the cloud reached him, and he had to close his eyes, and therefore could not find the stopper or the flask. Just when Jimmy was sure he would die like a doughboy in the trenches of Belgium, one of the senior girls calmly put on her goggles and walked over and put the flask in the sink next to the lab table and filled it with water. The cloud slowly dispersed, and by some minor miracle, Mrs. Cannon didn't see a thing.

Nate Northwoods left town mysteriously the following summer. He wanted it to be mysterious anyway and told Kilos he had been recruited by the CIA, and all records of his prior existence were being destroyed, so don't even try to find him. And if Kilos ever did manage to track him down, he'd have to kill him. When Kilos told Jimmy about it, Jimmy responded with two options. Nate was recruited by the CIA to be a chemical weapons expert, or he was full of shit. Kilos could take his pick.

RULE # 50 - *Always Question Generosity*

When Sonny picked up Jimmy that night after basketball practice, Jimmy was in no mood to go to the YMCA and watch Chance, Sonny and Bob work on their masonry skills.

"I'm starvin', Sonny," complained Jimmy. "I should just go home and eat."

"Let's go to Hardee's," suggested Sonny.

"With what?" asked Jimmy.

"Don't worry," said Sonny, "I'll pay for it."

Jimmy wondered why Sonny was buying him food but shrugged it off. With a full stomach and a head full of smoke, watching his friends lay bricks would be far more entertaining than watching TV with his family.

"Let's stop at Kroger first," said Sonny. Kroger was the grocery store next to the high school on Main Street. Students could reach it by walking through the school parking lot, so it was the main place they went for chewing gum. "I need some gum."

As it was after dark in February in Illinois, and Sonny's passenger side window did not roll all the way up, it was far too cold for Jimmy to wait in Sonny's car while he went in for the gum, so they went in together. Since he didn't have anything to buy, Jimmy stood at the front of the store and shook himself warm as Sonny stood in the checkout line with his gum in hand. Jimmy was staring out at the parking lot, reminiscing about what an idiot Nate Northwoods was, and did not see Sonny as he left the checkout line and headed for the door.

"C'mon man," said Sonny, slapping him on the back to wake him from his stupor. They left the store and headed straight to Hardee's; where each got burgers, fries and cokes, paid for with a crisp ten-dollar bill which came from Sonny's pants pocket, the same pocket he had stuffed the gum in.

Games at the Y were much like the Student-Faculty game, except the teams were not split between faculty and students. It was an adult league, open to anyone who turned sixteen before the end of the season, populated mostly by high school kids and young adults, with a couple of teams made up of guys in their thirties and forties. The referees had to choose between letting play get rough or turning every game into a free throw shooting contest, and they usually chose the former. This was the first and last game Jimmy attended, as he quickly realized once you've seen one Cheap Shot Festival, you've seen them all.

The next morning, he drove to school himself, and did not see any of his friends throughout the day, because he had to spend his free period at Goon River getting extra help. The first semester of Calculus was only slightly harder than the math classes he had taken before, an easy B, but the second semester was much, much, more difficult. They were studying the equations involved in calculating the volume created by revolving a curve around a straight line, better known (to math geeks, anyway) as three-dimensional integrals. This was the first time in Jimmy's life no matter how hard he tried to concentrate on learning something, he could not on the first, second, or third attempt unravel the equations. Kilos and Vonny-Yonny understood them, so he knew they could be understood, but not by him. It was also the first time in his life he flunked a math test, or any other test for that matter, and he needed to retake it.

After the extra help Jimmy still did not understand the concepts, but he memorized enough to get a C on the re-test, or so he hoped. He rationalized he would need to stop smoking weed for the rest of the year, plus quit the basketball team, to keep up with Vonny-Yonny and Kilos in Calculus. He was thinking this through as he walked in the back door of his house, and he had concluded he would prefer the C in Calculus to getting an A in Boredom and was smiling broadly at his solution when his mother met him, one step inside the door.

She had the angriest look on her face he had ever seen, which was saying something, because he had made her angry many, many times before in his life. She did not say hello. "Come with me," was all she said without any further greeting, and she turned to march into her bedroom, and slammed the door behind him once Jimmy walked through it.

"Sit down!!" she commanded, and when he did not sit fast enough, she pushed him down onto the bed. She bent over, nose to nose with her son, and asked him without waiting for a confirmation, "What were you and Sonny Mathis doing passing a bad check at Kroger's last night?!?!?!"

Jimmy was a genius. He always knew it, but on this day, he proved it to himself beyond any doubt. He put the most innocent, indignant, incredulous look on his face he could muster, as he knew the next words he spoke were the most important of his young life. "What are you talking about, Mom?" he asked, at first looking puzzled, then softening his expression to show he was thinking she must be joking.

"I'm not joking!!!" she shouted.

He knew she wasn't, but also knew to be convincing he had to act as innocent as possible. "What are you talking about, Mom?" he repeated in a softly serious tone.

"You know what I'm talking about!!" she concluded.

Jimmy said nothing. He had learned through experience when in a negotiation, silence was often a very useful tactic. He was negotiating for his life, so he was using all the tricks.

"Did you and Sonny go in Kroger last night?" asked his Mom, trying to pressure him into a confession.

Jimmy thought about it for an instant, then he decided he wasn't going to lie for Sonny. If Sonny was going down, he was going down by himself.

"Yeah, Mom, we did," Jimmy said, as if needing a moment to remember. "He got some gum before we went to his basketball game at the Y," responded Jimmy truthfully.

"Did you see him pass a bad check?" grilled his interrogator.

"No, I was standing at the front of the store. I didn't go through the line with him," explained Jimmy. "All he got was some gum."

"So why did you go in?" continued his mother. There was no let up to the pressure.

Jimmy tried to make light of the situation, and smiled and said, "It was cold, Mom, and you know Sonny's window doesn't roll up."

"Well, we need to go to the Kroger, right now!!" she shouted, grabbing her purse from the nightstand.

"What for?" asked Jimmy, not moving.

"Because the police are there, waiting for us. They've got Sonny and his mom down there already," said his mother, grabbing him roughly by the arm to pull him off the bed.

Jimmy did not know if the old saying his Gramma told him was true about your entire life flashing before your eyes in the second before you die, but during the five-minute period between walking out of his parent's bedroom and into the back entrance of Kroger, by the loading dock, his future flashed before his eyes several times, crashing to pieces all around him. He stared out the window and looked at the sun, shining brightly in the west in the last hour before sunset. It was Groundhog Day, and the groundhog had seen its shadow, and winter was going to last at least six more weeks. That seemed ironic on a warm February day like this, so warm he didn't bother to button up the green winter coat he had never taken off since his mother met him at the door. He was numb to inconsequential things like temperature at this point anyway.

After following her inside the stock room, Jimmy watched as his mother was met by a big, tall, white policeman, who greeted her warmly and sensitively, to ease his task of soliciting her help to persuade her son to confess to a crime. Jimmy looked past him and saw two other cops talking to Sonny and his mom.

When Sonny's mom saw the two of them enter, she shouted forcefully, "See?? He's wearing a green coat!!!"

That made no sense to Jimmy, but the cops looked slightly crestfallen. Then the cop who was being so kind to his mother explained the situation.

"We brought you down here because the manager of the store is accusing Sonny Mathis of passing a bad check," he said sternly. "We are not accusing your son of doing it, but he was with him and he knows what happened. We want to ask him some questions."

Jimmy looked at his mom and looked over at Sonny. He was furious at his friend for putting him in this situation, but he also realized no matter what the cops were saying now, he could end up being charged along with Sonny if their stories did not match. After staring at Sonny for a cold, hard, moment, Jimmy repeated the same story he told his mother to the policeman. Yes, he was in the store. No, he had never seen a Canton School District check in Sonny's possession before the crime. No, Sonny did not tell him he was going to pass a bad check. No, he did not see Sonny pass a bad check. Sonny's mother, who had drifted over to listen, said "See?? Just what my son told you!!"

"So," asked Jimmy's mother to the nice policeman, first somewhat relieved, but then becoming angry, "How did you figure out who did it so fast?"

"The store manager looked in last year's high school yearbook, and recognized their faces," admitted the cop.

"So, you looked in the yearbook and picked the first two black faces you saw???" asked Jimmy's mother. She had lived in Canton her whole life too. She was now very angry.

"Look, ma'am," said the slightly agitated policeman, "I told you we weren't accusing your son."

"Then why am I here? Maybe that's a question I should ask the N. Double A. C. P.!!!" she warned through gritted teeth, as if she had no choice but to call the NAACP.

That was a very strong threat to white people in Canton. Nothing scared them more than the NAACP. Just mention those letters to them and white people started stuttering. They knew the only reason black people would organize was to form lynch mobs, like the KKK, and the thousands and thousands of black NAACP members, if they all came to Canton at once, would kill every white man and rape every white woman in town before the sheriff could put a posse together and save them.

"Mrs. Williams," responded the now apprehensive officer, "Thank you for your time. You and your son can go now."

As they walked to the door, and quickly, Jimmy glanced at his friend, who had not been released so easily. He wondered if he'd be sharing a cell with his brother soon. He felt sorry for his directionless buddy until he was out of sight, then, as Jimmy walked to the car with his mother, his emotions boiled over into anger, and he vowed never to speak to Sonny again. That anger was already receding when his mother suggested on the ride home it would be in his best interest to stop hanging out with Sonny. By the time he woke up the next morning, curiosity had overcome anger and common sense, and he had to find out how things had fared for Sonny even if it meant driving to Lewiston during visiting hours. As it turned out, he heard the rest of the story that day, during free period. He and Sonny took a ride around Big Creek Park, so no one could hear the details.

"Good to see you're not in jail," said Jimmy, once they left school property.

"Yeah, that was close," admitted Sonny.

"So, how'd you get out of it?" asked Jimmy.

"The coat, man, the coat," replied Sonny. "It turns out the cashier who took it said the guy who cashed the bad check was wearin' a brown coat. The manager was absolutely sure it was me, but the checkout girl said no, it wasn't me, 'cuz I was wearin' a black coat, and it wasn't you, 'cuz you were wearin' a green coat."

"That doesn't make any sense, man," pondered Jimmy.

"It didn't make sense to me either, but then I found out later that Otis Mitchell was bangin' that chick," informed Sonny.

Otis Mitchell was ten years older than Sonny and Jimmy, about the same age as Sonny's brother Silas. He attended Mt. Carmel Baptist Church growing up like every other black person in town.

"I thought he was married to some white chick," said Jimmy.

"He is," responded Sonny. "But you know he's a player."

"No, I didn't," laughed Jimmy. "But I'm not mad at him."

"Hell no, Jimmy," chuckled Sonny.

So once again he was laughing and joking with Sonny as if Sonny hadn't almost ruined his life the day before. All was forgiven. One thing Jimmy knew for sure, Sonny had guaranteed he was flunking Boredom this semester.

RULE # 51 - *Bid Your Hand, But Use Your Imagination*

The Goon-Yers came in force the next time. February was dragging on and it was only the 8th, so their appearance was a welcome change to the routine. Kilos and Jimmy were in the middle of cheating their way through a game of Pitch against Watay and Chance the Anteater when they came in, led by the biggest of their big guns, Andrew Allstate Thomas and Don Craig, as well as the normal crew.

When Jimmy saw his ex-teammates walk in, he called out, "Allstate? And you brought State Farm with you too?"

The only way Don Craig could ever earn a nickname was by proxy, since he never did anything worthy of a nickname himself. Out of frustration Crazy Joe finally gave him the nickname State Farm because his best friend was Allstate.

"We've been practicin," declared Allstate.

"Anything in particular?" questioned Jimmy.

"Very funny, Jimmy," replied Allstate.

"This time we're gonna kick your..." proclaimed Dale Parton.

"HEY!!" shouted Table Muscle, who had been watching the confrontation from behind his desk. "Either play cards or get out!!"

"Whaddaya think, Whales?" asked Kilos. "Should we teach these Goon-Yers a lesson?"

"You mean another lesson," corrected Jimmy with a sarcastic grin. It wasn't a question.

The game began, Jimmy and Kilos against the Insurance Companies. For extra insurance the underclassmen positioned helpers around the table, to watch every move and every word said, as they thought they knew every trick the seniors had in their bag. There was no way they were getting cheated this time.

"Why don't you have that little squirt," suggested Jimmy, pointing at Dale, "Stand under the table and watch for foot signals."

The room had more people in it than Table Muscle could get to show up for his real classes. About twenty underclassmen were crowded around the table, standing or sitting in desks arranged in a circle. Other than Watay and Chance, no other seniors were there except the card players until Sonny and Bob strolled in, higher than kites. They arrived in time to hear Jimmy's joke.

"Foot signals!!" laughed Sonny as he walked in. They had used foot signals in the past. They could come in handy in certain situations.

"There's no way you can win without cheating," accused Norman Bates, in his trademark entitled tone; arrogant and snooty. Not even the other juniors liked Norman much.

"Hah!! We don't need to cheat to beat you goons!!" responded Kilos.

As the game progressed, it became clear the juniors had been practicing. To make matters even worse, Kilos was honoring his word and not cheating. Jimmy hadn't promised not to cheat and even if he had he would have cheated anyway, because by this point he couldn't play Pitch without cheating, as they had created so many Sig-A-Nols every word and gesture meant something to someone, and not giving Sig-A-Nols amounted to giving false Sig-A-Nols.

Midway through the game the juniors were ahead by two points, and drastic measures had to be taken. Jimmy, as always, was keeping score. He made sure to call out the current score after every hand and he did so because that made it easier to cheat. If he called out the wrong score, and no one caught him at the time, they could not complain about the score being wrong later. Well, they could still complain and in this case, they did, but it was an argument that was almost impossible to win. He took a point away from them the next hand and added a point to the seniors total the next, so the score should have been 14 to 11 Goon-Yers, but it was written down as 13 to 12.

It was Jimmy's deal, and the Goon-Yers were whooping and hollering, encouraging their boys to get the last points they needed. They were so excited about the bid they made in the last hand it had been easy to misstate the score. When Allstate saw his hand, he knew they had the game won. He had the Ace and King of Spades, the Ace of Hearts, and the Queen, Jack, and Nine of Clubs. He thought about bidding 3 in Spades, counting on high, off-jack, and game for his points, with the chance of his partner supplying the fourth point with a low spade. Being a conservative, he bid 2 instead.

Kilos had nothing. Nine of Diamonds, Six and Seven of Clubs, Deuce and Nine of Hearts, and the Nine of Spades. "Pass," he said with a shake of the head.

State Farm had nothing either. Five and Eight of Clubs, Deuce of Diamonds, Seven of Spades, and Four and Five of Hearts. He had to pass as well.

That left it up to Jimmy. No way, regardless of what he had in his hand, was he going to lose a game to these goons without bidding. He'd rather lose a bid than let them make a bid to win. He had a Jack of Diamonds, the Five and Ten of Spades, and the Seven, Ten, and Queen of Hearts. He did not hesitate before bidding "Three, in Hearts!"

Allstate laughed when he heard the trump. "Game over," he promised.

Jimmy led with the Seven of Hearts.

"Hah!!!" cried out Allstate, throwing his Ace with authority.

Kilos was crestfallen, but threw the Deuce and said, "That's Low," without much enthusiasm. If they lost the bid, the game was over, and not having the Ace on a 3 bid was not very encouraging.

State Farm played the Four of Hearts with a smile.

Allstate went for the jugular and played his Ace of Spades next. He wanted Jimmy to know how screwed he was immediately. Kilos played his nine of Spades, State Farm played his seven, then Jimmy, just to let Allstate know it wasn't over, played the Jack of Diamonds, the off-jack, taking the round.

"What else ya got?" asked Jimmy, playing his Queen of Hearts. When Allstate threw his Nine of Clubs he said nothing and began to squirm a little. Kilos threw his Nine of Hearts, and State Farm threw the Five.

Now it was Jimmy's turn to squirm. If State Farm had the King of Hearts, he was in trouble. But what could the odds of that be, when the Ace and Queen were already in play? He had no choice but to play the Five of Spades. Allstate regained his confidence with this play and threw his King. Kilos threw the Six of Clubs and State Farm, instead of throwing a game making card, threw the Deuce of Diamonds with a shrug.

Next came the Queen of Clubs, followed by the Seven of Clubs, and the Eight. Jimmy threw the Ten of Hearts to take the round.

"Looks like we're gonna make game," said Kilos, now encouraged.

Jimmy wasn't so sure. He still had the Ten of Spades in his hand. If State Farm had a trump, or either of the insurance guys had a face card in Spades, Jimmy was set. He threw the Ten with trepidation, but Allstate had the Jack of Clubs, and State Farm had the Five. Jimmy took those cards along with the Nine of Diamonds remaining in Kilos hand and said with some relief, "Do we need to count the game, or are the 2 tens enough? Looks like we just made our bid. I got low, off-jack, and game."

"So, what," said State Farm triumphantly, "We still win the game, 15 to 14!!!" He had been keeping the score in his head and didn't bother to check the official score sheet as the game progressed.

Jimmy studied the score sheet, then looked at State Farm and asked, "Aren't you in Pid's Advanced Math class? You can't even add!! Look!!!"

He spun the score sheet to show State Farm the total, 13 to 12, and then said, "Actually the score is 15 to 14, Seniors. You got High, so I'll add one point to add to your total, so you now have 14, and we got three points to add to twelve, so we have 15, not you."

Don Craig had a look of absolute confusion on his face. He could not dispute the math, but something wasn't right. His confusion turned to anger quickly. "Hey, that score's not right!!!"

Jimmy looked at him incredulously. He turned to Kilos and said, "Hey Kilos, what's twelve plus three?"

Don Craig's face was redder than Santa Claus's jumpsuit. He jumped to his feet and took two short, deep, breaths. He pointed his finger at Jimmy, who was smiling broadly. "You know you cheated!!!!"

Jimmy's facial expression changed to mock innocence and he replied, "You can review the score sheet if you'd like. I think you will find that my math is correct. Here, Allstate, take a look."

As Allstate ran down the list of figures, Kilos did the same. They could not find any errors.

"Looks correct to me," said Kilos.

"I don't care what the score sheet says, you cheated!!!" cried out State Farm.

"Quit being a sore loser, Don," warned Table Muscle from behind his desk.

That was too much for Don Craig. His Christian values were being tested to the limit. He spun on his heels and marched out of the room with his head held high, so he wouldn't have to breathe any more of the stench oozing from the mouths of the heathens inside. The rest of the underclassmen followed behind him, trying to act more upset about their classmates' loss than they were amused by the look on goodie-two-shoes Don Craig's face after it. As time went on, more and more had to admit they chose the latter.

"Those guys are something else," said Kilos after they left the room. "We beat 'em, fair and square."

Jimmy eyed him with surprise. He thought Kilos had known he had changed the score, just like State Farm had known, by keeping the score in his head.

"Hah!!" laughed Jimmy, "Of course I cheated on the score!!"

Kilos' body language revealed he was quite crestfallen. He said nothing, but the look on his face confirmed it.

"C'mon, Kilos," chided Jimmy with derision, "If I hadn't cheated, they would've won. There's no way I was losin' ta those little pricks."

All the other seniors in the room roared in agreement, while Kilos kept his thoughts to himself.

RULE # 52 - *If You're Going to Get Heckled Anyway, You Might as Well Get Drunk First*

B asketball season reached its merciful demise in late February, within a few days of Jimmy's eighteenth birthday. In 1977 turning eighteen was the start of legal adulthood in all phases of life, including the right to buy and consume alcohol. Only a few waited until the official start date to embark on their drinking life, most had imbibed by sixteen at least, but by the second semester more and more seniors were celebrating their eighteenth birthdays by strolling into liquor stores and buying whatever hooch they wanted, from near beer to Everclear. Bob made the mark in January, and after Jimmy did in February, Sonny would a few weeks later in March. Chance and Watay would have to beg until April and May, but by graduation day, all of them would be legal.

The team had won three games and lost seventeen by the last home game of the season. The players, the fans, the parents and especially Bucky were giddily looking forward to the last game and the merciful end to this nightmare. It was traditional for five seniors to start the last game and play most of the minutes, and since the team was looking at either 3 and 18 or 4 and 17, it didn't look to anyone like there was any reason to break that tradition, except Bucky. Jimmy was, for the first time in weeks, paying attention to Bucky's pre-game speech, because Crazy Joe told him to make sure he did. They were playing against Clinton, a team that had won only five games themselves.

Bucky began with, "We have a good chance to win this game, boys!" He was stinking drunk. Watay had declared it with certainty during warm-ups, and by the slurring of his words and his inability to hold his head still, Jimmy concurred. While Bucky continued his pep talk, Jimmy wondered if he was drunker than Jimmy was stoned, and concluded Bucky must be drunker, even though Bob and Sonny made sure Jimmy was higher for this game than any other.

"Are the seniors startin"?" interrupted Crazy Joe.

Bucky looked around the room and saw the five seniors who were dressed and ready to play: Egg, Crazy Joe, Watay, Carl David, and Jimmy. Carl Murphy's feet hurt, so he was in street clothes, and Paul Hunt quit the week before, so he wouldn't miss any of the baseball workouts.

"No. We're starting our normal starting five," he responded. That included Allstate and State Farm along with Carl David, Egg, and Crazy Joe.

"It's the Senior Game!!" shot back Crazy Joe.

"We have a chance to win this game," retorted Bucky.

"Are you sayin' if ya start the seniors, we don't?" asked Crazy Joe, standing up in anger.

"I'm the coach here!!" Bucky shouted back, realizing he was in an argument he shouldn't be, and he had to stop it immediately.

"All the seniors have had a chance to start this year except Spider. He deserves a chance..." Crazy Joe tried to continue.

Bucky cut him off, "Not while I'm coaching he doesn't!!" he screamed back.

With that Crazy Joe sat back down and muttered, "This is bullshit!" not quite under his breath and the tension quickly rotted into resignation. No more words were spoken until the Little Giants trotted out to the court for the introductions that followed.

As it was Senior Night, the six seniors, five in uniforms and one in dress pants and penny loafers, walked to the end of the court and stood under the basket nearest the Visitor's bench, instead of congregating with the rest of the team in front of the Home bench. Even though they weren't all starting, the seniors were to be introduced individually to the crowd. Their names were called alphabetically, and each walked slowly to the center court circle to thunderous applause from an even drunker-than-Bucky crowd; where Coach Farnak, in his role as Athletic Director, waited to shake their hands. With a last name starting with W, Jimmy watched all the others go before him, and when his name was finally called, and he took his slow stroll to the big C in the middle of the circle, the crowd noise was louder than it had been at any point of the season. The cause of the pandemonium was a long banner Kilos and Chance unfurled during Jimmy's amble. They had been working on it for a week. It read:

THANK YOU DOCTOR J AND WATAY

When he was halfway to Coach Farnak, the crowd erupted in a chant of: "Doctor J and Watay, Doctor J and Watay!!!" Jimmy waved and bowed and took as much time to walk to the center as he could, and the crowd whistled and roared and gave him encouragement he didn't need to drag his feet as slowly possible, and then delayed the game by refusing to stop chanting, even after the seniors had rejoined the team huddle and Coach Farnak had walked off the court in a snit. Jimmy didn't mind, as it was the last time he would stand on the court that night.

Then the actual starters of the game were announced, and the crowd realized all seniors would not be starting, and things got ugly. It was a good thing Bucky was drunk, or his feelings might have been severely damaged. The drunken senior class let out a ton of venom that night, and most of it was directed at Heady, even though Bucky was not in the slightest way spared. Bucky couldn't generate the hatred Heady did, even though the football team had a winning record and the basketball team stunk. The crowd made sure to let Bucky know what they thought of his basketball knowledge, however, and who they thought should be playing.

"Put Doctor J in, you idiot!!!!!" was one of the nicer comments.

"Hey, you bald, backward, motherfucker!!! You should have been startin' Whales from the beginning of the season!!" shouted Sonny, and everyone could tell whose voice it was quite clearly. He did not disguise it, so Bucky would be sure to know it was him.

Some offered encouragement to Bucky, like Yobs, who shouted, "Hey Bucky, do you need another beer? I got some in my trunk!!"

The only time the abuse stopped was when Watay was brought into the game. Then the crowd shouted "Watay! Watay! Watay! Watay!" until they were hoarse. Even though only a few knew the back story of the nickname, it had spread like wildfire.

Funny thing was Canton won the game. Crazy Joe and Carl David played furiously and dominated the boards, and Allstate managed to keep his hands on the ball long enough to make a few clutch shots, and they pulled it out by four points. The crowd managed some polite applause, but in general, they were not happy. The game had been boring, other than the heckling, and not seeing Jimmy play was worse to them than not winning. It wasn't like they could brag about being 4 and 17.

RULE # 53 - *Paradise for Most is Purgatory for Others*

J immy was employed for about two weeks. It would have been a dream job for most high school seniors, but for Jimmy it was torture that couldn't have ended soon enough. He was hired as a stock boy at a liquor store. It was quite strange how it happened. One day he was walking down the hall with Kilos, minding his own business, and he heard his name called on the intercom, with instructions to go to the office immediately. As neither of them could think of anything Jimmy could be in trouble for, he decided not to ignore it and go to the window where the secretaries sat.

He leaned on the counter, and when he was recognized he said cheerfully, "Hello, Mrs. Wastey...I mean Hastey. What did I do this time?"

"You signed up for a work study program first semester," she responded, just as cheerfully.

"I did?" asked Jimmy. He must have been stoned when he did it, because he had no recollection of doing so.

"Yes, you did. Here is your signature," she confirmed, holding up a clipboard with the signup sheet attached.

Jimmy just shrugged, as he could not prove it was forged, and it did appear to be his hand writing.

"Westside Liquor Store is looking for a stock boy," she explained. "It pays two-fifty an hour, if you're interested. You're eighteen, right?"

Jimmy was extremely interested. Now that he had his driver's license back, the seven-buck a week allowance his dad gave him was not enough to maintain his lifestyle the way he wanted, and with basketball practice ending, he would have the time.

He didn't realize how stressful being a stock boy could be until he started. The stated tasks of a stock boy were to help unload the supplies from the delivery trucks and stack them in the stock room, to keep the display cases stocked with each type of beer by bringing the beer from the back room to the front, and occasionally helping old ladies carry their booze rations to their cars, if they couldn't lift as much as they could drink. The unstated part of the job was to inform the owners which customers were not really eighteen and whether they had a fake ID or not, so they could call the police instead of selling them booze.

That was where the stress came in. First it was comical when he saw underclassmen, or better yet underclasswomen, come in with fake ID's. They all knew Jimmy even if he didn't know them, so they assumed Jimmy would know if their ID's were fake or borrowed from an older sibling. The looks on their faces as they first recognized Jimmy; then mulled over whether they should leave without buying anything other than chewing gum, was hysterical. Those who made it past that decision had to stand at the counter while the owner stared at the ID and glanced at Jimmy, to see if he would expose them. He never did, even though he had more than enough opportunities.

After the first week Jimmy was avoiding the owner's wife as much as possible, as she had made it clear someone like Jimmy could never be trusted. She had suspected a couple of giggling girls were not actually eighteen despite the date on the ID they presented, and when she looked at Jimmy for guidance, his noncommittal shrug was all she needed to see to let her know he could not be relied on.

It took her another week to convince her husband to fire Jimmy. During a lull period in the store she sent him out to the surrounding grounds to pick up trash. He was high at the time and looked for every piece of paper he could find and was occupied for half an hour. A rush of beer drinkers came in while he was out, and horror of horrors, the Budweiser ran out in the display case and she had to go back in the stock room and get a couple of cases herself. The next day was Jimmy's last, and thus ended his involvement in the school's work study program.

RULE # 54 - *Don't Forget to Bring a Towel*

"So, Jimmy," said Yobs as he sat in the cafeteria listening to Jimmy's story, "Since you don't have a job no more, you should try out for track!!"

Next to Yobs were Eubanks, Sonny, and Kilos.

"Fuck that," responded Jimmy. "What would I do that for? I've never run track in my life! Plus, you guys know I'm slow as hell."

"Because, track is more fun than any other sport!!" exclaimed Yobs.

"We're gonna have a blast, Jimmy," said Sonny. "Track meets are more fun than anything. You don't wanna miss out."

"What's so fun about it?" asked Jimmy, unconvinced. "I don't wanna have ta run all day."

'Whales, you're already in shape from basketball," countered Kilos. "It'll be a breeze."

"Yeah, right," argued Jimmy. "I don't even have an event. I won't get ta go ta the meets."

"Don't worry, Stick," soothed Eubanks. "I'll teach you ta triple jump. I'm the only triple jumper we've got, unless you count Norman Bates."

Jimmy looked around the table and realized he needed a better argument than he was able to dream up at that moment to avoid running track with his friends. The funny thing was he already knew how to triple jump, sort of. His brother had been a triple jumper as well, back when it was still called the Hop, Skip and Jump, and had taught him in the backyard one summer when he was in grade school.

"C'mon, Spider," pleaded Yobs. "You're a Varsity Man and we need you."

Everyone laughed at that.

"OK, I'll go ta the first practice, and see how I like it," agreed Jimmy. It wasn't worth arguing against such persistence. He figured he could back out of it later or some other escape would present itself. However, that got another laugh.

"You already missed the first week of practice," said Kilos.

The idea he could miss the first week of practice and still try out for track was instantly intriguing to Jimmy. He was getting hooked before he realized it.

"What do you guys do?" asked Jimmy.

"Me and Kilos are hurdlers," answered Yobs.

"You know I'm a high jumper," added Sonny.

"Don't you have ta be able ta jump for that, or can you just be high?" asked Jimmy.

"Fuck you, too," replied Sonny.

Heady was the head track coach. He specialized in coaching the sprinters, hurdlers and jumpers. He was assisted by Table Muscle, who coached the throwers, and BiteMe, who coached the distance runners. That meant all five boys reported to Heady once they exited the locker room and trotted out to the track, which ringed the football field, later that day. Jimmy had no clue what to do or expect when his tennis shoes hit the cinders.

"The most important thing," coached Sonny as they made their way out of the locker room, "Grab a towel and keep it wrapped over your head at all times when you are not competing."

Jimmy noticed each of his friends had a towel draped over their heads, hanging down like a terrycloth wig on either side of their faces, tucked into their heavy sweatshirts. It was not nearly cold enough for this type of protection, but they all did it. Jimmy grabbed a towel and did the same.

"And stick with me, Stick," said Eubanks.

Heady was standing inside the track with his whistle dangling from his neck. He was never without that whistle.

"What is this?" he cried, when he saw the group heading his way.

"Jimmy's tryin' out for triple jump, Coach," responded Eubanks.

"What??" asked Heady, "As a senior?? I don't have time to teach..."

"I'll teach him, Coach, don't worry," replied Eubanks, not letting Heady finish his sentence. "Don't forget, I taught myself."

Heady didn't have time to respond to that comment, as Norman Bates trotted up beside him and responded for him, "Hah!! He won't even be able to make the pit!!"

At that exact moment Jimmy decided he was joining the track team. Up until then Jimmy was leaning toward this being his first and last practice. At the same exact moment Jimmy made his decision, Eubanks decided he hated Norman Bates' guts. Before then, he had merely detested him. The next day Jimmy was in the store with his mother, buying track cleats.

RULE # 55 - *Some Things You're Better Off Doing Sober*

The test scores trickled in starting in March. The most important test for college bound high school students was the ACT test. It was the only standardized test score they needed to be admitted into most colleges. The more academically talented and competitive took the SAT, which in later years would become the more dominant standard test, but in 1977 it was considered by only a few elite colleges to be a requirement. Most of the Advanced Math class took it, of course. A few elite students, namely; Vonny-Yonny, Jimmy and Kilos; had been given the pre-ACT and pre-SAT tests in their junior years, which were used by colleges and educational foundations to identify and select scholarship recipients and National Merit finalists.

There was an unspoken competition between the three of them, as they had been very publicly singled out as the most academically gifted students in the school, that went well beyond being accepted by the university of their choice. Unlike their fellow classmates, who were sweating their scores and needed high ones to gain acceptance to the colleges they preferred, these three had been accepted by the schools they applied to before the end of January: Kilos by the University of Illinois in Champaign and Jimmy by Bradley University in Peoria; both to study engineering, and Vonny-Yonny by Tulane, in New Orleans, to study medicine.

"You'll see the first snow of winter at Tulane," said Kilos to her when she told them the news.

"Huh?" was her response. "It doesn't snow in New Orleans," she said matter-of-factly.

"It does if you're a coke dealer," responded Kilos. He had heard most of the blow entering the country passed through the swamps of Louisiana during that time.

When they looked at their ACT scores as they sat in the foyer at Goon River, they all had to laugh. They had the identical score of 29 out of 36. The SAT didn't prove anything either, as Kilos topped the trio in the first section, Vonny-Yonny in the second section, and Jimmy between the two. To their surprise they did not tie for the highest score in the school on the ACT test, it was Katy Widner, who scored a 31. She had been in Advanced Math but didn't make the cut when it came to taking Calculus, so it came as quite an ego deflator to the trio until she admitted, when pressed by Kilos, she had a copy of the test in advance. That score got her into Bradley though, bless her heart.

Jimmy and Kilos scored so high on the SAT test they were rewarded with another test. It was the Engineering SAT test, developed expressly to expose the aspirants with the most aptitude for engineering studies, and to award scholarship money to those who scored above a certain level. The test was given on Bradley's campus in Peoria, on a Saturday morning. Kilos picked up Jimmy bright and early. Not so early Jimmy didn't have a chance to smoke a bowl or two in his basement bedroom first, though.

"Wake up, man," said Kilos, "You look sleepy." Kilos had heard rumors of Jimmy being a stoner, and he most surely looked it, but he couldn't believe someone as smart as Jimmy would destroy his brain that way, and most certainly not before taking an important test.

"I'll try," was all Jimmy could muster.

Kilos' new favorite tape, Presence by Led Zeppelin, was pouring out of his speakers. Robert Plant was singing, "I got this monkey on my back, I got this monkey on my back, back, back, yeah. I mumble screech and make unintelligible scratching noises with my voice until I say: Nobody's fault but mine." And then Jimmy Paige riffed his way through the next thirty seconds.

Jimmy still had quite a buzz when the test booklet was placed on his desk along with the long, narrow, cardboard sheet with oval holes to fill in each answer and the clock was started. The questions were not that tough, and he answered the first few with little difficulty, but then his mind drifted, distracted by the veins on his right hand and why they were so different from his left hand. They were in no way mirror images of each other. The pattern of one bore no resemblance to the other. How could that be? He pulled up his sleeves to see the course they took down his arms to connect through his wrists to his hands, and the main lines snaking down the arms were the same, but once they crossed the threshold of his wrists, each hand had its own idea of where the veins should be routed. He glanced over at Kilos, furiously answering questions, to look at his hands to see if his veins were as disassociated on each hand as his were.

"Hey, quit looking at my answers!" scolded Kilos softly, but with a sharp edge.

That's when Jimmy remembered he was taking a test and was supposed to be answering questions. Tests like this measured how quickly the questions could be answered, not only how correctly they were answered. Jimmy contemplated if people who needed more time to learn something than he did understood it better because it took them longer. Maybe that was the more intelligent way to do it. He was skimming the surface, while they were plowing deep. After mulling it over for a while he returned to the booklet and answered more questions.

Jimmy had reached answer sixty-five of the eighty-five questions when the instructor called for the answer sheets. He scored above average, but not nearly as high as Kilos, who had finished all 85 questions, and was given a scholarship based on his score. This gave Kilos the right to brag, and he without doubt took advantage of that right, but it was not as fun as it would have been if Jimmy had disputed it or became angry over it. Jimmy humbly agreed with Kilos instead, because it was such a valuable lesson he couldn't dispute it. He now knew for sure some things had to be done sober.

RULE # 56 - *It Takes Two to Have a Fight, But It Only Takes One for a Beating*

Track practice was much, much, more entertaining than basketball practice, as most of the time was spent goofing off unsupervised. It started with a group trot, maybe once or twice around the track, at a pace of about ten minutes per lap. The normal group was Eubanks, Yobs, Kilos, Sonny, Jimmy, Brad Littlejohn, and Harry Roach. The practice uniform was hooded sweatshirts and sweat pants gathered with elastic at the ankles, and towels. After that, they loitered in a bunch stretching for fifteen minutes, and then sat in an imperfect circle stretching for another fifteen. Only after an hour of doing mostly nothing was any specific training done. There was plenty of time for gossip.

"Guess what No Sense told me yesterday," said Sonny as the group made their way around the track. No one felt it was necessary to guess, so Sonny continued. "Potsy's movin' ta Banner."

The rest of the group laughed. Banner was a town of maybe one hundred poor souls, located at a wide spot on the Illinois River, named Banner Lake, less than ten miles from Canton at the junction of Routes 9 and 24. Its only claims to fame were the liquor store and motel at the junction, and the fish in the lake. It was so small it did not have a high school, and any kid unfortunate enough to live there attended high school in Canton. There they were universally labelled as the Banner Rats.

"That's a good place for a Redneck like Chance," mentioned Yobs, thinking positive.

The boys hadn't finished cracking Banner Rat, Anteater, and Potsy jokes by the end of their opening trot. It was the third day of practice for Jimmy, and just when he thought he understood the practice routine, Heady changed the pattern by bringing the team together to make an announcement before the half hour of stretching he had expected.

319

"Gentlemen, I hope you realize the first meet is on Saturday, the Western Illinois Varsity indoor meet in Macomb. It's one of the biggest indoor meets in the state, and most of the schools within a hundred miles of Macomb will be coming. We can enter two people maximum per event, and we are taking one bus only. I'm posting the people who will be travelling outside my office after practice on Thursday," he said to the mostly attentive squad.

"Can we drive over, like some of the seniors did last year?" asked Yobs.

"If you are eighteen you can," responded the coach.

"You guys all eighteen?" asked Yobs, looking at the rest of the crew.

Eubanks and Jimmy shook their heads yes, and Sonny added, "That's affirmative!"

"I'm not," whined Roach, with his head down.

"That's not cool," said Eubanks, "You're the only one with a car in good enough shape to make it that far."

"I'm not either," added Littlejohn, but no one cared about him not being able to avoid the bus, since he didn't have a car.

"Maybe I can get my dad ta ask the school for special permission!" said Harry Roach, with more confidence than Jimmy thought was warranted.

"I'm takin' the bus," declared Kilos. No one tried to argue with him. A party might break out in the car, after all.

"Another thing," said Heady. "I have a prior engagement that weekend, and I won't be going to the meet."

"At the Banner Motel?" asked Yobs, disguising his voice. That broke up the crowd, and no one was fooled by the voice change.

"Very funny, Mr. Yardwick," said Heady to his beloved, hard hitting, starting safety.

"So, when's tryouts?" asked Eubanks, changing the subject. He was the only one who had thought far enough ahead to know everyone in the group may not be going to the meet, either in the car or on the bus.

"Don't worry, Mike. I don't think the county record holder needs to try out," shot back an amused Heady.

"Not for me," responded Eubanks, "For Jimmy. He should be the second guy triple jumping."

"What???" shouted Heady. "He's only been out here for three days! You and Bates are the two guys."

"What if he can beat Bates in a jump off?" countered Eubanks, not backing down. "That's the rule in track and field, isn't it?"

"Hah!!" scoffed Heady. "He won't even be able to make the pit!!"

"Hey Coach," said Bates, "I'm running the 880, so I don't need ta triple jump."

Heady's big face was turning beet red. "I'm not takin' some guy who can't even make the pit!!" he screamed.

"What, are you afraid ta have a jump off?" prodded Eubanks, staring at Bates. "I don't think you can beat him."

"Unless he cheats, there's no way he can beat me," responded Bates.

"Friday, Coach, Friday. I'll have him ready for a jump off on Friday," declared Eubanks.

Heady was so angry he had spittle in the corner of his mouth, but he couldn't deny his star triple jumper was right. In track and field, the only way to settle it was to have a jump off. Plus, Heady reasoned, until today Jimmy had not once managed to negotiate his way through the first two steps of the three required to complete a triple jump, let alone make the pit, so there was no way he could see Jimmy being able to beat Bates in a jump off.

"OK," said Heady. "The jump off will be at Friday's practice. If Stick can beat Bates, he can go."

For the remainder of the practice and the next, Eubanks patiently and positively took Jimmy through the jump sequence and taught him all the tricks and techniques he had learned, while Norman Bates, who was working on his jumps on the same runway, laughed at Jimmy's struggles. It didn't bother Jimmy, in fact it was motivation for him, but Eubanks was getting angrier and angrier at Bates' heckling. By the end of practice on Thursday, Eubanks and Bates were nose-to-nose and had to be separated by BiteMe and Table Muscle, and Jimmy had successfully completed a triple jump twice.

By the end of the school day on Friday, the Williams/Bates jump off was big news among the classes of 1978 and 1977. It was now much more than a contest between two guys to determine who would represent Canton in the triple jump at a track meet, it was another chance for the Class of 1977 to prove it was better at everything than the Class of 1978, and the Class of 1978's chance to prove otherwise.

There was a huge crowd around the jump pit, almost ten people, which was a huge crowd for a track meet tryout. That's a good crowd for a high school track meet itself. The Class of 1977 was solidly behind their man, but the Class of 1978 was conflicted, because most of them liked Jimmy more than Norman Bates, but they had to defend their class honor, didn't they?

Bates, before his first jump, said defiantly to Eubanks, who was staring at him like he had tripped his grandmother, on purpose, "What, are you thinkin' if I win you'll wanna kick my ass?"

"No," growled Eubanks, with a calmness that defied his mood, "I'm thinkin' about kickin' your ass either way."

Bates scratched. Jimmy ran down the track and made his moves and landed without scraping his heels on the edge of the pit, but barely. Bates scratched again. Jimmy duplicated his motions and when he took his third step he was so far along he knew he would make the pit, which was another first for him. He landed safely in the sand with almost a foot to spare.

Bates turned to Table Muscle, who was officiating the jump off in Heady's absence, and said, "OK, he's made the pit twice. Is that good enough? I think I might have tweaked an ankle on the last jump."

Table Muscle shrugged, and with that Bates trotted off without limping or taking another jump.

Kilos bounded up to Jimmy and said, "Looks like you're in! We'll have lots of fun on the bus!!"

"Naw, he's coming with us," countered Yobs, putting his arm around Jimmy's neck as they walked off the track, away from the coach's earshot. "Roach's dad got permission from Walter Matthau to let him drive to the meet tomorrow. Me and Eubanks are the chaperones."

"Yeah, Jimmy," added Sonny. "You, me, Yobs and Eubanks. And Roach, of course."

Kilos had picked Jimmy up for school that day and was taking him home, and he also agreed to take Sonny and Brad Littlejohn home while they dressed in the locker room, since their houses were on the way. The four of them were rolling out of the parking lot in Kilos' car when they saw Eubanks, walking down the sidewalk on First Street with his gym bag in his hand.

"Hey, Mike!" called out Kilos, as he pulled the car over, "Jump in!!"

"I only live two blocks away," shrugged Eubanks.

"So, what?" said Kilos, and since Mike could not think of another response, he got in, forcing Littlejohn to ride the hump in the back between Eubanks and Sonny.

Kilos had driven a block when they saw Norman Bates, also walking down First, and he honked so Bates would be sure to see Sonny's middle finger in the back window. They had gone another half block when Mike tapped Kilos on the back of the head.

"Pull over," he commanded.

"What, you gonna go kick his ass?" asked Kilos.

"Naw, man," replied Eubanks, "I don't need ta get in any more trouble. This is my house," he advised, pointing to the house on the corner.

Kilos stopped, and Eubanks exited the car, crossed the street and jumped up the stairs to his porch. Before Kilos could pull away, Bates reached the corner. When he saw Eubanks on the porch, he dropped his gym bag, balled his fists, and stood in the classic boxer's stance from the 1920's. When Kilos saw that, he put the car in Park and turned off the ignition.

"Well, are you gonna come down here and fight me or not?" shouted Bates.

By this point Eubanks had opened his front door. When he heard Bates' challenge he looked at him with disgust, and for an instant the audience in the car thought he would walk through the door and avoid the confrontation, but instead he responded.

"Go away, Bates," he said in a low tone. He did not want to come down off the porch, as he knew he would lose either way, but he felt he had to if Bates kept harassing him. The crew in the car watched intently.

"Are you afraid of gettin' your ass kicked in front of your friends?" baited Bates.

Eubanks had a mix of resignation, depression, and anger on his face, in that order, as he deliberately trudged down the steps and stood facing Bates with his hands at his sides.

"You better defend yourself!!" shouted Bates.

Eubanks eyed Bates with distain, shook his head slightly, and with a quick fury punched him in the mouth. The fight was over. Bates screamed while putting his hand over his mouth to catch the blood and teeth that were spilling out. Eubanks shook his head again and plodded up the steps, like he was savoring his last few moments in the sun before returning to his windowless prison cell. The boys in the car laughed hysterically as they watched Norman attempt to gather the parts of his face which had fallen to the sidewalk, but Kilos quickly realized it might be best to vacate the scene before any authorities arrived, and he drove off. He had another new tape, by Kansas. As they rolled down the street the speakers wailed out:

"Carry on my wayward son, there'll be dreams when you are done..."

RULE # 57 - *You Never Buy Beer, You Only Rent It*

All the cool guys bought the Kansas tape. Jimmy could hear it as soon as he opened the door of his house the next day, blasting out of the speakers of Harry Roach's car. As he walked down the front sidewalk, he could see Eubanks in the front seat with Harry, and Sonny and Yobs in the back. Jimmy lifted the hood of his track sweat suit over his head, to shield him from the biting wind blowing down from the gray skies. It wasn't raining yet, but rain was coming. The car arrived right on schedule, at 12:30 in the early afternoon.

When Jimmy reached the car, Yobs jumped out and said, "You're the skinniest. You gotta sit in the middle."

Jimmy leaned over to step into the car and saw a full case of Miller High Life, in bottles, in the middle of the back seat.

"Why don't you guys put that in the trunk?" Jimmy asked, never surprised to see booze or drugs in the hands of his friends.

"Because," explained Yobs matter-of-factly. "We're about ta start drinkin' it."

Sonny put the case on his lap, allowing Jimmy to slide in. Yobs jumped in beside him, and Roach pulled away from the curb.

"Grab two or three of them and pass the rest up to the front," Yobs instructed Jimmy and Sonny.

Sonny did as he was told, but Jimmy said, "I'm not drinkin'. Got any weed?"

Sonny responded, "Only enough for a few hits."

Yobs took five bottles from the case and sat them between his legs and on the floor in front of him. "Good. You take the hits, Spider, and I'll drink your share of the beers."

Yobs passed the remaining beers to the front seat to Eubanks, who handed a beer to Roach, then pulled a bottle opener from his pocket and popped each.

"Gimme that!!" called out Sonny, as Yobs pulled on his cap with his teeth impatiently.

By the time they turned on Chestnut Street, each had drawn their first below the necks of the bottles.

The trip to Macomb should have taken about forty-five minutes. Jimmy had driven it many times the year before, going to visit his sister before she graduated from Western Illinois U that year. Macomb was only thirty miles away, as the crow flies, but the road didn't take the same route a crow would. The route was simple enough, though: west on Chestnut to Fifth, south on Fifth to Hickory, and then west on Hickory, which became a two-lane country road out of town once past the cemetery. The road led to the little hamlet of Cuba, less than 5 miles away. That town was ten blocks long, and once through, a right turn on Route 95 led straight to Macomb after another thirty lonely miles.

The first part of this stretch was flat until the tiny hamlet of Smithfield was reached, and after that the road wound through hilly, wooded, countryside with large trees growing on either side of the pavement, spreading their limbs far over the roadway, giving it the illusion of a tunnel, especially at night when the car headlights reflected off the leaves. The effect was especially dramatic on wind-swept, rainy nights. There was a railroad that took a similar route, so for part of the course its tracks paralleled the road, and at certain points they crossed the road and angled away, only to cross again at other points later. After Smithfield came even smaller Seville and Murietta, and once out of the woods, New Philadelphia, which made Jimmy chuckle, because there was only a sign and not even the hint of a town was visible. Smithfield, Seville and Murietta had a couple of streets, at least. The lone purpose of the sign, in Jimmy's mind, was to signal Macomb was only a few miles further on.

It took the boys an hour and a half to arrive at the huge gymnasium on the campus of WIU. That's because of the many pit stops the boys needed as the beer they were chugging made its way out. Yobs, Eubanks, or Sonny would command Roach to pull over, and on roads like this there were many spots to do so, and they would retreat behind a tree or bush to relieve themselves and then shake themselves dry on the way back to the car.

"You never really buy beer," explained Yobs, "You can only rent it."

They had made three stops by the time they reached Smithfield. The drinkers were pacing each other and had reached their fourth by then. This time even Jimmy had to get out to drain his snake. He was in a good frame of mind after the four hits Sonny supplied between swigs, and his bladder was also full of poison that needed releasing.

As Jimmy watched his buddies stagger back to the car, he realized he had better pay strict attention to the road ahead, because Roach might be seeing double by this point. It was a good thing he did, because once they were a couple of miles past Smithfield, the road was blocked in the direction they were going, and Roach was not recognizing that fact soon enough to give Jimmy any comfort.

"Look up, Roach!!" he called out, as Harry's head was bobbing. He slammed on the brakes and skidded to a stop just in time. White and orange striped barricades with flashing lights blocked the westbound lane, which was the lane in which they were travelling. Past the barricades was a partially covered bridge, the kind with framework over the roadway extending the length of the bridge, but not enclosed by wood or some other covering. Since they had stopped anyway, the boys thought they may as well get out and pee again. Yobs walked past the barricades and onto the bridge itself.

"Guys," he called out excitedly, "Look at this shit!!"

The other boys joined him and saw the reason for the lane closure. The bridge was under repair. There was a large oval hole, five feet wide and seven feet long, in the roadway. The boys could see straight down through the hole to the water below.

"Man," said Yobs, "What if we were so drunk we drove into that hole?"

"Yeah, the highway department is all fucked up," replied Roach, whose dad owned a construction company and had inside information leading to this conclusion. "They should have a guy out here signalin'. Someone could get killed."

As the boys returned to the car, Jimmy noticed the sign on the bridge.

"We coulda' fallen inta the Spoon fuckin' River," said Jimmy, shaking his head.

When they returned to the car, the guys peered as far down the road as they could past the bridge, to see if anyone was coming before they crossed it in the opposite lane. The thought of what would happen if two cars were crossing simultaneously passed from their minds immediately, as Macomb was a few miles away and there was still plenty of beer left to drink.

The near-death experience at the bridge was enough for Sonny, and he stopped after draining his fourth, but the other three boys were not ready to quit by the time they reached the campus. They drove around the nearly vacant streets of Macomb while Roach finished his fifth, and Yobs and Eubanks chugged a sixth in the gym parking lot. After taking another piss standing next to the car, the boys marched into huge athletic facility, joining the troops of other boys doing the same.

RULE # 58 - *Always Avoid Risks Which Have No Reward*

The warmth of the building, after trudging through the biting wind outside, made the boys dizzy and disoriented. The gym was enormous, and hundreds of high schoolers were milling around, wearing a kaleidoscope of colors in a myriad of shapes. As the purple and gold clad Canton crew cruised through, Jimmy noticed the tone at the meet was not what he expected. The boys from different teams were mingling freely, laughing and joking with guys on other teams as if they were reacquainting themselves with old friends. If these have been football or basketball teams in such unsupervised proximity, brawls would be breaking out all over the place. Jimmy heard guys wish good luck to other guys on different teams, and it seemed sincere. He looked at Sonny for guidance.

"This is track, man," said Sonny. He felt no further explanation was necessary.

"There they are!" cried Roach, pointing to a familiar looking group in the balcony.

The bus with the remainder of the Canton squad arrived several minutes before the quintet in the car, even though it left Canton forty-five minutes after them, and the team was sitting in the balcony in the first few rows. BiteMe and Table Muscle stood in front of them, lecturing about something. Yobs found the stairs first and bounded up them, three at a time. Eubanks followed, then Roach, half tripping as he tried to skip steps. Sonny came next, then Jimmy. As Jimmy climbed the stairs, he had more than a premonition something bad was about to happen, and he knew better than to be too close to the action.

Yobs' breath reached Table Muscle's nose long before the rest of him. Before Yobs could even shout out a warm greeting, Table Muscle exclaimed, "You've been drinking!!"

330

Yobs was so drunk he did not, at first, comprehend what had just been said. By this time, Eubanks' breath reached BiteMe, then Roach's.

"They've all been drinking!!" replied BiteMe.

Now all five boys were standing in front of the seated team, facing the coaches.

"You guys are NOT competing in your conditions!!!" shouted an outraged Table Muscle. They were not only drunk, they were drunk while he was in charge, so he took it personally.

Yobs had recovered enough to realize what Table Muscle was saying, and he did not agree.

"We are not drunk!!!" responded Yobs. "I haven't had a drink ta drop all day!!" He could not hold himself still while he talked and wobbled like a top. He was obviously drunk.

"Yardwick, do you think I'm that dumb??" asked Table Muscle. He was shocked someone so drunk could be so adamant he wasn't. But then he realized only someone this drunk could be so adamant.

"You must be if you think we've been drinking!!" shot back Yobs.

"You are not competing!!" shouted Table Muscle with an air of finality.

Yobs would have none of it. He stepped up to the coach, put his face as close to the coach's as he could, and shouted back, "We drove all the way over here, and we are gonna compete!! We are not drunk!!"

Jimmy was amazed Yobs could be this bold. BiteMe stepped forward, and for a moment it seemed a fight was about to break out. Then something happened Jimmy would have bet his life would never happen.

A strange look came over Table Muscle's face, as he was trying to decide the course to take which would keep him out of the most trouble. He was afraid. Not of fighting Yobs, but of the

331

backlash to follow if he did. Plus, Harry Roach was the favored son of the kind of city father who could call up the principal and force rule changes on the spot. He could probably get teachers like him fired, too. He knew it was wrong to back down, but why should he take on any risk? He wasn't getting paid to be the head track coach. He wasn't even getting paid a dime extra to act as head coach while Heady enjoyed his "prior engagement", which he wouldn't be surprised was code for a chick on the side. He bet Heady's wife thought he was at the track meet.

"OK, Tom," he said. "You guys can compete. But you are not getting any help from us."

Jimmy's mouth dropped open. Sonny's did too, but he quickly realized the need to vacate the immediate premises as soon as possible and grabbed Jimmy by the arm and dragged him down the stairs. The other three followed seconds later, as they also realized the need to put distance between themselves and the coaches, so they couldn't change their minds. They met on the main floor of the gym and regrouped.

"I can't believe that shit," said Sonny, as if anyone needed to say that.

"What?" asked Yobs. "I can't believe Table Muscle could smell it on us!!" You'd think only a drunk could be this delusional, but Yobs was thinking as clearly as he did normally. "Then he backed down. He's got the balls of a eunuch."

Jimmy laughed a long, hard, nervous, laugh. Somehow, he knew he had better enjoy himself now, because this was not over, he was sure. And so, he did. They all did. Not that they competed well. Sonny made the opening height and that was it. Jimmy made the pit once, which was a personal best by default, and scratched twice. While Yobs managed to negotiate the high hurdles, he did not come close to making the finals, but he did better than Roach, who tripped over hurdle #3. If Eubanks had not made a jump long enough to make the finals on the last of his first three, they would have left the gym before dark.

While they were waiting for Eubanks' last jumps, Sonny found Scott Michaels, who Jimmy knew since little league, and Scott took pictures of the jumpers; Jimmy, Sonny, and Eubanks. Scott had ridden on the team bus, so he could take photos for the yearbook. They posed like body builders, gangsters, and samurai, but looked more like guys just out of the sauna, with the towels they had draped over their heads. The photo shoot turned out to be the highlight of the competition, as Eubanks could not match his third jump with any in the final, and he was left off the podium.

Other than Scott, they managed to avoid the coaches and the remainder of the team from the time of the confrontation on, except Kilos, who strangely did not comment on his classmates' condition. When they left the gym, they were all in a good mood. It didn't last until they reached the car.

RULE # 59 - *Stay Away from Crazy People or You Risk Becoming an Accessory*

Gloom enveloped them as they trudged through the parking lot. The wind was stiffer now, and raindrops were being slung through the air, although it was not a steady rain. The quintet's mood, buoyant while the lights of the gymnasium were shining on them, turned as dark and foul as the weather.

"I wonder what that fucker Heady's gonna do when he finds out," mused Roach.

None of the boys responded, because they all knew it wasn't going to be pleasant. As they walked down the aisle toward Roach's car, Jimmy saw the Canton team bus, parked one row over.

"I didn't see that on the way in," remarked Jimmy, pointing to it.

When they reached the car and opened the doors, the empty bottles strewn about the floor gave Yobs an idea. He grabbed a couple of empties and moseyed to a spot near the bus and threw one of them. It hit the metal side of the bus, breaking with a loud crash.

"Damn it, too low!" cried Yobs, and turning to his compatriots in the car, he jeered, "Target practice!!"

When Eubanks and Roach heard that, they each scooped up two empty bottles and ran to where Yobs was standing, aiming his second bottle.

Jimmy and Sonny were sitting in the back seat, trying to get warm. They looked at each other and shook their heads. They did not get out of the car.

The three others took turns hurling bottles at the bus until each had broken a window. This was not a feat they accomplished rapidly as Yobs and Roach had to return to the car for more bottles when they failed on their first two attempts. Once all hit their targets they came back to the car laughing and slapping each other on the back.

"Those fuckers are gonna freeze their balls off on the ride back home!!" exclaimed Yobs triumphantly as he sat in the back seat next to Jimmy.

Jimmy thought about Kilos and the rest, and how cold it would be riding on the bus with open windows in the cold and rain, with damp clothes on. He didn't think it was funny at all. Eubanks and Roach, however, thought it was hilarious. It tickled Roach so much he had another idea.

"Let's put empty bottles underneath the tires of a bunch of cars, so when they back out they'll get flats!!" he suggested, and the two other bottle throwers agreed, and they gathered the rest of the dead soldiers and placed them carefully under the back tires of as many cars as possible until all the empties were distributed.

Jimmy and Sonny were looking around the parking lot from their lousy hiding place in the back seat of Roach's car, sure someone had to have seen or heard the bottles and windows breaking and fully expecting to be hearing sirens next. Remarkably, the other boys finished their task and sauntered to the car laughing, not even trying to be quiet, as if they didn't have an inkling of the risk they were taking. Harry started the car and they left the parking lot, and Macomb, without further incident.

As they passed out of the city limits, Eubanks said, "We've still got three left, boys!!" He opened each and handed one to Yobs and Roach, keeping the last for himself. "I'm leaving you two out, since you didn't help dispose of the other ones," he said to Sonny and Jimmy.

Jimmy had been thinking about drinking one of the bottles he knew would be remaining when they returned to the car, but the other boys' recent actions had put him in a frame of mind which screamed out for absolute sobriety, so he did not argue. Sonny was thinking the same thing and did not challenge Eubanks either. Sonny and Jimmy, at this point, were only focused on making it home unscathed, without any side trips to the county jail, hospital, or morgue.

Once past New Philadelphia and into the woods, the trees were being lashed by the wind, bending and swaying and threatening to split in front of the car. It was the type of night horror movies were made for. They reached and crossed the bridge again safely, much to Jimmy's relief, but once over Yobs told Roach to pull over.

"You need to take a piss already?" asked Jimmy. The car was on the shoulder of the road a few yards past the bridge. It was pitch black outside, except for the dome lights and head lights of the car.

"Naw, something better," said Yobs.

He ran into the middle of the road and grabbed the nearest barricade. He walked onto the bridge and dropped it into the hole. Eubanks and Roach, when they saw what he was doing, jumped out to help with the other barriers. Sonny looked at Jimmy. Once again, neither one of them had any intention of getting out of the car.

"Are these fuckin' peckerwoods really this crazy??" wondered Sonny aloud. Since the answer was obvious, Jimmy didn't waste his breath on a response.

Before they returned to the car, the trio had cleared all the barricades, tossing them either over the bridge or into the hole and down to the water below. There was nothing to stop the next car speeding down the road that night from falling in, except an act of God. Jimmy said a quick prayer, in the hope that He would provide it. When they saw that next car in the distance, its lights reflecting eerily off the tree branches, Harry Roach decided not to stick around and witness the coming tragedy. He spun the tires as he punched the gas and sped away.

Three people laughed the rest of the way to Canton, finishing the last swigs of their beer without a care in the world, and two sat silently, hoping they would wake up from the nightmare they must be having, and what they had just witnessed had only happened behind their eyelids while they were sleeping. Jimmy felt such sweet relief when the car rolled to a stop in front of his house, he couldn't make it inside and peed in the bushes next to the front window.

RULE # 60 - *Listen to Your Mother. Every Now and Then She's Right.*

"I checked the paper the last couple of days," said Sonny when he picked Jimmy up for school the next Monday, "I didn't hear about any fatal accidents."

"That's good," responded Jimmy. He hadn't checked because he was afraid to know.

"I also asked Donny Google if he'd heard anything," continued Sonny.

"You didn't tell him what those crazy fuckers did, did ya?" asked Jimmy.

"Hell, no! I don't think I'll ever tell anyone about it," predicted Sonny.

As they walked across the parking lot, they saw Lurch standing by the back entrance, staring at them as they approached.

"Is Numb Nuts Lurch waitin' for us?" wondered Jimmy aloud.

It was as if he had a tracking device in Sonny's car, and knew they'd be arriving at just this second.

"Come with me, boys," he said, confirming Jimmy's suspicions.

The trio was silent as Lurch led the boys down the hall to his office without explanation. They didn't ask, because they knew why already; and he didn't tell, because he knew they knew. When they walked in and saw Yobs, Eubanks, and Harry Roach seated in the room, they had the confirmation they hadn't needed. Once they were all in place, Walter Matthau and Carl Manson came in behind. The room was so full of people it was hard for anyone to breathe.

"You all know why you are here," started Lurch. "We want to hear what happened."

Jimmy thought to himself there had to be some other reason they were here, because everyone knew no one was going to say anything.

"Jimmy?" asked Lurch, singling Jimmy out. "The coaches said they didn't smell anything on you. Tell us what happened."

Jimmy smiled and said, "When?"

"You know when," called out Manson, "At the track meet!!!"

"Oh, that," sighed Jimmy, somewhat relieved he wasn't being asked what happened AFTER the track meet. "I PR'd in the triple jump!!"

"You what??" asked Walter.

"PR'd," repeated Jimmy, "I set my Personal Record!!"

The boys all laughed nervously.

"This is no laughing matter, boys," cautioned Lurch. "If I don't hear the full story by the end of the day, you're all getting suspended!!"

The boys eyed each other, to see if anyone would break. Silence was maintained until Eubanks asked a question. "So, what if we do admit it? You're sayin' we won't get suspended if we admit it?"

Lurch didn't respond to the tricky question and the boys weren't surprised. A stare down ensued.

The vice principle broke the silence by stating, "OK, if that's the way you want it!!" and he pointed at the door.

With that the five boys vacated the office as quickly as possible. Kilos was standing a few feet outside, in the hallway. He had been informed of the meeting in progress and wanted to be the first to hear the outcome.

"We have been unjustly accused of consuming alcohol before the track meet," Yobs expounded, loud enough for anyone standing in the foyer to hear.

Kilos knew that already, as he had been at the scene of the original accusation. Everyone in the school who hadn't been there knew that part by now as well.

"So, we're gonna get suspended unless someone Narcs," Yobs turned to scan the crowd, searching for suspects.

"We are completely innocent," continued Yobs, "You know that yourself, Kilos. Did you smell anything?"

"Nope," responded Kilos dutifully.

Kilos took over from there. The crowd was expanding, and since he was a politician, he made a speech.

"Here before you stand five, fine, Varsity Men, unjustly accused, by THEM!!" and as he said the last word he spun and pointed to the offices behind him. "I know. I was there!! Standing before you are The Innocent 5 Tracksters. If they are suspended it will be an injustice that cannot be ignored!! We must stand up for our rights!!"

Jimmy looked at Kilos and wondered if he had made a mistake taking Calculus. He should have spent that time in Remedial Gullibility classes, from where Jimmy was standing. Even if Jimmy hadn't been there to witness it or smell it, he would assume Yobs had been drinking and was lying about it. That's who Yobs was. That doesn't mean Jimmy wouldn't put on a show like he believed Yobs, just like Kilos was, but no way would he be doing it as sincerely as Kilos seemed to be.

The next time he was alone with Kilos, he felt him out to see where his head really was.

"So, how was it on the bus?" Jimmy asked as they rode to Goon River.

"The ride over was great, but the ride back was horrible. Someone broke the windows on the bus, probably those jerks from Metamora or Kankakee, and I was freezing the whole time," recalled Kilos.

"Broke the windows?" asked Jimmy, remembering to act surprised.

"Yeah, three of them, all on the left side of the bus," said Kilos.

"That's really fucked up, man," replied Jimmy with sympathy. Jimmy thought it was fucked up when he witnessed it and hadn't changed his mind since.

"Not as fucked up as you guys gettin' accused unjustly," answered Kilos.

"True," agreed Jimmy. He rationalized if they had been unjustly accused, it would be fucked up.

"I'm not gonna let this die, Jimmy," continued Kilos. "I'm gonna form a protest."

Jimmy tried to pull Kilos off the ledge, unsuccessfully. "I don't think that's necessary, man."

"What?? Of course, it is!! You guys are no doubt innocent, and I'll swear to it on a stack of Bibles!!" screamed Kilos.

Jimmy realized the only way he could bring Kilos back to reality was to tell him the real, whole, story; but quickly decided that would be worse. The Air Force made the same decision at Roswell, so the precedent had been set already.

Before the day ended it was too late to turn back. As Jimmy ambled down the halls, he realized he may have been a well-liked, popular kid before today, but now he had been elevated to a legend. The Innocent 5 Protest was in full swing. Posters were going up, protesting the cruelty of the Terrible Troika, as one of the posters named them, or extolling the purity and virtue of the Innocent 5.

His mom did not think he was a legend when she received the phone call at work later that day, telling her about a meeting she needed to attend at the school tomorrow. He was called into her room as soon as she got home, but at least this time Jimmy knew it was coming, even though she managed to manufacture more fury than she had over the Bad Check Incident. Despite being ready for it, he might not have survived if not for the US Postal Service.

"So," she said in a tone letting him know she wasn't going to believe his next words. "Were you out drinking before the track meet??"

Jimmy had been preparing his answer all day. He even remembered to fold his arms belligerently for effect. "No way, no how, was I drinking that night. I did not have a drop." Then he glared at his mother with outrage, like she was yet another accuser in his face.

"What about the other boys?" she asked.

"I plead the Fifth," responded Jimmy.

"What??" replied his more than exasperated mother.

"I learned about it in Civics class," explained Jimmy, trying to make the conversation as cerebral as possible.

Then the mailman rang the doorbell. Jimmy ran out of the room not to get the mail, but to get a few tension free breaths outside of the interrogation chamber before having to go back in. And lo and behold, the deliverance from his current dilemma was in his hands.

As he walked back into his parents' bedroom, he said, "Three of these letters are for me, and two are from Bradley."

He opened the first as his mother stewed. She had patience and could wait through this stall tactic. It was on Bradley letterhead and said:

Congratulations on choosing Bradley University for your higher education. Please see the attached letters concerning orientation sessions and a scholarship interview.'

He read it out loud to his mother and then he went on to the next page. It showed three separate dates, two in July and one in August, for the three-day, two-night on-campus event. The last two sessions were the only ones which also included a chance to take College Level Placement Exams, which Jimmy wanted to take, as he had heard he could avoid taking English and other un-important classes if he scored high enough.

The last page was an announcement asking for Jimmy's atten-dance at an interview on Bradley's campus. He had been nom-inated as a Romeo B. Garrett Scholar, and if he did well in the interview, a scholarship of up to $2,500 could be his. Romeo B. Garrett was the only black professor Bradley had employed for thirty years, and after persevering for so many decades, a scholar-ship fund for black students had been established in his name, for those with financial need and academic excellence. He looked at the date, August 11, and that narrowed his choice of an orienta-tion session to the last one, August 10 through 12.

His mother softened, but she was still going to wring an an-swer out of him.

He opened the next letter, also from Bradley. It read:

Congratulations on choosing Bradley University for your higher education. We have recently been advised of your ACT test results and based on your score you have been awarded a $1,500 scholarship. This scholarship will be renewed each year, depend-ing on your grade point average remaining above 3.0. Good luck in your remaining high school classes, and we look forward to see-ing you on campus this fall.

His mother lost all her anger when he read that one. Brad-ley University was an expensive private school costing $5,000 per year and she and her husband had been clueless of how they would pay for it, plus the $1,500 per year they were paying for his sister JoAnn to go to Illinois State, a much cheaper state school.

Jimmy knew he could make pleading the Fifth work af-ter opening the last letter of the three. It was from the National Achievement Scholarship Program. When he opened it, even he was impressed with himself. It read:

In recognition of your outstanding scholarship and your promise for academic achievement in the field of Engineering as shown by your outstanding SAT test scores, you have been awarded a $1,000 scholarship sponsored by the Aetna Life and Casualty Company. This scholarship will be renewed each year, and the value may increase in future years. This scholarship also comes with a paid summer internship program which matches students with companies who contribute to the fund. You are not restricted to the company which sponsored your actual scholarship, any company on the list can be selected if a position is available.

Media outlets in your local area have been notified. Good luck in your future endeavors.

"Does that mean this is gonna be in the newspaper?" marveled Jimmy.

His mother took the letter from him and read it silently. "Yes, that is what it means."

She tried to get back to the task at hand but had no more fire in her belly.

"We have to go to a meeting with the vice-principal first thing in the morning," was all she could spit out.

Jimmy dashed out of the room overjoyed. It would now cost less for him to go to Bradley than it cost for his sister to go to a state school. No way could his dad punish him for anything anymore. He was a man ready to stand on his own two feet.

"So," Lurch said as he sat in his office with Jimmy and his mother the next day. "You know why you are here."

Jimmy and his mother were silent.

"We are not accusing your son of drinking, Mrs. Williams," clarified Lurch kindly. "But he is getting suspended for three days if he doesn't tell us what happened."

"Well, Jimmy," said his mother, "What do you have to say?"

Jimmy had practiced his lines before he went in, just like the Watergate guys did.

"I did not have anything to drink before, during, or after the track meet," testified Jimmy.

"We know that, Jimmy. You have to tell us about the others," countered Lurch.

"Who are the others?" asked his mother.

As Lurch read their names, Jimmy gazed out the window. He tried but couldn't stifle a snicker.

"See??" accused Lurch, trying to get Jimmy's mother on his side. "He thinks it's funny!!"

Jimmy could not help but correct him and said, "Naw, I wasn't laughing at that. Look outside. Someone painted The Rock again!!"

'Heady Sucks' was written in large white letters over a base coat of purple. It was positioned perfectly to be seen from where Jimmy was sitting in Lurch's office.

Lurch looked outside, then stared as sternly as he could at Jimmy and asked, "One last time, are you going to tell me what happened that night?"

Jimmy stared at his feet. He knew not to look up at Lurch or he'd start laughing again. All he could think of when he looked at him was the idea of him answering the door by saying "You rang?" like Lurch on the TV show. More seconds ticked away. Jimmy's mother said nothing.

"He won't talk!! He won't admit to what the other boys did!!" Lurch said to her, and then to Jimmy, "OK, if that's how you want it!! You are not allowed back at school until Friday. No makeup privileges will be allowed."

Jimmy and his mother stood to leave.

Lurch stood as well, and then stuck out his hand toward Jimmy. "I know this is an awkward time to do this, but congratulations on your scholarship. We've never had someone win this one in the history of our school. It was in the paper this morning. You should be proud."

Jimmy gave him the awkward handshake he deserved, and he and his mother walked out of the office, through the foyer, and out to the car, which was parked in front of the school, next to The Rock. The ride home was just as awkward. Jimmy's mother saw the light at the end of the tunnel and knew it could be a train. That train's name, in her mind, was Sonny Mathis.

"Why is it that every time there's trouble, Sonny Mathis is involved?" she lashed out at Jimmy.

"Sonny didn't have anything ta do with it, Mom," Jimmy replied.

"You need to stop hanging out with him, before it's too late!!" she shouted.

"I will, Mom, I promise," soothed Jimmy, "In August."

When he returned to school on Friday with the other Innocents, except Eubanks, who received two extra days for punching Norman Bates, Jimmy was given celebrity status. Not the Homecoming skit, not Hyde Park week, and not any of the many J Moves he pulled off during garbage time of basketball games, came close to gaining Jimmy the volume of at-a-boys and back slaps from the guys and admiring smiles from the girls he was awarded that day. Maybe not even all of them combined.

Kilos had organized a protest march the day before, from the parking lot down the main hall and stopping in the foyer for a rally. Kids had filled the foyer, were up the main stairs and half down the hall. They had Innocent 5 signs and chanted "Free the Innocent 5, Free the Innocent 5!!" and "Injustice for 5, Injustice for All!!" again and again, until the Terrible Troika and all the coaches formed a goon squad to break it up.

345

RULE # 61 - *Even If You Don't Hesitate,*
You Can Still Lose

When Jimmy entered Physics class that Friday afternoon, Mr. Davis reacted as if he thought Jimmy had been ill for the last three days.

"You missed the midterm while you were out sick, Jimmy. When will you be ready to make it up?" asked the concerned teacher.

"I can take it after school today, if that's OK with you," advised Jimmy.

If Mr. Davis hadn't been informed Jimmy wasn't supposed to have makeup privileges, Jimmy wasn't going to tell him, and the best way to ensure he didn't find out was to take the test as quickly as possible. Physics wasn't that hard, an easy B, so he wasn't worried about what was on the test and didn't feel the need to study. The sooner he took it the better.

"Another thing," said Mr. Davis. "Scott Johns signed you up for Senior Bowl. We start practice next week."

Senior Bowl was to dorks what the state high school basketball tournament was to jocks, except Senior Bowl crowned not only state champions, but also a national champion. It consisted of two teams of five students each, seniors only, hence the name, who sat at opposite tables and answered questions posed by a panel of adults. The questions ranged from math and science to history and the arts, and no area of academic study was off limits. Points were given to the team whose member answered each question fastest, and there were bonus questions allowing each team to discuss the answer as a group before the team captain gave a response. Each student had a buzzer to press after hearing each question, and whoever pressed it fastest had three seconds to give the judges an answer. If correct, the prescribed points were awarded, and if incorrect the same points were deducted.

"Are you the coach?" questioned Jimmy.

"Sort of, but more of a sponsor," responded Mr. Davis.

"OK, I'll do it," said Jimmy. He couldn't say no before the midterm.

When he returned after school to take the test, Mr. Davis was behind the lab table where he normally sat, instead of behind his desk.

"Why didn't you tell me you were suspended with no makeup privileges?" he asked Jimmy.

Jimmy stared at the teacher with a wry smile on his face. He wondered if Mr. Davis had also known before, in class, but didn't let on until Jimmy agreed to join Senior Bowl.

"Because you didn't ask. It's kind of embarrassing," remarked Jimmy, without the slightest hint of embarrassment. Plus, since most of the school had been bragging about his suspension all day, he didn't feel the need to brag about it himself.

"Well, you can't make up the midterm. I'm going to have to give you an F," said Mr. Davis, with little remorse. "See you at practice next week."

RULE # 62 - *It's Not Braggin' If You Can Do It*

Senior Bowl practice was not really practice at all. Most of the time was consumed by Jimmy and Kilos trading jokes and bragging about how much smarter they were than everyone else. The entire group of thirteen had been in the Advanced Math program. The top ten in grade point average were included. More precisely, it was the top twelve, plus Jimmy. Jimmy was down in the twenties, the lowest ranking student invited. No one in the room would dispute his inclusion, as none of them could keep up with him in real time.

By the second day Mr. Davis had had it. He had divided them into two groups, with Kilos on one side, and Jimmy on the other, and he was asking questions rapid fire. Jimmy and Kilos were taking turns answering most of them and keeping up a constant banter as they went. Mr. Davis brought the practice to a halt. He threw down the gauntlet.

"I'm sick of you two bragging," he sneered.

"It's not braggin' if you can do it," said Kilos in response.

"You're not as good as you think you are," the teacher counselled.

"Probly, but we're for sure better than you think we are," responded Jimmy.

"And how good is that?" asked Mr. Davis.

"The two of us can beat everyone else in the room combined," challenged Kilos.

"So, you think that the two of you can beat the rest of the team combined? OK, let's do it," said the eager teacher. If he could humble the pair, it would best for the team. They needed to learn they weren't invincible.

The two braggarts were placed at one table, while the remainder of the team sat in the first rows of the classroom. Nancy Naughton, Ken Farris, Vonny-Yonny, Sarah Hopper, Bob Fair, Scott Michaels and Natalie Brown were all there, a veritable Murderer's Row of Canton academics, but Jimmy and Kilos were unperturbed. They knew the winning strategy. The key to the game was to raise their hand as soon as the question was asked, before the answer came to mind, and then take the risk they would think of the answer before the time was up. They knew if they waited until the answer had formed in their minds, one of the others might beat them to the punch.

"What is the capital of Austr..." began Mr. Davis.

Jimmy's hand shot up. Whether it was Australia or Austria, he knew the answer, so why wait until he finished the question?

"alia?" continued Mr. Davis.

Jimmy's hand was raised before anyone's without dispute. "Canberra," he answered correctly.

"What is square root of..." asked Mr. Davis.

Kilos' hand went up.

"81?" finished Mr. Davis.

Kilos' hand was clearly up first. "Nine," he answered.

And so, it went. Kilos and Jimmy didn't let anyone else answer a question. They missed a few, but they knew they couldn't lose if they were the only ones answering questions. Mr. Davis saw this going downhill quickly. He changed tactics.

"Which classical composer wrote Clair de Lune?" he asked.

As soon as Kilos and Jimmy heard the words 'classical composer' they knew not to raise their hands. They and everyone else looked at Vonny-Yonny, expecting her to be the only one to have an answer. They were right.

"DeBussy!!" she said triumphantly.

Mr. Davis scanned the list for more questions on classical music, but he couldn't find any.

"OK, that's enough for today," he said.

"OK, what's the score?" asked Jimmy. There was no doubt who had won, as the larger group had only answered one question.

"I wasn't keeping score," replied Mr. Davis.

"It wasn't close enough ta need ta keep score, and you know it!" taunted Kilos.

Mr. Davis never tried that again. It was less painful to put up with the now increased bragging. He still had a plan for them, however.

RULE # 63 - *The Darker the Witness, The Lighter the Weight of the Testimony*

I t was May the 2nd when Jimmy was cleared to re-join the track team. For some reason, neither Lurch nor Kilos would let the track incident die. The suspensions had been served, the five had been kicked off the team, and no further action needed to be taken, but the two of them wouldn't stop agitating about it. Student Council meetings became debates about it instead of planning for Senior Week, and Lurch pestered Heady, BiteMe, and Table Muscle to stalk Yobs and Eubanks, to compel one of them to confess. Table Muscle revealed it to Jimmy after Civics class one day.

"I talked to Mr. Yardwick again, about the track meet," said Table Muscle. "I told him that a fine young man like himself should be willing to come forward and tell the truth. I told him he was letting you twist in the wind. You are being loyal to him, but he's not being loyal to you."

"Thanks, coach," was Jimmy's only response. He was trying to forget that night as soon as possible.

But after all this time, here he was, sitting in Lurch's office to once again discuss the incident. Jimmy couldn't believe it. This was the third time, and nothing was accomplished the first two. The other Innocents, except Harry Roach, of course, had been interrogated on even more occasions. This time, it turned out, was different.

"I want you to know that you are cleared to rejoin the track team," announced Lurch, as if it would be good news to Jimmy.

"The others?" asked Jimmy.

"Only you," said Lurch.

"How'd that happen?" asked Jimmy, not quite believing his ears.

"Mr. Yardwick came in and confessed," stated Lurch proudly.

"Confessed to what?" asked Jimmy apprehensively.

"You don't have to play dumb. He admitted the four of them were drinking and you weren't," said Lurch.

"Oh," exhaled Jimmy, with much relief.

"That's a load off, huh?" asked Lurch. "Mr. Yardwick is a real standup guy. You should thank him."

"And no one else admitted it?" questioned Jimmy. Sonny had told him he had gone in and told Lurch the same thing weeks ago.

"You mean Sonny Mathis? No, he didn't stick up for you at all," responded Lurch.

As Jimmy thought about who to believe, Sonny or Lurch, he weighed who had the most to gain from lying and picked Lurch. Sonny wasn't getting reinstated to the team no matter what, so he had little to gain by lying. Lurch, on the other hand, could try to use it to his advantage by causing a strain between Sonny and Jimmy.

Another reason to not believe Lurch was something Jimmy's Gramma had told him years before: the testimony of one white person carries more weight than the testimony of fifty black people. Maybe Sonny had told Lurch, but it wouldn't have mattered anyway, because Lurch believed what most white folks did, niggers would all lie for each other. One of the white boys had to come forward before anything official could be done.

Kilos found out before Jimmy. He was waiting in the foyer when Jimmy departed Lurch's office. "Let's go!!" he said to Jimmy with a big smile on his face.

"Let's go where?" asked Jimmy.

"Heady's office, ta get your uniform back," informed Kilos.

Jimmy would have never done this if Kilos hadn't been outside the office at that time. Jimmy was completely over the idea of triple jumping ever again. Kilos knew that, which was why he was outside waiting. He knew if he suggested it at that moment Jimmy might go along, but if he let any time pass, he wouldn't. As he had hoped, Jimmy was not in the mood at that point to pass up the chance for a good confrontation and went along enthusiastically.

When they reached Heady's office, he was sitting behind his desk talking to BiteMe, who was sitting in a chair next to him. Without a single word of greeting, Jimmy blurted out, "Give me my uniform back!" Kilos stood by his side glaring.

Heady looked at the pair with a cock of his huge head and said, "What?"

"Give me my uniform back, please!" repeated Jimmy, realizing his lack of manners.

"Who says you're getting it back?" asked Heady.

"Lur...I, I mean Mr. Vandervort told me I was cleared," explained Jimmy.

"He doesn't coach this team, I do," responded Heady. "We only have one meet left before the County meet. It's too late for you to come back."

"Come on, coach," interjected Kilos. "Let him back on the team. He's got two weeks ta get ready."

Heady thought about it, and decided it wasn't worth arguing with them anymore. What harm could they do in such a brief time? "If I let you back on, no shenanigans, or you're both off the team!!" declared Heady.

"No problem," said Jimmy. "So, are you giving me the uniform back or not?" he asked defiantly.

"Take it," Heady said, pointing to a pile of gear he had already set aside.

The boys grabbed it and hurried back out.

RULE # 64 - *Going Along to Get Along Leads You Straight to Hell*

A check of the calendar revealed Jimmy had less than two weeks, it was more like ten days. There were two days to practice before the last meet on May 5, and then the County meet was May 12. Both were in Canton, so no further bus rides or road trips were included. He had the runway to himself since both Eubanks and Bates were out for the season. Bates had dental surgery and was forced to wait until the next year to play any sports, to give his mouth a chance to heal. The day after Jimmy was reinstated, a rumor circulated a lawyer representing the Bates family had called the School Board President to advise him of the costs of their damages, including his fees, and the Bates did not expect to pay a dime.

Even after missing five weeks of practice, Jimmy was back in top form by the meet on the 5th of May. His eighteen-year-old body was a wonder of resilience and energy to whom running all day was second nature. His top form, however, was barely making the pit. That was why when he jumped clearly into the pit on his second jump, he was overjoyed.

The meet was like most track meets, with several teams competing together from schools in the local area. Jimmy noticed some of the guys he played basketball against trotting around the track, from Washington and Pontiac, and Olympia and Metamora. But it was the guys from Kewanee who befriended him. They were fellow triple jumpers, and watching him jump, and from his reaction, they could tell it was a new PR.

As Jimmy danced in celebration beside the pit, one of them, a tall brother with a tall Afro, trotted up and slapped him five. "Nice jump, man," he congratulated. "You got good form."

His teammate followed and slapped him five also, front and back. "Are you a sophomore? We ain't seen you out here befo'," said his friend.

Jimmy laughed. "Naw, man. I'm a senior."

That surprised the Kewanee guys. It was a good jump for a sophomore, not a senior. Plus, Jimmy looked young enough to be a freshman, as skinny as he was. Jimmy knew he needed to explain.

"This is only the second time I've jumped in a meet in my life. I never tried it until this year. I went ta the WIV meet and then I got kicked off the team," he detailed. "This is my first meet back."

The Kewanee boys were even more startled. This didn't look like the type of kid to get kicked out of anything.

"They must be real tough on brothers over here," consoled the taller guy.

"Yeah, we thought day was tough on us in K K Kaywanee," added the other.

"Man..." said Jimmy, and shook his head, and that was all he needed to say.

The next week of practices was upbeat. Kilos kept up a steady banter as they trotted around the track during the starting warm up and the ending cool down. He went on and on about how much fun the County meet would be, and how after three years of running the hurdles he would PR in the final race of his life. The peak would be when they announced his name over the loud speakers in the stadium before the race began. He knew he wasn't good enough, even if he did PR, to go on to the state sectional meet, so this meet would be the finale of not only his track career, but his entire athletic career.

That was probably why Kilos went so ballistic when Heady taped the list of competitors for the County Meet on the wall outside his office on Thursday, and Kilos' name was not on it. Jimmy's name wasn't either, but he was only mildly upset. But Kilos was so angry he dragged Jimmy into the vortex of it as well, and both went together to Heady's office when they knew he'd be there, late in the day before practice. As expected, Heady was sitting in his chair as normal, but instead of BiteMe it was Coach Campy Campbell sitting next to him. This time Kilos took the lead.

"Why am I not listed in the hurdles?" he asked with rage.

"Because you're not good enough," sneered Heady.

"What??" shouted Kilos. "I've been on this track team for three years. You've always let all the seniors compete in the County Meet, no matter what!!"

"Well, this year is a little different," replied Heady.

"I've got to be the best triple jumper on the team," threw in Jimmy, as he was the only triple jumper remaining on the team.

"You don't have a good enough jump to compete either. You'd be wasting your time," argued Heady.

"I've wasted my time on worse things around here," responded Jimmy.

He thought it was funny, but nobody else did, except maybe Campy, who had a twinkle in his eye. As far as Jimmy was concerned, this wasn't going much further, unless someone lost his temper and did something genuinely hilarious. He contemplated the best way to provoke it, but he never got the chance. After letting the steam in his brain reach the bursting point, his friend exploded.

"I can't believe you, Heady!!!" screamed Kilos. "I hate your guts!!"

"Get out of my face, you little jerk!!" roared Heady. "You think I don't know you're the punk who egged on Eubanks to punch Norman Bates?!?!"

The tension was broken, as both boys burst out laughing.

"What's so funny about that??? I have to pay for the kid's surgery out of my football budget!!!!" cried out Heady.

"Uuh, you called him Norman, not Mark," explained Campy.

"Get out, boys!!!!" shouted Heady. "I've had it with you!!"

On his way out, Kilos faked a sneeze, and the sneeze sounded a whole lot like "Heady Sucks!!"

Once they were out of range, Kilos told Jimmy, "We're goin' to the meet tomorrow."

"What for?" asked Jimmy.

"You'll see," replied Kilos with a sick smile.

Since the meet was at the track next to the school, it didn't take much effort for Jimmy to meet Kilos there. The boys ambled into the stadium, across the track, and into the infield and mingled with the crowd, talking to their many friends, not only from Canton, but neighboring schools as well. One of Jimmy's best friends from elementary school had moved to Cuba before junior high, and Jimmy chatted with him as he always did when they crossed paths. Kilos knew several guys from previous meets and sought them out, as hurdlers tended to know the other hurdlers after competing so many times together, but Kilos was only using them as a cover. He was stalking Heady, waiting for his chance. When he saw Heady saunter to the far side of the track to start the heats of the 220 Yard Dash, he made his move.

"Come on, Jimmy!" he called out excitedly. He grabbed Jimmy by the arm and sprinted toward the grandstand. The stands were sparsely populated with lounging athletes and a few coaches and fans as the boys leaped up the steps, two at a time. Kilos did not stop until he reached the top row, and then he hopped up the short flight of steps leading to the press box, which was perched above the highest row of the stands, at the fifty-yard line.

The box was twelve feet long and seven feet deep. It was sized for three or four people to sit in chairs behind the table which was pressed against the front of the box. The front was open to the air as the hinged vertical doors were propped open. A microphone sat on the table for Heady to use during the meet, and it was turned on and ready for action when the boys entered.

Kilos picked it up and declared, "I would like to make the following announcement!" he paused, waiting for the assembled throng to turn their heads, and continued, "Listen up, everyone. I would like to announce that HEADY SUCKS!!!"

Jimmy scanned the scene and spotted Heady across the track, waddling as swiftly as he could in their direction. Kilos saw him too and searched for inspirations for more mischief in the few seconds available before having to make their escape. He found a pen sitting on the table, and the forms used to fill out the event results, and scribbled furiously on one after the other, HEADY SUCKS then HEADY BLOWS then HEADY KISS MY ASS then FUCK YOU HEADY.

As he stood watching, Jimmy couldn't think of anything to do, but then his sinuses gave him the answer. He had a cold, and he had been spitting out thick green mucus for the last couple of days. A huge glob drained down his nose and into his mouth. He thought about spitting it out on the jacket Heady left slung over a chair, but that would not be good enough. Why not spit it into one of his sleeves, so he wouldn't see it, he would feel it instead when he put the jacket on? He picked up the jacket and spit down the sleeve from the shoulder hole. His sinuses cooperated enough to lay another one down the other sleeve for good measure, and then the boys were jumping down the stairs faster than Heady could catch them. By the time he crossed the field, they were out of reach. He instead went straight to the press box.

The first things he noticed were the friendly messages Kilos had left him. By this point the boys had returned to the infield and were mingling again inconspicuously, as much as possible, which meant they stuck out like sore thumbs. It's not like most of the people inside the stadium hadn't seen them running out of the press box.

Heady snatched the microphone off the table and screamed into it: "Will Scott Johns and Jimmy Williams please leave the stadium? Repeat, Johns and Williams, GET OUT OF THE STADIUM NOW!!!"

Jimmy glanced at Kilos and said, "OK Kilos, we can go now. Your name was announced on the PA system, just like you wanted. You said that was the best thing about the County Meet anyway."

And it was. Kilos exited the stadium saluting Heady as he marched out, twisting his body to turn his raised middle fingers toward the box.

RULE # 65 - *The First Conclusion Reached Is Usually the Best*

T he baseball and softball teams, on the other hand, were awesome. Both the boys' and girls' teams cruised through the county and the sectional tournaments and qualified for the eight-team Illinois State High School tournaments. This would be the first time in Canton's history this had been done. No other high school in Illinois history had ever done it. It couldn't have possibly happened before, as this was the first year Girls Softball had a state tournament. A new law nicknamed Title 9 commanded schools to split their athletics budgets equally between the genders, and in response, in the spring of 1976, Girls Softball was officially sanctioned by all Illinois high schools.

There was a short season the first year, with no conference titles or state tournaments. The Canton squad finished undefeated, 7 and 0, and in the first full season of Girls Softball, the 1976 – 77 school year, they were 16 and 0. As they approached the first game of the state tournament, the Canton girls' softball team had never lost a game in their history.

They were co-captained by Status Queens Hannah Hartford and Casey Queen, but the star was Laura Ashland, the Homecoming queen. Most of the student body was shocked at her talents, except the guys from Jimmy's old neighborhood. Before she became Homecoming queen material she grew up a tomboy who came from humble means and played baseball with the boys in Jimmy's grade school whenever they'd let her play.

The boys team wasn't unbeaten, but they did get hot at the right time, running off a string of victories at the end of the regular season and winning the conference title. The coolest of the cool athletes were on the boys' baseball team, led by their star pitchers, Paul Hunt and Pat Hampton. Once the tourney began they alternated starting, and both had won impressively each time they were handed the ball. Pat Hampton was good enough to have already been offered and accepted a full scholarship to Bradley. Paul Hunt was still hoping for one himself, at least to a state school, and winning a game in the state tournament might provide the impetus the recruiters needed to get his phone ringing.

The boys' finals were held in Peoria, on the brand spanking new diamond built for the Bradley Braves varsity team. After not supporting the team throughout the season; Jimmy, Sonny, Chance, and Bob felt it obligated to attend the first state tourney game. Plus, their buddy Watay rode the pines on the team, and they could use the opportunity to heckle him. He was a slick fielder but hit like Mendoza.

When they met to plan their strategy for the outing, Sonny insisted on driving separately and bringing Jimmy, and only Jimmy, along with him. Chance and Bob were forced to go separately in Bob's car. The reason, which he would not divulge before they were on the road and Sonny could speak his mind freely, was he was taking a side trip before the game to visit some friends of his cousin in Peoria, and he didn't want to be bothered bringing the crackers along.

"You know how they're always sayin' somethin' stupid, tryin' to be cool," explained Sonny.

"So, what's the deal?" asked Jimmy, wondering what kind of wild adventure he was embarking on this time.

"My cousin A. J. is bangin' this chick in Peoria that's got a bunch of brothers," said Sonny. "They're cool. I went over there a couple of weeks ago and met 'em. All their names start with a C: Curtis, Craig and Clyde. And their last name is Carter."

"What's the bitch's name, Candy?" asked Jimmy.

"Naw, man, Tamika," answered Sonny.

Jimmy thought he knew his way around Peoria. He had been going there since he was in the womb. Peoria was built on two levels, the valley along the river, and the bluffs above the river. The poor neighborhoods, as expected, were in the valley. Sonny drove past the turn Jimmy's dad made when they visited his parents, a course seared into Jimmy's brain from uncountable trips before. He drove far down Adams, before turning left, then right, then left again and then again, until Jimmy was confused.

They came to a street with an open field on one side, and a row of eight ramshackle houses on the other. The houses were almost identical, with the only difference being on which side the front door was, and were the common type for this region, two stories with big covered front porches and wide wooden steps leading up to them. There were at least ten people sitting on the steps and standing around the porch of the house Sonny stopped in front of, and the other seven porches were vacant. Jimmy waited for Sonny to get out before he stepped out of the car himself.

"What's happening, Clyde?" asked Sonny to a large boy sitting on the steps. He looked up at Sonny with a vacant smile. He did not respond.

"Sonny, what up, little brother?" hollered a voice from inside the house.

Another older looking guy, maybe early twenties, stepped out of the house. He had a big Afro with a metal comb sticking out of the back. The comb handle was topped by a Black Power fist. He was wearing a classic white, ribbed, sleeveless undershirt, cargo pants, and work boots. He was dressed like he had just come from a construction job.

"Come on in, Sonny," he said, and as the boys hopped up the steps, he opened the door for them.

He led them into the front room and they sat on the couch. People buzzed in and out of the house like it was a beehive.

"This is my main man, Jimmy," introduced Sonny, once they were in the room alone. "Jimmy, this is my main man, Curtis."

The newly acquainted slapped five.

"Jimmy's gonna be livin' here in Peoria in a couple of months. He's goin' ta Bradley," continued Sonny.

"You must be a bad muthafucka ta get in there," said Curtis, the highest of compliments.

"He's smart enough to know what to say to keep me out of trouble," responded Sonny.

"Your cousin said you'd be over," said Curtis. "I saved you some."

"Yeah, man," replied Sonny. "We're gonna go see the state baseball tournament."

"Cool," said Curtis, "You'll be up for it after you hit this." He pulled a nice size bag from his pocket.

"That's a dime?" asked Sonny, skeptically. It looked too big to be a dime bag.

"For you it is, man," said Curtis. "A. J. got me hired down at the plant. I owe him big time."

"Man, that explains the clothes. You're usually stylin'," concluded Sonny.

"Yeah, I'm gettin' some new threads as soon as that first paycheck comes," agreed Curtis.

Sonny handed him a ten and took the bag and rose to his feet. "Come on, Jimmy," he said.

"We ain't gonna smoke any while we're here?" asked Jimmy.

"Naw, man, not in the house!!" barked Curtis, with a horrified look on his face. "My old man's here."

Jimmy glanced at him with surprise. It was OK to sell drugs in the house, but he couldn't smoke a joint in it? A line had to be drawn somewhere, he guessed. As the boys left the house Curtis followed them out. Another brother was walking up the steps as they went down. He wore the same hair style as his brother, and had a toothpick hanging out of his mouth.

"What's up, Craig??" asked Sonny. He introduced Jimmy to the last brother as they walked to the car.

There was plenty of time to get up for the game between the Carter house and the ball field. By the time they met up with Bob and Chance in the parking lot of the stadium, they were in a fine mood to cheer, heckle, or ignore everything around them and just daydream.

The game itself was like most baseball games, with lengthy periods of boredom interspersed with moments of frantic action. The Canton side was up against what many thought was the best team in the state, from one of the big Catholic schools in Chicago. Their starting pitcher was a sure bet to make a living at it. Coach Farnak wanted to break the pattern of Hampton and Hunt alternating starts and select Hampton to start a second game in a row, but Egg cornered the coach and insisted Paul Hunt be given the start as had been the established routine. He told the coach in Hunt's fragile mental state of not having a scholarship yet, not starting would be a crushing blow from which he would never recover. The coach let his star player sway him and ignored his first thought.

Coach Farnak, Pat Hampton, and maybe even more, Paul Hunt, regretted that decision in the top of the eighth inning with two on and one out. The game was tied at two to two. The Brother Rice pitcher, a formidable beast of six foot four and two hundred ten pounds, was mowing down the Canton hitters with much more ease than Paul Hunt was dealing with theirs, but the score was none-the-less even at this late stage. It was at this point in the game, with everything to gain or lose on the next at bat, Paul Hunt threw the best curve ball of his life. The ball spun in and dropped from the height of the batter's waist to his ankles. The only response the batter could make after realizing he couldn't stop his swing was to hack down with his bat and connect with the top half of the ball. The ball bounced lazily, but with plenty of top spin, toward Paul Hunt. He watched it coming and knew this was the perfect outcome, better than a strikeout, a double play ball rolling right to him. All he had to do was to bend over and grab it and throw it to Grant Roper at second, who would then complete the play with a throw to first to end the inning.

But he didn't bend over far enough, fast enough. The top spin caused the ball to scoot faster on the third hop than the second, and he could only slap at it with his glove, which only slowed it down as it passed between his legs, and when he spun to pick it up he kicked it, and when he finally corralled the ball, he threw it off balance to first base instead of second and it sailed wide of the target and into Canton dugout. The result of the best curve ball of Paul Hunt's life was two runs scored and a man on third, still with one out.

It was also the last pitch of Paul Hunt's life in organized baseball. Coach Farnak trotted out to replace Hunt before another pitch was thrown, and Paul walked off the field in tears. Pat Hampton was called in and struck out the next two batters, which stopped the bleeding, but the patient was already brain dead. Six outs later the dream season of Canton baseball was over, at least the boys' half. The girls' half didn't end until later that day, when they lost their first and last game as well.

RULE # 66 - *Don't Repeat the Same Mistakes*

"Man, what a bummer," sniveled Chance.

"I almost feel bad for those fuckers," expressed Bob. That very neatly summed up the other boys' feelings as well. They would have been happy for them if they had won, but they couldn't be upset because they lost. Most of the baseball players were pretty much insufferable jerks already, and if they had won the state championship, their heads would have swollen to a size rivalling the football coach's.

"Can you believe Hunt blew the game by letting such an easy grounder go through his legs?" wondered Chance.

"Yes, I can, actually", said Jimmy, as a memory flooded back to him. "He did the same thing in his first little league game."

Then something happened that had never happened before, at least in the memory of Sonny, Chance, and Jimmy. No Sense had two sensible things to say in a row. "I'm hungry. Are you guys hungry?"

As they were all eighteen years old, of course they were hungry. They all nodded yes.

"I saw a pizza place when we were comin' into town," suggested Chance. "It was right on Adams Street, just before you get to Bartonville."

"I don't have any money for pizza," replied Jimmy.

"Me neither," agreed Sonny.

"Don't worry about it," responded Chance.

"Movin' ta Banner has made you rich?" asked Bob.

"Just come on and don't worry about it," Chance repeated.

366

The boys caravanned to the pizza parlor and parked their cars side by side. As they stepped out, a car full of high school aged girls parked across from them and did the same. Chance, ever the gentleman, ran ahead so he would be the one to hold the restaurant door open for them.

"Good evening, ladies," purred Chance as they walked in.

What were the chances four guys would walk into a pizza place at the same time as four girls? Chance didn't have the slightest idea which mathematical formulas could be used to answer such a question, but he did know he wasn't going to let the opportunity to chat them up pass him by. As he did have a tremendous gift for spouting meaningless compliments and lame jokes, it wasn't surprising the groups ended up sitting at adjacent tables, flirting and chatting while they munched their pizzas. As girls often do in such social settings, they rose to visit the ladies' room together, after they finished the last bites of their pizza, to discuss which of the boys they wanted to make out with.

"Well, whaddaya think?" Sonny queried his friends, in the same frame of mind as the girls. He had a selection in mind and wanted first dibs.

Chance burst out laughing.

"What's so funny?" asked Jimmy.

"I don't have any money ta pay for the pizza," replied Chance. "I'm thinkin' we should get the hell outta here before those chicks get back."

The four boys looked at each other and howled in laughter. They stood as one and headed for the door.

"Wait, I gotta take a piss!!" exclaimed Sonny. "Here!!" he said tossing his car keys to Jimmy, "Go start the car!!!"

Sonny trotted off to the bathroom. Jimmy stood still for a second, debating what to do, and quickly realized he didn't want to be standing there if the girls came out before Sonny. He ran out of the restaurant behind Bob and Chance and sprinted to Sonny's car. Bob was screeching out of his spot as Jimmy ran past, and he had to leap out of the way to avoid being hit.

'Later, Jimmy!!" shouted Chance from the passenger's seat.

Jimmy had never driven Sonny's car, and it took him a few seconds to start it and put it into gear. He just had it going when he saw Sonny inside the restaurant walking in a hurried but casual way toward the exit. Jimmy could see the manager behind the counter, and then he saw the women's restroom door opening and the girls giggling their way out. Jimmy slammed down on the gas pedal to get as close to the restaurant door as possible, so Sonny could dash out and dive directly into the car. His adrenalin got the better of him, however, and he shot across the parking lot and slammed into the back of the girls' car. Sonny opened the restaurant door just in time to see the collision and hear the clashing as the tail lights on the girls' car were smashed.

"Oh shit, Jimmy!!" called out Sonny, running toward the back of his car to inspect the damage.

"Get in, you idiot!!!" screamed out Jimmy. He could see the girls inside the restaurant. They had arrived at their table and were looking around to see where the boys had gone.

Sonny realized the need to vacate as well and dove into the back seat of the car because it was closest, and Jimmy sped out of the parking lot without turning on the lights. After he drove a few miles Jimmy pulled over underneath a street lamp, and they both jumped out to inspect the damage.

"You put a good dent in the fender, but none of the lights are broken," said Sonny.

"Good thing this car is such a tank," replied Jimmy.

"You fucked up the back of their car pretty bad, though. Let's get the fuck out of here," ordered Sonny. "I can hear sirens."

They passed a police car, lights flashing and siren blaring, going the opposite direction as they sped out of town.

RULE # 67 - *Leading is Not as Important as Succeeding*

The county Senior Bowl competition was two days later. The Canton team had gathered in the high school foyer, waiting to board the bus, when Mr. Davis made an announcement.

"We will be able to field two teams of five players, so I have decided to make Jimmy and Scott each the captain of a team, and they can pick the four others that will be on their teams."

"What?" shouted Kilos. "Jimmy and I have ta be on the same team!!!"

"Yeah, Mr. Davis. Me and Kilos and Vonny-Yonny can beat anyone!! We could go to the state finals, at least! Maybe the nationals!!" said Jimmy.

"Well, that's not the way I want to do things, boys," he twanged in reply.

"C'mon, Mr. Davis, you've gotta put us on the same team!!" pleaded Kilos.

"Well," said the drawling sponsor, "I have Jimmy ranked number one, because he's answered the most questions correctly during practice, and I've got you ranked number two, Scott. So, if you want to play together, Jimmy is the captain and he can pick you. I'll make Yvonne the other captain. OK?"

Kilos hesitated. He would be giving up the chance to be the captain if he agreed to that arrangement. Jimmy would be sitting in the middle and be the team spokesman on the bonus questions. It was a very difficult choice, and he needed time to think about it. He was Student Council President, wasn't he?

When Jimmy saw how difficult it was for Kilos to swallow being subordinate to him, he bristled.

"I'll make it easy on you, Kilos," he said, "I have first pick and I pick Yvonne. Who's your pick?"

Kilos stared at Jimmy and replied, "I pick Scott Michaels."

When Jimmy finished picking, he had Nancy, Kirk Morgan, and Ken Farris on his side of the bus along with Vonny-Yonny, and Kilos sat on the opposite side with his squad for the fifteen-minute ride to the county seat.

Upon arriving at Lewiston High School Jimmy may have thought he was being paranoid, but everyone really was staring at him. The top nerds from all the high schools in the county were there, and Jimmy was not only the darkest and easiest to spot, but also the most famous. They had all read the article about his scholarship in the newspaper and now they were seeing the flesh behind the headline. Could he possibly be as smart as the paper said? They were about to find out.

Just to rub it in with Kilos he wrote CAPT next to his name on the blank name card each person had in front of them as they sat waiting to begin their first matches. There were eight teams total representing six schools, as Canton and Lewiston were the only two allowed two teams each. The others were Havana, Cuba, Farmington, and Avon, all hamlets too small for more than one squad.

After the first round, only the Canton and Lewiston teams were left, and the four other schools were left to spectate. Jimmy's team had faced Cuba and won handily. They were so far ahead Jimmy stopped answering questions midway through to save his brain energy for the next round. The next round was against one of the Lewiston sides and it was closer, but not by much. The match was over quickly enough for Jimmy's team to have time to watch the conclusion of the other semi-final, between Kilos' team and the other Lewiston squad.

As he watched, something didn't smell right to Jimmy. He concluded either the Lewiston guys were all geniuses, or they had seen the questions before. One of the outcomes of the Pitch Festival was the development of a keen sensitivity to the aroma of cheating, so keen it could be sniffed before it was visible. In practice, the students had been asked hundreds and hundreds of questions from past competitions, some of which they knew would be recycled in the upcoming competition, while others they knew would be new. As the matches progressed and scores of questions were asked and answered, Jimmy calculated about half were questions he had heard before, and the others he had not. He could tell by the way the Lewiston guys were answering questions they had heard a lot more than 50%, maybe 90%, if not all the questions being asked of them. They seemed to be recalling the answers, not needing to think of the answers.

When Kilos' team went down, Jimmy took a deep breath and knew it was up to him to win the Senior Bowl for Canton. He would pay full attention this time around and take no prisoners. He would play like he was himself and Kilos combined. All he needed was a little help from Vonny-Yonny, and they would be able to lift the trophy.

But it wasn't meant to be. Lewiston was ahead by one point despite Jimmy's best efforts. He answered at least twice as many questions as anyone else in the competition, and had most of Canton's points, but they were still down to their last chance. The subject was Chemistry. Jimmy smiled, thinking Vonny-Yonny knew more about Chemistry than anyone. She was the one who was going to be a surgeon one day.

The moderator asked, "What are the negative particles in the outermost shell or energy level of an atom called?"

Jimmy glanced at Vonny-Yonny, waiting for her to push her buzzer, but she looked back at him and shrugged nervously. The Lewiston boys were huddling, but none of them could answer. Jimmy took a chance. He knew the negative particles of atoms were electrons, and there was only one kind of electron he could remember the Sheep Farmer talking about, so he guessed, "Valence electrons."

"Correct!!" cried the moderator.

The Lewiston guys broke their huddle and stared at Jimmy in amazement. He was just as smart as the paper said. Now it was tied, and Canton had a glimmer of hope to pull it out on the last question. It was a bonus question for Canton, so they would have fifteen seconds to answer it before Lewiston got their chance. If they formulated the correct answer, the trophy was theirs. His heart rose when the moderator stated the next question was about a famous piece of classical music. He thanked his lucky stars he had picked Vonny-Yonny.

"Who wrote the opera The Valkyrie?" the moderator asked.

Jimmy eyed Vonny-Yonny, knowing he did not have a clue this time. She stared back at him and slowly shook her head to show she did not know the answer either. They did not listen to any Wagner in her house. Jimmy did not want to give a wrong answer, as that would seal their fate, so he surveyed the Lewiston team, hoping they wouldn't know it either, but he could tell by the eager looks on their faces they did. The time ran out.

"Richard Wagner!!" they shouted in unison.

That not only clinched the match, but also Jimmy's conclusion Lewiston had a better cheat sheet than Canton did. No way did these hicks from the sticks know anything about classical music. To them classical music was the Grand Ole Opry. After the trophy was awarded, a swarm of geeks surrounded Jimmy like he was a sports star, to shake his hand and congratulate him, from the winning team and the vanquished.

"Wow, you really are smart!!" gushed the captain of the Lewiston team. "I thought you were gonna beat us by yourself!"

"Well, thanks," replied Jimmy. "I thought I could have too, except I don't know anything about classical music."

The boys crowded around him laughed.

"We don't either," answered one of them smiling. "We must have heard that question ten times in practice."

Jimmy shook his head.

As they rode back on the bus, Kilos sat next to Jimmy. Jimmy didn't feel much like talking to him, though. He couldn't get the thought out of his mind that they would have won if Kilos had just…

"Too bad we couldn't be on the same team," said Kilos. "Davis is such a jerk."

Jimmy glanced over at Kilos with an air of exhaustion and feigned taking a nap. What Kilos said didn't deserve a response. Jimmy felt it would be a waste of his time to even think about it anymore.

RULE # 68 - *Authority Rewards Only Those Who Happily Kneel Down to It*

T he Senior Honor Assembly, the last assembly of the Class of 1977's high school life, was on May 27, the Friday before Memorial Day weekend. For most seniors it was just another hour to get through, an excuse to get out of class, and maybe, just maybe, a chance to heckle the administration one last time. The faculty goon squad had sprinkled themselves throughout the auditorium, in hopes of stifling any such activities as soon as they happened. There was no need, because a very potent load of Lumbo Gold had been dispersed throughout the town a few days before, and the crowd was very mellow.

Of no surprise were the Athletes of the Year, Pat Hampton and Laura Ashland.

There was a minor surprise when Take-A-Nap won Teacher of the Year. He was the only person the senior guys were actively campaigning for, and the minor surprise was enough people supported the obviously sarcastic campaign and voted for a teacher they hated. The main thing he did to warrant the honor was to get fired as basketball coach and not have enough pride to leave town in a huff, and the second thing he did was to tell the Clap Joke in Health class.

The major surprise was the Student of the Year. Will Michaels won it. Since this award was given by the faculty, who did take it seriously, there was much speculation about who had managed to kiss enough faculty ass to impress their serious minds. Most of the speculators were split between sincere Bob Fair and shameless Kirk Morgan, the drum major in the band, and a few totally clueless handicappers picked Kilos. Since the Student of the Year had to have been a Student of the Month at least once, it couldn't have been Kilos. Another popular choice was Carl David, but more of his classmates wanted him to win than thought he would.

374

As Jimmy would find out again and again in his life, Will Michaels' claim to fame as an average student, average athlete, and average personality impressed those in authority more than the more talented, accomplished, and interesting people around him. He was so mediocre his future success was assured, and therefore they had to start rewarding him for it. Either that or he was the son of a rich, powerful, city father.

The last surprise was when Jimmy heard his name called. Jimmy was sitting in the balcony, which was not a place for anyone to be sitting who knew they would be honored.

"And last, but not least," said Walter Matthau, "We would like to recognize a student who has been awarded a scholarship for the first time in the history of the school, the National Achievement Scholarship for Minority..."

"Way to go, Whales!!!!" shouted out Sonny, before Walter could finish. For some strange reason Sonny was not in the balcony, he was in the middle of the main floor.

The crowd roared in laughter.

"...Engineering Students. Jimmy Williams!!" Walter finished.

Table Muscle, who was stationed in the balcony to watch over the worst of the worst, encouraged Jimmy, "You should take a bow."

Jimmy strolled to the rail of the balcony and waved.

As he stood there waving and looking at the other honorees standing on the stage, he had a flashback to the last assembly he had in junior high. He was one of the ones on the stage that time.

It was ninth grade, the last year of junior high before the Class of 1977 moved on to high school, much to the comfort and joy of the junior high faculty. Maybe next year they could have the Bake Sale again! Mr. Monahan had the forward-thinking idea the year before to have school wide assemblies throughout the next year and bring in a series of speakers of different disciplines to help motivate, stimulate, and inspire his students and share their real-world experiences and know-how. One was an architect who spoke about how he had designed the buildings at Spoon River College. Another was a violinist who spoke about her career in music. A third was a retired pilot, who spoke about the different airplanes he had flown. He, at least, had inspired Weedhopper.

By the seventh and last assembly, at the end of the school year, the students were no longer interested in being inspired or motivated, and they were plenty stimulated already. The sweetness of spring had filled their nostrils and they were on an epic sugar high, the kind that could only be brought on by May sunshine.

The speaker, entertainer, motivator, or sitting duck, depending on the perspective of the witness, was The Amazing Mr. Memory. He was a small but sprightly old man in an old suit and tie. Mr. Monahan was standing in the middle of the stage of the gymnasium, which doubled as an auditorium, to introduce him. The stage was a raised platform, deep enough to have the band sitting there, or plays acted out there, but on this day the curtain was closed, and the microphone stand was in front of it. The stage was as wide as the length of the basketball court and the gym floor had been filled with chairs filled with students, and the grandstand opposite was filled with row after row of students up to the rafters.

As TAMM waited off stage for his intro, seven students, all culled from the Advanced Math class, stood off stage with him. They had been excused from their classes thirty minutes earlier than the rest of the school, to meet with the speaker and learn their cues, as they would be used as assistants. It was Kilos, before he was nicknamed Kilos, and Jimmy, and Nice Nancy (she already had hers), Vonny-Yonny (Yvonne at that time), Kirk Morgan (before he became known as The Majorette), Bob Fair, and Sarah Hopper. They were picked because they were thought of as the most responsible and intelligent people in the class, the kind who could be depended on.

"And here he is, The Amazing Mr. Memory!!" boomed Mr. Monahan rousingly.

A group groan reverberated through the large echo chamber of the auditorium. A few managed a meager clap, and a couple managed not so meager boos.

In the minds of the hecklers in the room, TAMM started well enough, with, "Hello, I'm The Amazing..."

"What's so amazing about you??" shouted someone from the crowd.

TAMM stopped in mid-breath and smiled, then started again, "I'm glad you asked!!"

"I'm not!!" called out another.

TAMM plowed on. "I am amazing because I can remember anything. And I am here to show you how you can remember everything just like I can!!!"

The students behind the curtain were interested, because a better memory meant better test scores, and this group of seven was highly motivated to learn anything that helped. The rest of the student body? Not so much.

"I would like to call out my assistants," and then he rattled off each of their names and gave their birthdates as the seven walked on stage one after the other, as they had been instructed to beforehand.

"So what, I know their names too!!" was the response from someone in the crowd who wasn't very impressed.

"And birthdays?" asked TAMM. He should have known better at his age to be responding to the hecklers, but he obviously had never learned this wisdom, or had forgotten it.

"Naw, then I'd owe 'em presents!!" shouted another.

The kids on stage felt bad for the man, he seemed nice enough. Once again, the audience did not agree.

"I remembered their names because I used a memory technique called Word Association. Has anyone ever heard of it?" he asked.

"I think so, but I forgot!!" called out another heckler.

Despite their being ashamed at his treatment, the seven on stage couldn't help but laugh too.

"This is the rudest audience I have ever performed for," TAMM whispered to Jimmy, who was standing closest to him.

"Word Association is when you look at someone and associate something about them with their name. Kirk, over here. He has red hair, so I remember a red cap, and cap is short for captain, and a famous captain is Captain Morgan, so his name is Kirk Morgan!!" proclaimed TAMM triumphantly.

"If you shaved your eyebrows, you'd look just like Kreskin's grampa!!!" yelled someone from the bleachers.

At this point Jimmy was brought back to the present. He could hear Lurch's voice booming over the loud speakers.

"We have one last announcement to make. As you know, the seniors take their finals starting Tuesday and ending on Friday. At the end of the school day on Friday, all seniors must leave campus immediately, and are not allowed anywhere on school property from that point on until the day of graduation, June 14. Therefore, June the 3rd is the last day of school for the Class of 1977. If any seniors are seen on school property after that day, and that includes parking lots and athletic facilities, you will be arrested. Make sure you pick up your caps and gowns before Friday. Congratulations!!" he concluded with a flourish.

A collective gasp shot through the audience as the words stopped flowing from Lurch's mouth. It had been a tradition for many years for the seniors to take their finals a week early, and then have the last week of school to say goodbye to their teachers, have fun events around the school, and on the last day of the week, take a class trip to some fun place, funded by the Student Council and school district funds and chaperoned by members of the faculty. The Student Council had decided Six Flags Over

Mid-America would be the destination, so this was a bigger shock to them than anyone else. Disappointment among the Class of 1977 was replaced with anger, and then, in the enlightened few, a resolve to have Senior Week one way or the other. It was a good thing a few had it, because the majority didn't take long to find something very positive about having an unplanned week off, and their anger had worn off before they left school that day.

RULE # 69 - *Let Dead Dogs Lie*

Sonny sat in the death seat and Jimmy lounged in the back of the Montego as Bob cruised through Big Creek Park the next Tuesday. Jimmy had taken his last test of the day, and he welcomed the chance to take a toke.

"Have you heard about Peg Leg?" asked Sonny.

"What about her?" replied Jimmy.

"She called up a bus company and chartered two buses to take us to Six Flags next Friday."

"Who'd they get to chaperone?" queried Bob skeptically.

"No one," informed Sonny.

"You gotta be shittin' me, Sonny," answered Jimmy. "They're gonna let us take the Senior Class Trip without a chaperone?"

"Hey, we're all eighteen now," said Sonny. "The bus company said we didn't need one if everyone's over eighteen."

Jimmy didn't quite believe it, but if it was true, it would be awesome. There was always a catch, however, and Jimmy found it quickly. "If there's no chaperone, that means the school isn't sponsoring it, huh?"

"Yup," answered Sonny, "We gotta pay ten bucks for the bus and the ticket, so with food and stuff you'll need fifteen at least."

"Shit," moaned Jimmy, "No way can I have that kind of money by then. I may be able to scrape together six or seven."

"Don't worry, Jimmy. I'm gonna sell most of this bag," Sonny said while holding up a fat ounce of weed, "and I'll be able to cover you."

"Cool," said Jimmy.

When they reached the top of the hill, heading towards the park's north exit, Sonny told Bob, "Look over there. It's Dead Dog."

At the top of the hill were two baseball fields for little leaguers, with a short lane running alongside. Near the end of the lane was a wide gravel area for cars to park next to the farthest field. There they could see Paul Hunt, sitting in his car by himself.

"Carl David told me Hunt hasn't taken a bath or nothin' since he lost that game. They started callin' him Dead Dog, 'cuz he's startin' ta smell like one. Now he sits in that same spot for hours, takin' single hits by himself," said Sonny. "Drive down there, Bob."

Bob turned the car down the lane and they slowly approached Dead Dog's car and parked alongside. Paul was sitting in the front seat with his head back and eyes closed, totally zonked.

"Hey, Hunt!!" shouted Sonny, bringing Dead Dog back to life.

He opened his eyes and rolled his head toward the boys and smiled.

"You down here takin' single hits by yourself?" asked Sonny.

"Nah, man," answered Dead Dog. "I ain't got no weed."

Dead Dog's eyes were blood shot and his front teeth had a brown resin stain. He looked higher than any kite in the local area, including the three kites staring at him from Bob's car.

"OK, man," replied Bob. "See you later." As he pulled out of the parking spot, he said, "He's a lyin' sack a shit."

The boys laughed as they rolled toward the main park road to exit the park. Bob made the right turn and as he accelerated, a police car pulled up behind them. The cruiser had been patrolling the park and was coming up the hill as Bob turned. Sonny stuck his head and shoulders out of the window, turned his face toward the police car, pointed down the lane and mouthed, "Go down there and bust Dead Dog!" but he didn't say it loud enough for the cop to hear him. He was in such a good mood on such a fine day, he thought it was funny.

With that the police car's revolving hood lights came on. The siren was next, and as Jimmy peered out of the rear window he could see the policeman was pulling them over, not going down the lane to bust Dead Dog. Bob pulled over. The policeman did as well and turned off the siren but left the lights on, then he stepped from the car and strolled to Bob's open window. He rested his hand on his gun and leaned into the car, so he could observe each of the occupants.

"License and registration, please," he said, in the official police voice.

Bob had managed to find his registration card in his glove compartment before the cop's arrival and was fumbling in his wallet for his driver's license, afraid a joint or a roach might fall out. After a few tense moments, he was able to produce it without an incriminating incident.

The policeman looked them over, and said, "Step out of the car and follow me, sir."

Sonny and Jimmy assumed the cop was talking to only Bob, so they didn't budge. Bob stepped out and walked to the police car by himself. The cop motioned for Bob to sit in the car with him, in the front. Jimmy kept his eyes glued to the rear window, trying to determine what was happening in the car behind him. As the policeman sat in the driver's seat and Bob sat on the other side, the cop was doing all the talking, and Bob was shaking his head up and down mostly, and occasionally side to side.

"This don't look good, man," said Jimmy. Sonny did not answer.

Then a miracle happened. The passenger door of the squad car opened, and Bob jumped out. The cop turned the revolving lights off as Bob walked as slowly as he could for the hurry he was in. He dove into the car and said nothing until he put the engine in gear and drove out of the park.

"He gave me a lecture about hangin' out with guys like you," said Bob. "He said you'd get me in nothing but trouble."

The three friends laughed. It was a nervous, full of relief, laugh. They didn't really think it was funny. After making a few turns outside of the park and determining the squad car wasn't following, Bob said, "After that, I need another hit."

Sonny rolled his eyes at him and replied, "I swallowed it."

"You did what?" asked Jimmy, not quite understanding.

"When Bob went back to the cop car, I started eatin' it as fast as I could. I ate the whole fuckin' ounce!!" explained Sonny.

"Whaddya' do that for?" asked Bob.

"'Cuz I didn't wanna get busted," answered Sonny. "I didn't know if that fuckin' pig was gonna search the car or not, so I did what I had ta do while I still had the chance."

Jimmy couldn't believe Sonny ate the whole bag, but since he had his back turned the entire time Bob was out of the car, he couldn't disprove it.

"I'm startin' to catch the strangest buzz," said Sonny. "I guess you can get high eatin' this shit."

RULE # 70 - *Never Pull an Unloaded Gun*

"I got an idea," shared Sonny, the next day.

"Oh fuck, that's dangerous," complained Jimmy, "What about this time?"

"About how we can get the money for the Senior Class Trip," answered Sonny.

Now that he had eaten his source of income, Sonny was in the same destitute condition as Jimmy.

"Let's hear it," said Jimmy.

"I was over at Silas' house last night, and he was braggin' 'bout how him and Otis were takin' some white boys to the cleaners playin' Pitch," advised Sonny. "I told him that whenever he wanted to play against some real Pitch players to let me know."

"How long's he been out?" asked Jimmy.

"About a month now. I thought you knew," responded Sonny.

Sonny wasn't to be distracted. "So, whaddaya think, Jimmy? You said you had six or seven bucks. We can play for five dollars a game and once we win a couple a' games we'll be set. It's a sure thing!"

Jimmy had heard so many "sure things" sprouting from Sonny's mouth down through the years it was not encouraging at all. In fact, it had the opposite effect.

"Man, I don't know," said Jimmy.

"Don't worry, I'll cover you if we lose," promised Sonny.

"With what?" enquired Jimmy.

"I said don't worry," said Sonny. "Plus, there's no way we can lose with the Sig-A-Nols we got!!"

Jimmy didn't answer.

384

"You got any other ideas?" challenged Sonny.

Jimmy had to admit he didn't, other than not going on the trip. Now he had to justify the risk in his own mind. Neither Silas nor Otis could add past ten without taking their shoes off. Silas may have been playing Pitch every day for the last six months while he was in jail, but so had Jimmy and Sonny, and Otis was more focused on playing women than playing cards. They did have all the signals, and they were sure to let the math wiz keep score. What the heck?

"Let's do it," agreed Jimmy.

When they arrived at Silas's house a few days later, which was a block down Anderson Street from the house Jimmy grew up in, they parked in the driveway to plan their strategy. Johnnie Taylor was wailing instructions over the stereo through the screen door, "Shove it in, shove it out, move it in, roundabout, disco lady!!"

"Touchin' your fingers is Diamonds. Touchin' any other skin is Spades. Makin' a fist or tappin' the table means Clubs. Touchin' your shirt or chest is Hearts. Look up and down for high and low. You know the songs already, if they're stupid enough to let us sing," said Sonny.

"And I'll keep score," added Jimmy.

When they entered the house, Silas was sitting in the living room at the end of a long table. Otis was at the other end, with his back to the front door.

"What's happenin', young bloods?" asked Otis as he stood to greet them. Otis was decked out as usual, with his immaculate 'Fro matching his threads. He wore a wide collared shirt with a medallion hanging from his neck, and bell-bottomed jeans so tight in the crotch everyone who saw him knew his level of excitement at any given moment.

"Yo' man," said Sonny to Otis. "You are always clean!"

Both boys slapped five with Otis, and then walked down the table to do the same to Silas. Silas was enormous. The prison food must have agreed with him. At least a hundred pounds of belly could be seen above the table, and at least as much was below it. He didn't bother to get up.

"I hear you kept my brother out of jail," shared Silas with Jimmy.

"Yeah, me and Otis," Jimmy responded.

"Yeah, man," said Sonny, again to Otis. "Why are you messin' with that? She's not as fine as your wife."

"I gotta get me some strange every once in a while," explained Otis.

"Strange?" asked Jimmy.

"You know," chimed in Silas, "Strange fuckin'!!"

The boys looked confused. "Your wife's not a good fuck?" asked Sonny.

"Look, man," answered Otis. "You should never marry a white woman for any other reason than the money."

"Amen!" shouted Silas.

"I see brothers with poor white bitches and I just wanna take 'em aside and slap 'em," preached Otis.

"You should know that already, Jimmy," said Silas. "Your brother married one of the richest white bitches in town."

"He just told me they were dangerous," admitted Jimmy.

"Hell yeah they are, man. White women fuck the same way they dance," laughed Silas, waving his arms around his head like he was doing the jerk.

Otis chuckled and confirmed, "Yeah, I had ta hold her arms down the first couple a' times I fucked her, ta keep her from breakin' my nose."

"That chick at Kroger ain't rich," challenged Jimmy, testing the theory he had just heard.

"Well, there's another thing white bitches do," said Otis.

"Yeah, they suck a mean dick!!" roared Silas.

"I was takin' that bitch down ta the Banner Motel, just ta get my dick sucked," continued Otis. "I had ta cool her out, though, 'cuz she was startin' ta fall in love. The dumb bitch knows I'm married, but she's fallin' in love anyway."

"She's just in love with the dick, man," explained Silas.

"So she helped you guys out tryin' ta get some more of this," concluded Otis, pointing to his crotch. "I had ta fuck her one more time, just ta keep you guys out a' trouble."

"What a sacrifice!!" exclaimed Sonny.

"Are we gonna play cards?" asked Silas impatiently, "Or just talk about who's suckin' Otis' dick?"

"Cards, man," responded Jimmy.

"Four-point to 21 for five bucks a game?" offered Silas. "I heard about you goin' off ta college," said Silas to Jimmy. "Don't think you're so suave and de-boner that you can beat us, boy."

"You been learnin' French?" asked Otis.

"There was this cat from Loo-Ziana in the jail that would speak it sometimes. How dumb do you gotta be to come all this far just ta get put in jail?" wondered Silas.

Sonny picked up the deck from the table and said, "I'll deal, and Jimmy can keep score."

"No way, home boy," countered Silas. "I'll deal." He shoved the pencil and paper he had in front of him over to Jimmy. "Here you go, genius," he said.

So, the game began. Not only were Silas and Otis not smart enough to catch the Sig-A-Nols, they would stare at their own hands for lengthy periods and not pay attention to what Jimmy and Sonny were doing. They could have been mouthing words across the table and not gotten caught. It was an easy first game. The final score was 21 to 9.

"Another game?" asked Sonny, a bit too eagerly.

Silas displayed an even more eager temper.

"You think you're slick?" he asked his little brother. "Don't let me catch you cheatin', Jethro!!"

Silas turned to his left. The stereo was on top of the coffee table. He reached over and lifted the needle and started an album playing. It was the Brothers Johnson, Look Out for Number 1. "I want to know, just how you feel. Said I want to know, if what you feel is real..."

Sonny bobbed his head to the music with cards in his hand and twirled his thumbs with his arms close to his chest, the Diamond signal. Then he sang out, "I'll be good to you, good to you, good to you..."

"Stop talkin' cross the table!!" yelled Silas.

Sonny stopped singing in time to see Jimmy looking up. He had the King of Diamonds. That game was more lopsided, 21 to 7. As far as the boys were concerned, they had enough money and it was time to go. They picked up the ten bucks and tried to make an exit, but Silas was having none of it.

"Sit back down, boys," warned Silas, fully enraged. "We're gonna play one more game, and this time I'm gonna make sure you're not cheatin'!!"

"We don't have ta cheat to beat you, Silas," sneered Sonny with disdain.

At this point, side two of the Brothers Johnson finished playing, and Silas reached over to the coffee table. He did not reach for the stereo needle as the rest had expected, he instead stuck his hand inside the top drawer, and pulled out the biggest revolver either of the boys had ever seen. He sat the gun on the table in front of him and leaned over to his little brother.

"OK, you smart-assed, mealy mouthed, rubberneckin', mutha-fucker," he said with venom. "Now I KNOW you been cheatin'. Cheat this game and I'll blow both your fuckin' heads off!! We gonna play one more game for ten bucks, and I want the money back you stole!"

At this point, some of the deepest thoughts Jimmy ever had in his life paraded through his consciousness. He rummaged through his mind, examining his soul. He searched for the feelings of impending death his Gramma told him would be lurking in the nooks and crannies before his last days on Earth, and he didn't feel them. That did not stop him, however, from an inner dialogue on his current life choices.

As Otis nervously dealt the cards, Jimmy's thoughts shifted to what he should do next, in the next few seconds, not the choices he should make going forward in his life in general. What now? If they stopped cheating now and started losing, that would prove they were cheating before, so Jimmy decided they couldn't stop cheating. He glanced at Sonny to see what he was thinking. Sonny informed him immediately.

"OK, Silas," snapped Sonny, "One more game. But after we beat you this time, we gotta go. Why don't we play 5-point for ten bucks, so we can get it over with sooner?"

"Pick your poison, boy," agreed Silas.

Jimmy stared at his cards. He had the Ace, Jack, and Deuce of Spades. "I bid three,"

Silas eyeballed Jimmy, who was nervously smiling at him. "Say-Ler-Vee!!!" he shouted, "I pass."

Everyone else did as well, and Jimmy called out Spades and threw the Ace. Silas had a lone ten and had to give it up. Sonny threw the jack of Clubs. When the hand ended it was 5 to 0.

"Hey," said Jimmy before Silas could react, "Otis dealt, and I bid before Sonny even looked at his cards. I had the Ace, Deuce and Jack. What am I supposed to do?"

Silas gritted his teeth and growled, "Deal the fuckin' cards."

The game ended 21 to 5, as Jimmy and Sonny were dealt the kind of hands no one could question, other than whether they had stacked the deck. They would have won even if they hadn't continued signaling.

"Can we go now?" mocked Sonny.

Silas stared at his brother for a long time. "Well, I couldn't catch you sneaky motherfuckers, even though I still think you were cheatin'," he finally groused, and the others could see his temperature rising and knew he was contemplating picking up the gun and blasting away.

"Here's my ten," said Otis, tossing a bill on the table. He wanted to break the tension and for the gun to be put away as soon as possible. Twenty bucks were not worth his pretty face being messed up by a stray slug. He could count on his lady friends to give him more cash so long as that didn't happen.

When Silas saw his partner conceding defeat he pulled a ten out his pocket as well and warned, "Get the fuck outta here before I change my mind and shoot you fuckers."

Sonny and Jimmy rose quickly, scooping up the money before another change in plan could occur. As they reached the door, Sonny stopped and turned to his brother and said, "I know that gun wasn't loaded, Silas. You're not that crazy."

Silas picked up the gun and flipped open the cylinder to show his brother. Every chamber was filled with a nice shiny bullet.

"Only a punk pulls an unloaded gun, Sonny," advised Silas, "And your older brother ain't no punk."

As he drove away, Sonny broke into a sweat, and it wasn't long before his shirt was soaked. He pondered aloud, "I didn't think he was THAT crazy, or I'da never done that shit."

"Well," said Jimmy quite sensibly, "We better have one helluva good time on the trip!!"

RULE # 71 - *Occasionally Obedience Is Rewarding*

Sleepy-eyed seniors stumbled in ones and twos and threes out of a growing number of vehicles until one hundred and ten were huddled together waiting for the two buses to arrive at zero dark thirty on the morning of June 10. Since they were not allowed on school grounds, they met in the Kroger parking lot. The buses were late enough to make everyone nervous the bus company brass had an epiphany and decided to breach the contract, so when the buses finally arrived, a huge cheer was served up by the crowd. These were not school buses, they were charters. If the school had sponsored it, they would have been riding in rickety yellow buses with no toilets, not the sleek buses they would soon board, with high backs and thickly padded seats. Each bus held sixty in fifteen rows, four seats per row.

The delay in the arrival of the buses gave those who assumed the authority the time to make an all-important, crucial decision: To which bus would each person would be assigned? The Status Queens controlled Bus One, and their football/baseball player boyfriends were mandated to board it. Egg, Yobs, Crazy Joe, Hulk, Carl David, Nick the Greek, Grant Roper and Carlo, plus their boyhood chums Dana Pickman, Jasper Waldon and Wastey were all included. Once the Status Queens had seats for everyone who automatically qualified, they extended invitations to commoners below the guaranteed level to fill up the bus. Kirk Morgan accepted graciously, and so did Scott Michaels. Jimmy was asked, but he declined. Kilos was asked, and he declined as well, saying he was riding on the same bus as Jimmy. He was still attempting to be reinstated into Jimmy's good graces after Senior Bowl. Chance, having made it out of his rat hole in Banner just in time, was next in line and jumped at the chance to ride with royalty.

The Zit Queens controlled Bus Two, and Sonny proclaimed

Bus Two as the Party Bus. Anyone not willing to party for three straight hours should ride on Bus One. That scared a few, like Nice Nancy and Sarah Hopper, into Bus One, much to the relief of the main partiers, who included every remaining passenger on the bus except Kilos. Peggy led the charge, followed by most of the Zit Queens, Sonny, Bob, Kilos, and a host of freaks and geeks like Weedhopper, Pid, Chicken Hawk, Ron Williams and Carl Murphy, Worm Chow, Pigpen, Buddy Anthony, and Jesus.

Jimmy boarded after his friends, undecided on where he would sit. Kilos would be more fun to talk to, but Sonny had weed. As he walked down the aisle he could see Sonny in the last row and headed that way. Kilos popped his head up from the sixth row and said, "Sit here, Jimmy!"

About mid-way down the bus, a couple of rows behind Kilos, Peg Leg stood in the aisle and she called out, "Jimmy, I need you over here!!"

Jimmy had not checked in with her, so he assumed he had to sign in. He dutifully walked past Kilos to where she was standing.

"Sit down," she commanded. She pointed at a row facing backwards on the bus, with a table in front of it. She had the roster spread across it. "Let me in first," she continued.

She slid in and Jimmy sat beside her, his arms leaning on the table as he searched for his name on the sheets of paper.

"You know I've known you since kindergarten, Jimmy?" asked Peg Leg.

Jimmy stared at her with a quizzical look, but he couldn't remember.

"Of course, you don't remember me," she said. "But I remember you. We've been in so many classes together I've lost track."

She reached for her purse, resting next to her on the seat. Jimmy thought she was retrieving a pen, but she wasn't. She pulled out the biggest bag of pot Jimmy had ever seen and dropped it on the table, blotting out the roster. It was the biggest bag Jesus had ever seen as well. He was sitting across the table in row nine. He leaned forward to inspect it.

"Wow, how much is that?" questioned Jesus.

"Enough," Peggy replied. "About two ounces of good Lumbo."

After stashing the bag in her purse, she turned to Jimmy and said, "Any time I had a class with you, I always knew it was gonna be more fun than if you weren't in it, and I've always wanted to party with you, and this is my last chance. You're gonna sit next to me on this trip and we're gonna party the whole way," she said decisively.

Jimmy wasn't going to argue with her. He looked back at Sonny, and over to Kilos and shrugged and declared, "I'm sittin' here, fellas!!"

Once the bus was underway at slightly after 6AM, Sonny wanted to be the first to light up, so he snuck into the bathroom and took his single hitter. By the time he returned with a proud smile on his face, Peggy had rolled about ten joints. It was Jimmy's job to light each one, take a hit, and then pass it on to someone in another row. He passed the first to Jesus.

"Bless you, my child," he said to Jimmy.

Jimmy gave the next to Sonny in row 15, then the next to row 14, and so on until he reached row 6. He stood next to Kilos and took a huge hit from the joint in his hand. Kilos couldn't believe what he was seeing.

"Here," spat out Jimmy along with a puff of smoke, "Take this, Kilos."

"Nah, I'll pass," said Kilos. He was unable to fully comprehend Jimmy doing this. He couldn't believe he would do this. Why would he waste his fantastic brain this way?

Jimmy shrugged and went on to row 5. He could see the bus driver watching him through his mirror and wondered what he was thinking. Maybe he was a stoner himself, and was looking forward to the contact high, or maybe he couldn't tell weed smoke from cigarette smoke, as there were a few of those lit up as well. But he didn't appear to be judgmental in any way. In fact, he took the back roads instead of the major ones, as if he was trying to avoid the authorities himself.

By the time they reached Jacksonville, about an hour into the journey, there was such a thick cloud of smoke in the air it seemed like it would rain at any second. Jimmy was so high as he watched it he imagined lightening zapping Kilos on the back of his head. He attempted to engage him in conversation, but Kilos would only stare straight ahead, he couldn't respond. He had one hell of a contact high. Sonny even noticed it when he stepped up to take another joint from Peg Leg, and to offer her a single hit in response. She declined, so Jimmy hit it.

"What's the matter with Kilos up there?" asked Sonny.

"Man, I think he's never been high before, and he's got a contact," surmised Jimmy.

"We should make sure," suggested Sonny. "We should all blow our hits out on him."

Jimmy laughed, and Jesus blessed the idea as well. Sonny spread the word to everyone from row 7 to 15. From then on, after every hit, those in the back of the bus would creep forward and blow their smoke over the top of Kilos' head, or around the side of his seat, such that the cloud, getting thicker everywhere as time passed, was thickest in and around the seat which held the Student Council President. If he noticed, he didn't reveal it. He silently stared straight ahead for the next two hours.

By about eight o'clock all the passengers on the bus were higher than they had ever been in their lives, or at least as high as they could ever remember being. After passing out at least twenty joints, the exact count was lost somewhere between eleven and loaded, Jimmy had a tough time even conceiving how high he would be when Six Flags appeared, still almost an hour away.

Within the next few seconds he'd forgotten that thought and went on to ones even more random. Then the people on the bus who brought their own weed felt the need to share with Peggy, and since Jimmy was sitting next to her, it would be rude for him not to partake as well.

By the time the buses rolled to a stop in the Six Flags parking lot and the two groups rejoined before heading into the park, the only words Jimmy could utter to describe to Chance what happened in the last few hours were: "I'm so high I'm fuckin' wasted."

Chance looked at him and wondered how someone who looked so high could have even formed those words.

"On our bus we had one bottle of Jack to pass around, and that was it. I got a half a swig," he whined.

Jimmy didn't feel sorry for him. He should have known to follow Jesus.

RULE # 72 - *There is No Reason to Lie to People Who Won't Believe You Anyway*

"I think that girl over there is starin' at me," declared Sonny as he, Bob, Chance, and Jimmy stumbled through the park debating which rides they should try.

"Sure, she is," responded Bob, rolling his eyes.

The object of Sonny's pronouncement was partnered with another girl, and as Jimmy gazed at her, he thought she was staring at him, too.

"I'm gonna go talk to her," announced Sonny.

The girls were standing next to a concession stand, tearing off pieces of cotton candy from a bag they were sharing and stuffing it into their mouths. They were pleasant looking white girls, while not being overwhelmingly beautiful. Both wore shorts, the comfortable kind, not the tight, skimpy kind, and blouses which were not low cut, but revealed things had developed. There was no doubt they were staring.

Sonny strolled to the taller of the two, and smiled, and professed, "I sure would like some a' that!"

The girls smiled back, and the taller one, who appeared to be the leader, answered, "Who's your friend?"

"Don' 'cha wanna know my name?" asked Sonny.

"Not 'til you bring your friend over," countered the as-of-yet unnamed girl.

Sonny assumed she meant Bob, as he was the tallest of the three and usually attracted more girls than the others.

"Hey Bob!" called Sonny.

Bob turned his head and raised his arms with his palms up in the universal sign of 'huh?'

"Not him," said the tall girl. "The skinny one with the glasses and the Afro."

"You mean Jimmy?" asked Sonny. He couldn't believe what he had just heard, so he had to make sure. No one else fit the description.

The shorter girl smiled. Yes, she meant Jimmy.

"Come over here, Jimmy," called Sonny.

Jimmy headed to where the girls and Sonny were standing.

"I'm Marsha," said the shorter girl, speaking directly to Jimmy. "Do you want some?" she asked, offering him some candy.

"I'm Kim," added the taller girl. She didn't offer Sonny anything.

"Well, my name is S. A. Mathis," Sonny replied. "But you can call me Sonny."

Bob and Chance refused to become a couple and joined the group.

"These are our friends Bob and Chance," Sonny continued.

"Uh-huh," said the taller girl.

"Where're you from?" asked Marsha, speaking directly to Jimmy again.

"Canton, Illinois," answered Jimmy. "We're here for our Senior Class Trip."

"And we don't have chaperones, because we're too wild for that," proclaimed Chance, puffing out his chest and trying to look as dangerous as possible.

The girls ignored him.

"Where are you girls from?" asked Sonny.

"We're from Davenport," said Kim.

Davenport was across the Mississippi from Illinois in Iowa, less than eighty miles away from Canton.

"Are you seniors?" asked Bob.

The girls ignored him.

"Are you going to college next year?" asked Marsha, once again directly to Jimmy.

"Jimmy?" asked Sonny. "He's a genius. He's goin' ta Bradley ta study engineering."

Marsha turned to Kim and said, "See? I told you he was smart."

Kim turned to Sonny and queried, "We were about to get on some rides. Do you TWO wanna come?"

Jimmy had no clue how to react to this, but Sonny most certainly did.

"Hey, Bob and Chance, we'll catch ya later. And Kim, I'll come with you anytime."

First was the Ferris Wheel, next was the Tilt-A-Wheel, and then the girls steered straight for the Tunnel of Love. It happened so fast and he was still so high Jimmy didn't have the chance to get nervous, even though he knew he would be making out with a girl for the first time in his life as soon as the tunnel got dark. He put his arm around her as they stood in line.

"I thought you were never gonna do that," encouraged Marsha.

When the lights went out she reached over and took off Jimmy's glasses, and the two were locking tongues until the boat burst into the light of day.

"Man, Jimmy," laughed Sonny, who was sitting in front with Kim, twisted around to stare at his friend. "Come up for air!!"

Jimmy was more intellectually stimulated than physically, which is not to imply he didn't have a boner. He knew this would happen one day, and he couldn't think of a better way, with some girl he had never seen before and most probably wouldn't see after.

She was nice enough, and cute enough, but to a man whose future depended on laser focus, she was most assuredly dangerous. He wondered why his friends lost control over girls. He liked them, that was for sure, but he could never understand why other guys lost their minds over them. He could never lose his mind over anything. He'd tried, but he couldn't do it like they did. Even while he was deeply enjoying her tongue in his mouth, he didn't see the experience changing what he planned to do tomorrow or the next day. Maybe he was missing some hormones or something.

But it was a blissful day. In some ways it was the happiest of his life. He had to let everyone see what he was doing. When they rode the sky tram he shouted down to all the people he saw.

"Hey Egg!!" he called down to Pat Hampton, when he saw him walking below with Jana Gamble.

Egg tilted his head to see Jimmy and shouted, "What?"

"Ahh, nothing man!!" Jimmy shouted back. The point was for Egg to see him, not to say anything.

It went by quickly, much too quickly for Jimmy. Late in the afternoon, Bob joined them even though he was the fifth wheel. Chance had abandoned him as well, or rather he had abandoned Chance, when Chance befriended a group of girls Bob thought were too ugly to accompany through Six Flags.

"You should have seen them," described Bob, screwing up his face in disgust.

He watched silently as Jimmy and Sonny bid goodbye to their new friends by the exit of the park, as the girls' bus left earlier than theirs did. Marsha seemed sad and happy at the same time.

"I can't wait to see you again, Jimmy," she whimpered.

Jimmy kissed her in response. He could wait, forever in fact, so he wanted to spend as much time locking tongues as possible beforehand.

As they watched the girls board, Sonny questioned Jimmy, "Did you get her phone number and address?"

Jimmy wasn't thinking past forever, so hadn't even thought about it.

"Nope," he responded.

"Well it's a good thing I got both their numbers," lectured Sonny. "You can be so smart in some things, and so dumb in others."

With those words Chance sauntered up to the boys with a big smile plastered on his face.

"How'd it go, boys?" inquired Chance.

"OK," responded Jimmy. "How 'bout with you?"

"Man, you won't believe it," replied Chance. His friends knew, whenever they heard that, to not believe whatever came next, so he defeated his own purpose with that statement. "I met up with these wild girls from Springfield. They had everything. I had five beers, three joints, and I reamed one of them under the roller coaster."

The three guys listening, even the one with No Sense, confirmed, with sideways glances, this was the biggest lie Chance had ever told them. Maybe, just maybe, he found a group with beer and pot, but he squashed any trace of credibility by claiming to have fucked one of them under the roller coaster.

"You're dreamin', Potsy," jeered Bob.

"Yeah," added Sonny, "You're a fuckin' Dream Reamer."

"And not just any Dream Reamer either," chimed in Jimmy. "You're a Five Beer, Three Joint, Dream Reamer."

And so, a new nickname was born, even though there were no more school days left to harass Chance with it. Before they left Six Flags, Chance switched buses with Kilos, who no one had seen after he disembarked in a daze that morning. Chance was hoping for a repeat of the trip down, smoking someone else's pot from Six Flags to Kroger. Instead he took abuse for the next three hours. They even composed a new theme song for him, with Gary Wright as the inspiration.

> *Dreeeeeeam Reamer,*
> *I think you, can bullshit through, the ni-ight!!*
> *Hey-hey Dreeeeeam Reamer,*
> *Five beers and three joints got you feelin ri-ight!!*

RULE # 73 - *Don't Throw Away Your High School Yearbook - Unless You're Not in It*

Graduation day was the most beautiful day of the year. The late afternoon sun was shining, it was warm but not too hot, and the breeze bombarded everyone's nostrils with the scent of spring flowers. That made it even worse torture to stand in line, to march to seats, and most of all, to listen to boring speeches. It was held in the middle of the football field. Chairs had been set out in ten neat, straight rows of twenty, across the field, with the same stage used for the Holiday Dance placed in the end zone nearest the school parking lot. The home side grandstand was filled with grandparents, parents and those siblings unlucky enough to be too young to stay home alone.

The seniors and a few of the most important underclassmen mingled in the gymnasium, sifting through the crowd to find those who had not yet signed their yearbooks. The yearbooks were issued the last day the seniors were allowed on campus, and with much controversy, but many of the seniors didn't see them until graduation day.

For one thing, Sonny's picture wasn't in it. The only way to know he existed was from the group picture for FCA. There was no excuse for that slipup in his mind, as Dream Reamer was one of the main editors. Plus, Potsy was in nine different pictures throughout the book himself. Not oddly enough, the picture of the Senior Class Skit did not include the Sheriff, it was a full length shot of the Waco Kid. In fact, three of the other main editors of the book, Kirk Morgan, Jana Gamble, and Scott Michaels, were in even more pictures than Chance. Hulk, Pid, and the rest of the editors didn't hog that many, but they were not hard to find in multiple places.

By far, the Banner Rat took the most heat. When his former buddies tracked him down, Sonny lit into him.

"I can't believe my picture's not in the fuckin' yearbook, fuckin' Potsy!!" he snarled, pulling Chance away from the group of girls he had been flirting with until that moment.

"And there's a picture of you instead of me in the skit, you little prick!" complained Jimmy.

"At least you're in more than one shot," retorted Bob.

"Well, Sonny," responded Chance without the slightest bit of remorse, "I had nothin' ta do with that part of the book. And Jimmy, I worked on the yearbook all year and damn right I'm gettin' as many pictures of myself in it as I can get!"

The cover was soundly panned. The editors blamed Mr. Bishop, who was faculty sponsor. The silver color, the movie theater theme, not too many liked it. Some of the blank pages were black and a special silver pen was required to write on them, which was a problem if you didn't have a silver pen.

By the time the signal was given, and they lined up for the short walk to the field, most had the pages filled with the sentiments of their classmates, to cherish for a life time, or to throw away by accident or on purpose in a couple of years. Jimmy collected everyone's he wanted except Sonny's, and Sonny wasn't signing any yearbooks because he wasn't in it. Kilos filled an entire page and a half, reminiscing about mischief stretching back to fourth grade. Bob's message was laced with insults about Chance. The Innocent 5 and Hyde Park Week were repeated themes by others. Pid signed his name as Pid. All State signed as All State, but State Farm signed as Don. Annie Royal was gushy. Vonny-Yonny admitted she would miss the teasing. Watay wrote about J Moves. Yobs scribbled something in code. A cute sophomore cheerleader signed. Potsy was not allowed to sign, since Jimmy didn't want him taking up any more space in the book than he already had. It was all good.

They marched out of the building for the last time, and no one fell or looked the slightest bit wasted, like they were afraid of one last detention and wanted to get the thing over with without any further incidents. They walked down the track on the cinders, then filed row after row onto the field and into the chairs. Jimmy couldn't decide which was harder, the chair he was sitting on, or keeping the cap perched on top of his Afro.

Speeches came next. First came Walter Matthau, then a priest, then Kilos, more nervous than he ever was before in front of a crowd, then Jana Gamble, and to cap off the entertainment, the main speaker was Vonny-Yonny as valedictorian. Nothing memorable was said by anyone. No astronaut or senator followed to give a longer, even more boring, keynote address. The last task was the march across the stage to receive the empty shell made to hold a diploma, flip the tassel to the other side, and it was officially over.

"I'll see you on Monday, man," said Sonny, as they parted on the field after the ceremony.

RULE # 74 - *Shit Flows Downhill*

The Metropolitan Sanitary District of Chicago had a problem. They had way more shit than they knew what to do with. So, they bought acres and acres of fields outside of Canton, fields made worthless by past strip mining, and sold the idea to the locals of excreting it over them to recreate the top soil the mining companies had scraped away decades before. They didn't have any research to show this would work and didn't care, the real goal was to dispose of tons of shit. The former owners of the land thought it was an awesome idea too, as MSD paid them twice as much for the acreage than farmers with usable land could get for theirs.

After MSD had acquired the many, many, square miles they needed to "develop" the site, four gigantic holding tanks were sunk into the ground and partially filled with water. Piping extended deep into the tanks, and a control station was built alongside from which operators controlled the valves and pumps. Tanker trucks filled with treated, supposedly bacteria free, liquefied shit arrived in a constant stream from Chicago to fill the tanks from the bottom up, so the shit stayed covered by water in a theoretical attempt to keep the smell down. Pipelines were routed from the station to each sector of the site, and from there smaller piping to each field "under development". The station operators opened and closed valves and turned on and off pumps to direct the shit out of the tanks to whichever fields it was to be spread on that day. At the edge of each field the solid pipeline was terminated with a hand operated shutoff valve, and from that point, temporary steel piping was connected to extend the line across the field itself. The temporary pipes were made in fifteen-foot lengths, six inches in diameter, and joined together with metal Marmon clamps. The piping was laid a length short of the far edge of the field, and a two hundred-foot long flexible hose was attached, the other end of which was connected to the manifold of the plow of a huge tractor.

When the operators hit the buttons and the valves were opened, shit flowed out of the holding tank, through the piping system, and into the tractor manifold. A driver would slowly, maybe three miles an hour max, drive back and forth across the field spreading shit into the grooves made by the plow. After the tractor made as many passes as the length of hose would allow, the valves at the edge of the field were shut, the hose was disconnected from the end of the pipeline, and a section of pipe was removed. The driver maneuvered the tractor to allow the hose dragging behind it to be connected to the new end of the pipeline, and then the valves were turned on and the tractor spread shit back and forth across the next fifteen-foot wide section of the field. This was repeated until the last section of temporary piping was removed and the tractor had spread shit across the entire field.

Jimmy and Sonny were hired when the NAACP in Peoria discovered such a big project was going on and no black people had been hired to work there. An organizer visited Mount Carmel Baptist Church one Sunday a few weeks before school ended and asked if anyone was interested. The graduates started at the bottom, which meant they were valve men on a crew of four. A crew was headed up by a foreman, the next on the pay scale was the tractor driver, and bottom rung were the valve men. Their job was to connect and disconnect the temporary pipes and then to open and close the valves at the end of each pass when instructed by the driver. The tractor driver had a walkie-talkie for this purpose, and another was kept by a valve man, so they could communicate. The driver had to negotiate the turn by backing up and bringing the tractor around without running over the hose, which was quite difficult considering either the tractor or the plow was constantly getting stuck in shit. The valve men disconnected each pipe length as the tractor driver finished that section and tossed them into a pipe holder which was connected to the back of a smaller tractor. Once all the pipes were removed, the foreman would drive the small tractor to the next field, and the valve men would connect them all again and start over.

If it wasn't the shittiest job in the world, it was in the top five. When each pipe section was broken by pulling on the Marmon clamp, shit flowed out of the pipe in all directions. It took two men to carry the section to the pipe holder, and they had to toss each on top of the others as they piled up. If the pipe was not kept exactly level, shit would flow out of the lower end onto whoever was holding it. It would fly out when the pipes were tossed through the air. No matter how long it was tilted up on one end after it was disconnected, there was always a little shit left in the pipe. When the hose was connected or disconnected, it was the same thing. Walking across fields thigh deep in shit didn't help either. The MSD issued knee high rubber boots were routinely breeched.

But it was also one of the best jobs in the world if your criteria were to make a lot of money (twice minimum wage), get time and a half and double time on Saturday and Sunday, and not only being allowed to get high on the job, but to be encouraged to get high on the job by your foreman. His most important job responsibility was loading up his crew every morning at six thirty, and when the tractor driver got bored during the day, to walk across the field and smoke a joint with him.

The tractor was large enough to require climbing two steps to enter the cabin and moved so slowly it was easy to catch up with walking. The hardest part of the job for the valve men was not falling asleep while the tractor made each pass, so when the driver called, one of them was awake. That was made easier if the driver and valve men were trading insults over the air and kept their minds occupied thinking of the next crack. It was made more difficult by the amount of pot being smoked. There was a delicate balance to be maintained. Something had to be done to keep the driver's sanity, as the tractor engine's roar was so deafening he could sing as loudly and offkey as he wanted, and the valve men could not hear him over the rumble. No one thought of ear plugs.

Each morning the first shift met in the parking lot, to be given their assignment for the day and pick up the equipment they needed, which was usually just a walkie-talkie. Depending on how many showed up for work, several fields were worked at once by different crews. Sometimes a crew finished a field at the end of the day and brought the small tractor back with them with the pipes in it, so in the morning they could be driven to the next field by the morning crew. There was a morning shift that started at daybreak, to which Sonny and Jimmy were assigned, and an afternoon shift, which started after lunch and worked until dark.

The walkie-talkies had two channels for use by the field hands, and the chatter from all the crews could be heard on one of the two. That allowed others not in the same crew to join in the conversation, and the best insults could be shared with everyone. The highlight of the summer was the day someone from the second shift crew left their walkie-talkie at the valve Jimmy was sent to man the next morning, and when he keyed the one he had been assigned to make sure it worked, he heard the distinctive crackle of the second one.

It had been announced during the morning meeting a walkie-talkie was missing from the day before, and the crews were supposed to be on the lookout for it. Losing a walkie-talkie, each of which cost hundreds of dollars, was one of the few ways to get fired from MSD. One of the others was using bad language or verbal abuse over the open airwaves, which Sonny had been issued a warning for in the first week. One of the tractor drivers had a problem with his voice and could only talk in a high-pitched warble, which sounded like soprano goose honking, and Sonny quickly started responding with high pitched goose sounds whenever the driver in question spoke over the air. They were not even in the same crew, which was another no-no. When Jimmy heard and then found the lost radio, he knew he needed to do something fun, but couldn't figure out what, so he turned off the errant walkie-talkie and put it in his lunchbox. After work he and Sonny were driving home when Jimmy pulled the walkie-talkie from his hidey-hole and showed it to Sonny.

"Guess who found the missing walkie-talkie?" asked Jimmy, holding it up.

"Naw, man," said Sonny. "And you didn't turn it in?"

"I figured we should have some fun with it first," suggested Jimmy.

One of the things Sonny did with his first paycheck was buy new speakers for his car, the kind which allowed the police to hear him long before they saw him, and from the moment the last wire was soldered they were set to full blast. The Commodores were on, singing, "Love is slipp'ry when its wet! Love is slipp'ry when its wet." And then a drum solo that went on and on. Sonny had the idea to key the walkie-talkie in the middle of the solo, and leave it keyed to give the second shift crews a concert to listen to. The boys cruised the roads surrounding the site for the next hour, blasting music to the bewildered crews still on the job.

The next day Sonny found out the guy who lost it was going to get fired at the end of the week if the radio wasn't recovered, so Jimmy waited until the general foreman came around to check on the crew, turned the walkie-talkie on and slipped it into the bed of his pickup truck without anyone noticing. About an hour later a call came over the airwaves, announcing the walkie-talkie had been found and a job was saved.

RULE # 75 - *You'll Never Understand the Importance of Practice Until You Haven't*

B y the time of his Bradley orientation session, Jimmy had made enough money to have his college wardrobe in his closet, a cushion in his savings account, and enough left over to buy a full ounce of weed from Silas, who exacted some revenge for the card game, as he charged him thirty dollars for the worst weed ever grown in the state of Illinois. It was so bad Jimmy was forced to use the strawberry flavored papers in order to mask the taste. Using a pipe was not feasible, as the harshness would overwhelm before a buzz could.

The session began with a meeting in the newly constructed gymnasium, Haussler Hall. Roughly seventy perspective students clustered on the main gym floor with the university staff in charge of the proceedings, and as Jimmy scanned the room he saw a group of black kids standing together, laughing and chatting as if they had known each other for years. There were two guys, and five girls, and Jimmy was immediately impressed with the way the guys were holding the ladies' attention, especially the shorter and darker of the two. When he saw Jimmy hovering nearby, he called him over.

"It's good to see another black face in the crowd besides us," he said, reaching out to shake Jimmy's hand. "I'm Brian Wrightwood. This is my boy Danny Brimstone."

Brian had the kind of beard best described as a chin strap, with the line of hair stretching from one sideburn down under his chin and then following the edge of the bottom of the chin and up to the other sideburn. He looked like a guy who would be bald in ten years from the look of the top of his head, which Jimmy could clearly see, as Brian was six inches shorter. Danny was taller, lighter, and better looking, but couldn't hold his own with Brian in the all-important gift of gab department.

"James Williams," he responded. He'd decided he wasn't going to be Jimmy in college.

"We need a third person to share the room with us, Jim," continued Brian, without sharing the names of the girls. "And since none of these honeys will agree to sleep with us, how about you?"

Jimmy eyed the girls and they were smiling, so Brian must not have offended them. They were cuter than any of the girls he had grown up with. Jimmy had always known there was a bigger world out there, so he was not surprised intellectually, but he wasn't prepared emotionally for the multitude of beauty he was confronted with now, at orientation, no less. In one glance he felt vindicated for his choice to not get involved with any of his admirers in Canton. They just couldn't look this good. However, he also realized he should have at least practiced with the hometown girls, because he wasn't confident enough to talk to the ones he was standing in front of now.

"Sure, man," agreed Jimmy, "It's three to a room? I thought it was two."

"Yeah, when we come back in the fall it'll be two, but for orientation, they're makin' it three," explained Brian.

Before he could ask the names of the girls, a staff member called the group to attention.

"Welcome to Bradley University. You have made the right choice. You should know the orientation schedule by now, but if not, it is posted on the wall outside. If you have made your roommate selections, please step up to the desk and sign-in and collect your keys. Those of you who have not, please wait and we will make the assignment for you. If any of you are taking the CLEP tests, you need to be in Jobst Hall in one half hour, so you need to get a move on. There is a list of activities for those of you not taking the tests that are great ways to help familiarize you with the campus. I suggest the scavenger hunt. You can ask any of us with the green nametags for help. That's what we're here for! Enjoy and good luck!"

"Well, I'm taking the tests," said Jimmy to his new friends.

"Us too," replied Brimstone.

"Yes, ladies," sang Brian to the girls, "I hope you don't miss us too much. Come on, Jim."

Brian was obviously comfortable being the leader. The newly formed trio marched to the table, signed in and took their keys. They were assigned to Harper Hall, room 206. The entire campus was two blocks by three blocks, so even though the gym was on the west side of campus, the dorm was in the northeast corner, and Jobst Hall was in the northwest corner of the campus, they had time to go to the room and drop off their stuff before heading to Jobst.

"Did you just meet those girls?" asked Jimmy as they walked across the quad.

The other boys laughed. "Naw, man, we all went to high school together," chuckled Brimstone.

"We're smooth, but we're not that smooth," admitted Brian.

"Where was that?" queried Jimmy.

"Lindblom High School in Chicago," answered Brian, with much pride, "Ever hear of it?"

"Naw, man," responded Jimmy. "I'm from just down the road in Canton. I know you never heard of that."

"I heard of it," countered Brimstone. "Canton Ohio, right?"

"Wrong. Illinois."

"OK, never heard of it," admitted Brian.

It turns out Brian was the Senior Class President at Lindblom, and was attending Bradley to study electrical engineering, same as Jimmy. What were the odds of that? Then they went on to the more important topic of the honeys they'd just left behind. It seems none were their girlfriends, but that wasn't stopping them from targeting one for some temporary titillation.

They were still debating the pros and cons of each when the trio entered Jobst Hall.

The CLEP tests were split into four sections and achieving a high score on any section resulted in receiving four credits hours and eliminating the need to take the corresponding classes in College Composition, American History, Natural Sciences, and Social Science, all basic required credits for graduation. Jimmy thought they were easy, and he was completely sober. He breezed through them so quickly Brian, who was sitting next to him, thought he had given up and was walking out.

"Man, aren't you gonna finish? Don't get discouraged, brother," he asserted. He was committed to inspiring the less accomplished than himself.

"I am finished," countered Jimmy. "I'll see you guys back in the room."

Brian and Brimstone eyed each other skeptically. Either this kid was super smart, or he was completely full of shit. They would find out the answer, and a few others they hadn't thought of, before the orientation session was complete.

Jimmy happily bounced to the room, ready to reward himself for doing so well on the tests, by rolling and smoking two joints. He could have walked to his car and smoked, or driven to a nearby park and smoked, but he could think of no better way to spend the first hour of his dorm life than lighting up in the room.

The dorm was designed similarly to the others Jimmy had visited over the last few years. His two older sisters had been in at least six different ones over that span, and they all looked like this one. Except they had taken one of the desks out of the room and replaced it with a third bed. Jimmy pulled the chair from under the remaining desk and placed it next to the window, which he opened. And then he lit up. When he exhaled he realized the flow of air was coming in, as the smoke swirled into his face instead of out of the window, but he didn't worry much about it. His sisters had told him it was illegal for anyone to search their rooms for drugs on their campuses, so he assumed it was OK even if the smoke did go under the door and out of the room, which of course it did. By the time he was finishing up the second, he could hear voices in the hall outside his room.

"Do you smell that?" asked Male Voice One.

"I sure do," responded Male Voice Two.

"We should go to the Resident's office and report this," declared Male Voice One.

Jimmy heard the sounds of footsteps walking away, and he tiptoed to the door and looked out. The hall was empty. He assumed the voices would return with the school authorities and they would knock on his door, and he didn't want to be there when that happened. He had the bag of weed in his hand, and quickly decided it would be better to stash it in the dorm room closet, on the top shelf, behind the bags stored there, than to take it with him as he left. He calculated it would be worse to be apprehended with it on his person. He hid the bag, and quickly slipped out of the room, down the stairs, and into the parking lot where he had parked his car and drove off without anyone seeing him. When he returned two hours later, after going to the mall to see if anything else needed to be added to his wardrobe, he returned to an empty room. No Brian, no Brimstone, and no bag of weed in the closet. Jimmy was asleep before his new friends arrived.

RULE # 76 - *They Won't Kick You Out If They Don't Have Your Money Yet*

The next morning while they ate breakfast in the Geisert Hall cafeteria, Jimmy, along with Brian and Brimstone, were summoned to Swords Hall by one of the green tagged advisors they had met the day before. Geisert was the newest dorm on campus, built a couple of years before, across the parking lot from Harper. Brimstone's older brother, who was also a student at Bradley, was staying in that dorm during the summer school session. That was why Jimmy had been left in the room alone the night before, the other two had been hanging out in Geisert. They hadn't come back to the room until well after midnight.

Swords Hall was the campus administration building, where the president's office, the registrar, and the financial offices were located, among other things. It was on the south end of the campus, tucked between the library and the new science building, Olin Hall. When Jimmy walked into the office he had been told to report to, he saw a large man, in a Table Muscle sort of way, not an intimidating way, wearing black, thick rimmed glasses, sitting behind a long table studying a piece of paper. Sitting next to him was a woman with a big hairdo and pointy glasses wearing a frilly white blouse. In unison they directed very concerned looks toward Jimmy as he approached. He stood watching them watch him until the man broke the silence by instructing him to sit down, and as he did he wondered what the other guys were thinking, getting blindsided this way. At least Jimmy knew what this was about already.

"Did you bring drugs onto the campus with you?" asked the man, once Jimmy was seated in the metal folding chair across from him.

"No," answered Jimmy.

"Did you bring fireworks with you to campus?" questioned the man more sternly.

"No," replied Jimmy, quite astonished by that question. Who would bring fireworks to a college orientation? That had to be a trick question.

"Did you bring marijuana to campus with you?" probed the woman.

Jimmy thought about lying, but then realized he would be dragging the others down with him if he did, and they knew nothing about what he had done and didn't deserve it. They had befriended him, after all. He thought of all he had been through in his eighteen years, all his dreams and hopes, all the dreams and hopes his parents had for him, all the hopes and dreams his grandparents had for him. All the people in his church who had watched him grow up and predicted a remarkable future for him. All the friends and neighbors who had bragged he was the one who would make it. How would he tell them he'd been kicked out of college before the first day of class? But he couldn't think about that now. All he could do now was to be honest, and not ruin anyone else's dreams. Honesty, since nothing else seemed feasible, was the best policy.

"Yes, I brought it," he admitted.

"Was it in a baggie, with red colored rolling papers inside?" continued the man, looking at the paper again.

"Yes," confirmed Jimmy, "That was it. I brought it."

The two interrogators looked down at the paper once more and spoke softly to each other.

Jimmy did not think he had gone far enough to clear the others, so he volunteered, "The other guys I'm rooming with know nothing about this. I didn't show them I had it, I didn't tell them I had it, and they were nowhere around when I smoked it."

The woman looked up and over her glasses at Jimmy and said, "Thanks for telling us the truth. This is an ongoing problem here at Bradley, and we will not tolerate the usage of any illegal drugs on our campus. If you had been fully enrolled, you would have been expelled, but since you are not officially enrolled yet, we have decided to give you a censure."

Jimmy was confused. A censor was the guy who wouldn't let people curse on TV. What did that have to do with getting busted with pot?

"What's a censure?" asked Jimmy.

"It is a formal notice that your current behavior will not be tolerated in the future," clarified the man.

"A notice?" pondered Jimmy. That didn't seem like much of a punishment to him. There had to be more. "So, I guess you're gonna notify my parents," concluded Jimmy. He thought he was stating the obvious.

"What?" cried the woman, "We can't do that. You're over eighteen. We cannot notify them by law. Only you can tell them."

Jimmy couldn't believe he could be getting off with what was sounding more and more like a wrist slap. There had to be more.

"What about my scholarships?" asked Jimmy. That had to be the catch. He didn't have to tell his parents about the censure, but he'd have to have one hell of a story to explain how he lost the scholarships otherwise. "I got some scholarships for my test scores."

The man looked at him with astonishment. This kid had scholarships for test scores? "It won't affect them," said the man.

"OK," shrugged Jimmy. "Can I go now?"

"Yes," responded the woman. "You can go, but don't bring anything back when you start the semester. We'll be paying special attention to you, to make sure you don't. If you get caught again, you will be kicked out. No second chances. Do you understand?"

As college was supposed to be a learning experience, Jimmy wanted to maximize the educational aspects of this encounter, so he asked the question that had been bothering him since he discovered the weed was missing. "Well, I do have one question," he said. "How was it legal to enter the room without a search warrant?"

He thought Table Muscle would be proud of that question, as he had spoken at length about the rights of citizens in Civics class.

The woman stared at him sternly and replied, "This is a privately-owned university, not a publicly owned one. Since every building on this campus is owned by us, we don't need a warrant to search any of the rooms in any of the buildings."

Now Jimmy understood. The search would not hold up in a court of law, but this wasn't a court of law. Bradley could kick him out based on it, but not have him arrested.

"But what about the others? They're in the clear, right?" asked Jimmy.

The man shook his head. "No, they have their own problems."

Jimmy walked out of the building and into the sunshine and couldn't believe what had just happened. The smile on his face may not have been permanent, but it was stuck on so hard it seemed like it could be. He had a while to wait for the Garrett scholarship interview in Bradley Hall, so Jimmy sauntered to Jobst Hall to see if the CLEP test scores had been posted yet. They had. Jimmy reviewed his and realized the tests were as easy as he thought. He passed all four, giving him sixteen hours to add to the eight he had from his Calculus classes. Twenty-four college credit hours made him a sophomore. What a life college was, thought Jimmy, smiling even more broadly; busted on the first day, a sophomore on the second.

It was then he saw his roommates striding across the quad, and it made the smile disappear in an instant. They attempted to avoid him, but Jimmy caught up to them.

"Guys," he called out. "Sorry to get you involved in this. I took total blame for bringin' the weed though. But they told me you guys were in trouble anyway. What happened?"

"When they searched the room for the weed, they found the firecrackers I brought with me," confessed Brimstone.

Jimmy couldn't believe it. In his mind bringing pot was much more sophisticated than firecrackers. The city slickers brought firecrackers and the country bumpkin brought pot? That didn't sit well with Jimmy, as he thought they would be the ones ahead of the curve and teach him about life, not the other way around.

"What the hell did you bring firecrackers for?" asked Jimmy, still bewildered.

Brimstone shrugged. "I don't know, I thought there might be some place to light 'em off down here."

Brian piped in, "They were a lot more pissed off about the firecrackers than the pot. They said we could have burned down the building or something."

"So, what did they do?" asked Jimmy.

"We got censured," divulged Brimstone. "What happened to you?"

"Same thing," laughed Jimmy, then changing the subject, "Have you checked your CLEP scores yet?"

"Yeah," moaned Brian. "A waste of time. We didn't get any credits out of it. How about you?"

"I'm a sophomore," declared Jimmy. "I got all sixteen hours, plus the eight I got from the Calculus classes I took at community college last year. I was a year ahead in math, so they let me take college math in my senior year."

The other boys stared at him with a mixture of shock, awe, and disbelief. Those tests were hard. What kind of kids did they grow in Canton? They did not have a response, other than to open their mouths.

"Gotta go," said Jimmy. "I need to be in Bradley Hall in five minutes."

"What's goin' on in Bradley Hall?" asked Brian, not wanting to miss anything.

"I gotta go to a scholarship interview," explained Jimmy. "Catch you guys later."

Jimmy walked away and left them gaping and climbed the steps of Bradley Hall.

After the interview, which turned out to be as easy an interview as Jimmy may ever have in his life, he wanted to celebrate. He decided to take a stroll down Main Street to Co-Op Records, which was located across the street from the campus, about two blocks further down Main, to buy a tape or something. It was the same place No Sense bought his bong. As he ambled down Main, a gold colored Deuce and a Quarter drove by, with music blasting out of it, Parliament's We Want the Funk. The car was occupied by three brothers, with arms hanging out of the car, bobbing their heads. The one in the front passenger's side had a toothpick hanging out of his mouth. He stared hard at Jimmy as they rolled by. When he stuck his head out of the window to stare even harder, Jimmy flinched.

"Hey, Jimmy!!" the guy with the toothpick said.

Jimmy kept walking and tried to ignore him, but the car slowed down.

"Hey, ain't you Sonny's friend Jimmy?" asked the guy hanging out of the car.

Jimmy stopped in his tracks, and knew the face was familiar.

"It's Craig, man, Craig Carter!!" the man called out. The car was now stopped on the side of the road.

"Hey, what's happenin', Craig?" asked Jimmy, now remembering where he saw this face before.

"Just cruisin', man," he said. "Jump in, we'll give you a ride. Where ya goin'?"

Jimmy jumped in and told them the whole story of the bust, but not about the tests he had just passed. He knew his audience. When he finished, Craig said, "That's fucked up that they took your stash, man. You wanna get hooked up again? I know a guy sellin' nice dime bags."

Jimmy thought about it. He had the ten bucks. He had been told several times in his life you've got to get right back on the horse after you fall off. He was finished with his tests and other official business. Why not?

Craig had his friend drive to the spot, and Craig took Jimmy's ten and jumped out. A few minutes later he was back with the bag and handed it to Jimmy.

"Thanks man," said Jimmy, smelling the contents, "This smells good!"

"Here's a pipe, fill yourself up a bowl," offered Craig. Jimmy took him up on it. By the time he had them drop him off at Co-Op, Jimmy was feeling all right again with the world.

So, thought Jimmy, this was turning out better than he thought. If he had tried to smoke the rest of the bag of weed he bought from Silas before school started it would have killed him, and if he brought it to school it would have ruined his reputation as a connoisseur. The weed he had now was so much better! Knowing what he needed to do next, Jimmy bought some papers in the head shop, then walked to his car to roll a couple of joints, and then went to the dorm room to give them to his roommates as payment for the heat he brought down on them. When they weren't in the room in Harper he tracked them down in Geisert.

"Here he is!!" yelled Brian as Jimmy walked down the hall toward them. Two other guys, one who looked like Brimstone and another who didn't, were standing in the hall in front of an open dorm room door staring at Jimmy skeptically. He could tell they had been told the story of the last day, and they didn't know what to make of this Wildman walking toward them. Jimmy didn't care. He knew he had a reputation to uphold.

"I got something for you guys," he said, transferring the joints to Brian with a hand shake. Brian held them in his hand like they were scorpions.

"You're back in the box already?" asked Brian incredulously. He didn't know anyone this wild where he came from. Maybe he did know guys this wild, but none of them could get into ANY college, let alone a school as difficult to get into as Bradley. Let alone breeze through tests in an hour he couldn't pass in ten and become sophomores before their first official day on campus. College was turning out to be even more amazing than he imagined!

"Don't worry man, just take it off campus and light it up. You won't be disappointed," instructed Jimmy. "I wanna do something to make up for the trouble I got you into."

Now it was Brian's turn to be inspired by someone.

RULE # 77 - *Keep the Promises You Make to Your Mother*

When Jimmy returned to Canton he didn't tell any of his friends what happened. He didn't even tell them he was back. He had enough weed to last him the next couple of weeks if he took it one hit at a time, and his plan was to sit at home and not spend another penny until his moving day. He had spent his last day at MSD before orientation, and his last paycheck had been cashed, so the money he had saved by this point was all he was going to have until the day he left Canton behind.

Sonny called him on August 16, a couple of days later. His tone was more subdued than Jimmy had ever heard it.

"Are you going to the memorial service today?" asked Sonny.

Jimmy assumed the sadness in Sonny's voice was artificial and rummaged through his mind to determine what the punch line would be. Then he realized the joke.

"No, Sonny, I didn't get invited to Elvis' funeral," deadpanned Jimmy. It had been all over the news that day. 'Elvis, Dead at 42, from an Apparent Heart Attack.'

Sonny did not react the way Jimmy thought he would. He was quiet, much too quiet, for the next few seconds. "You didn't hear?" he asked after the long pause. "Carl David is dead."

Jimmy now knew Sonny wasn't joking. He couldn't comprehend it, though. All he could get out was, "What?"

"He got killed in a car wreck while you were outta town," said Sonny somberly.

"What?" repeated Jimmy, his mind still trying to process the information.

"The wake is at the funeral home a couple of blocks from your house," continued Sonny. "It starts in an hour. Want me ta pick you up?"

Jimmy was still trying to piece it together. "Are you sure?" he asked, not about Sonny giving him a ride, but about the death.

"I saw the car at Google's junk yard. It's all fucked up," confirmed Sonny. "The driver's side door was smashed all the way across to the other side. The others were lucky ta not get killed too."

"Others?" asked Jimmy.

"Dana Pickman was with him, and a couple of the sophomore cheerleaders," revealed Sonny.

Jimmy was finally prepared to accept Sonny's story.

"Naw, Sonny," he replied, gathering his wits, "I'll just walk over."

So, the first reunion of the Class of 77 took place a lot sooner than anyone had planned. The location was not foreseen either, the Greenwood Mortuary. It was not even a block from Jimmy's house; it was just beyond the row of houses across the street. Jimmy crossed the street, walked between the houses, climbed and jumped over a five-foot tall chain link fence, and he was in the white gravel parking lot of the mortuary. That is where he met Bob and Sonny, exiting their cars. They didn't say a word to each other as they walked in.

The mortuary was laid out like a church, with rows of pews and an elevated stage at the far end. In the middle front of the stage stood the altar, and below it, at the same level as the pews, was an ornate casket with the lid open. As the boys approached, they could see Carl's dad standing to the side, looking like he had not stopped crying until the tears ran out and had not slept since. He looked completely haggard and sad but was trying to be as dignified as possible.

Carl seemed so alive as they peered down at him it was hard to believe he wouldn't wake up if he was shaken, but his eyes were closed, and he looked so peaceful none of them tried it. His head was misshapen, as if the mortician had piece it together after it had been broken into fragments, but it was still clearly Carl David. After a few seconds, the trio had seen enough and turned to

Carl's dad to shake his hand. He had words to say to each of them, spoken so softly they had to lean close to his face to hear them.

"Congratulations on your scholarship, Jimmy," he said to Jimmy when it was his turn. "Carl told me he was proud to have you as a teammate and a friend."

A tear almost fell from Jimmy's eye at the words, and one would have fallen from Carl's dad's eye if he had any left. Jimmy could not think of a response that would make Carl's dad feel any better. "Sorry for your loss," was all he could muster. He was too shocked to cry. What could his dad be thinking? Jimmy was about to embark on a new life, full of the promise of the future, and he had to put his own son in the grave.

As they walked out to the front porch of the mortuary, the boys saw Dana Pickman standing there sobbing, trying to hold it together. He was wearing his best designer jeans, a polyester shirt with the top buttons open, and a medallion hanging from his neck. He was dressed like he was headed to the disco, except his arm was in a sling and his forehead was scraped up.

"So, what happened, man?" interrogated Bob, without the slightest tact.

"He probly don't wanna talk about it," responded Sonny, with surprising compassion.

"Naw, I can tell you," said Dana, "It helps ta talk about it." He took a deep breath and told the story. "Well, me and Carl had a double date with a couple of the sophomore cheerleaders, you know, the cute ones. I was supposed to get the weed, but I couldn't score, so we bought a case of beer instead. We took 'em over to Peoria and hung out for a while, then we drove back on the back roads, so we could drink and have some fun. We came to the intersection of Smithfield Road and Stone Church Road, you know where you turn left? There's never anyone on that road. Carl had just turned to tell a joke to the girls in the back when...when..." Dana choked up and had to take a few deep breaths to compose himself. "We never saw the car until it was too late..." he continued before drifting off into a strained silence. "He never had a chance. The car plowed right into him. It's all my fault. If I'da just been able to score the weed like I was supposed to, Carl would still be alive. All the times Carl saved my ass, and I couldn't save his."

"Man, it's not your fault," said Sonny, now without much compassion. Dana never called him to ask if he had anything to sell. He could have hooked him up.

Then Annie Royal walked up and gave Jimmy the longest, deepest hug she could muster.

"When are you leaving?" she asked.

"Another week," answered Jimmy.

"Well good luck," she said. "I hope I get to see you again, but if not, I know you'll do great in college." She turned without hugging the others and entered the building to pay her respects.

The boys lingered on the steps for another half hour, trying to figure out their next move, and greeting most of the senior class as they came and went. Not many words were spoken, silent handshakes and pats on the back were mostly what was communicated. When the parking lot thinned, and they were left standing by themselves, Sonny had an idea.

"Wanna go see the car at Google's?" he asked. "I got some smoke."

"Sure, why not?" answered Bob, and they turned to walk toward their cars.

Jimmy held his ground.

"You comin'?" asked Sonny, turning his head toward Jimmy.

"Naw," Jimmy responded, shaking his head. "I'll just walk back home. See you guys later."

Bob and Sonny walked away and climbed into their cars and drove off, the last time Jimmy would see them before he left for college. It was August, after all, and he had made a promise to his mother.